A native of Porstm_____ng interest in naval h_____ur acclaimed novels under the pseudonym Frank Kippax – *Underbelly*, *The Butcher's Bill*, *Other People's Blood* and *Fear of Night and Darkness*. Under his real name, he is a TV scriptwriter and an author of award-winning children's books. His previous novel, *A Fine Boy for Killing*, also features Sea Officer William Bentley.

THE WICKED TRADE

'The reader is up to his knees in the viscous ooze of Deptford Creek where mouldering timber hulks and mouldier specimens of humanity are engaged on His Majesty's Service . . . It's fly-on-the-wall, warts-and-all, fast-and-furious stuff.'
Water Craft

'A pacy, tautly written tale. A no-holds-barred world and don't spare the blood, grime and grot. History with the accent on sordid realism. *More please.*'
Huddersfield Daily Examiner

A FINE BOY FOR KILLING

'Exciting drama . . . in this enthralling novel the tension builds and the characters are drawn into a destiny of fear, love, hatred and horrifying tragedy. This absorbing study of life on board ship two hundred years ago is the first in a new series of naval adventures – I shall look forward to the next.'
Yorkshire Gazette & Herald

'Terrific, wonderfully detailed stuff – for those who don't mind a salty story whose saltiness comes from the taste of blood . . .'
Oldham Evening Chronicle

BY JAN NEEDLE

A Fine Boy for Killing
The Wicked Trade

BY JAN NEEDLE WRITING
AS FRANK KIPPAX

Underbelly
The Butcher's Bill
Other People's Blood
Fear of Night and Darkness

JAN NEEDLE

THE WICKED TRADE

HarperCollinsPublishers

HarperCollins*Publishers*
77–85 Fulham Palace Road,
Hammersmith, London W6 8JB

The HarperCollins website address is:
www.**fire**and**water**.com

This paperback edition 1999
1 3 5 7 9 8 6 4 2

First published in Great Britain by
HarperCollins*Publishers* 1998

Copyright © Jan Needle 1998

The Author asserts the moral right to
be identified as the author of this work

ISBN 0 00 651115 5

Set in Linotron Meridien by
Rowland Phototypesetting Ltd
Bury St Edmunds, Suffolk

Printed and bound in Great Britain by
Caledonian International Book Manufacturing Ltd, Glasgow

For my Uncle Les,
who brought me stories from the Seven Seas,
and all the other Brices, young and old

THE WICKED TRADE

1

The two men, Yorke and Warren, were talking in comfort the evening they were taken, when they'd thought at last that they could see an end in sight. Their mission had been long and arduous, their need for secrecy a constant strain. But earlier that day, on the shores of Fareham Creek, they had met a man and made an offer, and backed it with a string of names. They were venturers, they said, and they wished to join the trade. They had information that they'd gathered in dire secrecy, and they used it as a lure. Now, feet into the fireplace, Mrs Cullen preparing them a meal, they were contented.

'He said his name was Saunders,' said Charles Warren, musingly. 'But it is not, it is George Felton, his home is in Cowplain. But Saunders is a name I know from Kent, one of the eastern crews. I wonder what significance there is in that?'

Charles Yorke was comfortably amused. He selected a new clay from the table rack, and began to pack it, for after dinner. Mrs Cullen had provided them with fresh tobacco, in a box, and boasted, with fetching naivety, that it was 'from the trade'. Whatever, it was good tobacco, lately cured.

'None at all, I doubt,' he said. 'A name he plucked from out the air. Although Saunders may well have been high up in his mind, if we are right about the Kentish men. Perhaps it was a test, to try us for reaction. I suppose if you had let on that you recognised it, that could have set suspicion in his head.'

Charles Warren was fifty-six years old. He was a stocky, quiet, sombre man, with eyes of fierce intelligence.

3

'No, I think the time for tests is past,' he said. 'I think tomorrow or the next day we will get to see the men we need. Let's hope they don't demand the stake in sovereigns, there on the table. If they make me turn my pockets out, the very fluff would cry out my true profession!'

He was a riding officer in the normal way – and if success was paid in bounties, was deserving to be rich. But his wage was tiny of itself, hardly enough to keep him in the class of horse he favoured – good horses were his only weakness, it was said. His origins were humble, also, which was why Charles Yorke, at barely twenty-five, was in command of him. There were ways to get wealth while doing Customs work, but Warren shunned them vehemently. Officers who accepted gifts instead of blows could wear good cloth and ride fine horses; also stay alive. Charles Warren, it was known, would court death, rather.

Yorke, hungry but impatient, leaned into the fireplace and took out a glowing stick. It was a warm evening, almost summer still, but the smouldering logwood enhanced the parlour and gave off a pleasant smell. He felt the brand's heat on his cheek as he sucked the clay. Truth was, he'd smoke while eating, if he fancied it; he was fanatick for the weed.

'We're businessmen,' he said, around the pipestem. 'To make free with our money in a trade like this, unless we had an army at our back – now that would be suspicious, with brass knobs! No, we'll deal in talk and promises until we've met them, to the very top. Then the gold will hit them, like a ton of bricks. Ah Charles, we're getting close to it, I really feel we are. Today I had a premonition, a solid premonition. I think that we are coming very close.'

The men were friends, despite the social gap and protocols of service and command. For two months or more, on this occasion, they had quartered this stretch of coast not as riding officers but in the utmost secrecy, from east of Selsey to beyond Keyhaven in the west. Before that they had wormed deep into the eastern mysteries, from whence the threat was being made. Warren, too, had felt excitement mounting in the past few days. His circumspection, though, was stronger than Charles Yorke's.

'Aye, aye,' he said. 'At the very least I think we're closing in. This inn is good and secret, Mrs Cullen's lack of curiosity is capital indeed. However –' he cleared his throat, as if to give a shout – 'However, she could be a little prompter with her suppers!'

Outside the low, dark room there were noises. Horses stamping in the yard, and voices. There was a sudden spattering at the thick window glass. Rain had been in the air all day, despite the warmth. It had arrived.

'They've timed it well for shelter,' Warren said. 'In Hampshire, tell me, does it always rain?'

'I am a Surrey man,' Yorke chuckled. 'Let it come down!'

Then the door crashed open, and four men burst in, preceded by a wave of brandy, a veritable sea of stench. Outside there were more voices, male and loud, and a brief woman's scream as Mrs Cullen rushed from her kitchen to see what might be going on. Yorke caught a glimpse of her, white kerchief at her ample bosom, white features flushed and anxious, as she was pushed behind a door unceremoniously. A large and ruddy man had pushed her, a man with whiskers and a pigtail like a seaman, although his coat was tailed and upon his head a shallow, curl-brim hat. He held a pistol in his hand, a long and wicked thing, with a semi-bell.

'My God,' said Warren. 'We are discovered, Mr Yorke. We are betrayed.' His voice was low, filled with anxiety. But then he rapped out, in a hard and fearless tone: 'Quit off from here instanter, you drunken sots! We are armed!'

The men were also armed. More pistols had appeared. A knife. Two more pushed in, one with a cutlass. Warren and Yorke – who had not produced their weapons – stood watchfully, and waited. The smell of brandy was underlaid by damp clothing, sweat, of man and horse. No fear, though. The ruffians did not smell of fear.

'You are Customs men,' said one. He was small and bright-eyed. 'You have come to spy on us. We have found you out.'

From outside, strangely, there came a high-pitched, shaking scream. Then muffled shouting, and the screaming stopped. One of the interlopers lifted his arm, and in his hand a bottle. He raised it to his mouth and drank.

Yorke spoke. His voice was brazen. It rang in the low room like a bell.

'We have come to meet your masters, fool,' he said. 'We are the reverse of Customs, we are venturers from London, come to help your trade.'

Desperate times need desperate remedies, thought Warren, at his side. Saying the unsayable to unknown men with guns.

They were not impressed, apparently. The body of them surged forward, and their looks were bestial. It was clear that they had been drinking for a good time, and with purpose. Now there were seven in the room, and the door was bursting with the weight outside. Yorke reached for the inner pocket of his coat, wherein he kept a pistol, always primed. It was a Cyrus Rollins, made for him especially, bespoken by his uncle and protector, with a special cover on the priming pan, a neat device that made – said Cyrus Rollins – misfires history.

But Warren saw the movement, and spoke so only Yorke would hear, with calm authority.

'No. They will kill you if you touch it, they are beyond control. Leave it, Mr Yorke.'

Into Yorke's head came the thought that, drunk, mad or sober, the open barrel with its promise of a monstrous ball of lead might act as a bucket of cold water in their faces. If it came to shooting matches they would win, that was not in dispute. But one of them would die first. Who would be the one to risk it?

'Charles,' he said, but hesitated, and they were lost. There was a surge, apparently involuntary, a group movement that occurred without an order being given. Two tables squawked as their legs scraped across the flags behind the weight of men, and a heavy settle went over backwards with a bang.

It was Warren who got his weapon out the quickest, his sword was cleared before the deadly little Rollins was even firmly in Yorke's grasp. Quickest, but too late. A fellow to the left of him made a movement, low and sweeping, with what Warren, before it hit him, thought was a flail. By luck or horrible facility it took the hanger blade almost at the guard and broke it neatly off. As Yorke's blunt pistol emerged into the light his chest took the full weight of two men, both of whom attacked his head with clubs. Drunk or not, a third man caught the Cyrus Rollins as, knocked from its owner's hand, it described a graceful arc over the mêlée. Its patent pan-guard had not been displaced.

Overwhelmed and clearly helpless, both men avoided fighting back beyond saving their faces from too-deadly hits. They were to be taken, they assumed; this party was not likely to be the instigators, there must be men behind them, the men, maybe, they'd sought. Yorke's eyes, one bruised and closing, found his older consort's, frankly to be reassured. To kill them would be purposeless, surely?

But the men were wild with rage and drink. They tore Charles Warren and Charles Yorke from out the snugroom with the utmost savagery, smacking, kicking, hitting them with knobby clubs. By the time they had them in the yard, both were bloodied, the younger dazed almost to the point of disability. Warren, still *compos mentis*, tried to get a fix on faces, for the future satisfaction that would come from hanging them, but they came and went, and thronged and throbbed, and hallooed deafeningly as they rained down blows. It was raining, too, black and steadily, hissing from the leaves all round the yard in the windless silence of the summer night, gushing from the gutters, falling in a curtain from the thatch. He picked out the large, loud villain in

7

the curly hat and pigtail, he noticed several times the small man with the shining, vicious eyes, he saw a ginger fellow, a country stumbler who stayed back a ways, face set and maybe showing fright. But mostly it was jumble, men in coats, some wigged, some in heavy cloaks, some in short seamen's breeches, slops. All, or almost all, consumed by anger.

There were lights still in the inn, dim through the country glass, but no further sounds, no screams from Mrs Cullen or the hare-lipped girl who helped her. There had been men around to drink the nights before and in the mornings, but Yorke and Warren had no hopes by this; they would either stay well clear if they heard or saw this mob or – more like – had set it on or were a part of it. No aid from travellers, either; the inn was on a road more fairly called a track, which led from nowhere great to somewhere less important, as Yorke had coined the jest some days before when they had chosen it as perfection for their purposes. Not so perfect for survival, though, as they stood and stumbled in the rain, their feet and wrists jerked free of clothing to receive their bonds. They were to have one horse between them, it would seem, a big horse, extremely strong, that Warren caught himself admiring, in spite of all, and drunk or not, the bumpkins did their knots like angels. Not angels, seamen. Not bumpkins, men of free trade. But men, it looked, of awful wickedness.

Yorke, struck in the face by a flail armed certainly with lead and truly deadly, was unconscious when they put him up. His eyes were open, now and then, but they did not see, and one bone of his cheek appeared collapsed, to fill out slowly as a great black livid swelling bloomed and blossomed. The horse stood stolid in the rain while they jerked and slid him into place, snorting only gently as a rope was fastened underneath its belly and hauled taut, a rope that held Yorke's ankles fast together. His chest, raked by spasmodic coughs, was laid along the horse's neck, his joined wrists bent underneath his belly. Warren was allowed an upended cask to step up from, and swung his leg across with some sort of dignity. He sat motionless as his ankles were lashed underneath, and tried to pull Yorke's torso upright to save him from falling sideways when they should set off.

As the assailants mounted, Warren did a head count, not complete. Ten at least, probably more, but as they bucked and wheeled around the blackness of the yard accuracy became guesswork, more or less. There seemed to be nobody in command, and no idea of any form of discipline, or sense. Warren assumed they were being taken off to talk to someone, otherwise why not just have killed them where they sat? But as they moved out from the inn, his confidence grew less. Some of the men had whips, one a flail, three had cudgels. Defenceless, gripping the fabric of Charles Yorke's coat to try and steady him, Charles Warren played the stoic as the blows and cuts came on to him, and he wondered at their frenzy and their hate. A whiplash split his cheek, a rough stick grazed his temple, then dislodged his wig, then raised his scalp. The head in front of him, lying on the horse's neck, received repeated blows, and one bold hero prodded at it with his swordpoint until Yorke's blood ran thickly on to the horse's hair.

In the Hampshire rain, in the noisy, drunken silence of the peaceful, violent night, Charles Warren began to doubt that they would ever see the light of day again.

2

Miles to the north of them, not far south of London, the rain was soaking and insistent, though similarly soft and almost silent, undriven by the faintest wind. William Bentley, drenched through his cloak and coat right to the skin, was saddle-sore and weary, and sick at heart. He was on his way to join a ship in Deptford, and he had been riding there since morning. He was not alone, but almost wished he could have been.

The man beside him, tall and ungainly on his hack, was something of a prattler. Preceded by an express the night before, he had turned up at the crack of dawn, and gone about the house as if he'd been at ease. He had taken breakfast like a long-lost cousin, chattering to William and his father before formal introductions had been completed, and bowing to his mother and his sisters in a rather ill-bred way, and smiling. William was going back to sea again, he did not want to, the girls were heartbroken, and his mother had to keep her own opinions to herself. Midshipman Samuel Holt, though surely much too old to have not yet made lieutenant, was like a careless youth. He even did not fade or merge, or drift into the scenery, when the last farewells were made, and William reached down to touch his sisters' fingers one last time. Father, as a contrast, had gone about his business on the farm ten minutes previously.

At first, the weather dry and decent, the two young men had travelled side by side. Sam Holt had brought up many gambits, little snippets of his life and times, many opportunities for Bentley to respond, but the conversation, in the main, had been one-sided. William, aware, had explained he was not a talking sort of fellow, who spent much time alone. But he was also aware, at times, that his demeanour and expression spoke something different, of disaffection and a mild distaste. Truth was – and this he could not tell a stranger, even hint at – the idea of resuming the naval life, which had been disrupted violently for him some years before, was a form of mental anguish. So Holt, out of politeness, perhaps a desperation of his own, had talked the miles away, and had not seemed to mind Will Bentley's taciturnity. The rain, however, when it came, might have been a relief, who knew? As the road bogged and the horses tired, they could ride apart, in damp cocoons of silence, where Will, at least, could brood and ponder.

It was cash, the oldest, sharpest goad, that had resealed his fate as Navy officer. He had wanted, and tried, to leave the service, had refused all blandishments, cajolings, threats for some long time. His relations with his father – never warm – had frosted, and a dip in Bentley fortunes – never explicated – had led him to a realisation that threats of excommunication from the family and the home were not idle ones. On paper his sea-time was good, to their lordships – who knew not the half of it – his experience was excellent. He had been ill, true, a good excuse for the hiatus, but now his bronchial problems were all cleared up. Uncle Daniel Swift, roped in to take a hand in it, insisted that if he worked hard at navigation and 'got in the thick' again, there was no reason in the world he should not resume his rise. William, who refused point blank to contemplate his uncle's aid, or get advancement on his back, or even consider any offer of a shipboard place with him, made his own approaches to the Office and the Admiralty, speaking in his letters more of desire to resume than bleak necessity. Truth was, he did not want to starve.

There was a war on, nor had he come ashore through reasons of dishonour. But although the first responses had been prompt, it seemed to him a weary time before the process was got running. And then the job had come, the place, position, the assigning to a ship. It was a small ship, the sort of ship that no one, he could imagine, would join from choice, a tender based in London River, another weight upon his heart's unease. Bad enough to have to serve, but that was that. But how much worse to join the Impress Service, so universally reviled. Then, last evening the express, and here he was on horseback, alongside this lanky, stupid man, this prattler.

To be fair though, William argued with himself, Samuel Holt had maybe prattled for discomfort's sake, and indeed had not spoken now for something like an hour. In fact, as they jogged along, he it was who felt some need for conversation. Normally, William was happy to be silent, and spent the main part of his hours in lanes and byways, on horse or foot, in peaceful solitude. He had a boat as well, an open yawl with leg o' mutton rig, that he sailed endlessly in the soft wildernesses of Langstone and Chichester havens, or out into the Solent and beyond the Wight. He fished, as he had to have a reason to be out there, no one sailed for pleasure, naturally. Him neither, in the last analysis, perhaps: William sailed because he needed to. Now, he had a need to know.

The rain had broken through the last defences of the felted wool around his neck, and was moving in runnels down his chest and back. Below the dampness was a band of discomfort, almost pain, around his waist, and below that still a spreading, jolted ache and soreness. They had ridden solidly, changing their hacks some thirty miles back, and William assumed and hoped that they were near their destination. London was not unknown to him, and the Portsmouth road a good one in the summer months at least, but this night was darker than the Shades. He had no inkling where they precisely were, and he needed rest. It was a way to frame his question.

'Mr Holt,' he said. 'What is this ship like, when we get to her? We will have a place to lie and sleep, at least?'

Holt, up ahead, had given him some details of the ship

before, in the early stages. A brig, quite old, quite small, but not unhandy. He swivelled in his saddle, looking back.

'Mr Bentley, yes! That is to say, the Biter has such things, cots for the officers, all comforts of the home. Yes, there will be beds for us; I hope.'

'But what do you mean by "hope", sir? Pray tell me more, and sensibly. What sort of ship is she? How run? Is it a bad ship?'

Through the rain there came a muffled laugh. Holt eased his pace, dropping back until they went side by side.

'Hereabouts,' he said, 'there lives a man I know. He is a rich man, a baronet, a trader in the East. His house is large, and ornate, very comfortable, the alpha and the omega. To be frank with you, the Biter, sir – is not!'

He dug in his heels, and his horse moved back ahead. Before its rump, wet and rhythmic, could disappear Will Bentley clogged his horse also, to draw up alongside. As he did so, they emerged from out of a clump of roadside trees and saw a long vista of rolling grass and hedge as the moon gleamed through a thinner patch of cloud. No buildings, no outer village of the Great Wen, but just the road, more like a river in the misty light, and another copse ahead.

'So,' he said, determinedly. 'What is your meaning, or must I wring it from you? Should we stop again? Would this merchant welcome us, or is there an inn hereabouts for getting warm and dry? How long are we from London? How long from Deptford and the ship? You make her sound a fright. Is that true?'

He was thoroughly annoyed with Holt by now, a vulgar, laughing thing that would not give him answers. For hours he had talked too much, now there was no sense from him, just evasions. If there were truly no good berths on board, William was determined he would sleep on shore, at least for one night more.

'I've told you all I can,' said Samuel, suddenly and tersely. 'Good God man, the Biter is my ship, Lieutenant

13

Kaye is my commander, what should I say to you? If it were my choice, we would stop off at Dr Marigold's and get some wenches, or feather beds if Hampshire men prefer them for lying on! It's above an hour, maybe two, to London Bridge, then a wherry to the tiers at Deptford. Then you will see the Biter for yourself, for your approval or disdain!'

In silence, Will Bentley held his station, but a little chastened. Holt was right in one thing, but it gave him little comfort. If he disliked the vessel never so much, he could hardly say so to his new and fellow midshipman. Will felt he ought to make amends.

'There is necessity,' he mumbled, 'and speed is of the essence is the theory. We are under orders, after all, to join the ship. This Dr Marigold – he is the merchant, I suppose?'

Holt let out a hoot of joy, all animosity evaporated.

'The merchant! Marigold!? Nay, Mr Bentley, that is capital! The merchant is my ... well, a kind of benefactor, a gentleman who has done me aid and kindnesses. Dr Marigold has a gay house in the Blackfriars – you know, maids for hire, harlots. He is a whoremaster!'

He was laughing, so William joined in, to hide confusion. The use of whores, although he'd seen it on his uncle's ship when lying in St Helen's Roads, was a thing beyond his own experience, or even comprehension of such harsh desires.

'Lord,' he said. 'When next you see him – the good man, not the bad – please you don't tell him my mistake.'

Holt threw a glance at him.

'Well, that's not likely, anyway,' he said. 'My times for talking to Sir A ...' He stopped, and wiped rainwater from his eyes and face. 'Nay, private things, sir. Men like you have no need of benefactors, I suppose, and men like me are insufficient grateful. Nay, wrong again, I do him wrong again.' This last was almost muttered, but he flashed a bold smile, adding loudly: 'He has a sense of humour, does Sir

14

A, but perhaps to call him whoremaster would be a shot too far. There is much he disapproves of in my life, I'm sad to say. No matter, then.'

So they would not go to the great house for their comfort, nor to a gay house neither, that was settled. Will dropped his horse behind as the road became a narrow, sodden bottleneck, and tried to fathom out. Earlier his strange companion had talked too much on shallow subjects, then he'd uttered cryptically on deep, while now he did not talk at all. Under it there was embarrassment of a sort, thought Bentley, there must be. He decided the offhand manner was not perhaps innate vulgarity, but more like a social cover. Holt was above him in the Navy pecking order, but not in any other, clearly. He had prattled earlier of his lawyer father, who had gone to Virginia but had died 'before he made his fortune', and said it with a laugh, engagingly. But the fact that he had gone, and his son had stayed at home, argued that the unmade fortune must have been a sad necessity. What's more, Holt had got his naval education at 'Christ's Mathematical, where all the jolly paupers go!' – and made another jest of that. Momentarily, Will felt a blush begin to rise. When Holt had breakfasted at his father's house, much at his apparent ease, Will had remarked the stains and grass stalks on his clothes, and Samuel, drinking tea, had chuckled that he'd slept in a hedge the night. Could it be he had not spoke in fun?

'Sir,' he said. 'Mr Holt.'

'Or Samuel. Sam for short.'

'Yes. Samuel. Look, you must call me Will, and do forgive me if you think I'm a grumps, but it is hard for me, you know. This is my first ship for a damn long time, and my last one was the Welfare; you have heard of her no doubt, and of my uncle who commanded her. As you've been frank with me I'll tell you frankly that I go to sea, between us two, out of necessity. I have an older brother lives in Wiltshire who will inherit what I call my home. I have no other means of income, but I can do mathematics,

15

and don't get mortal sick in ships. The Biter is a tender for the Press. She is . . . it is not what . . .'

Holt made a harsh noise in his throat. Amusement.

'Not what you were bred to, William. No, I do well believe it! I have heard of Daniel Swift – who has not? – and know that he's your uncle, and the Biter's not his kind of ship, I'll warrant you. She is a collier, out of Sunderland I think, cut down because she's of a certain age. She's old and dirty and a little cranky, and she's on the Impress, which is a pain to other men than you and me. Nay, I am being far too open maybe, so are you, but to hell with it, we're shipmates and we'll stand or fall together, so keep it up, say I. We are due on Biter by tonight on pain of God knows what, but when we get there Lieutenant Kaye won't be on board, he'll be off whoring – lord, there's frankness for you! So if you'll risk it, friend, we'll go for the young maids' bodies also, and the meat and drink – even the feather beds if that's your preference! What say you?'

As he had spoken there had been a squall of wind, warm but unexpected, to batter fresh, heavy raindrops in their faces. First one and then the other turned the horses' rumps into the gust, huddling in their sopping cloaks. The beating rain made answer useless for the moment.

William, at last, said: 'Samuel. It is not that I am being nice, but . . . Truly, I have never even thought . . .'

In the dying gust, they both heard noises. Odd sounds, like a bellow and a scream. The horses heard it, lifting their heads into the falling drops, one flicking up its ears. The wind died, and the sounds died with it. The two young men glanced at each other, both quizzical. Then Holt pulled his horse round to face the northern road.

'Ah, whatever,' he said, with a note as if regretting the frankness of his speaking. 'She is a Press tender, men will hate us for the things we do, but we have to do our duty anyway, we must earn our meat and drink. The Biter is a fine ship, let us say, and I am proud to serve in her. So let us go and greet our lord and master.'

The breeze blew, and a scream came, faint but clear. It was high and pure, a young scream, probably a girl's. Then a bellow, male and powerful, then a second screaming voice, that broke into a sob. The breeze died and they both dug heels in horses' sides. Outlined against the sky there was a dense black copse ahead. It was not far away, perhaps a quarter-mile or so, and the horses, as if sensing purpose in the movement, surged and snorted. The weak light through the breaking cloud held up, and when they reached the woodland they could see an entry through the undergrowth. As they slowed to go into the trees William caught a fire's glow a hundred yards inside, and a horse snickered when it caught their own mounts' scents.

The shouting and the screams were to the purpose now, bold and definite. One woman's voice was bawling loud abuse, the other howling. Among the deeper shouts they heard blows being struck. It was a mortal struggle.

'God, Will,' said Holt. 'Is it a tinker camp? Let's not stick our nose in anything of that.'

They reined their horses to a halt while they considered. Had it been footpads or men of the highway, they would have gone in headlong, but a family quarrel, however violent, was a different thing. In the glow from the fire both could see the outline of a cart, a covered living van. Bentley touched the hanger at his side. There might be many of them; it was his only arm.

'Do you have a gun? They—'

There came an awful scream, pain-filled and wrenched. The other voice screeched, 'Murderer! Murderer! Help, he's killing us!', and both men spurred, all doubts forgotten. The horses, more circumspect, responded to the goad, but cautiously, feeling the ground before they put their weight on it. They came into the clearing not on a gallop but sedately.

The scene before their eyes was wild, however. In the darkness it was a question of shapes and shadows, but there was a man, a vigorous terrier of a man, in a black

17

cloak, scuttling between two girls or women, pulling at them, flailing with an arm that held a cudgel. For a moment the three fought and struggled, moving round in circles between van and fire, the movement punctuated by grunts, by silence, and by screams.

'Hold!' shouted Samuel. And William added, 'Enough! Enough, sir! Stop!'

The shock was startling. Immediately the three figures sprang apart and all noise ceased. Only for an instant, then the man roared incoherently, while one of the maidens let out a wail, lower than her cries of earlier, full of pain and misery. Then the man, as if with great intent, rushed at their horses, arm and club raised as if to strike, eyes glaring furiously. Will's horse, of its own volition, stepped back a foot or two, before he could control it.

'Go before I kill you!' roared the man. 'Private business, private! Get off from here!'

In Samuel's hand there was a heavy Navy cutlass, the blade already hacked significantly. William struggled to get his sword out, but the horse was not for fighting, it was a master of retreat. The man ran up to Samuel's horse, then had to stop. The prattler did not move. The Navy blade reached forward past his horse's ears, pointing at the waiting throat. The throat was knotted angrily, the muscles worked.

'You go,' invited Samuel, almost as if to a friend. 'I do not like to see men threaten women. You go, sir. Go now.'

But the women were the ones to run. One darted to the other, whose face was covered with her hands, and clapped an arm around her and tried to drag her off. As they moved, the cloaked man moved to stop them, and Samuel leapt neatly from his saddle and sent the blade over his head in a whooshing arc. At the edge of the clearing one girl fell, giving out a cry of misery, and the other stopped to help her.

Bentley was down now, sword out, trying to restrain his horse with a rein. The other horse was standing quietly, watching the old nag tethered to the cart. For a moment, there was just the sound of water dripping through the leaves. William noticed that no new rain was falling. It had stopped.

The cloaked man faced Samuel, but the wildness in his eyes was almost gone. He raised a hand, a sort of friendly gesture, or submissive, if half-hearted. Holt stepped forward, all aggression, the cutlass raised and ready.

'Drop it,' he said.

'These women,' the man began. 'These two whores—'

Samuel stepped once more, lowering the blade, its position very deadly.

'Drop it!'

With an imprecation that was lost in passion, the man threw the club – not down but straight at Samuel's head – and turned towards the women. With a burst of movement he scuttled across the clearing and levelled a great clout to the head of the stooped one, who fell across her friend in a jumble. Then he was gone, through the undergrowth into the trees. William Bentley and Samuel Holt stared at one another.

Slowly, the two young women rose to their feet. One, enveloped in a sodden cloak with hood, appeared to look at them. Her companion, however, did not. Her face remained covered. From beneath her hands came sobs and sounds of pain. William, the rein still in his hand, took two or three steps towards them, but imperceptibly they edged back towards the clearing's edge. He stopped.

'We are not here to hurt you,' he said. 'We thought you might need help.'

'Are you a surgeon?'

The maid's voice was odd, or struck him so. He hardly understood what she had said. There was a note like scorn.

'You're from the north,' said Samuel Holt. 'Who needs a surgeon?'

'He's had her teeth,' the girl said. She glanced at her companion, and both men moved forward, gently. William, with a jolt, saw blood underneath the hands, blood moving on the chin, on to the neck and breast. 'She's been bleeding hours.'

'Her teeth?' said William.

'There's a village,' Holt said. 'I'll help her up on to my horse. Mr Bentley will take you.'

The girl turned her head to William, and the cloak hood fell aside. Another jolt struck him as he looked close into her eyes. She was young, and lustrous, and distracted. But her eyes, though troubled, locked on his, and held them. They were brown, and deep, and speaking, beneath thick eyebrows in an oval face, and he felt somehow robbed of sense, as if a charge of heat had gone between them.

'He has gone there,' was what the maiden said. 'To the village, there's an alehouse, he'll get men. We ran away. They'll kill us.'

Then the other maid collapsed. As she fell into a heap in the mud her hands dropped and her face was uncovered. It was white and bloodless, with violent bruises and torn, broken lips, barely parted. But as she lay her mouth fell open wider, and it was filled with blood, that dribbled down her cheek. Her gums were empty, blood rising in the ragged sockets where her teeth had been. Just three left at the back on one side, on the other four.

'I know a place,' said Samuel, quietly.

3

In Hampshire, now, Charles Warren and Charles Yorke were near the end. Of their road and suffering, Yorke hoped, but he feared another end might be in store. They had come miles, and every yard a torture and a beating. His face was whipped to pieces, one eye blind, his cheek-bone numb the last hour or more. He had been in and out of consciousness himself, but his older friend behind had borne the brunt of blows and taunts and whipping, and of startings with the points of many swords. At one stage Warren had slipped sideways with a sudden, weighty rush that Yorke had been incapable of preventing, and it had caused great whoops and yells of jubilation.

The horse, bone-weary after many miles across soft muddy fields and dense leafy pathways leading to the west, had mercifully stopped. Yorke had twisted round as best he could, to see Charles Warren's legs arched round the belly, his feet above the back, lashed with thin, biting line. Underneath, he could make out the trunk and head of Warren, with his lashed wrists dangling down towards his chin. Had he been in his senses he must have screamed, the pain would have been unbearable. But he made no sound.

The men did, the smugglers, free traders, savages. They yelled and yipped, kicking their horses round about the tired one, lashing and poking at the body hung below. Almost absently, one or another of them would take a slash at Yorke's own face, but he felt little pain – except for his companion, which was a different thing. As the horse was lashed into a stumbling forward pace, the back hooves struck poor Warren's head, first one and then the other, rocking it back and forward, side to side, at every kick. Until he, Yorke, began to roar and shout and rock so hard the horse put down its head in fear and refused to go another step. Much as the drunkards raged and beat him, Charles Yorke would not desist, until at last some of them dismounted, and pushed Warren back upright on the horse's back and held him there until he showed some life. The rain had stopped, but they dashed water in his face from a puddle in the grass and smacked and fanned him with their hands. Like Yorke, Warren was bareheaded, neither wig nor hat remaining. They caught each other's eyes, but did not speak.

How long did it go on? Neither of them knew. Yorke judged it must be nearly midnight when they stopped, but that was a notion, only. They were on a wide heath, still windless, with a waning moon above them as the grey bulked cloud dwindled. The horsemen, less noisy, not so boisterous, moved off some distance, which gave them hope, but neither of them spoke, still. Both had fought before, with desperate and determined men, but nothing they had ever known had been like this mad vindictiveness.

What now? Bottles were passed – they heard the clinkings – but the scene had lost the aspect of a gin-house or a sailors' drinking den. Was this the place they were to meet the men behind the rumpus, the secret powers that they'd hoped to gull? Both men knew beyond a doubt that they had lost that gambit, whatever lay behind the failure. Betrayal was the likeliest, betrayal or some first-class spying work. From loss of blood, ill-usage, hunger, Charles Yorke felt coldness creeping into his bones. Behind him his companion, rock-hardness melting into mere humanity, began to shiver violently.

Still no sign of movement from the huddled wildmen. Still no sign or sound of anyone's approach. Yorke mused on his good uncle, up in Surrey, and wondered if he would ever see him or his home again. And he brooded on betrayal.

'I have heard of it, admitted,' said Sir Arthur Fisher, moving forward from the blazing logs. 'Heard of it, but never thought it might be true. Truly, my friends, we live in foul times.'

Samuel Holt and William, still damp although their outer layers of protection had gone to be force-dried, nodded as if sagely, clutching mulled pots of metheglin. Men had brought the maids down from the horses, women had carried them inside for care. Sir Arthur – Sir A, as he insisted – had called for more fire, dry blankets, drinks and food. There had been wood smouldering already in the hearth, but it was soon blazed up, while servants bustled round with great solicitude.

William, after introductions, had been treated with most easy courtesy, while Holt explained the situation to the baronet briefly, dwelling rather on the problem of the mountebank than the injured girl. William, who on the journey from the copse had elicited almost nothing save the maidens' names and their deep fear of being sought out and attacked anew, questioned if there might be some way indeed their place of refuge could be fathomed by the man. Sir A deemed it most unlikely, as they had not been followed, but called in his steward Tony, a quiet, watchful, stiff-built sort, and told him to maintain a guard and have the gatehouse discreetly manned. The maidens' names were Deb and Cecily.

It struck Bentley, watching Sir A and Samuel talk together, that there was a strangeness between them that was on Samuel's side more prominent. Their host was a tall man of considerable age, quite elegant, but remarkably warm and intimate. He had greeted Samuel as a confidant, but Samuel had stayed stiff, with circumspection even in his smiles. But then, thought William, Sam Holt's an

23

odd fish; I've already come to that conclusion, haven't I?

The housekeeper, a fat and homely creature he'd looked upon indulgently when she'd come in all a-bustle and officious, soon proved herself formidable indeed. She had not only cleaned Cecily and eased her pain, dosing her with tinctures and the normal remedies, but she had spoken long and hard with Deborah, extracting information. She gave an account of all of it without a trace of censure or surprise, even on the most appalling details of the operation, and spoke most vehemently of Deb's fears for the near future: in short, her strong conviction that the mountebank would hunt them down.

'Oh nonsense, Mrs Houghton,' cried Sir A. 'How could he find them? Far more likely that he will take his chance to flee. These young gentlemen confronted him, did they not? He's unlikely to imagine they will abandon the poor creatures to their fate.'

'She says there are associates in the vicinity, sir. Ruffians with whom he's dealt before. Why should I mince words? It was a close call if they should be sold to them for play-things, or "pay their debts" by the selling of their teeth. I think the maidens chose, and he accepted because the fee was greater. Better to lose their ivory than be tossed to that crew, was their opinion. Now she says the crew will come for them and take them willy-nilly. Her "just desserts", she named it, on account she was the second string if Cecily's teeth proved useless or broke up, but she tried to run and hence the beatings in the woods. I think she has a bitter turn of jest.'

Sir A stood thoughtful, and sucked his lower lip. William, worried, could none the less picture Deb's face. Surely, he thought, the condition of the girls was horrible. Sam Holt sipped metheglin.

'There is another thing,' said Mrs Houghton. 'I said you'd have the law of him if he should even dare to do the slightest little thing. She laughed. She said, sir, that the man who bought the teeth is a magistrate himself. And asked me how the law would ever help them.'

Sir A had stiffened slightly, contemplating his house-keeper gravely and in silence. He pushed his fingers up his temples, beneath his wig.

'Oh dear,' he said. 'A magistrate. A magistrate whose wife has rotten teeth. Did she say how far from here? Did she know? Is there anyone would fill that bill, think you, Mrs Houghton? Any rumour?'

Mrs Houghton pursed her lips. She was not about to assume the mantle of the local gossip. Sir Arthur Fisher sighed.

'Well, keep them comfortable, if you please,' he said. 'Nay, I know your excellence in that department, it is a form of words only. Tell them that they are safe with us, explain that Tony has a dozen men. Oh dear, poor maidens, to have been brought to such a pass. How old, Mrs Houghton? Did they vouchsafe?'

She shook her head.

'The one that speaks, the one that *can* speak, says seven-teen or thereabouts. Knock off a year or two, I'd say. They're grown, but still quite slight.'

'Children,' said the baronet. 'God's blood, let's keep them safely if we can. Tell them that, please, Mrs Hough-ton. Tell them I'll keep them safe until they are fit to move, and then I'll transport them safely wherever they might want to go.'

'Which is where?' asked Samuel, oddly. 'They come from the north if I know accents. Who will get them home again? You cannot guarantee them that far, sir, surely no one can? You cannot give all people succour in every cir-cumstance.'

It hung strangely like a jibe. Mrs Houghton gazed at Samuel a long moment before she spoke.

'Aye, from the north,' she said. 'Hatter girls from Stock-port way. They ran off from home as young folk do, and were saved or preyed on by this mountebank, whose name is Marcus Dennett, she believes. Oh, they have folks in London, that is their story, as it most always is. Friends of last resort, if they could ever find 'em! Sir, I will do my best. At the very outside we can keep them safely here. The hurt one may need a surgeon, if her gums go bad; they sometimes do, when teeth are ripped. I'll go to them.'

When she had retired, Sir A mulled over details of such transactions, such 'monetary extractions', repeating several times that he had come across such awful things before, by hearsay if not in concrete. But he was deeply affected, muttering of 'dark times, foul times' distractedly, and grinding his wig down on his skull. Then, suddenly, he turned from the fire to face them, an expression of grim frankness on his face.

'You see, I think I know the man,' he said. 'I cannot be sure, but . . .'

'What? A neighbour, sir?' cried Holt. 'But . . . but surely no magistrate would . . .' He tailed off, reddening. Bentley's expression remained stolid. Sir Arthur noted it.

'You do not seem surprised, young man,' he said. His tone was peculiar. 'Is this sort of outrage rife, where you hail from?'

It was William's turn to flush.

'I have never heard of such a thing before, sir,' he replied. 'Indeed I scarcely can believe it happens. It is only that I . . .'

He faltered. There was a weight of history on him, that he did not wish to make a song of. His history he preferred kept under boards. It was his, not anybody else's.

Sam Holt spoke lightly, but somehow he made the words sound like a mild rebuke once more.

'William is a midshipman, sir,' he said. 'Younger than myself a shade, but the action he has seen has been a good deal hotter. He was in the Welfare, sir. His uncle was her captain, Daniel Swift.' To lighten it, maybe, he added: 'He is a Hampshire man. Near Petersfield. They are not noted, as I've heard it, for their bestiality.'

Sir A's gaze did not falter, but his stance was modified. He nodded gravely, everything explained. He made no comment, for which William was grateful. Over the intervening years, where ships were talked about, the Welfare's fate was always known, his uncle was a bogey or a hero, nothing in between. Bentley, from interlocutors or acquaintances, craved indifference.

'A Hampshire man,' the baronet responded. 'I have a man in Hampshire this very day. Do you have dealings with the Customs down your way?'

Strange question. Down his way? Perhaps Sir Arthur did not know the geography.

'The Portsmouth men, sir? Unfortunately not, it is near twenty miles distant from my house. I . . . my dealings with the Navy have been rather slight these last years.'

'To say nothing of the Navy's with the Customs!' said Holt, amused. 'You know how well those two fine bodies rub along together! This man, though, sir? Would that be Charlie Yorke?' He smiled at William. 'Sir A has a . . . well, not a son, precisely.'

Sir Arthur nodded.

'I am his uncle, but to me he is a son,' he said. 'Sam understands it very clearly. Yes, it is Charlie; he is a riding officer, sir. Or rather, he is down there on Customs House business, he and another man.' A cloud passed across his face. 'It is near two weeks since I heard news of them. It is a desperate venture they have undertaken.'

William looked expectant but polite. Sir A shook his head, as if to clear it. There was no more forthcoming, apparently.

'It is a wicked thing, the trade,' he said. 'Are you bothered with it, where you live? Petersfield is on the London road, I think?'

Will nodded. He did not want to talk of smuggling; that brought back hard memories, also.

'My father's house is off the beaten track, sir. We are not bothered by it nearly. It is quite small beer thereabouts,

27

I do believe, being the distance to France is great and the Lowlands greater. Not the wild armies that I've heard of to the east.'

'Ah,' said Sir Arthur. But he let the thought die off, as if he'd changed his mind. He cleared his throat. 'And why are you young gentlemen along this road tonight? Are you for London or going for the coast?' A smile at William. 'Young Mr Holt could tell me more about his engagements but no longer cares to, do you see? Own life to lead, eh Samuel? Own life to lead!'

Samuel smiled stiffly.

'Not a bit of it, Sir Arthur, it is just I have been busy for a month or two.' To Will he said: 'Sir A has done much for me, in times gone by. If it were not for him—'

'No!' said the baronet quite sharply; but his eyes were kindly still. 'Samuel, you have made your way, not I. I did my bit when you were younger and had some small need of it, now I'll hear nothing more. Mr Bentley, Samuel will pass for lieutenant whenever he is called to be examined, and his only course is up. If you are to be shipmates with him, you are lucky. You will never find a better man.'

It was handsome, but Sir A avoided possible embarrassment by begging their presence for a late supper and then a bed. What business, he demanded, could get them out upon the road once more, at this late hour? Nothing!

But there was, and Holt was determined they must go about it. The matter with the maidens had cost a good two hours, and at the very briskest pace, he said, they could not reach London till well past midnight, even given clear roads and no more excitements. Their horses would be rested, they were fed and full of inner comfort from the glass, and they must off. He added, with a strange shyness, that he had collected William from his home to join him to a ship in Deptford, where they would indeed be shipmates.

'Then how well I know you, Sam,' said the baronet. 'For I wagered that you'd go, whatever blandishments I tried to offer. You will not take your horses, they are blown, so Tony has prepared two for you from my stable. Young man, be so good as to tug that bell-pull, will you?'

'But, sir, our hacks,' William began, to be silenced with a gesture. He jerked the bell-pull.

'There is a coach-inn five miles away,' Sir Arthur said. 'Your hacks can go there in the morning, and you can lodge mine at the Bear's Paw near the bridge, you'll go to Deptford down the river, yes? I'll have a man or two in London in the week, it's normal traffic in my line. What ship is she? The one you're going to?'

Involuntarily, the young men swapped a glance, and on the instant Will Bentley understood at least some part of Samuel's reticence. He did not want to name the vessel because, quite clearly, he thought Sir A would know her and her line of duty. Like William, it now became apparent, he felt it keenly as a sort of shame. Strangely, this reaction reassured Will. New warmth towards his friend-at-arms coursed through him.

However, Samuel did not shirk for long. He turned a clear eye on Sir A, although his lips were tight.

'She is called the Biter, sir. Lieutenant Richard Kaye, commanding. He is expecting us by the hour.'

Sir Arthur Fisher may have looked askance, but William did not know his face with sufficient intimacy to read his thoughts from it. There was a pause though, a thinking pause; then he made a hum.

'Mm. The Impress Service, eh? Well, boys – very necessary, very. These bloody, bloody wars. Samuel, how find you Kaye? I know of him.'

Holt's answer was slow coming, and Sir Arthur turned a polite look on William.

'I have interests in the ship direction,' he said. 'Mayhap Sam has told you?' He chuckled, not with clear humour in it. 'I have some certain dealings with the Press, from time to time.'

'I find my captain . . .' started Sam. 'I find him as a midshipman should. We have as yet seen little action. I have been on board of her but seven week.'

'Seven weeks? No action? Hhm.'

'She has been at the dockyard, sir, for some of it. She is . . . not a young ship, sir.'

'Press tenders rarely are. The Biter was a collier, unless I mistake me. North-eastern built, on cat lines. Big and slow and roomy. Well.'

'Aye,' said Samuel. 'Well. But beggars can't be choosers. Can we?'

It had got uncomfortable, but they passed it off. Tony took them to the horses shortly, with Sir A making his farewells from his fireside, tall and dignified and full of kindness and good words for the road. Outside it was dry, although still cloudy, and their outer riding clothes were warm and fire-steamy. Tony had already tied Will's dunnage next his saddle – his chest was due to come up later with a carter – but before they kicked off he handed each a narrow canvas bag. Horse pistols, with powder horns and balls.

'From my master,' he said, in his country accent. 'There'll be a lot abroad up London way, Mister Sam. You can shoot the buggers, can't 'ee?'

He laughed and smacked a rump. The horses, wistful at leaving home so late at night, set off without enthusiasm.

4

William thought of Deborah, while Samuel thought of God knew what. For the first half-hour he did not even stay close to his companion, making it quite plain that talking was not his pleasure or intent. A pity, William found that, for he was keen to explore the attitude to being in the Press that he figured had been hinted at in Sir Arthur's parlour. To Samuel, earlier, it had seemed a laughing matter, to be spoken lightly of in the manner seamen had when talking of their ships. With Sir A, though, Will had sensed a touch of shame.

The knowledge that the ship he'd been put down for was a tender had filled him with a heavy gloom, when the news had come. His mother, even, had responded with excuses, and a delighted 'la' that had spoken little of delight. His father, with whom William spoke hardly anything on Navy matters, had merely grunted.

'What does it mean?' had trilled little sister Martha. 'The Impress Service? The Biter is a fine name for a fighting ship though, Will!'

'Hah!' had said his father, quietly. 'A fighting ship indeed.'

'Lord, sir!' had said his mother, lightly. 'It is a ship! You're off to sea once more, William. You will make the best of it, as you always do.'

His older sister Lal, who was exceeding sharp, had winced imperceptibly at this, and touched his hand.

'Near waters, though,' she'd put in gently. 'If she lies at Deptford, where will you . . . ply your trade? Surely not far from London River? We will see you home sometimes. Why, perhaps you will even come into Portsmouth. Then

31

we shall all go on the ship and visit him, Martha! Won't that be fine?'

'What *is* the trade, though?' asked Martha. 'Won't *no*body tell me? It sounds . . . impressive. William! Lal! Mama! It sounds im*press*ive. A *jeu de mot*!'

They had laughed, save father, who had left them for his study when the news was fairly broke, and it eased the matter till William, too, could escape the womenfolk to stand at his open window and watch the light across the home copse trees. Later, both girls had sought him out alone, and cried, but not because he was in the Impress Service, just because he was going to leave. Lal, further, because she feared for him. She could still remember her brother before he'd gone to join her uncle's ship. Bright, bumptious, uncaring and a joy. While he had recovered afterwards, in his bed, she had often come to sit with him, and talked, and talked, and never seemed to mind the lack of answers.

Out of the blue, breaking his reverie, Samuel spoke. He had slowed and dropped astern, with William hardly noticing. He muttered, gruff and bitter, but it came through pretty clear.

'If wishes were horses, beggars would ride,' he said. 'And here we are on horseback, eh? What made you of Sir Arthur Fisher, Will? My benefactor?'

There was a pause before the 'benefactor'. Holt's voice was loaded with a type of aggravation.

'Sam, I do not know the man,' said Will, most carefully. 'I stood and steamed for him in his fine parlour, but that is all. He is rich, he is courteous, and he is very kind – we ride his horses, do we not? Am I to leap to condemnation?'

They jogged along quite fast. The highway was wide hereabouts, well made, and the blackness of the night had diminished as the clouds had faded, although the moon was almost down. Will hoped they could not be far from London's villages, at least.

'Nay,' said Samuel, after some thought. 'Nay, not condemn him. Sir A is a good man, I believe, a very good one. It is just – oh, somehow he oppresses me, I almost hate him. Beggars can't be choosers, I said to him just now, and I know he had my meaning. He saved me from despair and poverty, without him I should be a tinker now myself, like that man Dennett, or more likely a cadaver, in an unmarked grave. My father went to Virginia, I have told you that already, I believe. My mother and two small boys died shortly after him, of scurvy or the bloody flux, and I was left with Christ's, a pauper-scholar and scarce enough to dress myself. One day he visited, not grand but kind, and took me up in some way.' Holt paused, looking across between the horses, his expression neutral. 'Not for my arsehole, neither, which is what a lot of gentlemen expect for such advancement. Nay, it was my mind Sir A was after. Let's say – my soul.'

He lapsed. They jogged. Sir A's face was not that of a lecher, Will had noted that himself. But the talk of soul he found . . .

Samuel must have shared the thought. He grunted, half amused.

'Nay, I make it sound like playhouse flummery,' he said. 'Sir A was lonely, true, he is a lonely man, but he seeks to help young men, not have them, in whatever way. He has made a habit of it, I cannot find a better word instanter. Three or four have benefited, and some are easier with it than I. Most, indeed, I guess. Perhaps I should feel shame about myself, I cannot tell for certain, but I find it . . . hard. I want to be my own man, Will, not beholden. So I play the ingrate, refuse to see him almost unless forced, go against his wishes and advice. And end up – off my own pig-headedness – in the Impress Service, which the baronet so dearly, clearly thinks despicable, as who does not, these days?'

To this line, William could say nothing, when denial or acceptance equally would cost his dignity. Samuel spoke plain, and Samuel accepted the Impress as an inferior situation. Will Bentley must keep mum.

He did say, 'Why so lonely, though? He is rich, his house and lands enormous. Why bother with young men at all, indeed? We're ingrates all, if you believe my father; it is in the bone!'

The jest eased him, but Samuel stayed dour.

'He had three sons, all dead years ago. He is a shipper, his wealth comes from the East, he is connected with John Company, I believe. One day he sent his sons out to Batavia, a passage from Calicut, and they were dead within a week, from the ague. Then three months later, when she heard the news back home in Langham Lodge, his wife went, oh horrors, very quickly, not above five days I think. Mrs Houghton, the housekeeper, once named it as a broken heart and who could argue, in this case? She sat there in her room, and gave up food, and drink, and everything. And life.' A pause. 'He is a good man, William. I can despise the rich, it was my father's training, although one day one wants to be up with them, I suppose. But Sir A is neither pig nor toad, venality and corruption touch him not. One day, perhaps, I'll reconcile myself, stop being my own man or trying to so hard. But first there's the Biter, eh? After the Welfare you should eat her, Will! By God, though, she will not make you rich on prize money, nor me neither. Lieutenant Kaye is rich already, so he don't need to try!'

Samuel's mood, perversely, had lifted at the prospect of the ship he dearly hated and the service he, like his would-be benefactor, so despised. This time, when Will asked him leading questions, he would honestly respond. The Biter was the sort of ship his sort of officer – men without interest – went to as if by natural law, he said. She was dirty, vile and poky, with a crew so low they would not have pressed themselves, even, if they'd come upon themselves blind drunk in the gutter one dark night. Sir A had known her name by her reputation, which was why Sam had hoped to get out of the house without vouchsafing it. Sir A had known that he must be in her not out of choice, but out of sheer necessity. He should have passed for a lieutenant long ago, and been called to greater things, but he had clashed with the baronet with monotonous frequency when he'd thought string-pulling had been mooted. He was a prig and fool, it served him right to end up on the Biter, there was no argument about it, none at all.

William was discomfited to his soul. And what, he wondered, must their lordships think of *him* to place him on this ship? He asked feebly: 'But if she is dirty, Sam, is there no one who will see her clean? Surely Lieutenant Kaye . . . ?'

The laugh was harsh and short.

'Lieutenant Kaye has his own reasons, I believe, although I know them not. She's not a King's ship, though, she's under charter from her owner for a fee, he sails on board as master, and has last say in many things, including cleanliness and fizz. John Gunning's not a very cleanly man.'

William was mystified and showed it, but Samuel took it very easily.

'It's not unusual in these days,' he said. 'Wars cost money so we're told, and ships to build cost hundreds, even thousands. So Mr Gunning gets his charter rent, the Navy gets his seamen for a crew – with the best protection from the Press that any man could have! – and the Biter has a navigator and a pilot all in one, which is fortunate with Richard Kaye as captain of her, for he could not navigate a paper hat across a puddle in the sun. So everyone is satisfied – save us!'

William said, awkwardly: 'But there is some honour in it, surely? You make it sound . . . well, we are at war, and the Press is very necessary, otherwise there would be no men in our ships, no men at all. And there are legal ties, and rules, and so on. You're not suggesting . . . ?'

'I'm not suggesting nothing,' riposted Holt. 'Aye, sure it's legal, they taught us that in black and white at Christ's; and the moral side. We rehearsed the moral side till our tongues clove to our mouths, although my father, rest his soul, would not agree, I'll warrant me. Nay, the service has its good points, so does bold Cap'n Kaye, come to that. Between him and John Gunning we spend a lot of time in Deptford, is one for instance, and we spend a lot of time on shore. Lieutenant Kaye's a great stickler for liberty, at least of that sort, and if you don't believe in pressing centum per cent, then he's your man, as the Irish say, for he has the air of a fellow with better things by far to do, especially if drink and whores are in the question. That's where he will be now, our good commander, you might depend upon it. We'll get to the ship as ordered, foot-sore and arse-weary, and Slack Dickie will be stuck in some neat strumpet, lucky bastard. Don't call him that to face, by the way, he wouldn't catch the joke. But as I told you, he has his good sides, don't you see!'

A vision of Deb's face, exhausted, bruised, exquisite, arose behind Will's eyes, sudden and unbidden. He forced himself to moral things again.

'Your father,' he asked, awkwardly. 'Why would he not agree about the Impress Service, that it is just? Was he a victim of it?'

For a while there was no reply. Just the sound of horses' hooves on mud and stone, the creak of leather. Holt sighed.

'He was a lawyer. He went to Virginia, among other reasons, because of a spirit who had preyed on villages around where I was born and raised. That is, near Lewes, you may have heard of it. He had a strange belief the law could help wronged people. His passage out – theirs, he would not leave my mother and the littles – their passages were paid by subscription, the families of wronged parties, friends, well-wishers. Who knows, if he had lived . . .'

'A spirit? I have heard of Lewes, but forgive me. You do not mean a ghost?'

'Hell, William, I am the bumpkin, not you, man! Nay, I mean a rogue who kidnaps poor sufferers and sells them to the colonies as slaves. Indentured servants, Seven-Year Passengers, you must have 'em down in Hampshire, surely? This man, this *agent*, as he styled himself so grand, scoured the land around Lewes for two years till he was murdered by a man whose sons had been taken and despatched on transports. The man was hanged, of course, but my father was approached by many other families and resolved to go to the Colonies himself to try for rescues or releases of the victims he could prove coerced by fraud or violence. Those who answered the handbill and the advertisements of their own volition – well, naturally he held out little hope for them. You Hampshire people have a song for us Sussex men, I know. If *your* country clods don't get spirited, perhaps it's right and we are stupid, after all.'

Will did not suppose it, so he merely smiled. Too tedious to tell of the isolated, simple life he led much of the time, so little knowing of the world at large.

'I thought the slaves were black,' he merely said. 'Except the odd convict, naturally. Negers out of Africa.'

'Aye, Negroe or Irish mainly, although to be an orphan in the port of Liverpool, or Bristol, so I'm told, is a very dangerous thing, an orphan or a bastard or a whore without protection. Our spirit, the one who had his throat cut in Hailsham High Street and my father and my family died for, had a special trick of relieving henpecked husbands of their shrewish wives, or disappearing drunkards and other feckless fellows who had outstayed their welcome in the marriage bed. But mainly innocents. The young and silly and the poor and weak. Poor father would have relished saving them. He was a man for moral things.'

The moon was gone, but up ahead of them something was glittering, not constantly but there. Inn lights, maybe, or houses through the trees.

'What o'clock do you suppose it is?' asked Holt. 'You do

37

not have a timepiece, do you? I wonder, if Richard Kaye is not on board, if we would be, in fact, too late ourselves.' He grinned. 'I mean the gay house,' he said. 'Your old friend Dr Marigold! Could you stand a little whoring, after all?'

'God, Sam!' said William, covered in confusion. 'God, Sam, you are an odd fish! You talk of morals, your father righting wrongs, and then you talk of whoring in one breath! But truly, I know nothing of that pastime, nothing.'

'What of that maid, then?' Samuel mocked. 'The one you glued to on your horse and couldn't take your eyes off, hot as coals? Deb, was it? There are better whores than Deb at Dr Marigold's!'

'There you are!' cried William. 'First moral talk, then you debase that poor child, you slander her on no excuse at all! You are a cynic after all! Why call her a whore? What of poor Cecily, who has lost her teeth? Is she a whore?'

Sam Holt was not all hard-case sailor man. His cynicism might run deep enough, but he recognised Will's hurt and hurtability, and reined back his exuberance. While marvelling at a Navy officer so naive about so prime a Navy interest.

'William,' he said. 'Don't take on so, it's only half in jest. Look, man, the flesh and pleasure are not problems, we must take pleasure where we can, and when. It's like sleep to seamen, is it not – we must snatch a half a second, however hard the weather, or we'd never sleep. So Cec is not a whore, or if she is, a most unusual one to sell her teeth for five pound once, and not her body, which is a time and time again commodity. How long will five pound last, think you?'

William felt sick at heart. Better, surely, to have sold her body.

'Five pounds?' It came out faintly. Samuel shrugged.

'A guess. Five for her, more for the mountebank, perhaps? More than she would have got him as a toy among the ruffians that we were threatened with. Or perhaps he is a spirit, also. Perhaps the alternative he offered was a cruise to Maryland or Massachusetts. He would sell her, and Deb as well presumably, to the captain of a transport, who would sell them on for servitude or slavery when they reached the Colonies. They realise now, I warrant, they'd have been better stuck in Stockport, making hats.'

Will said nothing. The beauty of Deb, in his memory, was faded. His back ached, his behind and legs ached, in his heart just dull regret for both the maids.

'I don't mean Deb's a whore, or Cecily, but if they have to be, what of it, it's the times,' said Sam Holt, quietly. 'They are maidens, women, just human creatures like ourselves, who must eat or die. What were they doing with the mountebank? How desperate must you be to sell your teeth, how desperate to track down two hundred miles or three to earn a living? A living, Will, think of the word, think what it means, a *living*. How much do you have in a year? Thirty? Fifty? And the chance to earn some more, even the chance of prizes, although hardly in the Impress Service, but bounties do accrue if Kaye can be rousted into action. Deb and Cecily, even as whores, even with a full set of ivories—'

'Sam,' said Will. 'Enough, I beg of you. Enough.' Mrs Houghton had said they'd left the north to seek adventure, had run away from dull routine. But every awful thing that Sam predicted for them must now be right. Except – Sir Arthur Fisher would look after them. He had forgotten that.

Sam agreed, when he put this to him. Smiling, he agreed the maids were saved. But he still insisted ('I am a pedant, and a pedagogue!') that his friend should face the 'fine philosophy of the whole affair, and grasp it'. Which meant, it seemed, that Will must sleep with Deborah.

'You will allow,' he told his silent companion, 'that to lie with a girl like that, for her to sell her body, might be quite wonderful, but would in no wise be *important*. We cannot marry whom we please, can we, but we have to do the other thing; you have to, William, you're a human, you're a man. And such girls, what do they do, such girls as Deb and Cecily? Their aim is not end up in the gutter if they can, but to marry someone rich and powerful, to marry or become the plaything, mistress, concubine, and it can happen, if they have the brains and beauty and the luck. But most of them, they do end in the gutter, don't they? If you lie with Deb, and give her money, you ward off that evil day, you leave her with her chances open, well fed, well dressed, with prospects. It is your duty, man, your duty. To keep her from the gutter!'

No need for answer. Sam, once more, had made himself content by flight of fancy, then moved on merrily. William, slightly ashamed, caught himself in the thought that Deborah was safe at Sir Arthur Fisher's house, and he and Sam had horses that might be returned there, if the time allowed. With the thought a quick remembrance of those eyes, that hair, that face, despite the knowledge that she meant nothing to him, absolutely nothing, and he much less to her, it was all a dream. To Cecily, poor Cec, he apportioned not a thought. Deborah was safe.

Later that night, though, in the pitch-black early hours, Deb left her warm, soft bed with Cecily, still drunk with brandy, still bleeding, still in pain, and crept down through the servants' rooms and out into the dim back yard. Deb had noted earlier where the nearest dogs were, and where the animals, and where the stables, and where she might find an ass or a mule. The run was not an easy one, nor was it particularly hard, although poor Cecily could only stumble clumsily, letting out small cries when jogged. Deb had run before, especially in the last two months, not always with the mountebank directing. Her latest run had been that day, while Cec had screamed and weltered with his cruel hands in her mouth, and Milady had lain silent, white-faced and stoical, waiting for the plugging in of her new teeth. Deb, almost as drunk as Cecily, had known then that she'd never do it, no, not even for a thousand pounds, and seized an opportunity amid the blood and shrieking to slip out and get away. Not far and not for long. Dennett knew he would find her, that she could not leave her friend despite this small betrayal, and he was right. But Deborah could run with Cecily. They were getting good at it.

Perhaps outside the park, both knew, the mountebank was lurking. Perhaps he'd gathered men to hunt them down, perhaps this run would be a short one, not a great escape. But Deb was eaten up with shame at her abandonment, and she had a great determination. After half an hour, with Cecily on the ass and her ahead, they were a mile away at least, heading north, sometimes on the road, more often near the edge of cover. They had liked Sir Arthur's house, and his kindness, and Mrs Houghton and her girls and men. But the magistrate had paid for more than he had got, and Marcus Dennett would be made to suffer surely, if Deb's teeth should be needed and could not be had. In any way, Dennett would say he owned them, they were his, and he would have somehow come to the great house and got them, by force or trickery, there was no doubt of that.

At least the night was dry by now, and still quite warm. In London they could truly disappear.

5

Charles Yorke was still alive, just, but he thought his friend was dead. They were lying in a stinking brewhouse outside another inn, in Hampshire still as he imagined it, but perhaps in Dorset or in Sussex for all he really knew. They had travelled long in the night, although they might not have travelled far. There had been much stopping, much gathering of drunken men to beat and gawp, much ill-treatment at many hands. At each stop they had been misused and then abandoned in a corner while more drinking had gone on, and each time they had hoped to meet the men they were intended for at last.

It had not happened, though, and they had got weaker as the night wore on. Yorke had lost consciousness from time to time, while the older man had lapsed for longer periods, which filled Yorke with despair. After his first long hanging upside down, beneath the horse's belly, his tormentors had not allowed a repetition, which argued that they did not want him dead. Charles Yorke, in fact, had thought him so the first time they had righted him, so drenched in blood was he. His face, wiped down, was cut and bruised beyond recognition by the horse's hooves. He had teeth missing and one eye closed entirely. Oh God, thought Yorke; that we should have come to this.

At one halt, tethered to a post beside a stream while the drinkers went off for some more refreshment, they had found themselves half capable of speech. For moments, they had leaned against each other, both panting as if they had run, not ridden. They had had new beatings, although not full-hearted ones, which acted – Yorke had noticed this before – as a kind of stimulator, strange to tell. But the men had moved away for further cannikins minutes ago.

'Charles?' Charles Yorke was tentative. His friend was desperately low. For moments there was no response. 'Charles, how do you?'

'You do not need to ask,' Warren said, eventually. It was an attempt at jocularity, but Yorke was too tired to be moved. The older man's breath came uneven, with a rasp behind it. They were touching. That was the only comfort.

'Do you think they mean to kill us?' Yorke said. 'It is hours now. I thought to have been presented to the venturers. This round is endless, it does not have a purpose or a point that I can see.'

In the silence, each noise extraneous was made larger and discrete. Across the yard a horse moved its feet on stone, then there came the uneven spatter as it dropped fresh turds. After that a sighing, a kind of yawn, then the high scream of a vixen. In the silence after that sound a dog barked half a mile away, a heavy, thudding bark. A burst of laughter from inside the house. Then a gentle breath of wind, that brought the fresh manure smell to them, sweetly familiar, unendurable.

'Oh God,' said Warren, 'we are doomed to die this night, I think. This is a progress, a triumphal round to show us off, and put some mettle in the Hampshire and West Sussex men. We are not intended for the venturers, I guess. They have proposed, their people will dispose of us. It is to warn the fainthearts, and a celebration, both.'

Charles Yorke considered this. They had been betrayed, no doubt of that sad fact. But surely they would not just be paraded, done to death, without some questioning? Good God, he thought, we could be innocent! He caught the thought, and was amazed by it, and sourly amused. They could be innocent, but they were not. If they were to be destroyed as spies against the new free traders, who sought to bring harsh Kentish ways into this local scene – then so they were.

They did meet more important men, however, in the end – not after that halt, nor the next one, or the next – but by this time Warren was too far gone to be worth questioning, and Yorke was not much better. They saw the men at a manor farmhouse, not a country tavern, and the rowdies stayed outside. They were pushed, half carried in the case of Warren, into a fine large kitchen, where two gentlemen – in looks at least – were seated at a long scrubbed table. Warren, released, dropped to the flags in silence, hitting his head against the table with a bang. That, for Yorke, was sufficient. His only thoughts were hatred and revenge, if thoughts they counted as. He was rational enough, certainly, to stare at the faces opposite, burning them on his mind and eyeballs. It was said that a murdered person's eyes retained a picture of the perpetrators, although he hardly thought it to be true. In case it was, he stared. Perhaps he would survive, in any case. If so, these men would be remembered though he lived to see a hundred.

One was fattish, one was thin, one wore a fullish wig, the other man was bald. The thin one had a glinting greyness in the eyes, which caught the candle-flare, the fat one had had the smallpox bad, and bore the pits and scars. The fat one had on a stretched waistcoat of dull stuff, enlivened by a silver chain that would have tethered a treasure ship so enormous were its links. He took snuff. His chin was stained, his nostrils reddened. He must use it constantly.

Indeed, before either of them spoke, his two fat fingers snaked into his fob, returning with a box of figured silver, which he opened with dexterity, tapped, and penetrated. Then a double snort, the box instantly disappearing, and a large lawn handkerchief smothered his nostrils with a flourish. Yorke watched and waited, eyes like gimlets. He tried to meet the thin man's gaze, to crush him with the weight of hatred, but the thin man knew, and kept his eyes averted. The fat one, nose well polished, was the first to speak. His voice, like his form, was large and strangely comfortable.

'My friends,' he said. 'How good of you both to take the trouble. Had you let us know in advance, we would have prepared some sweetmeats.'

This was mere unpleasantness, so Yorke ignored it. The thin man made a gesture of impatience.

'No, all jollity aside,' went on the fat. 'You have put yourselves through much to be here with us. We understand from our friend in Fareham that you have proposals. He talked of cash to sink. He talked of business. So tell us – what have you in your minds?'

For one wild, mad moment, Charles Yorke had a rush of hope. Maybe they did not know, maybe this ill-treatment was a . . . was a what? Warren lay in front of him, unconscious and grey-faced. This devil was just playing, for his sport. However:

'You think in some wise we are what we are not,' he said. It came out thickly, his lips were suffused with blood. 'I guess you think that we are agents of the Crown, but I promise you, we are in the business like yourselves. If Mr Felton told you otherwise, he made a grave mistake. We are honest like yourselves, which is to say . . . that some . . . might call us . . . rogues.'

A glance had passed between them, though, a glance of some significance. He had lost their interest and attention even before swallowing his last and dangerous words. The slight man touched the big one's arm, but he was already quivering with laughter. It came out as a grunt and snort, and he ended it by taking in a bolt of snuff. Through the noise, the thin man's voice cut nasally. He did not sound amused.

'So, Mr Felton is it?' he said. Yorke felt the bottom of his stomach drop away at his mistake. 'To you his name was Saunders, I believe.'

'I . . .' He stopped. The big man trumpeted into his handkerchief.

45

'Aye,' he said. 'Aye, aye, aye indeed! His name is Saunders, and yours is Yorke. And his is Warren, and your proposition is a load of yeasty shit, sir! You are spies, you are Customs House, you have heard of our new ventures over here and you wish to put your oar in, isn't that the truth?!'

'Tssssssh!' went the other man, quietly but sharp. 'Pah!' returned his pock-marked friend, but stopped. He stared at Yorke and panted, dabbing at his nose. They know our names, thought Yorke. It had surprised him for a moment, but it depressed his spirits more.

'You need not die tonight, you know,' the thin man said, suddenly. His voice was low, but very clear despite the nasal timbre. 'We want some information, that is all. Who set you on to us? It is not a lot to tell to save you, is it?'

But dull rage burned in Yorke. He was leaning against the table, hardly capable of standing upright. Warren, on the floor, was breathing badly, stertorous but uneven. While this swine offered him a bargain.

'Us?' he said. 'And who are "us"? Why should I tell you?'

The words came badly through his cut and broken mouth, and the forming of the words sent agony shooting through his cheekbone. Nausea rose hard inside him, causing him to sway. The fat man waved a hand towards a chair.

'Sit down,' he said. 'Fall down, for aught we care. You will suffer long if you do not stop shrewing with us. We mean to know.'

He did not sit, but waited for the nausea to pass. With it passed the rage, leaving him able to weigh up. He wondered if they would be allowed to live, whatever information they could offer these two men, but he did not think so. They had done enough now, probably, to hang, and they must know he would identify them the minute he was free. In any case, he had no information. He and

46

Warren had been set on at Customs House, told what it was *thought* was happening, ordered to become a part of it and find the main men out if possible, to join them and win their trust until they could be destroyed. The intelligence that had started it would have been bought, for certainty. But from whom – most naturally – no inkling had been given him or Warren. His interlocutors must know this, too; it was the game.

'I could give a list of names,' he said, 'but what of that? How would you know I did not lie?'

The fat man smiled.

'Give us the list and we will see,' he said. 'At least we will spare you until we have checked on them. Now there is an offer you should not slight.'

'And if you find I lied, you kill me, naturally.'

'Well, naturally.'

'So to be sane I should tell the truth, and then you'd kill me because you would not have to check. My friend needs a physician, he is sorely hurt. If you have him tended, I will tell.'

Fingers into fob, then snuffbox, then the nostrils, left and right. This time the fat man coughed, behind his handkerchief. The thin man drew out a watch and studied it.

'I should say your friend was nearly gone,' he said. 'It is late for you, as well, we have more revellers due here any minute. There is a surgeon in the house, though, if a little full of brandy. Now – what other men are out in your capacity? You should not be alone in this venture, I suppose? Who are the other officers, are they too masquerading as men of business like yourselves, where are they staying? Tell me that, and your friend will see the surgeon. He may yet be saved.'

After several seconds, the fat man stood and walked around the table. He was rather deft of foot despite his bulk, and brushed snuff powder off his breast daintily as he moved along. He stopped in front of Warren, and extended one foot, in a neat, fine-leather shoe, until the point was very near his face. Yorke straightened his back, raised a hand; but weakly lurched. The big man smiled then, and withdrew the polished shoe. He turned back towards his companion.

'We waste our time, George. I knew we should. Leave them to the dogs, they've served their purpose. Who else dares follow in their footsteps after this, of their persuasion or of ours? They've done the job.'

'Have mercy at least on him,' said Charles Yorke. His voice was almost breaking. 'He is a good, an honest, man.'

There was a pause. The thin man looked at him with great seriousness upon his face.

'As are not we all?' he asked. 'Our trade and our desire, young man, is to bring no harm to anyone. Do not you understand that? There is still time to save your life, and even his perhaps. A man in your position could be worth his weight to us. In gold, you take my meaning? You are not dead. You will have time to think about it, will you not? I wish you luck.'

Yorke had on a stubborn, bitter face but ten seconds later, before he had a chance to open mouth, the men were gone, and upon the instant three bully-boys came in to drag Warren to his feet, and both of them into the crowded yard. They were thrown on to a horse, their feet were triced underneath as usual, the whippings and the beatings instantly began. By the time they reached the next inn, to be dumped inside the brewhouse, he was almost sure Charles Warren's life had fled.

'Mr Warren?' he said. 'Charles?'

There was no reply, no sound of breathing, not the slightest fluttering of movement.

'You are dead,' Yorke said. 'They have killed you, Charlie, and they'll soon kill me. Oh Charles, we live in wicked times.'

Somehow that gave him comfort, to use a phrase his uncle and protector used. He thought of Sir Arthur and his great, beloved house. He had spoken of this mission to him, they had discussed its many dangers, which had now come true. He felt Charles Warren's face, and it struck cold on his fingers. He leaned across and touched his cheek to it.

'God be with you, friend,' he said. 'I swear that you will be revenged.'

6

They left their horses at the Bear's Paw, and they made their way to the stairs at Tooly Street on foot. It was not far short of midnight by this time, and Bentley was astonished by the level of activity around the bridge and river bank. He did not remark it, though: Holt took it with indifference, so he must do the same. Ditto at the inn, which lay just off the road Sam called The Borough a bare furlong from the bridge. William had imagined knocking up the people, or tethering their mounts to sort themselves out. But there were coaches, carts, foot passengers of every degree, touts for the water transport, and a throng of ordinary folk, behaving as if it were broad daylight. Sam had used a tout – told him their destination and agreed a price – and the man had shouldered Bentley's bag and set off six paces in advance. Thank God; for Will, on his two legs once more, could hardly bear himself, to tell the truth.

There was no more talk of Dr Marigold's because both men were tired, but on the river, legs stretched, backs straight along each side of the sternsheets, they recovered the desire to communicate and to enjoy. Despite himself, William had excitement bubbling inside at the prospect of seeing his new ship, an excitement oddly mixed with dread. He had not wanted her, Sam's reports of her were terrible, the Impress Service was the last thing in the world he would have chosen. But she was a ship, and he was joining her, he had been broken willy-nilly from his decision to watch his life glide by. No, not decision; he had not decided anything, just let it glide. The smell of the river, the dense foresting of masts along the north shore, dense clusters on the south, the constant traffic on the waters, of wherries, ferries, barges, keels and deep-sea traders slipping down, brought an unexpected gladness to his heart that he, too, was soon to be at sea. He had not, truly, known that he could miss it, or want to be in ships, at any rate. His own small boat was his love, his life in many ways, his talisman of sanity, but he had not known he hankered still for size. The tide was ebbing, and the two strong oarsmen shot them downriver at a cracking rate, and he was full of happiness and fear.

'Jesu, Will,' said Samuel. 'Isn't she beautiful, this river? And what a bastard smell! Look! Over there. It's a dead sheep, isn't it? Or mayhap a shepherd!'

More probably a dog, although now the moon was down the blackness was extreme. To William it was just a shape, blown and revolting, accompanied by a blast of corruption that made him gag, covering his mouth. Samuel did likewise, for fear of ague or some like infection from the foul air, although the boatmen rowed on heartily enough. Indeed the general smell was hardly less disgusting, and the surface of the ebbtide water was a litter of vile objects, dimly discerned. All around him on the banks were solid clustered buildings, outlined by lights, and on tiers and piers and buoys were ships, some discharging cargo despite the hour, all discharging their general filth to mix with the effluvia of the great city.

Beautiful, he thought? But so it was, astonishingly so. It had a brooding aspect, the black water snaking, bubbling along with enormous muscularity between the crowding, crouching town and the dark hulls below the massed spars and upperworks, even the most silent of them somehow full of purpose and intent. Sometimes, also, the dully filthy smell was cut by gentle breezes, aromatic zephyrs like veins of purity sent, he imagined, from fields and woods and water not far beyond the teeming southern riverside. He fell to imagining the lower reaches, beyond where they were heading this night. Once below the giant city – near half a million of souls, so it was said – there would be wide open empty spaces to the estuary, then the sea. He could hardly wait.

Near Deptford things were blacker, on the river and the shore, with areas of total darkness, flat shores bereft of human habitation or moored ships. As they raced down upon the area of the dockyard sparks of light appeared once more, and the loom of ships could be sensed and seen. There were fires in some places, and the smell of burning wood and melted pitch.

'Sam? It is the middle of the night. Are men working here?'

Holt laughed.

'Some say they never work at Deptford,' he replied. 'The shipwrights have their own disease, called "Wake me later". It will be fires set off in the day, most likely. Their business arms will be engaged in lifting pots if anything.'

'What ship?' one of the boatmen grunted. It was the larboard man, a not unjovial type of forty years or so; who had not raised a smile, however, at Sam's pleasantry about the dock workers.

'Again?' said Sam, who had misheard.

'What ship? This is Deptford, in one minute. If we over-shoot we must row back agin the tide, and that should cost you. What vessel are you seeking?'

'The Biter. She is a—'

'I know the Biter. Jack Gunning's ship. So – you are the Press.'

Both men rested on their oars, despite no spoken signal. Bentley saw clear dislike in their expressions.

'Aye,' said Sam Holt, clearly. 'We are the Press and you are watermen. I paid you fares, not the King's bounty. No doubt you have protections, but we do not want to see 'em, ferrymen are not for us. She's over there, I see her. Beyond that pink.'

Perhaps they had not been threatening, merely pausing to get their bearings on their target. Whatever, both fell to pulling straight away, to crab across the current. Bentley, vaguely relieved, studied the tiers ahead. Out of the darkness emerged a darkened ship, not long but bulky, with high bulwarks and high stern. No lights were apparent, but at her gangway two boats were moored, bumping gently against the high black side in the tideway. Still wordless, the boatmen spun their craft to head the flow, which pushed her sideways till they ranged beneath a boom rigged outboard from the gangway, with pennants hanging down.

'The watchman does his job, I see,' Holt muttered. 'She's like a grave, if not so welcoming.'

The boat bumped gently, as the bow man seized a pennant to steady her. Moving forward, Sam grasped the boom and jerked himself up to sit on it, ignoring the ladder down the Biter's side. Now the ferryman did smile.

'There we be, masters,' he said. 'Go you up, sir, and I will pass your dunnage.'

William, despite his tiredness and bruises, could still play the seaman, so he hoped, so swung himself up after Samuel, who by now was balanced upright on the boom and striding for the deck. Through the gangway in the bulwark, Sam turned to watch, then put his arms out to catch the soft bag as it flew. That dropped, he reached into a pocket and flipped a coin. Dark night, moving water; it was snapped out from the air like magic even as the boat crabbed sideways and astern.

'Goodnight to thee as well,' said Sam ironically, as the silent men pulled off. They went for Deptford steps, he noted, in hope to get another fare, or maybe wait in a tavern till the hardest of the ebb eased off. William, beside him, felt live timber beneath his shoes, felt greater excitement, strange mixed sensations rise within him, his eyes only for inboard, the wherry and the river quite forgotten. The deck moved beneath him, and it was *his* deck. His eyes sought everything, as he became accustomed to the local dark. This was the Biter, this was his. What sort of ship would she turn out to be? And what sort of man her commander, so unloved?

That night, as Samuel had predicted, he was not to know. Sam shouldered his companion's bag, and picked his way with care across the Biter's waist. It was cluttered, filthy, strewn with half-cut wood, uncoiled rope, and spars. A topsail yard, it looked like, lying stripped of furniture, supported by the bulwark and by trestles, while from above loose cordage hung down in festoons, silent only by virtue of there was no wind to swing it. Bentley glanced aloft, and against the starlight saw confusion, yards akimbo, some sails but loosely stowed on them.

'Are we called to sail tomorrow, Sam? Surely not, it would be impossible.'

'Hey!' Sam shouted, not loud but gruff and threatening. 'You there! Are you the watchkeeper?'

There was a noise ahead of them, not unlike a pig at trough. A jumble of deck gear transformed before Will's eyes into a sailor – nay, a shoreman, doubtless from the yard, a lanky, rheumy wretch well in his dotage, or possibly in drink. As he unrolled himself into an upright shape, a sweet unpleasant smell of body greeted nostrils. The man's eyes were ringed in pink, gleaming in a sallow, whiskered face. Good Christ, thought William, let's hope he's from the yard. I have seen too many sailormen like him.

'Do you know me?' barked Holt. 'I am first officer here. You are asleep and drunk on duty. I will have you flogged.'

If the threat had weight in it, the watchman failed to shrink with fear. He cleared his throat, and spat on to the deck – an act that William found shocking. The gob of phlegm gleamed, uncomfortably near his shoe, ignored by its projector and by Samuel, as if it had no weight at all, not even as a gesture. Sam made a movement of impatience, solely at wasted time.

'Is the captain not on board?' he asked. 'We are expected. Have the yard then done so little? It is extraordinary.'

'Captain's in his crib,' said the watchman. 'Not yourn, though, master. Won't be pleased to see 'ee, neither.'

'We'll see,' Holt said, briskly. 'Now get you to your post, you sot. I shall speak about this conduct to the yardmaster. Come, Will. Careful as you go.'

As they moved aft, the watchman hardly stirred; till finally he merged into the dark from whence he'd come, seated beside a stack of lumber for a bottle or a sleep. Discipline, thought William, is unusual on this ship. Or then, mayhap the discipline he knew was the oddfish; he must wait and see.

'Insolent old toad,' said Samuel, easily. 'The power of command, eh William? With Kaye on shore I am in charge here, don't you see? Which is why, doubtless, he trembled at my every word.'

'But he said the captain's in his cabin.'

'He said not "ourn", he said the master. Gunning. In Deptford, as in anywhere I guess, who pays the piper calls the tune. The master's in the captain's cabin, where he should not be. At the very least I must check what's afoot, Lieutenant Kaye is very stiff about his cabin, you will learn these little protocols. Catch hold your bag, I must not seem like a chapman, must I? Better still, let's leave it on the deck. John Watchman there will keep it safe from footpads!'

The Biter, although small, was not flush-decked, and they stood now at the poop-break, by a door. From around it light was leaking – that boded not well for the cabin in a seaway – and to his surprise William heard the piping of a flute, played lively but with several slurs, as if the man behind it had taken a glass or two too much. Before Holt raised his fist to knock, the tune was ended, and they heard applause, not many hands, and female laughter.

'Here goes,' said Samuel, and he knocked. Looking rueful, he added: 'That old sot was likely right, I guess. They won't be pleased.'

Behind the door was silence for a moment, then a strong, loud voice roared, 'Who is that knocking?' Then, 'Come you in!' The two men stood there, though, a thought too long. There were loud steps, the catch-ring rattled, and the timber door jerked open. 'Ah!' said the voice. ''Tis you!'

Sam was tall, but the denizen of the cabin was a greater bulk. He was dressed in seaboots, wide trousers and an open shirt, and his stomach had a dew of sweat on it. As he moved backwards, the light revealed his face as fringed in curls, as if a wig had never graced his head. His mouth was red, lips full, teeth shining in among the wetness. In one hand was a metal tavern-cup, the other one was empty. Not the fluter then, William inconsequentially thought.

'Mr Gunning,' said Holt, half formally. 'I am reporting back as ordered by Lieutenant Kaye. I expected to find him here; in his cabin.'

If offence was intended or implied it washed right over Gunning. He had stepped back farther, and flung wide his empty hand. On a long settle at the transom, softened by many cushions, sat a young woman with a recorder, her features flushed. Her hair was disarranged, her handkerchief displaced, with fine full bosoms thus amply exposed. Beside her sat a young man with a black glass bottle, held by the neck, dressed something like a clerk or secretary, also red of face. By the cabin's outer wall, the topside of the Biter's stern, sat another young woman, dressed gaudily and rouged. There was rouge on Gunning's face as well; his mouth was smeared with it.

'My friends,' said Gunning, 'let me make the introductions. This fair young man is first lieutenant here, or would be if their lordships so ordained. First officer, then, although a midshipman, right hand of Captain Kaye, I've told you of. This young man is—' He shook his head, as if astonished, but it was only masquerade. 'Good God, sir, do I know you? No, I don't!'

The women enjoyed the show immensely, as did the clerky-fellow. They laughed uproariously as Gunning made a bow. William was flustered by it, but Samuel took it all in part.

'Step forward, William,' he said, courteously. 'Mr Gunning – and honoured guests – may I present you Mr Bentley, our new second officer? But Mr Gunning, you must forgive us, please. We have travelled very far today and we are weary. We rouse early in the morning – which is today – and we must rest. Ladies. Sir. Your humble servants.'

But it was not to be. Gunning, not drunk-aggressive but with clear intent, took up a bottle and advanced towards them.

'Nay, sirs, but I insist. We know your names, you must know ours. Sal – get the gentlemen a glass apiece. Gentlemen – Miss Sally Marlor, a spinster of this parish. Her father is churchwarden at St Mark's.'

More gales of laughter, and the rouged young woman tripped forward with two glasses. When she had given one to William, and before Gunning had filled it, she reached for his cheek and pinched it, not ungently.

'Ooh Jack,' she said, to Gunning. 'This one is a peach. Can we have him in our bed tonight?'

'Hush Sal! It is a respectable young fellow, a virgin surely! Whatever next!'

This from the flushed maid on the settle. But she stood also, and came up to Will and Sam. She poked Sam's belly with the recorder.

'I am a married woman, sir,' she said. 'Pray don't look at me with them hot eyes.'

'Mistress Ellen Cash,' said Gunning. 'She is with Master Edward Campbell there – although he is not the husband she's cuckolding. Master Campbell is a Navy clerk, sirs. Play fair with him and you might one day get a berth upon a rater, who knows!'

Taking his cue from Holt, William retained a smile, but only just. A pleasantry, a jest, an insult – what mattered was that Sam did not care to retaliate, whatever. Will could see that Gunning, drunk, could exercise his power cruelly, but of Campbell he was not so sure. However, if the man did work at the Office . . . well, perhaps he should be borne in silence, likewise.

'Good wine,' said Samuel, tasting it. 'Now, Mr Gunning, tell me please, where is Lieutenant Kaye? Has there been a change of orders, or is the plan to sail today? Where are the people, ditto?'

Gunning was not that drunk. He looked at Sam quite coolly, as if deciding whether he should mock or hold a conversation. Then he gestured round the cabin.

'Does this strike you as a state of readiness?' he asked. 'Did you not observe the deck? The shipwrights and the carpenters have made non-progress the world's new wonder of the day. This dockyard is disgraceful.'

Campbell interjected: 'I am here to put some vim in 'em. Sent by the Secretary himself. Tomorrow there will be such ructions, you'd not believe it!'

For all his inexperience, Will decided he did not, already. He took in the state of the captain's cabin for the first time, properly. It was a mass of uncompleted work. Such work, though, as he had never seen before. The alcove which contained the cot appeared to have the makings of a double bed, damn near four-poster size, its bare, unfinished wood festooned in blankets and soft coverings. Maybe they planned an orgy in reality. He did not intend to be the rouged maid's peach!

'Where are the people?' repeated Holt. 'Is work afoot in town? Lieutenant Kaye is at the rendezvous, perhaps?'

Gunning laughed shortly.

'Perhaps. I doubt it though, don't you? The men have liberty, some will end up at the Lamb no doubt, too drunk or idle to get their arse downriver. I am in charge meanwhile, I am looking after everything.' Infinitesimal pause; a glint of humour, directed slyly at Will Bentley's face. 'I am looking to what is my own, amn't I? To keep it safe.'

Sal Marlor was on her feet again, intent on plying Will with more wine, which was red and heavy. Despite of himself he had drained the first glass, tired and thirsty as he was, and had felt it rising headily from his empty stomach. She, however, was quite blatant in her movements, which Gunning did not care about at all. William covered his glass rather feebly, then with more firmness when she persisted. Sam backed him up.

'No more, mistress, nay, no more! Mr Gunning, we must bid you all goodnight. Ladies. Mr Campbell. Till some other time.'

Sal's disappointment did not last her long, for as the door closed behind them she was chattering and laughing with the rest. The air outside struck damp and fresh in contrast, but very welcome. Will was ready for a bed, although his head was full of questions, to be sure. They stood and looked across the river, sprinkled with starlight now the cloud was almost broken. The smell up here was mainly fair, clean water and wet fields.

'Well,' he said. 'What sort of ship is this you've brought me to? I'll say this: she is not like any one I've knew before.'

Holt opened his mouth for an answer, but a mighty yawn broke through. It was some moments before he conquered it.

'I said we should have gone to Dr Marigold's. Though had you laid your hand down right I think you would have shared the captain's bed with Mistress Redlips. Do you imagine Gunning had a pile of us in mind? Six in a bed, and devil take the hindmost! By God though, he is daring. Our Richard loves his cabin, and his bed, which the carpenters are building to his instructions as you saw. Gunning is an insolent, a dog, a bloody interloper!'

'But the ship is his,' said William, with a certain ambiguity. 'He likes to make that clear, I think.'

Holt ignored it as a comment, and merely grinned. 'The strange thing is,' he said, 'that he's a quiet dog when he's not in drink, lives sweet and frugal in his little hutch and lets friend Kaye get on with it. He is a hard man, do not mistake me, he takes the contumely of his chosen trade quite easy, despite men hate him with a bitter hatred, aye, and women too when lovers, husbands, sons are pressed. He's not above vindictiveness when times demand or chance arises, either, so they say. Running a tender does allow a man to settle scores. Some of his own crew on here have found themselves sold to His Majesty, at unexpected moments!'

'It is not safe to cross him then?'

From the far shore, borne on a breeze, they heard dogs barking, perhaps a half a dozen. Then it faded. Silence but for creaks of rope and timber, gently flowing tide. There was a mudbank smell emerging. William loved the smell of harbour mud.

'Not safe, not unsafe,' said Sam. 'He is naught to do with us at all. Let Kaye fall out with him if he will, but I will not.' He studied William closely, in the dark. 'She is not a tight ship, is that what you mean? She is not the normal run of Navy ship, not one that your famous Uncle Swift would recognise as such.'

'Good God,' said Will. 'Uncle Daniel! Well, good God, I can't *imagine* what he would have made of that bazaar in there! The cabin alone, and that enormous bed! Those painted doxies!'

'But you're a peach!' Sam crowed. 'A peach dunked in red wine. No, from what I've heard of Uncle Dan, he would not have smiled like you did. It is the style see, Will, the style of vessel and the way she is commanded. Where you have been, men probably showed respect, and fear, and deference: here they don't. You expected Gunning, I suppose, to call us sir, and scrape, and so on, but we ain't that sort of vessel, friend, the Biter is a very different ship. Even the Navy men are . . . well, you shall see. I tell you though, if we are free tomorrow night thanks to the Deptford yard – I'll show you dames will make Sal Marlor look as pale and drab as whey. What say you?'

'Bed,' said Will. His mind and heart and body all said bed. Sam took him by the arm and guided him across the cluttered deck towards a scuttle. Will could hardly lift his bag from the filthy planks.

'We'll need a glim,' said Holt. 'I'll go before and make one. Just stand there.'

Five minutes more and Will was hard asleep, in a cot behind a screen, with Samuel on the deck, ever the gentleman. Tomorrow they would fair it up, he'd said. Tomorrow, had thought William, as he'd dropped down the sheer wall to infinity. God, tomorrow I will see this awful ship in daylight; no, today. His last thought was of Deb, but she meant nothing any more. A memory.

Comfort was a memory to Deb. Comfort and ease and her old belief in a bright and lively future. She stood with Cecily, up to her knees in water underneath a bridge, straining to hear something above the gurgling of the water, wondering if the ass would be found, wishing she had set it free, not tethered it. Beside her Cecily was trembling, with cold and fear and tiredness and pain, almost at the end of everything. They had been in the water, Deb estimated, for one half of an hour, maybe more. Beyond the stream bed, still, might be the men.

They were not the gang roused out by Dennett, of that she was fairly certain. In the first two hours after their escape they had made good progress on the way to London, unpursued. Every now and then, Deb had led into a covert and sat Cec down on a log or stone, and pushed herself through the thickest to observe the road and listen. Her ears were good, conditions excellent, still hardly any wind. After quite a short time she was sure Dennett, for whatever reason, was not in pursuit, which satisfied her mightily. After all, why should he be? More likely he'd have gone to Sir Arthur's house if he was serious, and tried his luck with Tony and his boys and hounds.

Escape. That was a strange word, she thought, as the water-chill numbed her slowly higher and higher up her legs. Their outer clothes had still been sopping when they'd recovered them at the house, but the warm night had eased their situation. Not now, though. Now she was like ice, and miserable. Only her determination kept her from despair, her adamantine stubbornness. She was determined for herself, determined for her violated friend. One man had cost Cecily her teeth, her beauty, possibly her future. She would die before these other men made free with them, whatever was their sport.

This lot had found them when Deb had been returning from her lookout the last time. As she had approached from one direction she had heard the ass bray, which had startled her but been no cause for much concern. Till – when it stopped – she had heard men's voices, and a note of curiosity. She could not hear the words, but the intent was clear as crystal: there is an ass in this covert. Why? Let's go and find things out. Deborah had run pell-mell to gasp her news, and seized the ass's rope, and Cecily, and made them both scoot, as quietly as was possible. The men had heard, but the wood was thick, and luck for once was with them, so it seemed. They had spotted no one, nor been spotted, but had found the river and the bridge, all overgrown. They would stay here, where they were, a good while yet, she thought.

That was not to be. Cecily, without a sigh, dropped into the water, first to her knees, then pitching on her face, full-length. Almost at the same moment the ass snickered, then began to bray, harsh, jerkily, perhaps startled by the splash and Deb's muffled cry. She heard voices on the instant, a view halloo, but had time for nothing but to try and rescue Cecily, to drag her face clear of the water, her body upwards on the bank. At first she could not even make her room enough to breathe plain air, she dragged her hair and collar in a frantic effort to make her safe. Then boots appeared before her, and strong hands and arms lifted Cec clear into the air, water cascading from her dress and legs.

They were villainous, there was no question of it. Bluff

men, in dark, loose clothes, with neckcloths, and hair in pigtails. Not like her two young lovely gentlemen of the day before, but sailors for a certainty, rough, sea-going men. They carried clubs or cudgels, and curved, heavy swords. Pirates, she thought, although she did not know seamen. She heard one gasp, as he upturned Cecily's poor face.

Deborah was shivering. Unlike Cecily, who had none, she had teeth to chatter, and they did. She was grey with fear and cold, she was shivering with terror. These men would use them, they would kill them. Oh Christ, what hopes they'd had, what hopes!

'God's mercy on us,' said one of the men. His voice was thickened by emotion, but Deb did not hear that. 'See what they've done here. Jim, give me your cloak. I've got a blanket at my saddle. Where are the beasts? God's bones, her face is quite destroyed.'

'Do not hurt us, sir,' said Deb. 'Please do not hurt her more.'

In tears and soaked and freezing, she was not beautiful at all, just a sobbing little girl. The smuggler, big and strong, put an arm about her shoulder.

'Do not fear, maid, do not fear. But tell me, child. Her teeth. What happened to her teeth?'

But Deb could only sob.

7

In the morning there were sailors, when William rolled out, and they fitted Sam Holt's strictures on their condition and their type quite horribly. In the scuppers there were four, one smeared in blood and one in vomit, all as near death as he ever hoped to see live men. At the boom was moored a six-oar gig, that they'd 'come home' in. He wondered how far they'd rowed, and who had done it.

It was a lovely morning, a crisp, clear late summer morning, and the view across the fields and river enchanted him. From clumps of white mist sheep and cows appeared, at the bankside opposite he could make out domestic girls at washing, and from scattered houses streams of smoke rose vertical from chimneys – another windless day in store, this time without a cloud in view. It was quite late – gone eight o'clock – and the surface of the river was a mass of vessels, from rowing boats and barges going down, to sea-going ships drifting or using sweeps to get advantage of the tail-end of the flood.

In the dockyard also there was activity. All over the yard fires were being lighted, and swarms of men were moving round the two ships in construction, their high bare sides not yet faired and capped, but displaying timbers like rows of yellow teeth. Just off the shore were men-of-war in tiers, most with everything struck except their lower masts. On two, men were already working on the deck, while at another a flat barge full of yardhands was roping alongside a low pontoon.

Samuel, then, was by his side. His face was gleaming with drops of water, his short hair damp.

'What say you to a trip ashore? There is a coffee shop

behind the yard, if you'll believe me. Damn little chance of anything to eat on here.'

I could say much, thought Bentley. I could say, 'But where's the captain? What about the dockyard crew? Is there not work to do?' The thought of coffee was a tempter, though. He could use a privy, too. He did not imagine there were private heads on here, not heads you'd want to use in sight of shore and all the traffic.

'Shall we take a boat?' he asked. 'Or hail a wherry?' But before he'd said the word, a piercing whistle had come from Holt, and a boatman had altered course for them. Before he arrived, Samuel moved easily to the forward scuttle and dropped down it out of sight. A minute later he returned, grim humour on his lips.

'Drunk, every mother's son,' he said. 'Taylor will rouse them out, though, he is a good man, Taylor. Hey, Jem! We'll be one hour, not a second more. First man out, get him to light a fire for some breakfast, then rig the pump. Hose down the drunkest, then hose down the deck. Lieutenant Kaye will be here soon, and the shipwrights.' Quietly, to Will, he added: 'Pigs might dance a hornpipe. Jem Taylor is the boatswain. You can trust him.'

Before Will had time to take him in, however, the cabin door was opened and a strange sight was revealed. John Gunning was seen first, and he was like a meaty marionette, or perhaps some cadaver, fleshed and animated. His eyes were bloodshot, his skin was pale – except for smears of rouge – and there was an air of pain about his features. He walked as if his feet were not his own, as if he thought before essaying every step. While behind him, bold as brass, bright-eyed and lively, stepped Sal Marlor, hair awry, face licked completely clean of redness (save a natural tinge around the nostrils), her gaudy clothes as brazen as a bell. Behind her came Mistress Ellen, a picture from a tragedy with eyes down on her sallow cheeks, and Edward Campbell drew up the rear, looking neither here nor there, unscathed by liquor, undefiant.

'Your face,' hissed Samuel. 'Will, mend your face! You have not seen a ghost, 'tis Gunning. I told you we were better off in our own cots!'

The shore party – for so they guessed it was – came up to them at the gangway, and Samuel made a tiny bow to the young ladies.

'Sir,' he said to Gunning. 'Here is a wherry I have bespoke. Pray take it and Mr Bentley and myself will call another.' He winked slyly at his friend: their need is greater, don't deny it!

Gunning did not speak, nor did the women. Campbell acknowledged the kindness, as he handed them down to the boatman, Gunning being apparently beyond giving a hand. Unexpectedly, as the boat pulled away, the pale-cheeked Sal (pale with freckles, Will had noted absent-mindedly) made him a little wave. Which he ignored.

'Now,' said Sam, amusedly. 'Another boat, before we are too late. Oh God, here come the hordes.'

It was an old ship's cutter, paddled out from the dock-yard by an unruly gaggle, not one shipped oar between them. To nose it round the stern, one man held a broken bottomboard, another used a bailing tin. From the middle somewhere, a young carpenter with a bag of saws in hand hurled up a rope without a warning, which Jem Taylor, coming up behind his officers, caught in the air and bent on round a stanchion.

'There lies a bumboat near the other side,' he said, in a gentle burr. 'Shall I get un for thee, Mr Holt?'

'Better not,' said Sam. 'We need someone to oversee this— Oh, to hell in clogs! Jem, keep 'em at it for me, won't you? We shall not be long, just coffee and a shave. Will – down the other side, man. Let us escape this cesspit. Come.'

They did. As the dockyard men swarmed over the lar-board bulwark, Sam and Will ran for the starboard, hailed the bumboatman, and dropped lightly down the steep side into his craft. Within minutes they had been dropped on some hard-standing, picked their way up through the labouring men, and were seated in a small and smoky shop eating hot bread rolls and blowing aromatic steam from off their coffee. William had even managed a quick visit to the privy, hard beside the kitchen wall – reserved for customers, not dockyard toilers, and hence not unrespectable.

'This is the life eh, Will?' asked Samuel, through bread roll. 'You'd never know there was a war on, would you?!'

Will was happy, and he could not understand it. His service in the Navy had shown him many sights and many situations, but nothing, none, like this. In twenty-four hours, give or take, his notions all had been turned topsy-turvy. Across the table top, the young man he had scorned smiled at him like his one true friend, and spoke of war as of another jest. There was a war on, and they had left their posts, and it did not matter, because their King's ship was not ready, and she had no commander, no proper company, and only half her rigging. She was not even the King's – and the man who owned her had gone ashore after a night of whoring in the captain's cabin.

'Sam,' he said. 'I think that wine I had last night was drugged. Is Gunning a drunkard, by the way?'

'Of course he is,' said Sam. 'Did he not look wonderful just now? We will not see him more today, I doubt, depending on which day of his debauchery is reached. Normally it is three days and then, you'll see, he is drier than a prioress's privates till the next time. Do you suppose such parts are dry? I have seen some very pretty nuns myself. Oh! You have your prudey look on, Will!'

William felt a blush arising, but he raised a laugh. In truth, he did find Samuel a little raw on the subject of the sex, although he no longer considered him in all things low and of a vulgar quality; indeed, he was ashamed to remember his earlier opinion.

'No, but – you said he is a good man, too, a useful master.

Is that true? I can hardly credit it. He is so . . . so very *lax*.'

Sam was supping coffee, and snorted into it.

'Oh, lax! Will, the Biter's lax, Lieutenant Kaye is lax, the men are lax. There are hard jobs in the Navy, there are hard men doing them. There are easy jobs to which soft men come flocking, moths to the candle flame. Some men have talent, some men have guts, some men are mad, some men are parasites. In six months before this latest refit, I am informed, the Biter saw action of a sort just thrice. Two boardings and one short chase. Nobody killed, nobody hurt, a very minimal number of good seamen taken. Shore parties since I joined her not much better, although Jem Taylor is a useful man and some of the people can crack heads together when all's said. Good God, Will, our men have liberty near every week – shore liberty, it is unheard of! Why don't they run? Because there is no call to! Their life on board is like a paradise. They would sell their grandmas to be in the Navy! Their sisters' honour! The ship is lax, Will, not just sottish Gunning. The Biter's lax, and all who sail on her.'

A woman came out of the kitchen, fat and indifferent. She took their coffee pot away, leaving another, hot one. Sam poured and drank.

'Go on, ask it then. Am I lax, too? No, Will, I'm not. I'm not and never will be. I hate the ship, I hate that master Gunning, I hate most of the men, and most of all I hate Slack Dickie Bloody Idle Kaye. Why do I tell you this? Because I think I like you, Will, and I think that you will see the merit of my views in double quick time. And you, like me, will wish, and want, and hope, and strive to find some mettle and to grasp it. I want to fight the enemy, that's what I want and wanted from my service here. And the Biter is a shitty ship, a filthy and corrupt ship, that needs some iron in her soul, and I would like to be it.' He stopped. 'I speak too much, and far too openly. One word from you to Kaye on this and I am finished.' He was not one whit abashed. 'You have not met him yet. He too is rich. Perhaps you'll find a kindred soul, and then I'm finished ditto. Ah well, a short life and a merry one. I can always sell my arse.'

'I am not rich, Sam. I—'

'No matter if you are. I'm not. I'm damn near destitute. I mentioned parasites just now, did you notice that? I can be bitter, I have prejudice, please guard against me on that score. Richard Kaye is not a parasite deliberately I do not think, but he is very, very rich. I do not know why he needs the Biter, he uses her somehow like old King Charlie used his yachts, in golden days. I do not trust him, and I hate the way he uses her. Now I grow confused, ignore me. I need the privy, then a shave. Do you bother?'

William, for reasons he could not have quite explained, made a joke.

'Indeed I do, Sam. Indeed, I went just now!'

Perhaps it was a kind of indicator, to tell Samuel that he, himself, was not so very grand, that they should be open friends. Samuel, calmly, held his eyes.

'I am very blunt, like a poor sailor,' he said. 'Do not feel you have to emulate. I don't think badly of you, that you are well bred. Think well of me despite that I am not. Pay the reckoning, although you are not rich. The barber is a furlong down the way. But first the jakes.'

Will Bentley finished his coffee slowly. And while he drank, he thought.

In the breakfast room at Langham Lodge, Sir Arthur Fisher took tea with Mrs Houghton, and pondered gloomily over the fate of Cecily and Deb. He had known for two hours that the maids had gone, but had not known what definite action, if any, he could take. Mrs Houghton had been set on to sound the household girls and women, while Tony and his cohorts had searched the park and grounds, then asked out on the roads if anything was seen or heard at night.

'The general feeling,' said Mrs Houghton, ' is that they

deserved their fate. Our girls, as usual, sir, are hardly charitable.'

Both Sir Arthur and his housekeeper smiled ruefully. They knew, indeed, the girls would have raised their eyebrows even at this sight. It took some of the country people time to adjust to the baronet's modern notions. A woman who, at bottom, was just a servant taking tea with the master led sometimes to jealousy or disapproval, and endlessly to speculation. Sir Arthur was a wisp, the woman like a hard, fit pudding, who had never shown a moment's interest in a man. Never mind: folk speculated happily.

'Maidens are such peaky things,' said Sir Arthur. 'But do they know what that fate might have been, deserved or not? Did any of them hear anything, or see movement at all? Maybe some of them talked the night before. Were there no hints?'

'Liza said they were spirited,' replied the housekeeper. 'They were all much taken by the figure of the mountebank, who it is assumed was using the maids' bodies throughout the journey south, and Liza says the hurt one told her he would come for them whatever, that he could glide through walls.'

'Which of them is Liza? Am I wrong? I thought Liza was the sensible one?'

Mrs Houghton nodded.

'She is, sir, you're not wrong. The others were twice as daft. In short, they all know nothing, so fantasticals are rife. Both maids are pregnant, says Harriet, and the man had to have them so to sell the babies for a devil-worship celebration due at Kingston on Black Sunday. I boxed her ears most soundly.'

'Are they, though? With child?'

'Lord, how should I know, sir? Deb in her shift was well formed for her age – I take her for sixteen or so – she is even luscious. Her nipples were quite pale though, if I may be so frank, and her belly only rounded as you'd expect from such a shape of maiden. Cecily I bathed, and she was but a little slip, although well-breasted. Nipples also very pink and flat. Unlikely, sir, unlikely.'

Sir Arthur sighed.

'I never had a daughter,' he said.

No, you had three sons, thought Mrs Houghton, and her heart was filled. Sir Arthur shook his head, as if to clear it.

'Most like they ran,' he said. 'I feel keenly I have done them ill, you know. They expressed a worry, I dismissed it. That was bad in me.'

'No, sir.' She moved her head from side to side, slow and emphatically. 'Their worry was absurd. An unknown magistrate, they claimed, who did not know where they were taken by Mr Samuel and his friend, but who was going to track them here to Langham. Absurd on every count, sir, even the first. Surely you do not believe the story of the teeth?'

He studied her round, taut face for seconds. Mrs Houghton did not get flustered but her eyes dropped, and, imperceptibly, her shoulders.

'Poor Cecily's teeth were taken,' he said simply. 'Someone paid the quack to rip them out. Such a business does cost money, I would guess, and not a pauper's portion. It might be absurd to think the perpetrator or his quack would find out they were here and come for them, but they would see it differently, perhaps. All they know is that some rich man – living hereabouts – would want them back, or Deb at least, because he had been cheated.'

Mrs Houghton said, with passion, 'But you would have stopped them, master! You have not done them ill, you took them in, protected them! To even think that is to do you ill! Ingratitude!'

Sir A did not respond. She stopped, then quickly coloured.

'I beg your pardon, sir. I should leave such nonsense to Liza and to Harriet, perhaps. They were not ungrateful, but—'

'But afraid. Indeed.' He sighed again. 'Call Tony for me, Mrs Houghton, please. I will send him out again to look around and ask more questions. I have some idea as to who might have done this gross transaction, as do you. But we must not leap in the dark. It is a very bitter thing to think of someone, very bitter.'

When she had gone to fetch him Tony, Sir Arthur thought about the girls, and the wide and wooded country locally, and hoped the ass they had 'borrowed' would help them gain their objective, which he guessed would be London, not many miles north from where he sat, and where the streets – to girls like Deb and Cecily – were paved with gold, a tradition set in stone. He doubted, sadly, that he would ever see them more, but hoped they might survive to tell a tale to ones who loved them. Which thought led him to his nephew, and another worry. He was south, down Portsmouth way with good Charles Warren, and Sir Arthur had expected to have heard from him before this. Truly, dark times, he thought; foul times.

At about this time – broad day, warm sunlight getting warmer by the minute – they buried Warren in a field. Not in a grave, a hole in the ground however shallow, but in a haystack, that was hard and wet. Charles Yorke, from fifteen yards away, watched without discernible emotion, indeed hardly capable of structured thought. He lay along the horse's back, head resting sideways on its neck, too dulled by ill-treatment and exhaustion to do more than gaze. He found the antics of the murderers more interesting than the fact of Warren's death; they were like dervishes and ghouls, but slowed down by exhaustion in their turn. Three or four just sat apart, lost in the thick steam arising from the soaking grass, immobile in the aftermath of drunkenness.

They had no tools except their swords, and the ground and sodden grasses had resisted their attempts to grub out a shallow hole. They had turned to the rick in expectation, and been maddened by its own resistance. The hay was old, hard-packed and blackened, with the air of being derelict. Warren also, abandoned like a broken doll in front of it, his head at an angle, his behind grotesquely in the air, one arm snapped askew.

It was the big man, Peter, of whom Yorke had been conscious on occasions during the long hours of their drab ordeal, who broke through the hard black outer layer of the rick and gave a cry. Others thrust in arms next to his, tearing out lumps of sodden hay they then cast to the ground before plunging in for more. Their renewed whoops, although triumphant, tended towards the hollow in Yorke's ears, as if something was coming to an end. Indeed, the rampage had been on for untold hours; if Warren were to be stuffed out of sight at last, it must be huge relief to them. One man gone – mocked, outraged, abused, despatched. Which left just him. Charles Yorke watched them pick up Warren's body, still without emotions. The gentlemen had said that he might live, if he would throw his lot in with them, become a secret agent for the wild men of the east, a cancer in the heart of Customs House. What was he meant to do? Ask these half-drunken savages? Indicate that he had come to a decision? Or merely wait, until they spoke again of it, more clearly? He did not know, but thought more likely they would kill him, in the end. It was not, somehow, a quite unwelcome prospect.

Warren's corpse disappeared fast and suddenly. Seven or eight men surrounded it, lifted it, and thrust it home into the rick headfirst, like a ramrod. The feet, in their black muddy boots, stuck out, then were seized and pushed by several hands, with added shoulder thrusts, then covered with wet hay. Now me, thought Yorke, but could not move, despite he wanted to sit up to face his nemesis.

But no. Not him. The men struck flame and tried to fire the rick, which at first would hardly smoulder. No breeze, many hours of a downpour, old, rotten hay. They conferred, he watched them at it, there was some argument. At last they brought some brandy from their saddlebags, poured it on liberally, bottle after bottle, which spoke not just of easy come but wretched surfeit, as if they'd drunk furlongs beyond their fill. This time the rick did take when fire was applied; at first slowly, then with appetite. In two or three minutes after ignition it was going from the heart, although the smoke was black and heavy, not blue and dancing like a normal summer rick set off by men in drunken rage against their betters.

Rick-burners hanged, thought Yorke, but doubted in his heart that these men would. If they did, though, he would not be there to see it. Poor Charlie Warren. He could see his boot, twisting in the sun. And hear it crackling.

8

Life on the Biter was an easy life, Bentley could see that and he could comprehend it. He could not, however, quite believe it, and he passed the next few hours in expectation that the truth would be revealed. For William's truth, from his experience, was that life was hard, especially Navy life. As the day wore on no hardness came, and the general tenor of the ship and crew, if anything, became more comfortable, not less. The missing last ingredient was Lieutenant Kaye, her commanding officer; so William built his fears on him. Lieutenant Kaye would provide the hardness, whatever Samuel said.

Lieutenant Kaye turned up that evening, at after six o'clock, by which time the midshipmen, between them, had achieved a remarkable great deal. Sam Holt had mustered the men – 'the walking wounded' – when he and Bentley had returned from their 'coffee run' ashore, and introduced them to their new officer in a parody of the formality that William remembered from his days in Welfare. He had lined the people up beside the gangway, and told off their names without any prompting from Jem Taylor. Silas Ayling, Tom Hugg, Tom Tilley, Billy Mann, John Behar, Joshua Baines, Geoff Raper, cook. There was another in the scuppers still, Peter Tennison, and five more not on board, including the carpenter and the sailmaker, who was in love and probably in tears somewhere (which joke of Sam's had the men in tucks). They were, Sam told him loudly, good men all, who took their orders, were keen and clean, and most of all were sober. Amid renewed merriment, he told Jem Taylor to set them to on the essential tasks, behind the dockyard men: all cordage checked and coiled, misplaced rigging overhauled, and filth and mess cleared up and overboard. Then, stripping to his shirt, he chose a crew of four and pointed to the mast.

'Mr Taylor, I will take this task, you take the foredeck and the bowsprit. Mr Bentley, might I suggest you go alone and tour from top to keelson and get to know her lie? At dinner we will confer.'

Throughout the day Will looked, and searched, and crawled, and wandered. In the large hold, with its ranks of chains and irons for the Pressed men, in the bilges, where he noted several gushing springs among the seams – and a dockyard team with mallets and oakum tending them – in the steering flat, the lazaret, the powder room (unlocked and empty), the sailmaker's store, the carpenter's workshop, the galley. He came to this just before midday, and was spoken to by Geoff Raper, a thin, shaking man with only half a left leg – no peg – one eye, and a Scotch way of speaking he could make hardly head or tail of. The broth was good though, strong enough in smell to mask the spirit-stale that rose from Geoff and others of the people, and he had baked bread of sorts – flat but very tasty.

At times he spoke with Samuel, now sweating like a common man himself. William also, when he'd finished his tour, had peeled off his outer garments of a gentleman and pitched in, which apparently had gone down well with most of the people. Dressed, he looked rather soft, his face unlined and only lightly whiskered, but in his shirtsleeves he was a different matter. William sailed alone and frequently, winter and summer, and often in the sun went lightly clad. His hands were rough from rope and rowing, his arms were brown and hard and muscular. But it was his facility with the common seamen's tasks that most impressed them. He could splice and whip with the fastest and the neatest, and his eye for necessary tasks or small improvements was like lightning. It was a commonplace that young officers and gentlemen should learn sailors' tasks by doing them, and even more a commonplace that they did them like ham-fisted dogs (whatever compliments were passed for form and safety's sake). But William could do it all, and passing well. Most liked him for it; and in men's way, some would loathe him, for obscure reasons. This afternoon he got the benefit of the doubt, he thought. The men worked well, and not unkeenly, and the tasks got done. As in the morning, he felt an unaccustomed pleasure on this grubby little vessel.

Geoff, the hopping cook, served them tea late in the afternoon, with a batch of cakes spread liberally round the company, and some left over for the dockyard men. Samuel and Will, by now, had rinsed the dirt off, and were smartened up and formal, within their lights. The tide was full, almost on the turn, and the weather had stayed beautiful. The Thames was a mass of vessels, of every shape and size, with the first big traders coming slowly down to be shot out to the Nore and then the Downs when the tide should start to run its fastest. The two young men were leaning on the rail looking at the southern shore where young girls were herding cows.

'What do you think of them?' asked Samuel. 'I mean our stalwarts, not the maids. You played a good hand, mucking in like that.'

'It was for pleasure, not to make my mark,' said William. 'Indeed, they seem a handy bunch. Whatever else they are not lax! Jem Taylor handles them right well.'

'He does. As boatswains go, he is a treasure. Lieutenant Kaye thinks him too familiar, and says he ought to drive them more. Consequently . . .'

'Consequently?' asked Will, after a time. He followed Holt's gaze. Ahead of them, two cable's-lengths, came a small skiff, lean and fast, with four men at the oars, another in the bow and two in the sternsheets, barely visible. 'Oh. Is that . . . ?'

'Our Richard Kaye. It is. Consequently, we must shut up. Consequently, in answer to your first, the boatswain will become ... Well, you shall see. Jem!' he shouted, standing upright. 'Mr Taylor! Lieutenant Kaye's approaching. Clear away that tea, for God's sake. Look alive.'

There was, at present, no chance of real formality. The Biter was on the dockyard tiers, swarming with yardmen, with attendant noise and mess. Some of them were singing, a raucous row that increased perceptibly as the boat bore down upon them – an indicator that the men of Deptford were not Navy servants, had no fear of blue-coated martinets, took their discipline (if they even knew the concept, let alone the word) from no sailing officer, especially not an Impress man, and sang and skylarked exactly as they pleased. Kaye's own men, ranged up on either side of the gangway, took their cue directly from these freer spirits, their reluctant surliness quite surprising William. While Jem Taylor, before his eyes, became a different man; slack-shouldered, dull-visaged, somehow unjointed. As the skiff rounded up smartly underneath the boom, the bow man slung the painter across the rail with unerring aim – and Taylor dropped it.

'Jem, Jem,' Sam admonished, below his breath but loud enough for William. And added: 'Consequently, will become a shambling imbecile.'

William, for all that Sam had said of him, realised he had no idea at all what kind of man he might expect in Kaye – except a rich one. Certainly, from above, he had not the air of violence and unpleasantness that he knew so well from many other officers he'd met. He stood up in the well and wreathed his face in smiles as he glanced up at them. He was a handsome man, bulky but with narrow shoulders, with a roundish face, slightly lop-sided, and an air of boyishness. William guessed his age at twenty-three or -four, but the skin was smooth, unlined by ravages of weather or of care. He skipped quite lightly across the thwarts to reach the ladder, quite lightly but almost clumsy with it, and scooted up the Biter's side in quick order. There he stood, resplendent in blue coat and white-powdered wig, with eyes for them alone, ignoring the common sailors ranged up to honour him with a blank completeness, as if they were not there.

'So! You are Bentley, then! Your Uncle Daniel has said much of you, and I am pleased at last to engage the flesh! Your servant, sir!'

William Bentley, in that evening sun, felt the warmth drain from himself, to be replaced by a hollow certainty he found sickening. So Daniel Swift, whose offers and whose overtures he had so strongly fought, his savage Uncle Daniel, whose very forgiveness had filled him with a creeping dread, knew Richard Kaye and so had got this ship for him, behind his back. Not merit, not service, not even shortages of officers in time of war; but interest had put him here. In the Biter, in the Impress, and with a man Sam Holt most roundly hated. Why? He put his hand out because he had to, but his heart was crushed. His face, he guessed, must look a pretty picture.

If Richard Kaye noticed, though, he showed it not a whit. His round eyes, brown like hazel nuts and slightly protuberant, shone with enthusiasm as he pumped Will's unresisting hand. He was laughing.

'I know your weaknesses!' he said, aloud for all the world to hear. 'Your uncle has done me the signal honour of recommending you to me, with all your background, the good sides and the bad! Between us, sir, I confide we shall go far!'

William's bow and smile were models of control. Good Christ, he thought, imagine that I called Sam vulgar. This man, from speech and bearing, comes from a family that's impeccable, and he is rich. Corrupt, and rich, and as Sam says, a stupid, useless man. So why has Daniel Swift put me to him?

Lieutenant Kaye, his captain, still had hold of his hand. The skiff still hung in the water, at the boom, her boat's crew looking round indifferent. Samuel harrumphed significantly.

'Sir,' he said. 'We have done our best, but the ship is not yet in a state of readiness to go downriver, as you may see. The dockyard men are far from finished. While Mr Gunning—'

'Yes, yes,' Kaye interrupted, carelessly. 'No matter for that, Holt, we are going nowhere this evening. Look, man, get these idle dogs whipped up to shape, can't you? Bob! Get up here this instant, you idle rogue! Sankey; start him, can't you?'

Dropping Will's hand, Lieutenant Kaye moved to the gangway and peered over. From the sternsheets of the skiff, with sudden speed, a small black shape, black boy, appeared, and scampered for the ladder, which he quickly climbed. He was dressed in black velveteen, with a black cap on his head, and went shoeless. In front of them, he stood with downcast eyes. Although he smiled, his smile seemed empty, a mask of lonely misery.

'Mr Bentley,' declared Kaye, pompously. 'Meet my little man, my servant. Black Bob, make a bow, sir!'

Black Bob did, but never raised his eyes. He was eight years or so, maybe seven, small and beautiful, but very, very sad. Kaye reached out and took his hand.

'Black Bob,' he said. 'We go now to the cabin, where I need my head rubbed with those aromatic oils. Sankey!' (another yell) 'Get that boat tied and tidied, then I'll need another suit of clothes!' He turned his face to William – ignoring Holt – and gave out his soft, lop-sided smile. 'In my cabin, in thirty minutes, sir, we shall take tea. I have another surprise in store. It will delight you.'

Sankey, Holt explained, was the commander's coxswain, but treated like a servant or a slave. He was no good seaman, having come with Richard Kaye into the service from the great estates in Hertfordshire, his man from early years. For Kaye was of a landed family, and yes, exceeding rich, despite he was third son and might be thought to have joined the Navy from necessity, therefore. In fact, Sam

80

held, he had joined because he 'had had naught else to do', and was a great embarrassment to his father, a duke or something other mighty, because he'd failed to rise. Although it was a secret, it was believed that he was twenty-eight, and had passed for lieutenant – God knew how, skulduggery was suspected – some several years before. He had not made post, and never could or would in Sam's opinion, because he was 'so hopeless; a playboy, lazy, and a fool'. At the end of all which, Holt gave a sudden grin.

'Mark you,' he guffawed, 'I am not speaking as an enthusiast! His breeding, on the other hand, is excellent. You may go together like a horse and cart!'

It was the black boy, though, that had shaken Bentley most. He had heard of this quaint fashion, much indulged in by rich men in the city and some of their wives and mistresses, but he had never seen one in the flesh. Black men at sea he'd heard of, men of Africa and the Colonies who had kept or won their freedom through some special merit, but this was a child, a sad-eyed little toy. When questioned, Samuel was dismissive.

'I guess he bought him from a trader,' he said. 'Black Bob's been with him since before I knew the man, although 'tis said he used to have a parrot. He keeps him in a box beside his bed, or sometimes in it, for all I care. On ship he is a waste of space and vittles, but then so is Kaye in most men's eyes. Black Bob is harmless, though. He speaks no English that I've ever heard. He'll fetch and carry, though, if Kaye is not around, so I guess he understands an order, don't he?'

The dockyard men were ranging to the gangway. Two had gone down into their cutter to bail her out, and there was bantering and insults being swapped with Biter's crew. The chaos on the decks was of a different order from the night before, but still pretty comprehensive. But the damaged yard was finished, ready to be rigged and furnished, and its sail bent on. Aloft the hempen cordage had been gathered in, the standing gear all shipshape, most of the running hardened home to pinrails or belays. Will could see that with a good crew and some hours, the vessel might be almost fit to sail.

'Tomorrow?' he asked Samuel. 'Do you imagine that is the surprise?'

'That would be one indeed,' Holt replied. 'You do not know this dockyard. I should say another two days, then there is water, food, shot and powder. Most like, if we are lucky, we will get liberty tonight. I have told you, Kaye loves the London life, and relishes high society. Hence, we may enjoy the same, although I doubt so high. Unless . . .' He paused, his expression strange. 'Will, if he invited you, would you care to go with him? That, indeed, might be the excitement. For certain, he was not including me.'

William expressed it with a look, and Samuel laughed. Truth was, though, that care to or not, he'd have to go if asked, there was no choice. O desolate possibility . . .

'Then there is Gunning,' Sam continued. 'He did not ask his whereabouts, which means he does not need a sailing master, does he? Except he finds a shift or garter in his bed from Sal or Ellen, by God, then he'll roar! What's this of Daniel Swift, though? Is he behind your place on here? A strange honour for a favoured nephew, isn't it? A bloody ship like this!'

It was exceedingly direct, but then, it seemed, Sam's method was to do with frankness. William was aware he'd put himself at his mercy with the confidences of earlier, and could not find it in himself to play the icy tightlips in reply.

'Ah, Sam,' he said. ' 'Tis hard to talk of, harder to nail down. I own he must be, most like, my . . . benefactor, should I say? But . . .'

'But such a ship,' said Sam. 'Such a ship and people, such a captain, such a job. Does he hate you, when you see him – do you see him, even? Tell me, Will. I do not understand.'

Will did not either. He saw Swift infrequently, not least because he was a serving officer, and it was plainly known within the family that he would not accept him as a source of help, he saw him as a tainted source. There had been many bitter altercations over it.

'Fact is,' he said, 'he lectured me till he was blue in the face that I should go to sea again, and called me a viper in the family bosom that I so long refused. My family, contrary to some opinion you have formed, is strapped as bad as you are where younger sons come into it. But if he *is* behind my calling to this ship it is a kind of . . . well, where is the money in the Impress Service, where are the prizes, the advancement?' Will stopped. 'In any case,' he said, 'it can't be he, we've heard naught of him for months, he sails in distant waters. If he was near enough to pull those strings we must have known of it; he has a house at Fareham, not so far from us.'

'But Kaye spoke of him—'

Kaye spoke of him again. As the two midshipmen watched the yardmen paddle their leaky craft away, Black Bob turned up like a silent wraith, and led them to the cabin. Half an hour after that word was brought of a pinnace hailing them, and Coxswain Sankey shot away to muster a receiving party. Lieutenant Kaye, resplendent in silk and blue, the mids in blue and dingy linen, stood stiffly at the gangway while the smart boat, with a smarter crew, laid close enough alongside for the smartest man on board of her to skip briskly up the Biter's ladder. Captain Daniel Swift, short, and hard, and arrogant, raised his face and fixed them with strange eyes, grey and brilliant. His nostrils flared.

It was the first time Bentley had seen him on a ship since men he loved had hanged, and guilt and shame had almost drowned him. Warm day, blue sky, the sound of moving water. The truth had been revealed.

9

That night, some men got liberty on the Biter, as predicted. Lieutenant Kaye went seeking high society, accompanied by Captain Daniel Swift. But Samuel Holt, and William, and all but two of her active Navy men, went to the receiving hulk upriver, where they were issued with two-foot clubs, a brace of pistols for the officers, and handcuffs. They got a talk-to, also, from a lieutenant as hard and old as seasoned timber from the mother of all men-of-war, a man called Coppiner.

'Mr Holt,' he greeted Samuel, when they walked through her entry port from the pontoon landing. 'This is an unexpected pleasure, unlooked for. Next you'll tell me Mr Kaye himself has graced us with his presence.'

It sounded like a pleasantry, but William had been warned beforehand. Samuel's face was held expressionless, his body stiff. Around him members of the Biter's crew became deaf men, flowing silent into the hole cut in the hulk's old timber. Samuel, indeed, did not reply.

'More like he's at the Lamb, however,' continued Coppiner. 'He'd rather press a harlot's belly than a topmast man, who can deny that, eh? Well, I give them joy of him. And who is this?'

The eyes, on William's, were dull yet burning. He had the expression of a man consumed with anger, ignited long ago deep down inside, unquenched by years of dousing and control. His face was cragged with years and bitterness, lined and dark, with bushy white hair – unwigged – and bushy eyebrows.

'If you please, sir,' responded William, 'Midshipman

William Bentley, newly joined with the Biter. Lieutenant Kaye sends his humble compliments.'

This was true, and he had been aware receiving the instruction that it was some sort of jest, or at least a coded form of slight, or insult. However, he delivered it directly, with a steady gaze, and the old man – sixty, if a day – made no comment. He held Bentley's eyes with great steadiness himself; and did not smile.

'Well to hell with him, say I,' was his reply. 'And you may tell him that yourself, young man. Now' – to Samuel – 'you are well sent tonight, *sans doute* by accident of that painted popinjay. We need forty men by Tuesday for the Claris, and we are told the Bell, the Cheshire Cheese, the Waggoner and the Old Top Drum are all alive with likely men. Young fellow' – to William – 'if you like cracking heads, tonight's your night. One word – there are two ships in from the East, and the service tried to milk them off of the Ness. There was bloodshed, one man crippled, revenge is in the air. I only tell you this, you will observe, to make you keener. For every man you take without a passport, there will be ten men with to try and take him back off you once more. I wish you luck.'

He turned abruptly, stamping off along the dim-lit alleyway to 'do his papers'. Within five seconds he had disappeared, the flickering horn lanterns making a hole to swallow him completely, and leaving Will and Samuel quite alone in the 'tween decks. Through the entry port there came a little light, from the sky, but without the glims, the inside of the hulk promised pitchy blackness. For a moment, both stood silent.

'Christ,' said Will, at last. 'The stink. What is it, Sam?'

The question was rhetorical, in one sense. The smell was sewage, mixed with river mud, mixed with permeating dankness as if the old ship's timbers had been steeped in damp for tens and tens of years. But she was a ship still, just, so how could it be borne, how had it grown so all-enveloping? Sam relaxed.

'Like the Fleet Ditch after a storm in summer, eh? It's shit, old lad, deep-laid and festering in the bilge. It amuses Coppiner sometimes to unshackle the young hopefuls and give 'em exercise on the chain-pumps, which makes it ten times worse. They stir it up, and spread it across the deck to the drain ports, and it runs down like treacle into Old Father Thames. What did you make of Coppiner? He's sixty-two, they say, and still lieutenant. The hatred in that man would swamp a battleship.'

'Where is he now? Gone to get drunk?'

Sam laughed.

'How well you know the service! But no, that is another string to the old man's bitter bow. He is a drunkard who can no longer drink. The story is – and it may be just that, but I think not – the story is he cannot even wet his lips with liquor, be it never so dilute, without he vomits it out of every pore and every orifice. He was taken once – another story – by a crew of young men he was releasing to a frigate, and they forced some brandy down his throat, they held him down and filled him through a copper tundish, like a Strasbourg goose. He shit like a firework – they tore his trowsers off – and vomited from nose and mouth, and bled through his ears and round his eyeballs. The story is not true, though. He would have killed them after. Which is, I promise, not a joke. Avoid him, Will. He is wholly hazardous.'

There was a noise not far from them, and voices William could recognise. The seamen, who had flitted off without an order, began to reappear. Before, they were a cutter's crew – a good one, to his surprise, despite the fact no one issued orders, and Sam played passenger, not command – now they were a band of desperadoes, armed to the teeth. It occurred to him, that apart from the blue he and Samuel wore, these could be a gang of men from any ship, intent on mayhem. If other men avoided them, as sure as hell they would, who could blame them for that, or gainsay them if they gave fear as their excuse?

'Hell, Sam,' he said, 'it is a gang of pirates. Tell me again how we're within the law.'

He said it as a joke, and Sam responded with a laugh, but grimly.

'The King needs sailors, but the dogs won't come,' he said. 'Merchants want protection, but they won't give up their sailors; indeed, they pay them more than we do and they let them go on shore when they're not sailing. The law is this, Will: certain people we must leave alone, like children, watermen, sailors outward bound, apprentices, bona fide men of business, clerics, all persons with a pass that says they're clear. Those we take, we pay; we offer bounty before we force them, and on board we give them money in advance, or a ticket for it, anyway. Look at it in this fashion – the Navy needs the men, and if we don't do it someone else will, harder. Alternative: we starve.'

The men were gathered round them now, and some were getting restive. There were eight of them, led by the boatswain Taylor, the small, squat man of Irish face who seemed to merge rather than lead, which may have been bare wisdom in the case of one or two. One – named John Behar, Will was to learn – was tall and bony, his loose limbs all point and knuckle, his face a picture of affronted cunning. Tom Tilley was yet larger, of enormous bulk and heavy tread, with deep-set, unpleasant eyes and a twisted mouth. Indeed, on close inspection, they were all formidable, all held their cudgels with anticipating love, and all were mixing for a violent fray.

'We're ready, sir,' said Taylor, as if summing up a mood. 'We're fit to crack some heads for King and country!'

Taylor's bold statement was maybe meant to mock them, and as he issued it, he and his cohorts moved forward as a body, crowding them towards the entry port. William was aware of the issued pistol heavy at his waist, and he saw Sam's knuckles tighten on his club. But they were pushed backwards – not touched, but moved as if by a human tide – and emerged almost willy-nilly through the port on to the pontoon alongside which the cutter lay.

Outside the air was clean and warm, although a certain nip of autumn touched the skin, and the smell off the river was ten times sweeter than the reek inside the hulk. She lay above them like a sheer black cliff, not a light along her length save at the quarter windows, behind which Lieutenant Coppiner presumably sat and nursed his hate and grievances. And waited, thought William, like a spider in the centre of his web for flies, or sailors, or innocents abroad, to be thrust into the sticky, massy darkness where he could feed on them.

'Sir?' The boatswain glanced at him, a sideways look. He was already at the tiller, and two men were holding the pontoon, waiting to let slip. William lightly stepped on to the gunwale, then joined his fellow officer in the well. The cutter – without an order – was freed, sliding sideways and outwards from the receiving hulk until all the oars were shipped and clear and the men began to pull towards the shore. Silhouetted against a starry sky she was enormous, high from the water because empty of all heaviness, and sporting only one stump of mast, abaft of midships. The rising moon threw a white glare as it slipped from behind a cloud, but she still had no reflected beauty. She had been a ship, and lovely as ships are. Now she was a floating, rotten dungeon.

'Are there men on board?' asked William. 'Surely not just Coppiner?'

'That ent a man,' said Jem Taylor, unexpectedly. 'That be a black spirit, run away from hell.'

'He's a bastard, sir. I beg your pardon.'

There was laughter from the boat's crew at this – William had no idea who had spoken the latter sentences – and no sense at all the apology was meant. Sam Holt was smiling, too.

'Just Coppiner, and a crew of four or five or so. His imps, perhaps, if Jem is right about their master! They're wrecks, or mad, or drunkards anyway, there's no gainsaying that, they act as jailers, to his command. Us and the other tenders provide for him, and bring the muscle when it's needed. Tonight, say. We'll go out and fetch them in, and Jem here and the lads will chain them in the pens while you and me go aft with Coppiner to his office and sort out cash and papers. We'll sign them over, he'll sign them in, we'll go out for more.'

'Ho ho,' came from the middle of the boat, quiet but distinct.

'Depending on the time and circumstance,' said Samuel, unperturbed. 'There's none on there tonight, if that's what you mean, though. I guess our being here means there's a flurry on. What did he say she's called? The Claris, was it? I don't know the ship.'

A voice from forward: 'Forty gun; Captain Anderson. She lost a hundred in the Straits. The smallpox.'

Further aft: 'Then sixty more from scurvy, coming home. She lies at Sheerness.'

'Well, we can't ship 'em down there,' said Samuel, cheerfully. 'That's one bright aspect, if we find some rogues. On short-haul trips like this,' he explained to Bentley, 'pressed men can be a deal of trouble. Drunk, furious, with friends and wives and sweethearts ready to row out and take them off of us. But Biter's stuck down in Deptford, so we take 'em back to Coppiner and away like buggery. He has some soldiers, of course, as well as his imps, eight or ten or so, in case of boarding parties in a rage. But we'll sleep like quiet babies in our beds.'

It was black once more, the moon behind a bigger cloud. They were slipping past moored merchant ships, and ahead of them were wharves, and yards, and docks. Huddled houses right down to the bank, and wherry traffic, watermen's boats, activity. Bentley did not know the river, but this was seaman-land, and with a vengeance. Dark though the night was, the sense of life and fervour was enormous, growing greater as they approached the public stage. One end was set aside for mooring boats, and Taylor nosed the cutter in amongst them as the bow man made ready to put a rope ashore. There were two or three shoremen on watch, but none offered to take a line. A Navy cutter with armed men aboard most likely meant the Press. William saw one of the watchers, younger than the rest, merge with the dark and vanish out of sight, and as they climbed the stair into the dock-street proper he noted that – although the place was swarming – men in sailor's garb were few, and kept their distance.

Holt stopped when they reached the level, with the men all gathered round him. About them moved foot passengers of every degree – except that they all were pretty low, thought William. Costers, tradesmen, servant-types, beggar-boys and merchants' runners. Carts also, drawn by oxen, and mules packed with goods. He studied them, wondering how they were to choose potential targets, but Holt and the gang ignored them. They had other fish to fry.

'Now lads,' said Holt, 'the Old Top Drum's the nearest, so we'll go there first. There's a way in down that little jigger behind the skinman's shop as I remember. Am I right?'

'Plain to see where 'ee do drink, then,' came a mutter from the back. Holt dutifully joined in the chuckle.

'We'll split up into three till we get close,' he continued. 'That way the spies won't maybe spot us for the Press. We'll have to go in front and back when we've joined up, so we'll use the pie shop as a rendezvous, it's half a furlong from the alehouse. We'll meet there in ten minutes, divide in two – and pincher them.'

'Lawks, I 'ave forgot my fobwatch!' said another voice, and the laughter was renewed.

'Do it by your thirst,' said Holt. 'Ten minutes is a long time till a drink. If we strike lode I'll stand you one.'

Will went with him and Peter Tennison, a thin man who looked more like their servant than a man-catcher (he stank of liquor, also, from his night spent in the scuppers), and they kept their weapons obscured from the public gaze. Sam said the level of activity in these streets was not unusual, despite the lateness of the hour, but that the men they wanted would, by now, be well ensconced. The 'spies' he'd mentioned were usually small boys, who watched for Press patrols by local custom, and ran from pub to pub to tip men off. Hence, he added, if they did badly at their first stop, their chances of success would be diminished, at least for hours.

'Dead drunkenness is our best ally, Will; that and surprise. Lucky for us that Jack likes to sup on liquor.'

The gathering outside the pie shop was well done. Will saw it up ahead – still open, in the London way – with not a Navy man in sight. As he and Sam and Tennison arrived, so did Jem Taylor, from an alleyway, then from across the road came John Behar and Tilley, on their own. Jem Taylor whistled, and his crew showed themselves, ready and keen. Sam took the two big men, with Tennison and Silas Ayling, and put Taylor's team in Will's command. It took three seconds, but 'Quick!' he said. 'Mr Bentley and Jem Taylor through the back, us through the front. Now – look alive!'

Plucked by the arm into the jigger, William found himself pursuing Taylor and three others through liquid muck and garbage, the 'leader' damn near failing to keep up. He was well shod, they were ill, but the loathsome nature of the track worried them not at all, nor fear apparently of jagged stones or cutting things. Within two hundred yards they found a wall, and within the wall a wicket. There was no ceremony of seeking a response. Billy Mann, Josh Baines, Alf Wilmott combined their weight and threw it at the door, which clattered open – probably unbolted. In the darkness of the yard a blacker shape dashed for the wall, ascended it like a topman, and was gone. First loss.

'Draw your pistol, sir!' urged someone, hoarsely. 'Shoot'm if they tries fer't run!'

This was mad advice, and Bentley knew it. He drew his

club out though, and forged – again a follower – through the cluttered yard. There was a dog, within an outhouse, barking ferociously, crashing against the inside wooden wall, a huge and heavy dog. But they were past, and Jem Taylor booted in the back door to the scullery, and they were in. Here was dark, also, and Will heard screams and bellowing, and glimpsed one fat old woman, and a girl or so. He smelled sweat, sharp and excited, come off one of the men, sudden and distinctive, and Baines, a small man, rather ratty, was wild-eyed, almost yapping, like a spaniel at a rabbit's throat.

To William, though, it quickly seemed a useless way to take men unawares. Like other alehouses he knew – more so than most, indeed – it was a warren, of doors and passageways and nooks. The men were wild and quick, but their quarry, in the main, was quicker. As they bundled down one long passage, side doors sprang open, heads popping out like actors in a play. Bodies ditto, to scamper off away if they had need to. While others, men and maids, moved out into the thoroughfare and wedged in solidly, stoic in the face of threats and cutlasses.

In the biggest parlour they found Samuel and his crew, and the makings of a general brawl. Here were prime seamen, no doubt of that, and many of them almost incapable. There were others though, whose faces were alive with joy at the roughhouse in store. At the moment William put his face into the room a bottle missed it by an inch or less, smashing on the doorpost to spray him with a spirit and some shards of glass. Baines, behind him, ducked underneath his arm and shot across the room like a dervish to pay the thrower back. Blood was pouring from a gash beneath his eye.

'Cease this brawling!' shouted Holt, his voice sadly unrewarding. 'We are here in the King's name! I offer bounty for all able-bodied men, and three months' wages in advance!'

Wrong time, wrong place, wrong men, it would appear.

The room was full of sailors, and they were full of drink and cash and (judging by the doxies at their sides) explosive lust. However attractive wages and bounty might sound to destitutes, these men were here to spend. William, to his surprise, found himself propelled into the middle of the room, firm hands had pushed him from the ruck, and he was face-to-face with roaring homeward-bounders.

For an instant he was seized by fear, and for the same bare second the parlour, in his brain at least, went deadly silent. In face of him, burly as a bear, shoulders forward in a fighting crouch, there stood a man about to spring, to tear him into pieces. The lurch inside himself was sickening; the red-eyed, raw glare, the drunken jubilation on the savage face took him back to other places, other violent men. Neither Samuel – who might have tried – nor the Impress crew – who might not? – had time to move before the figure, as swift as it was massive, came at him with hands outstretched like claws. William saw both the bare feet come off the ground, the man was flying. And the noise came back, an enormous roar burst on his eardrums.

William was calm as ice now, and each move he made outstripped his conscious brain. As the face came towards him, level with his own, his arm with weighted club swung back and sideways in an arc behind his right leg, then flashed across his own face to strike the sailor's with a crashing blow. Then, neat as a dancer, the small blond man stepped back and sideways as the flying ape flew on, to scatter the Press gang and crump into the wall. Another roar arose, half of it cheers, and his men barged past him into the centre, their own clubs jubilantly raised.

The man was breathing blood from nose and mouth, but was conscious. His eyes caught William's, and he smiled. But surely not, thought Will; but surely not? A young woman came at him then, more claws, more hatred, but John Behar's hand, a bone and sinew nightmare, caught her by the neck of her gown, which tore across to reveal a full and handsome bosom that, by dexterously turning her, Behar managed to catch in one hand, then in both. Another wench – happily, thought William – then bit his leg.

The fight was general, and impossible. Everyone, save William and Holt perhaps, enjoyed it immensely, although some of the women screamed, as if for form's sake. Will could not tell at all if they were going to 'gain the day', or how they'd know, or tell. Then the third man not enjoying it, the man who owned the furniture and glass, put an end to it (though not immediate) by dousing all the candles and the other glims. There was a fire, for the friendly fug it made presumably, but it glowed dim. After some minutes men rolling on the floor were the only combatants, and that died off rapidly. Very soon the parlour seemed less crowded, as it was in all reality: there was little that could stop those bent on going, for nobody could identify his nearest fellow, certainly. When the landlord brought in fresh lights, there were the Press gang and five other men, three on the floor, one seated at a broken table, one standing. Five men whose ages added, at a guess, to damn near three hundred years, and one of them with only half a starboard arm.

'What is the bounty, sir?' asked one of them, and the boat's crew screamed with mirth.

'Five pound to age of forty,' Holt improvised. 'After that, a whore's dug or a groat in hand; it is yours to choose. Landlord – a jug of ale here, and some cannikins. What drink you, Mr Bentley, wine or brandy?'

Josh Baines the rat, and Tilley of the twisted mouth and giant hams, were facing Will, close in.

'You got yon bastard with your bully stick a lovely clout,' said Tom Tilley, in a sort of rough admiring way, if grudging. 'You didn't look the man to smash his teeth, begging your pardon. Sir.'

'You should have got him on the ground though,' added

Baines. 'You could've cleaned the lot out easy, swung from above. Toothless men don't bite, they say.'

Despite himself, Will could not control his face. His feelings were disgusted, and the men could plainly see it. Baines merely sneered and turned away, but Tilley's expression, already ambiguous, grew visibly more dark and dangerous. The deep eyes glowed, with bitter antagonism. William, whose disgust was with himself much more than them, yet clearly saw the dangers. He had known too many men like this.

'You step above yourself, the pair of you,' he said. His voice, though light, rang with authority. 'If scum have teeth want smashing – any scum – stand back. Baines! You, sir! Turn and face me!'

Baines did, and all Navy eyes were on the two of them. Will stared at him, until he dropped his eyes; in truth, no major battle.

'Aye, sir?'

'Keep your mouth shut with me until your opinion is solicited. Or you might taste my lead-lined stick some time. And you too, mister. You shall not presume.'

Afterwards, after the Old Top Drum, they tried the other taverns Coppiner had named, then three more possibles. They took the five old sailors they had caught – a hot Press was a hot Press, and the King's ships had to sail, whatever – although one of them slipped his bonds while they assayed their business at the Nag. They got three more, one young and prime and half-dead drunk, who said he had a passport although he could not find it, but did next morning sober; so good a one that even Coppiner made haste to let him go, they later heard. Three more from seven alehouses, all of which had mysteriously emptied as they chanced along, and in terms of proper men, in Bentley's book a wasted night, completely, utterly.

But he did not converse with Holt about it until much afterwards, until they had rowed downstream at last to where Biter lay silent on the Deptford tiers. In the boat –

its crew half drunk and rowdy, but still with ears – he kept his mouth shut, except on lighter matters than the Press. Samuel was quite euphoric, and had suggested, despite the lateness of the hour, that they should give the men their liberty, and go themselves to Dr Marigold's. He jested, though, for Kaye had ordered them straight back, and Swift had been a brooding threat hung over them. Both Samuel and Will had figured earlier that the sudden onset of conscientious duty Kaye displayed in sending out a gang had something to do with Swift's presence on the Biter. Even in the people's eyes he had glittered like a diamond, although he'd stood completely at his ease upon the quarterdeck then disappeared below.

The ship was dark, the ship was guarded by the sleeping yard nightwatchman only, on their return. John Behar woke him cruelly with a kick, then the men tumbled to their hammacoes, waking their fellows who had stayed on board and yarning for a while. Sam and William listened outside the cabin, although no officers' boats were at the boom. Lieutenant Kaye and Captain Swift were at the fleshpots maybe, perhaps even at the Rondy, at any rate not here. Sam went in boldly, for a bottle, and jumped nearly from his skin at a sudden scuttling from behind a curtain, like an enormous rat. It was Black Bob, naked in the half-built giant's bed, starkly visible in the white light of the dropping moon.

'Where is your master?' Gruff, but kind. The child of Africa did not reply. 'Don't tell him – nay, that's no matter.' Sam's voice dropped away, and he pulled the curtain back across. There was a bottle on a table, half drunk, which he picked up. To Will he said: 'Let's go outside. The air is pleasanter. Poor lad.'

The moon was setting, but the stars were out, the clouds completely gone. They leaned on the rail, lords of everything, and watched the water flowing black below them. Will told Samuel of his feelings when he'd struck the man, of the months of brutishness he had endured on the Welfare. He had had to do it, he had known he had to, because the man would have killed or crippled him. And then the man had smiled.

'Oh, Sam,' he said. 'It is so impossible, this question of good men and bad. Once I believed all were evil, all the common people we had foisted on us, then I learned that was not so, at all. Then mayhap I went the other way, but then again . . .'

He stopped, and Sam, instead of helping him, drank deeply from the bottle's neck.

'And then he smiled,' said William. 'I saved my life or eyesight, and I smashed his mouth, and he was amused by it. We burst in there like dervishes, and they enjoyed the roughhouse. We were there to rob them of their liberty, but —'

Sam interrupted.

'But they escaped. Surely no wonder they—'

'Not all! We took seven to the hulk. Seven men were put in chains by Coppiner. And the ones who did flee might not have done if we'd been luckier! God, Sam, that man has lost some teeth and blood! To what end? For what purpose?'

Sam let the passion take its course. He took another drink. Then he wiped his mouth and tossed the empty bottle overside.

'I doubt the seven men in chains will be there after their breakfast,' he said, drily. 'You don't see it, do you, yet? The young one has a passport or I'm a Spaniard. The others are too old or useless to bother with. They were in seamen's clothes though, and could have scuttled like the rest if they'd been minded to – perhaps they need a ship on account of aged or infirm. At least they'll get a bounty, if they volunteer; who knows, Captain Anderson of the Claris might even pay wages up in front, it has been known, it is the law.'

Tiredness and drink had William fuddled.

'Are you saying . . . ?'

Sam gave a snort.

'I'll say this, friend: we have to get a certain tally, or Lieutenant Kaye in his new-found smartness will have our balls for baubles. Sometimes, as you'll find soon enough, Press work can be vile and bloody and abominable. When we get the chance, let's play like Christians, shan't we? The one man we hurt tonight was smiling, so you say. Well, very good, say I.'

On which note, Sam suggested – a piss into the river, and so to bed. Which they did.

10

It was gone midday before the Surveyor General arrived at Langham Lodge – much trouble on the road from London, he told Sir Arthur over a glass of tea. The day was fair, the double windows open to the rolling lawns, and gentle breezes blew. It did not take him long, however, to notice his host's state, and to comment on it. They were not close friends, but had had dealings over many years. In one way, Sir Peter Maybold was responsible for the rise of Charles Yorke within the Customs service.

'Fisher,' he said, 'now spit it out, man. What precisely worries you? I should be surprised, in fact, if you had heard from our friend Yorke.'

This was disingenuous, and both men knew it. Sir A had sent express to Customs House the day before precisely because he had heard nothing, nothing for days. Which meant he had expected to. He stared at the florid face across from him with a little perturbation.

'Let us not beat about the bush,' he said. 'Yorke is my nephew. Whether I am meant to know or not, he and Charles Warren are on a secret mission in Hampshire or the Hampshire/Sussex border. They passed through here on their way down, and I have had intelligences since. I have not dragged you all this way upon a whim. Please take the matter serious.'

The fat man had been cold in his carriage, a problem with breeze through the bottom board across his stock-inged shanks. Now, with tea in hand and Sir Arthur's keen eyes on him, he started to get hot. He blew his cheeks.

'Hhmph,' he went. 'I take it bad in you you do not think I am. Blood, I would not traipse all down here for anyone, you know. On a horse it's bad enough, but I'm too fat for horses now, except across the park. I can't tell you nothing, sir!'

Petulant, Sir A observed. His heart sank. Maybold was Surveyor General of the Riding Officers, but it was a grace and favour rank in many ways. His wife Laetitia had young lovers, it was held, and so Sir Peter dabbled in his offices to keep his mind engaged, instead of leaving all the hard business to his juniors, more competent by age and brain. On the other hand, if he knew anything, it should be winkleable, so to speak.

'I beg your pardon,' he replied. 'Forgive me, Maybold, I do not mean to be insulting. You know my feelings on the wicked trade, you know it touches me both as a merchant and a man. Indeed, you know the debt I owe you for the hand you have put behind my nephew, the fillips you have vouchsafed him in his calling. Of course you take it serious, and I am truly grateful. Your perception, sir, was exactly nice: I am beside myself with worry. I beg you; reassure me.'

The fat pink face was wreathed in smiles. Sir Peter thrust his chubby legs out, nodding. As he did so, he shook his jowls.

'I was right, you see. A good judge, is my dear wife's opinion. But Fisher, I really cannot tell you anything that you do not – naughty, but I'll forgive you! – that you do not seem to know. Let us say that I confirm for you that the Charleses Yorke and Warren are "under the cloak" on this one. Well, if they are, then what of it? They've gone to ground, let's say, they've taken cover. They are both stout men, sir. Charles Warren has for many, many years been acting as a . . . well, let's say below the parapet, shall we? Fisher – Sir Arthur – do not worry, sir, I beg you.'

Sir Arthur sipped his tea, and tapped his nail, and worried. Sir Peter was a foolish man, he thought; but then, what in this instance could he give away? Yorke had spoken of a bold new undertaking, an uplifting of violence

100

being brought in to the Hampshire trade, and said that he and Warren were to win some confidences, get close in with some dangerous, ruthless men. He had also given notice of a 'final meeting', and promised news of it, good or bad. Both men had horses at the Lodge – Warren was quite mad for horses – and papers, too, and spare clothes and everything. If they failed, they'd said, they would retire here – a place of secret safety – to regroup.

All this he thought about, but did not say. After some long moments, he tried another tack.

'Sir Peter, you are an honourable man, and I count you as a friend. My feeling is, your men are overdue. They marched into danger and – for whatever reason – they have not come back. The Collector at Portsmouth is not unknown to me, nor is the man at Chichester, and I have other people further west. I must tell you, I will contact them.'

The eyes narrowed in their fat. Sir Peter Maybold sighed. He made a gesture of acceptance, which meant, Sir Arthur guessed, that he would learn little going 'directly to the servants', so to speak. He dropped a name.

'Lord Larcher has his nose in every pie down this neck of the woods. Especially when it comes to Customs business. Perhaps if I asked him? We have been . . . very close.'

It was a lie. Embarrassment as blackmail was the ploy. Lord Larcher was a model of vapid indiscretion, whom Sir A had only ever heard of, never met. He'd heard, specifically, that he had rogered Maybold's wife. Yorke, much amused, had told him that. The eyes slid downwards, to the chubby lap. Sir A said quietly: 'It is not a lot I ask. Reassurance would be the best of it. But if they have gone missing . . . well, that would have to do. They have gone missing, have they not?'

Sir Peter Maybold sighed once more, more heavily. He nodded, and his eyes were sad.

'We have by no means lost our hope,' he said. 'Charles Warren is well versed in this life, very well, and Yorke –

your Charles . . . well, he is stout indeed, a stalwart officer. We have brought in men from Dorset and the Isle of Wight, we have informants, we have people on the seek. I may guarantee, in two days or three, we'll . . .'

He stopped. Outside they heard a bell, a small bell, tinkling. It was a signal from Mrs Houghton to Sir A that a luncheon was ready, if he should want to share it with the visitor. Sir Arthur's heart was heavy. Guarantee what, that was the question. Just what could Maybold guarantee? He did not wish to share his food with him. He wished him to begone, begone and do some good for Charles and Warren.

'There is some luncheon, sir,' he said. 'Something light and cold. I wish that you could find the time to take some with me? You have been very kind and generous.'

'Well quickly, then,' replied Sir Peter. 'I must stir myself betimes. But Fisher, let me promise this. I will keep you in the picture, if I can. Indeed I will, sir.'

'You do me honour, sir,' Sir Arthur said. 'My gratitude is boundless.'

The Biter, when Sam Holt and Bentley had arisen that morning, was little changed, and little like a fighting vessel, still. When Kaye returned before the forenoon watch was ended, she swarmed with dockyard men, while Taylor and his seamen worked desultorily at shipkeeping tasks the two midshipmen found for them. Kaye seemed little interested in any progress they had made, and hastened to his cabin and Black Bob. It was not until an hour later, when the men were eating, that some smartness entered in with the arrival from upriver of Swift.

He did not come on board. His men hung on their oars while he spoke to William, the penetrating power of his voice transfixing all on deck. It was suggested that his nephew come with him immediately – put on a coat beforehand – as he had urgent business between the pair of them. William, whose body was for use of his com-

102

mander, not his uncle, was in a quandary, until Kaye's door came open to reveal Black Bob, nodding vigorously.

'He's saying go,' Samuel said, quietly. 'Here; your coat. You've smudges on your face; wipe 'em.'

In the pinnace, which Swift, he said, had borrowed with its crew, William sat uncomfortable for some while. His uncle's face was pale, as if from drink, and his mood appeared extremely brittle. William, even after all the years and all the thinking he had gone through, knew that he was afraid of this man, and guessed he always would be. He considered him as relentless, ruthless, cold; and feared the most of all that he had been his hero and his aspiration.

'Well,' said Swift, at last, 'how do you find your new ship? You have settled in?'

It was a loaded question, its barbs well hidden. Glancing at his uncle's face, he could only guess at what the answer should be, to be correct. But he knew, he thought he knew, the high opinion Swift held of Richard Kaye.

'She shapes up, I think,' he tried. 'Of course, the dock-yard hands are slow, and there is much to do, but—'

Swift made a noise, dismissive, aggravated.

'She is a tub. She is filthy, slow, and ancient. One good blow and her bottom would drop out, with everybody in her. What of Kaye, then? What do you think of Kaye?'

They were pulling down the river, and the tide was low and slack. The acres of exposed mud, black and green, exhaled a rich and pungent vapour. Christ, thought William. What sort of truth?

'I hardly know him well, sir. He has a very . . . a very easy condition with the company.'

Slack Dickie. What would his uncle make of *that*? He caught the stroke oar's eye, which slid away immediately. But not before Will had sensed a gleam that could be humour. Swift, to make him suffer, maintained his silence.

'Mr Holt, my fellow, rates him highly. He . . .' Oh blush for shame, he thought. To misuse Samuel so, to play for time. He said, decisively, 'Nay, uncle. How should I know?

He is well bred, a pretty talker, he pleases their lordships, else how would he command? I have seen him doing nothing that would let me form opinions, and if I had it would not be my place. When we go downriver, when we get stuck in whatever we are looking for, why, then I'll tell you!'

Swift smiled, for the first time. He was very handsome, in his face and in his body, and the smile lit him like an angel. His eyes were clear and grey.

'Between us, my boy, he needs attention. He is extremely rich, his family is of the very highest quality. He commands that ship because he —' The grey eyes narrowed, and Will caught their direction. Stroke oar, once more, let his eyes glide away. But Swift harrumphed, and took a different tack.

'No matter. We are heading for a yard now, and more of that later. These men are good men, nephew, but they are not mine, I've got the loan of 'em. For all I know they've ears that flap like turkey wings, and gobs like seven bells. Ain't that so, mister?'

The stroke oar smirked, and pounded on. Next bend, across the mudflats, Bentley saw a village and some yards with vessels on the stocks. His uncle nodded, and ten minutes later they came ashore. While the boat's crew found grass to sit or lounge on – some chasing crabs, barefoot in the muddy shallows – the two of them approached the keel and timbers growing on the slip. It was a vessel of a certain rakishness, or would be. She had a good slope to her stem, was narrow at the entry, and the stern was shaping slim.

'She should be fast,' said William. 'But whose is she, sir? May I guess Lieutenant Kaye's next craft?'

Swift threw back his head and barked. There were men inside the timbers, who looked at them, then returned indifferently to their tasks. Still no one had approached the Navy officers.

'Lieutenant Kaye pays charter for the Biter,' said Swift.

'She is well matched to his task. Why think you he should want a ship like this?'

'Well, sir . . . Well, you said he was rich, and commanded her because . . . And then you stopped. If he is rich . . .'

Swift nodded.

'A fair assumption. But no, she is not Kaye's, she is mine. Mine and . . . certain others'. Well, yes, I suppose it might turn out that Kaye will buy a share, but I doubt that. I have other things in mind for Kaye.'

William knew better than to try and probe. His uncle was of uncertain temper, and his affection for his nephew was itself uncertain, now. Swift blew air out from his open throat, a sort of sibilant indication of moving on.

'Oh, my boy,' he said, as if tiredly. 'I can't tell you the half of it, it is not meet at present. Listen – I was a private ship, you know that, don't you? My frigate was attached to nobody, these eight months I've been away. I had a good voyage – you know my meaning there, I trust? – and I amassed a good amount from it. I thought to stay in England for at least a while, to oversee this building among other plans, but their lordships want me at the Straits to join a squadron; so I must go. It has been precipitate, too precipitate, and leaves me with some ends not rove. Frankly, Kaye is one of them.'

He locked his eyes on William's, almost a glare. This was more like old times, and he felt a tiny tremor of discomfort, some frisson he did not completely understand. Blood will out, he thought disconsolately.

'In many ways,' said Swift, 'he is a very fine young man, our Richard Kaye. He does not need the Navy, he has no need of anything for that matter, he is exceeding rich. But he has ambition, nephew, he desires most extremely to be post. Now – frank again – this cannot, at the moment, come about. His father's name and power is not, for historic circumstances, with the Admiralty. Their lordships have opinions and they cannot, seemingly, be swayed. I have connections, as you know; massy ones. I have heard Kaye described, my boy, as this: a playboy, a fool, and lazy. As feckless, foolish, weak, corrupt. There. What think you of all that?'

This was mischievous, the cue to be amused, which William acknowledged with a nod. There were questions he could ask, but he thought it safer, still, to wait. Swift pulled a timepiece from his fob, flicked it open, then shut and pocketed it all in a movement.

'What I want from you is this,' he said. 'You are my sister's flesh and blood, if wayward, and you have grown up very cool. Also, I believe you conscientious, with the air and mien and the makings of a seaman. You know discipline, you can make men jump to do your bidding. Listen – this war will not last for ever, do you take my meaning? We must have other irons in the fire, for the peace. Influence. Interest. Power. Those are the vital things, my boy; the vital things.'

No reply to this, because there was none. William composed his face, hoping for elucidation. Captain Swift shrugged impatiently.

'When Kaye is post,' he said, 'his rise becomes inevitable. We have shared interests, he and I, I will put it at no greater pitch than that. With our help, with your talents and encouragement, with your *backing* shall I say, we'll put some fire in his belly, and some iron in his soul. Then, when he rises, and his wealth is matched by power – why then, he'll help us in his turn. He will be admiral, nephew. Once on the rungs the way is only up, and his father is a duke who has a million and more. Wars do not last for ever, Will. Do you read my meaning now?'

Bentley did, and it occurred to him, as it had occurred before, his uncle might be slightly mad. But his uncle did have interest in the higher echelons of the service, the highest echelons, and if anyone could get a dough-head promoted above his abilities, then surely it was he. To become an admiral in his turn! The first sea lord, mayhap?!

God, thought William, with a sudden chill, why did his uncle feel he *needed* such insurance?

'He's not a coward,' said Swift, suddenly. 'I would not give a shit for him if so. He's not a booby even, very much. With good officers, the Biter will do very well. The Press is considered greatly important in these times, and will get more so. What sort of man is that tall one, Holt is it? He seemed not of the very best, more like a blessed pauper than a gent, too damn familiar with the people. I'll have Kaye make you up over him, if you wish.'

'No, sir!' It came out half explosion, much too high. But Will was scandalised, amazed. 'No, sir,' he said, more levelly. 'Mr Holt is experienced above his years, is honest, and he's full of pluck. I shall learn from him, and take it as a privilege.' He almost laughed, surprised by the jollity of the thought. 'With me as second under him, Lieutenant Kaye would never make a captain, I declare. Sam Holt can even navigate, and should be lieutenant, save he has no cash or interest. I will learn from him, uncle.'

Swift humphed, and set off for some buildings up the slip.

'Aye,' he said. 'And navigation, that's another thing. Kaye cannot navigate to save his life or yours, he takes it as a joke, the great poltroon. He has a sailing master, who also owns the ship, who also drinks his life away. Where was he yesterday? Where today? Why cannot you navigate, sir? Why?'

'Because,' said William, but an answer was not needed.

'Because you've wasted time! Because you've dozed around on shore like a crying baby or a maid! You *will* learn navigation, Mr Bentley, and Kaye will have a navigator! There, sir! *There!*'

Luckily, it seemed to William, they had reached the shed that Swift was making for. They entered, and a man in leather apron bustled down to them from the far end. Taking his cue from Swift, this man, the master-shipwright it would appear, ignored William and entered into animated conversation about timber, dates, supplies. After half an hour he was desultorily introduced, then had to say a quick goodbye before they hustled out again. Swift gathered up the boat's crew with a shout, and five minutes later they were shooting upriver on a rising tide. There were questions William would have liked to ask, but the stroke oar still had ears, and his Uncle Daniel was preoccupied. Why should he not be? thought William. He is a Navy captain, yet a ship is being built for him. A fast ship and a handy. And Swift was off to join a squadron in the Straits . . .

Daniel Swift had one more surprise in store for him that day, and it was the stiffest of them all. When they reached the Biter's deck, he barked an order before William had time even to open his mouth, and a seaman scuttled aft as if it was his own commanding officer who had spoken. In truth, Swift's name and fame were known to all on board, and sailors take no chances with such people. Within seconds Samuel Holt appeared, then behind him the small black boy, whom Swift glanced at with disdain.

'Bloody pantomime,' he muttered. 'Will, my boy, that's why you're here, d'you see? Now' – to Samuel – 'is Lieutenant Kaye on board? And my man Kershaw? My apologies to Mr Kaye, but I am short of time.'

Samuel made the slightest bow.

'You are expected, sir. Bob! Bring hot water from the galley. Hot water! Tea!'

'No time for tea, no time for nonsense,' snapped Swift. 'Mr Bentley, follow here. This is for you.'

He almost leapt aft, pushing Black Bob roughly to one side. Will and Sam exchanged a look, but had no time for conversation. William got in the cabin behind Swift, and Samuel after him. Kaye, a trifle strained about the lips, was already on his feet.

'Ah, Captain Swift. Capital to see you. How did you with the business at the yard?'

'No matter of that, excellent, right well,' he said. 'Kaye, we'll talk tonight, sir, I must fly. Now, Kershaw. Have you explained yourself?'

In the cabin dimness, William had not seen the man. He came forward hesitantly, not a little odd. He was not old – forty maybe, maybe less – but he had the air of someone for whom age was an irrelevance. He had suffered something, something devastating. He had one hand only, and a blinded eye, but the damage was not physical, thought Will. He was strung up like a racehorse, overbred. Captain Swift touched him gently on the arm, and he somehow flinched.

'Explained himself? Not much he has! You are too shy, sir,' said Swift. 'Mr Bentley, by the kind permission of Lieutenant Kaye here, Mr Kershaw is the man I told you of. He is a good man – indeed with stars and sights and compasses and quadrants he is a genius – and he has sailed with me before. He is to be your tutor, to mug you through your exam to be lieutenant. You are getting old, sir, and you bid fair to disgracing us! Mr Kershaw will whisk you up to scratch in no time.'

William's face was blazing, and he blessed the lack of light. But he would not drop his eyes from Kershaw's face, and all he saw there he distrusted. The eyes were slant, and slippery, the expression cant. The mouth was wet and nervous, the tongue unstill behind the lips. Christ, you bastard man, thought William of his uncle: you have got me on this mad ship for some reason, and this is your spy. You bastard, bastard man.

11

The hole they made for Charles Yorke was not a grave, nor yet an *oubliette*, in theory. There were men among his captors who wanted him to die, but there were others, by now, who could not bear the thought. Yorke lay in the weakening autumn sunshine, beside a rocky bank, and heard them arguing. He wondered, off and on, which faction would win the day, but there was part of him that almost did not care. Charles Yorke was weary, almost unto death.

The sequence of events he'd been a part of was very hazy as he lay there. He remembered leaving London, he remembered stopping with his uncle at the Lodge, and talking through the plan. He remembered that he and Warren – dear, dead Warren – had talked to people Charles had known before, who were worried over something. He remembered meetings with some leaders, and promises of more. He remembered that they'd said that he could live.

When was it, though? Two nights? Three? A week ago? The men who'd held them, the drunken band, had changed, had grown and dwindled, ever on the move. The only constant thing had been the drinking, and the blows. In barns and inns and scattered villages words had been said, spirits taken, and cruel, savage punishment meted out upon their bleeding forms: see these men, these spies. They are the enemy, they oppose. Learn what we do to those who will defy us.

There was a big man, a fat, strong, tall man who had been there many times, if not all. At first he had seemed a terror, a man without compassion in his soul. Since Warren's burning, Yorke thought, he had changed. Twice or three times he had mopped Yorke's face, dipped bread in gravy and helped him take it down, tried to express something perhaps, then given up on it. Yorke could hear his voice as he lay in the sunshine, deep and hollow, somehow hopeless. We have gone too far in this, he heard him saying. We must not kill this man, it is not possible. It is inhuman, it is cold blood, impossible.

They were in a clearing, in a scrubby wood. Yorke lay on a stony rise, beside a rocky outcrop, full of caves and fissures. The sun shone through branches, dappling the grass. If he moved his head he could see some of the fellows, although not the big one. Another one he recognised, a ginger man, was staring at the ground between his feet, face grey with days of alcohol and fatigue. A third man was weeping, face clutched in his hands. Weeping for me, thought Yorke, peculiarly. For my fate, or his own dilemma. How extraordinarily strange.

Then voices rose, and men began to shout. Yorke closed his eyes, afraid of what he might see if anger turned into more blows and kicks for him. He had a longing, enormous and unfathomable, not to be hurt afresh. His body shrank upon itself, he prayed, he prayed they would not set on him.

'He will find us out!' roared someone. 'If we don't kill him, they will track us down and hang us!'

'They will track us down and hang us anyway!' yelled another voice. 'God's blood, do you think they will applaud!'

'Oh God, oh God!' a young man cried; almost a boy in fact. 'They said that we must save him, didn't they? Oh God, why have we done this dreadful thing!'

'Oh shut your din, you coward, and let us kill him now! At least with only corpses to accuse us we have a better chance.'

And the big man's voice chimed in, an ending knell.

'So will you do it then, Tom Littleton? Will you cut his

throat, or what? For if it's killing for the sake of argument, count me out. It is too late, too late.'

Wrong, though, to say Yorke felt hope renewed. He felt nothing substantial, his mind was all aswirl, thoughts came and went, hope, fear, indifference, non-understanding. He could see a bird perched on a branch, but could not make out its colours or its kind, which disappointed him. Shouts came with murmurs, tears with shouts, then slowly they were mixed with movement, and the clunk of rocks. Men were moving, men were shifting stones, the argument had died away.

This went on, he imagined (or imagined he imagined; he was in a dream) for a time interminable. Sometimes men came to him, their faces swam before his eyes, sometimes he was left. By the time they came to move him the sun was high, judging by the heat. But their numbers had diminished. He saw the big man, Peter, and he tried to speak. But no sound came, no words, and the face was closed and shuttered anyway.

It was a sort of cavern they had made for him. He was lifted, for he could no longer walk, and transported not ungently across a rocky patch, then down into a cleft. Three men lowered him, and underneath him more took his weight, then eased him through split walls of stone that glittered with some kind of mica. As his new world darkened, Yorke came to some sort of senses, and dark foreboding rose in him. He would have screamed, but he saw a face close by his own, and something in it kept his mouth shut. It was a face that could turn to anger and to evil if he made a yell, and they would have killed him, he thought, upon the spot. Sometime, not long afterwards, he wished they had.

They put him in a fissure, with horse blankets under him. Without a word, they indicated a small trickle of a spring that wet the rock, beside a stone water jug they'd brought, and a flaxen saddle-bag, full of bread. Two of them, one ginger, the other very young, crouched above him as he lay, as if they might speak or say farewell and have some friendly conversation. But in the end they turned away, and clambered up the narrow rocky chimney he'd been brought down, their boots sending dust and stones cascading. When they were gone, enough light still spilled in for him to see the food and water, and the walls, and for a time he could hear feet and voices. He also heard rocks being manhandled, rocks clonking down, to block the passage was his only guess. The light did dwindle, in fits and starts, but when they stopped he still had enough to see by. Not that there was much to see.

Charles Yorke, lucid for a while, tried to think what it all meant, and whether this cleft was intended for his tomb. But he thought of Big Peter, and the red-haired man, and the crying youngster, and it gave him hope. He had water and food, and with water by itself one could survive for many days. Then there were the leaders, who had offered him a trade for information. Someone would return when he was softened up enough. If they did not, even, some-body else must surely chance along.

Men are not animals, he told himself, men are not beasts. They would not leave me here to starve to death, they could not. In any way, that was not their plan.

That night, after Swift had been rowed upriver and William had tried to 'settle Kershaw in', it looked to him and Samuel as if they might find liberty. Word seemed to be, among the dockyarders and the people, that the work was almost finished, and it would be 'out on service' soon, or at least a trip to victualling wharf and then powder and supplies. Indeed, before he'd left, and in despite his hurry, Captain Swift had had some private words with Kaye, that had been apparently galvanic. The man had strode about the quarterdeck, and issued orders, and even done some shouting, in the great tradition. Some men had even jumped, Sam pointed out, laconically.

'It cannot last, though,' he said. 'God knows what your

uncle said to him, but Kaye will relapse by nightfall, he must. The fellows too, I haven't seen them move like this for aeons. They will need a night in bed.'

Kaye did relapse. After disappearing to his cabin in late afternoon, and sending Black Bob to the cook to get him ham and muffins, he sent word for them to attend on him for a little wine. They found him lounging across a settle, in silk shirt and linen drawers, with a mild sweat on. Languid was the word, but a fresh clothes suit was laid out, and Black Bob was labouring with a silken cravat and a pleating iron.

'This is beastly, men,' he told them, when they had seats and glasses. 'We have worked ourselves like slaves, the men have been like Trojans, and now there's nothing for it but to wait.'

Sam Holt and Bentley did not demur. The wine was good, the view across the river soothing. Most likely, they had the feeling, they would be sent ashore.

'So where is Gunning?' asked Lieutenant Kaye, rhetorically. 'Where is the master and his men? He had word yesterday to be here today, he knows the work is almost done. It is too bad, too bad. Your uncle' – was this slyness, gleaming in the blandness of the eye? – 'your uncle, Mr Bentley, would be in fits.'

William, although he had not had chance to tell it to Samuel, had a fair idea of the stimulus for the lieutenant's keenness. Before he had left, Swift had called him peremptorily to one side, to give him 'final information' on the way ahead. He was to dine with Kaye on shore that night, then in the morning would take coach to Plymouth and his ship. He would be away a year or two, and in that time Will Bentley had this task to do: serve Kaye, but serve him to the purpose, as explained. He was a good, rich man who would one day be a lord and have great power – but he was lacking.

'That navigator,' Swift said. 'That tutor whom you looked at all askance. He is for you, undoubtedly – I know your attitude to honest learning, and it does me pain – but he is for Kaye as well. You were a way to get him on this ship without an insult. Lieutenant Kaye will rise to post if only he can fail blotting his copybook, if you take my meaning. You must help him. That is your bounden task.'

Swift beamed, although Will's face could have hardly asked for it.

'Ah, my boy,' he said, 'how glad I am to see you on board a ship again, and grown so keen at last! Ready for service to your King and family after all the wasted years. Rise through your work and education, pass for lieutenant, pick Kershaw's brain. He still has one, doubt that not, despite what he suffered as three years a Spanish prisoner; do not underestimate him. Rise, help Kaye to rise, and then we'll talk again about that ship I'm building, and of dynasties, and wealth! Remember what I told you, my sister's son: wars do not last for ever, and there are fortunes must be made.'

He had wrung Will's hand then, and – startlingly – embraced him with vigour. Before he dropped into the borrowed pinnace, he said lightly: 'I have kicked Kaye's arse this afternoon, between us, William. I told him what he has to do to please their lordships, and rule one is a hard and busy ship. You will see a change in him; to you I look to keep it up. Tonight at dinner I will go at him again.'

It was the coming dinner, possibly, that made Kaye spoil their own plans. The blow fell as they sat and sipped his wine and watched the traffic on the river. His grumbles about Gunning and his 'infernal slackness' finished, Kaye had wandered over victualling, the badness of the Deptford rigging crews, the quality of woodwork the yard had 'botched up' in the cabin (at his own expense, which was the worst of it by far!) and the general inferiority of everyone and sundry.

'Indeed,' he said, 'while I'm on shore with Captain Swift tonight, there is much labour to be done, and not just on board the Biter here. Labour! What do I say, it's "duty" is the word! I fear, my friends, a certain slackness has crept into *your* souls while we've been at Deptford, perhaps that rogue Gunning has infected you. Last night you went out with a crew and picked up pensioners and cripples, as Coppiner has told it at the Lamb, and that the first time that you'd served him in a week! Mr Bentley, you are new, but that is no excuse where Coppiner's concerned, he is an ever-open maw. Your uncle warned me – I have to say this, sir – that you can be too pure, pedantic, prudish with the common man, and said I should have no truck at all with it. There now, it's out – and you must put yourself together, pull your weight.'

The strangest thing about this ambush of his uncle's was the way it was delivered. Kaye's bulbous eyes, bright with something that was not brightness, avoided direct contact with William's, as if what he said was not really meant for him, and in any case was not of great importance. It was as if he was recounting something he'd heard about another party, who was not there and did not matter anyway. The upshot, nevertheless, was clear. That night they were ashore once more, with an Impress crew, and they were expected to do better. Meanwhile, as a measure of his new-found love of duty, their captain would stuff his head on shore with Daniel Swift, and afterwards God knew what debauchery by way of pudding. This joke – the burden of Holt's song as they trudged the muddy streets of Wapping in the rain – helped keep their spirits up, but it was a dispiriter from start to finish. They took no able-bodied men, three wrecks worse than the night before's, and were all quite bruised, some cut about by stones, when they were ambushed in an alleyway.

Next day the dockyardmen finished without benefit of Kaye's presence at all, John Gunning returned on board at suppertime looking like a plague victim turned out of a charnel house, and the cutter's crew, without a by-your-leave, all ran ashore to go upon the bever. Samuel and

William, by nine o'clock that night, decided that the runners had the right of it – and hailed a waterman to row them up to London town.

'So have you ever done the deed?' asked Sam.

They were at the foot of a long, low hill, by the bridge, and the night was turning chill. William thought of an inn, a glass of toddy, something hot. Sam, after thirty seconds, snorted.

'So, not. Well, how old are you? Old enough to have men flogged, to die for dear old England? Of course. And a countryman, to boot. Hampshire must be a strange country, though. Where I come from, such matters seem to be in the blood. I was fourteen when I was first seduced. The maid who did the cows on Sweeting's farm. Maid! She was eight and twenty if a day, and she did me for a wager.'

The stage and stairs were bustling, the approaches to the bridge a throng of vehicles and foot passengers. Samuel, as he mocked, pulled William away from the waterside, on to the roadsmeet. There were hackneys to be hailed, nags for hire, costers and small children selling food, sweetmeats, and anything.

'The fact is,' Samuel went on, 'that you have to make a choice. We have skipped the ship, we have spent good money on the wherryman, and you've got duller and more gloomy by the minute. So you haven't done the deed, that is established. So now the question is – do you want to? And if not, what in hell's name do you aim to do instead?'

William watched the myriads pouring on and off the bridge. Sam had picked the northern shore to land, and had done so for a reason, beyond a doubt. The questions were just cant, the main decision made already. Unless he argued strongly to the contrary.

'Yes,' he said, 'you have the right of it, I am a countryman. But in country matters I hold my hands up, perhaps the maids round Petersfield march to a different drum than

117

yours. The females that I know are too demure, they go to church on Sundays. In any case, our milkmaids pull too hard for comfort, I should say!'

He did not know, he truly did not, what he desired from the night. London, to be quite frank, he found exciting, the dark swirling masses, the cries, the shouts, the animals, the smell. Part of him drew in upon itself, but part reached out to try the wild unknown that was configured all around him. Even the doors of houses on the streets seemed beckoning, most of them open, with dark corridors just behind, as if anyone could go in anywhere, for any reason. He was moving upward, with Samuel, they were moving north and westward from the bridge, without him really knowing where or why.

'The best thing,' Samuel said, 'would be to come and look. All right, I hold my hands up, also, I was disgraceful in these matters, I was taught too young and got the taste for it, it has cost me. But for one with scruples such as yours, there are many other pleasures not so gross. There are gaming rooms, there are eating rooms, there are viewing rooms, there are the tableaux. Good heavens, come to think of it, it is an all-round education. There is a woman there, a Mrs Putnam, who will even discourse to you about your morals. And another, Mrs Lewis, who will give you correction if you stray.'

They were closing on a city gate, and they were walking to a purpose. The vile smell of the Fleet was with them intermittently, although some fresher, grassy air blew through the dark, cramped streets.

'Most, I think, I would relish a strong drink,' he said. 'I may be scrupulous, but I notice you do not mention liquor in your breakdown of delights. I take it Dr Marigold does run to ale and wine and spirits? I take it it is Dr Marigold's you have in mind for us?'

'Oh yes, Dr Marigold's indeed,' Sam replied. 'Where else is there so fine in this metropolis, or all the world? Will, I promise you, you will love the place, your worries will all fade away the moment you set eyes on it. I promise you – for virgin or for rake – it is the alpha and the omega, the very top! Look, see up there. Where that white horse has just come out. That is the spot. I promise you – you will not be disappointed, whatever you decide to taste.'

From the outside, Dr Marigold's was not unusual, or conspicuous. It was in a fairly wide road, for those parts, with an enclosed yard reached through an arch of stone. On either side the front walls rose high, with many windows, all dark or shuttered, and at the end of the front elevation, a lower, older building stretched away around the corner of an alleyway or street. Overall there was the smell of smoking coals, and dung, but nothing very horrible. From the yard, Will could hear horses, and the ringing of a blacksmith's hammer, despite the hour. Sam, however, ignored the yard and knocked at a low black door. As William waited nervously, he smiled.

'We all must start somewhere,' he said. 'You won't regret it, I— Ah, here we are.'

Inside, the doctor's house was like a labyrinth. The door opened suddenly, and they were drawn into a dark and smoky corridor by a figure William could not fix. Along the passage there were glims, but it was darker than the orlop of a man-of-war. It was hot and aromatic, a heady mix of coals, tobacco, roasting meat and perfume, and there was a wall of jumbled sound, not loud but solid, of talk and laughter, and rhythmic thumping which could have denoted dancing feet and music, a hint of song. Within seconds both of them had gone from cold to hot, within seconds more to sweating. Sam's face beamed at Will, and Will, suddenly, was beaming back. This was all new to him, and – well, he felt it would be wonderful.

There were Navy men there – but only officers – and there were men in regimentals, too. The bulk though were in civil dress, not many of them young. William, blinking sweat as Samuel led him to a parlour with a servery, decided that money was their character, the thing that

119

named them for a group. Not country rich – or country trying, as they said in Petersfield – but merchants, men of the world of ships and goods, men of the world of cargo shares and profit, of money that accrued invisibly. They were quite old, in the majority, quite fat, and rather drunk. There appeared in the servery a young woman with a thinnish face, almost severe, and creamy, enormous breasts, unfettered by a handkerchief, even the brown nipples open to his gaze. And William felt his stomach lurch, and his mouth go dry.

They drank ale at first, to regulate their temperatures, then they drank hot spicy wine to 'set them going' when they were acclimatised. They sat at tables for a while, eating the hot meat newly off the spit, that more young women scattered liberally from trenchers, and they held a conversation, though only of a sort, because William had become fascinated by the maids who made so free with parts he'd never seen before, so close. Samuel seemed amused by him – his mockery was very mild – and promised better sights to come. The maids, though, were indifferent to his smiles. Within an hour, maybe less, he felt rather drunk.

Sam took him everywhere, to all the rooms, and introduced him to several people. Two lieutenants of the Press, who used the Lamb as rendezvous as did the Biter, so he said, three midshipmen, an officer or two or three or four of the seaborne soldiery, rather low and very, very drunk. There were higher forms of life in evidence, post captains and a lord, but naturally enough Sam Holt did not go near to them. And in all the rooms, except the dark and sombre ones where men sat hard at cards and dedicated drinking, there were maids. Out in the yard, where they'd wandered for a breather, Samuel brought them up.

'Well,' he said. 'What say you, William? You've got a glow on, you've seen the sights but haven't touched, you're like a boar held off the swill-pail. On that side yonder, there are the quiet rooms. I aim to spend a little in the dear old way. Will you?'

William did have a glow on. He was almost steaming. Away where Sam had nodded, far side of the courtyard, was a lowish building, but extensive, like living quarters. The windows were mostly dark and shuttered, but some few were open to the air, with lights glimmering inside. A sailor on shore, thought Will. God, this is what the seaman did, that he had once despised. But truth to tell, he was afraid. Drunk though he felt, he could not be sure of reacting in 'the dear old way'. His tongue clove drily to his palate.

'Money,' he said. 'How much have we spent, Sam? How do we pay? The meat and drink aren't given free. Is there a reckoning?'

'Aye,' Sam laughed. 'A slate. Pay by the week, the month, the year for all I know; Marigold don't care. Look – tonight so far is all on mine, it's little enough in any case; the meat *is* free, ditto the salt they douse it in to make you thirsty. But if you want to have a maid, it will not cost you much, depending on what you want to do, and who to do it with. But decide, man, soon. I am getting . . . hungry.'

Inside the house, Will met Mrs Putnam – 'Mistress Margery, to my friends' – and instead of acting like a cavalier, became a poltroon, entirely. Samuel, having introduced him, hung at his side out of loyalty for some while, although his impatience mounted by the second. Margery, a comfy dame of fifty at the least, flapped him away from the table where she sat at last.

'Oh dear,' she said, to William. 'You are not a master in this field yet, are you? You do not have to try your luck, you know. There is no hard and fast rule for a whore – though come to that, that's not a bad one in itself! I do a lovely cup of chocolate, if you prefer.'

She was a mistress in her field, and that was parting gallants from their money, and training up the young when necessary. She could see that she might lose him if she went too strong, so made it clear the chocolate was a joke (he was far too much a man for *that*, any old fool could work it out!) – unless of course he really fancied . . . but no, of course he didn't. She fussed about him like a mother all the while, putting up possibilities as if she were discussing with him whether he should try serge or fustian for his latest coat. And yet the things she said were scandalous, unmentionable, in the normal way of things: the merits and demerits of thin scraggy girls over fat juicy ones, the need for gentlemen to maintain a proper rectitude however wanton the demands put on to them by saucy hussies, the guarantee of complete discretion that made Dr Marigold's a toast throughout the land.

'Be assured, sir,' she told him, 'that nothing said or done within a maiden's bedroom walls in here – or thighs for that matter! – will ever see the light of day outside. They are the acme of discretion, so they are, the very zenith and the soul. They are respectable! Lord, and now you're laughing. Well, very good.'

He was laughing, relaxed enough to be almost open with his fears.

'Respectable for whores,' he said, agreeing. 'But that's the problem, is it not? They're whores, and we have countless warnings against the breed. On my last ship, women came on board in bumboats, and our surgeon held a muster every week, a pr—' He broke off, embarrassed. Margery was not.

'A prick parade, aye, aye.' She was a shade abrupt, as if he had offended her somehow. He had, or that at least is what she made him think. She said severely, 'Our maidens are not whores, sir, not in that way. They are chosen, hand-picked by Dr Marigold himself, perhaps with aid from me or Mrs Lewis, Mistress Pam. If you wish the rough end of the trade you are not in the proper house; sure, Master Samuel would not have brought you here. Our maids go on to great things, some of them; some of them have married out of here, or got protectors of great power. All of them, sir, have mothers, we do insist upon that point. Whores they may be, in a word, but they are not common whores, nor do they spread distemper to men's parts. Why, we have the tableaux, and Greek dancing, some of our girls have taken parts upon the stage, much admired by the public.'

In the end, coddled but unsure, Will settled for a type of peepshow, where he could look, and ponder (and anything else he wished to do alone, by implication) without the slightest interference or embarrassment. It was an exhibition set up by Dr Marigold for just such a case as him, for 'suchlike shy young persons of artistic bent, for the contemplation of the female form and beauty'. Here Mistress Margery nodded very earnestly. The young maiden he could contemplate – in silence, in the dark – was of the very highest loveliness, most extraordinary, she avowed. And a whore? Nay – she was as virginal as the driven snow, as virginal (said roguishly) as the young gentleman himself. Her face was always covered, and her modesty entirely intact. Dr Marigold looked after her, and her parts were not for sale. She was destined, said Mrs Putnam, for infinitely higher things. Before she led him to the peeping point, she gave him a clean napkin, and a glass of port.

It was a room, a small, dark room, and to William's surprise and slight discomfiture, there were already two men in it, one in a wicker chair that creaked noisily as he moved. It was too dark to see them properly, and they were very quiet, so he allowed the firm clasp of Mrs Putnam, as she led him, to be a comforter. She took him round an angle in the facing wall, so that he could barely see them anyway, and patted a straight-back chair with a good stuffed seat. Beside it was a little table, and before it, in the wall, an eyehole, nearly square, three inches wide or thereabout, two deep. It had a flap on it of polished wood, already open.

'There,' said Mrs Putnam. 'You'll be private here, sir. Do keep quiet, though, no speaking is the rule, most particularly no speaking to the maiden. Remember, sir, this is a privilege you enjoy. This is artistic contemplation.'

After she had gone, Will waited several seconds before he used the peephole. First he accustomed himself to the feeling of the place, its heavy, perfumed smell, overlaid with tobacco, though neither of the men was smoking at the moment, then to the vague movement sounds, the creaking of the basket-chair, the rather stertorous breathing of one of the watchers, who must presumably be fat. He glanced about him, but the lighting was discreet, just one small lantern, or a candle, behind a thick horn shade. If he craned, he could make out the curved back of a man, but that was all; why should he crane, in any way? But he was reassured. To all intents, he would gaze on this fair form alone.

And, oh God, it was fair. William moved his head at last, and applied his eyes, and had no idea at all why he was doing it, or what sort of sight he'd see. He knew now – he'd faced it in himself in talks with Samuel, even – that the female form, the very *thought* of it, could make him ache, but in no wise was he prepared for the reality. He put his face up close, he looked through the wood-framed hole, and he was struck in the belly, it was a blow of concrete physicality, that which he saw quite simply robbed him of his breath.

She was lying, this young woman, on a bank of pure lawn, or it might in fact have been a silken shroud. She was lying on a white bank, a roundish sofa covered in a field of white, and she was facing him almost directly, which is to say one leg was stretched towards him, with the other crooked out at an angle so that the knee was to his right hand, pointing to the wall, and the inside of her thigh, round, cream-white and elastic, led from the bended knee to the fulcrum where her body cleft. It was not the cleft itself, though, that held his gaze, took his gaze and tortured him, it was the thicket of black hair, a gleaming lustrous triangle in the light of the many candles ranged around her bed, of such a thickness, such soft density, that he knew it was the origin of the world, he gasped at the deepness of desire that it hollowed out in him.

A shroud. The cloth she lay on was spread beneath her, its starkness setting off the browner whiteness of her skin, the devastating blackness of the curled and tangled hair. But above the thighs and softly bulging belly, just above the breasts, her neck and shoulders and her head were all cut off by it, it was draped over the upper part of her, and her arms were hidden in it as if in sleeves. It could have been a shroud, or a prioress's habit with the front pulled up to reveal her nakedness, then piled softly on her face, the arms laid down beside her, encased. She faced him with her soles, the angles of her spread limbs drew his eyes to the forest and the dark joining of her just below it, and her breasts lay placid on her ribs, the right one pointing directly upward, the left, weight eased by the slight twist of her attitude, pointing to the left, its nipple soft and almost pink. She faced him with a total surrender, masked and oblivious, and William could hardly bear to look, nor could he take his eyes away. She was lovely. Oh God, oh God, dear God. He found her loveliness itself.

He must have sat there twenty minutes, maybe more, unmoving, still – as, fascinatingly, so was the maid. Flames of the candles moved, a breath of air from time to time blew over them, and patterns on her still flesh danced beneath dark lines of twisting smoke, but she lay as if asleep or dead. He knew she was not dead – William had never, ever, in his years on earth before seen anything so full of life – and he found her stasis extraordinary. After his first shock was past, he examined her, inch by inch, inch by loving inch, like a surveyor charting a new-found land. When the spell was broken, by one of the other men, he was shocked anew, quite horrifyingly.

The man approached him – not the breather, and not with heavy tread – while William was utterly absorbed in the soft curving glory of the round dome of the belly, crested by a tiny curl of hair around the umbilical dip. He spoke quietly, with his mouth not three inches from Will's ear, which made him jump so hard he nearly slipped from off his seat. His eyes jerked up and his hand, involuntarily, shut the peephole cover with a woody snap. The man's voice was thick with drink and scorn.

'You would think she'd move, though, wouldn't you?' he said. 'All that to shake at us, and she just lies there. Christ, I've been watching *you* ten minutes past, like a moonstruck booby. You ain't seen her face, then? Now *that'd* be a sight to look at, and a half!'

William was on his feet, crouched forward, shaken. The man's breath, meaty and rich with wine, washed over him. He was a short, fattish person, in a sober coat and breeches, fairly gone in liquor. He stood facing him, a friend, a confidant, swaying comfortably, uncomfortably close. And smiling.

'She's beautiful, the maid, eh? Well, from the neck down she is, she is indeed. But you can't have her, see, because she's new in from the north! She come in here two days ago or so, and they cover up her physog because she's sold her teeth! So beautiful, so soft, so lusty – and so fangless! She's only been a day or two, but there's a list for kissing two mile long already, when she's healed!'

William's untouched glass of port went over as he got away. For the second time this maid had kicked him in the stomach, so it felt. He was sick with horror, with pity and revulsion. He did not know or care how, but it must be Cecily he had been staring at, ogling, falling half in love with on the craziest of grounds. The room in front of him was empty, the other ogler must have gone unnoticed, and behind him the meaty one was laughing, liquid in his throat.

'Aye, she'll be a lovely kisser won't she, if you've got a shilling and you like it like the French! No fangs, but tongue and gum aplenty! Hey! Do not forget to button up, young man! You meet some devils in a place like this!'

Oh Christ, poor Cecily, thought William as he ran. He ran down passageways, he stamped down stairs, he found blind corridors and locked doors, and then he found a door that opened and burst through it, dying for fresh air. It was a room, though, a kitchen and a parlour for the denizens, the maids, the whores. There was a cooking fire, and in front of it some women, old and young. One, in a shift only, threw up her hands and screeched, while another gasped as if transfixed. She had a cloth in front of her, and on the instant gathered it in both hands and conveyed it to her face to cover it. Too late, for he already knew her, as she knew him, and this third shock nearly took his heart from out his body. Her face was bruised and ruined, mouth torn and sore. Even the eyes he recognised, above the balled cloth pressed into her chin. Cecily, the maid who'd sold her teeth. So the maid upstairs, then? The naked, lovely maid? She'd also sold her teeth, and her face was covered, too. Deb. Who else but Deborah?

12

The yard at Deptford, and John Gunning both, had suffered
much in terms of denigration. The men were idle was the
bottom of the gossip, idle, prone to disappearance into
holds or holes, and dishonest in the great dockyard tradition. John Gunning – owner, sailing master, drunk – was
praised in general only for his choice of whores. But by
next morning, when William woke up, the ship was ready
for a trip downriver, and Gunning was a man renewed.

William was aroused, in fact, by Samuel Holt, who shook
him roughly from a drunken sleep. Light was Will's first
sensation, arising from the depths, then pain as it flooded
through his eyes. No time to groan, though. Samuel
wanted him alive, and upright.

'Get on your feet, man! We are dropping down to Woolwich straight away! Look, Gunning's in control, and
they're expecting us. There's a breeze to hoy us down the
river but we need two kedges clearing, just in case. Your
job; we're still short of a hand or two.'

'But—'

But Sam had gone. Will lay there, in the cot, for only
seconds more, then dragged himself upright. He felt sick
and dizzy, perhaps not sober still, but the noises up above,
the crashings and the runnings, made him aware, for the
first time since he'd come on board this ship, that there
was a Navy way, and by some miracle it had arisen from
the dead. His mind flashed over the last evening and the
night, but he allowed it no space to grow. There was a
Navy way of sleeping when you found a minute out of
nowhere, there was a Navy way of clearing your mind of
clutter for the job in hand. He remembered Robinson, the

128

dour master of the Welfare, who had used to say to the midshipmen 'you may concentrate or die; the choice is yours,' with his hating little smile. Even that strange, good man William now cleared out. He pulled his breeches on, splashed water on his face from out his canvas basin, and licked his teeth to get the taste from off them. Of last night's liquor, and debauchery.

On deck, to some extent, the Biter was transformed. The yards and canvas, newly rigged and overhauled after the ministrations of the dockyardmen, were loosed off and ready, for hauling or for dropping from the yards. Men were up aloft, and the hands on deck had flaked and coiled halliards, braces, tacks and sheets. Compared with the ships that he had sailed on before, the men were few indeed – he counted eight he knew by sight, excluding Holt and Gunning, who was standing by the wheel. But there were four or five he did not know – Gunning's own, perhaps? – and Kaye's boat's crew were not there for counting, either. Neither, he was taken by the realisation, was Lieutenant Kaye himself. What bizarre episode was this, to go to Woolwich to take on gunner's stores without a Navy officer in full command?

Mind clear again: Sam came to him with Jem Taylor, boatswain, to elucidate. They had split the people into their customary watches, and shore-based slackness was at an end. Taylor's watch had cleared anchors and mooring gear to a large extent, with a little detail left to oversee – Will's task. Now his hands were put to pull-and-tailing, mostly, while others cleared and bailed the cutter and the yawl, ran in the boom from overside, and overhauled the towing warps. The breeze was favourable and light, the tide unlikely to give them seizures, but towing would be inevitably necessary when they reached Biter's new berth, and might be so before if things went awkward. Mr Bentley should work with Taylor, Mr Holt suggested delicately, but with the proviso that if need be Jem would be overside like the proverbial, and the midshipman – how grand, how grand! – would be on his own. Except he'd have some hairy arses to control. The implication – of course unspoken – was that he might not be up to it, for whatever reason. Will knew Samuel expected him to make a statement, to set his stall out, as it were: the idea being, to let the people know his mettle. Mind clear, and working quickly, Will made his choices.

'Mr Holt,' he said. 'For all I care Mr Taylor can go over the wall this very moment, and take whoever with him that he likes. I've anchored bigger ships than this before I've had my breakfast. Mr Taylor – just tell the men who stay that I can smell a slacker at a cable's length, and I am all for retribution. However – they are seamen all, that I can see. There will not be any trouble.'

He was aware how small he was beside the general seamen, how small and slight. Once on a day he had been small and slight and vicious, he had been famous for it, and some parts of that memory haunted him. He also knew that sometimes hardness was a weapon for an officer, sometimes the only one. He had struck the sailor down while on the Press gang; it occurred to him he should be glad he had. Now he held Jem Taylor's eyes, unwavering, to drive the message home.

'Aye, sir,' responded Taylor, mildly, and dropped his eyes. He was a powerful figure, although not much taller than William, and pretty equable, it seemed. Sam was satisfied as well, judging by his smile. At a sign, Jem Taylor went away.

'Now,' said Sam, 'how is it with your head? It's not the way you handle men that worried me, but the way you look! Dog's breakfasts are not in it, Will! How is your spirit?'

'It will do. Sam, who is in command here, you or Gunning? Has Kaye not yet come back, or is he in his cabin with Black Bob?'

'Then where's his skiff, and where's his cox? No, they're all adrift, as usual. Your uncle's fire-breathing didn't wreak much renewal, did it? Although there is a chance he's done it by arrangement with John Gunning, and will meet us down at Woolwich. One thing you never know on Biter, Will, is this: nothing!'

'But is John Gunning—?'

'Oh, at this lark he is perfect. If his self-control was one whit as—' He broke off. 'And, ho! He has a man to oversee him! His very own admiral of the fleet!'

Will saw his tutor, too, a strange vision of embarrassment and diffidence, approaching Gunning at the con, who signally ignored him. He was not ill dressed, looked like a gentleman and a seaman rather than a walker on dry land, but there was a scraggy, scarecrow air to him, enhanced by the oddly hanging sleeve that ended in a stump. He had been commissioned a lieutenant, William understood from some impatient sentences of Swift's, but now was on the sick and hurt, a pensioner officially unfit. Both Samuel and Will took him for his uncle's spy, so left him well alone when Swift had gone, until some move was made by him. Strange spy, though; since then he'd been entirely indifferent.

Gunning had men up on the fo'c'sle and the stern with the warps – now singled up – and turned to face them with a crooked smile.

'Mr Holt, there. Mr . . . Bentley, is it? We are set to slip and I hope you're ready. I want the headsails hoisted and backed in to larboard, foresail up and ready in its bunt. The tide and breeze shall set us out, I'll hold her stern in on its buoy until I get a slant. Five minutes, sir, till slip.'

'Aye aye,' said Samuel, automatically. 'Will, get those kedges and their cables set. You've got Hugg and Mann, they're all right. Now, brave boys!' he shouted. 'Man jib halliards, there! Behar! To me, to me!'

The men themselves, as well as William, must have been rotten with the alcohol, shot with it through and through. Like him, though, they had a method, call it experience, or work. They laid hands on the gear as necessary, sometimes to orders, more usually because they knew to pull or shove or belay was the thing required on that instant. William missed most of it, as he checked the flaking of the cables with his two men, and saw the anchors loose-lashed on the bulwarks clear to cut and slip if need arose. He heard the tramp of feet as yards shot up, the shout of 'back those heads'ls' from Gunning, who looked calm and keen and properly in control. He felt the Biter heel as she laid off to the breeze, watched the fore braced round and sheeted, and took time to marvel in her quiet beauty as she cut out and swung round to take the seaward flow. Ugly old tub; and full of quiet beauty. Beneath his grinding head, he felt his spirits rise.

And then last night. As he stood there, with the Biter slipping down the stream as easy as you'd wish, he remembered the shock and the excursions and his lips grimaced without him willing it. For the while now he had no duty but to stand and watch and wait for problems, so his mind rolled back the curtain, and he saw Cecily's face again, and the parlour, and the roaring girls. He had stood there like a muffin, horrified and bewildered, until a quick concerted rush of them had pushed him through another door, and he'd been in a small back lane outside the courtyard, outside Dr Marigold's altogether, sans help or company. But *he* had to help, or to find out, or enquire. Cecily was there, her face a sight to weep for, and Deb had lain upstairs, stark naked, while he had stared at her; and toothless too. Despite himself, now, on the Biter, he could see her form, and the vividness of it filled him with shame anew. She had been brutalised, debauched and robbed, and still he could not bleach that picture from his mind. He felt he had loved her when he'd met her; he felt now that that, however bedlam, was still in some wise true. He had to see her, speak to her, effect a rescue or some help.

Sam had found him at the coaching entrance, called and alerted, so he said, by Mrs Lewis, who was 'pretty mad' at all the goings-on. Sam, however, was a valued customer (he said) and had explained that his young friend was new, a country bumpkin, and probably insane with lust. William, far from appreciating this line of jolly conversation, gave a response so cold and miserable that Sam sobered quickly, and asked what was the business. Which, explained, he still had difficulty taking quite seriously as a tragedy to shake the world.

'What, Deborah as well? Lying stark and bare and naked like a babe, except she had a cloth piled on her head? Well, the things they'll do for money, these young lasses!'

'She has lost her teeth! She has sold them too, or had them dragged out by the mountebank! Good God, Sam—'

'Good God, Will, it cannot just be true! We saw them only . . . when? Yesterday, the day before, Tuesday, was it? How can it have happened, they were at the Lodge! Sir A would not have let them be betrayed!'

'But they are here! I saw both of them! Well, I saw Cecily and . . . Oh Sam, for Christ's sake, we have to go inside again and talk to them!'

It was quiet in the courtyard, and it was growing cold. There were ostlers in the stable, but no other passengers. From inside there was music, laughter, shouts, but the smaller part, where the women plied for money, was silent as the grave. What should we do, asked Sam, setting out the hopelessness before them: go and demand to see poor Cecily? Be conducted back into the peeping room and start to shout? Tell Mistress Pam or Mistress Margery we need conversation with the girls? Mistress Margery was a pleasant woman, and she would understand. She'd call them drunk and pack them off, and if such sweet talk failed, would call the men who did such things.

'Such things as what?' asked William, although he guessed he knew. Sam did not bother to reply. He touched William lightly on the arm.

'Look, friend, what do you hope to win by it, in any case? So we saw these young women, and we rendered some help to them, and you went all mooncalf over Deb on her looks alone, you booby. And now you've seen her in the natural and so what? Do you intend to marry her, for the sake of Hades? Or merely jam your club in her, like a normal Christian? But Will, she's toothless now! So why go back? Surely you don't want mating with a toothless crone!'

It was so harsh and thoughtless, that William could not reply. He hardly knew himself, to tell the truth, but he was moved, he was truly anxious for Deb's fate, for both the girls'. Anxious? Moved? And still the image of her nakedness burned in his mind, and – shamefully – he was glad that that transcendent beauty had not been Cecily's but ... oh great heavens, thought Will; I am cracked indeed.

'Look,' said Samuel, 'let's go home and think this over, shall we? I'm cold, it's late, we've had our drink and meat and whoring – well, I have, what you've achieved the lord in heaven knows! We can't get in there now without a row, and you've no idea if we did, what we would try to do, have you? Spirit them away? Kidnap them? Take them back to Biter and install them in the captain's cabin? We'll come back tomorrow, if you're mad enough. It boils down to this: if you want her, pay for her. That's the way it works, my friend.'

'But she isn't whoring!'

'Bah!'

'Nay, Mistress Margery said she was a virgin, being kept for higher things.'

'Aye, gums and all! Will, you are drunk so I forgive you. If Deb was a virgin six months before we first clapped eyes on her, I will kiss your arse and eat your hat. She is here for sale, man, they all are. That is how they earn their bread, I've told you, that is how they live. We pay to use their bodies, or they die. No more, the Biter's miles away and I need sleep. Or a drink, at least. We will drink when we get back on board, to drive this from your mind. This rank insanity.'

Will was drunk, and he did get drunker before he slept. Holt too, although not as drunk as he, and they prattled on about love and things for some long time. Sam's angle was heartening in one way, but disheartened him also. No shame should be allowed to taint sex dealings with the fair, he said, because it was natural and inevitable and necessary, females as much as males knew that, and tried to use it for their own ends if they could. But sentiment and strong attachment – call it love? – was a toy for idle men, or very wealthy, and in any case largely a delusion and a snare. What Will had, he insisted, was a strong dose of new-grown lustiness, like a young bull turned into a field of season heifers after a winter growing up. You have the money in your pocket, he wound up. Buy her, if you have to. If you like suppurating gums!

Will went to sleep in a torment, their dark, partitioned den turning giddily each time he closed his eyes. He believed Sam yet did not, he thought he would buy Deb then could not bear the thought, he could see her lovely body in great clearness, but could recall her face only as being of great beauty, with eyes that had called out to him. And also, Margery had said she was a virgin, not for sale, though Sam had shrieked at that, from great experience. As he slid to sleep he thought he would go back and buy her – but, what for? But definitely . . . he must.

The short drop downriver to the loading wharf at Woolwich passed off uneventfully, and Lieutenant Kaye – by what miracle no one knew – was there before them, and had bespoke a berth and loaders, even a launch to help tow and nudge the Biter in, all sail doused beforehand, no need for kedges, all smart and shipshape enough for the greatest stickler in the land. Also miraculous, the balls and powder were to hand, not hidden in a distant magazine by some grumpy clerk, and the loading crews pitched in with a will. For the next few hours the Biter was a veritable hive, which set the men a-grumbling, sure enough. Dame Rumour too; for by early evening it was noised 'for definite' that they sailed that very night. William, when he heard it, was strangely hollowed out. He had avoided thought on the Deb problem all afternoon, but now it seemed he could not seek her, willy-nilly; which doubled his desire and determination.

'Can it be true?' he asked of Sam, as they stood sweating in the waist. The shot and powder was all stowed, and some cable Kaye had had brought in by lighter was being snaked below into the cable tier. 'Have you had a hint of it, at all?'

'Not I,' Sam replied. 'Which means exactly nothing, does it not? We'll have a useful ebb till about the forenoon watch tomorrow, so it makes sense if he has a reason to be out there.' Will's face was blank, so he explained his thought. 'Sometimes we get intelligence from an agent or a tout. A ship is in the offing full of useful men, perhaps. Kaye gets his fee for each man he takes, and good information's worth a cut of that, d'you see? He must have some sort of network, all the time he spends ashore!'

'But are we ready? We have shot and powder, but I thought we needed food and water.'

Sam grinned, but almost sympathetically.

'Hell, man, if we do go we'll be soon back. I've told you, Kaye loves a bed that only moves when he does, not the ship. We can go out half-watered and with naught to give the dogs but tack, because we stay so close to rendezvous. She'll still be there, you know, whenever you turn up.' The grin hardened. 'And still a virgin, naturally!'

Will, though, was like the people on this score, despite he did not join their muttering. They were paid to sail, were fed and lived on board, but could hardly bear the thought of casting off and going from the shore. He gazed on Woolwich – a bleak, unfriendly aspect, as bleak as man could wish – and he wished he were on shore there, or better still, pulling upriver with a handy crew. Deb filled his mind, sometimes naked, sometimes wet and draggled in the rain. Come what may from it, he had to see her, had to test the truth. It was a *pro bono* act, he told himself, he must find out if she had suffered from some crime again, if she was being held against her will and needed aid or succour. A slight warm glow from that, until he realised he gave no thought at all to Cecily, who was as deeply injured. So clear the mind, and work.

At the end of the first dog watch, Lieutenant Kaye let it be known, with no formality at all, that they would finish all the stowing and the overhauling of all gear that evening, and would slip moorings and away at eight bells in the first – midnight's witching hour. The grumbling increased, both from the Navy men and Gunning's crew, both sets as confident that there would be no retribution from their slack captain. There was a certain grudging admiration for his method, though. He had brought them down to hell-on-earth (or Woolwich), too far for most of them to hope to reach their stamping grounds to drink before they sailed. Added to that, enough gear and clutter still about the ship to give them three or four clear hours' work. William felt merely miserable.

A half an hour later, Kaye put the cap on it by disappearing, first to public stairs obscured from the powder wharves, then by four-oar wherry to the heart of London. Most strangely, he vouchsafed the news only to the so-called tutor, Kershaw, who stammered as he passed it on to Holt.

'The man is crazy,' Holt said to William. 'Kershaw's crazy too, the whole damn lot of them are crazy. Apparently, it is a secret to be kept from Gunning, in case he takes it into his own head to go off drinking, too. Kaye insists he'll be back on board for midnight, no argument. And pigs can dance the Irish jig!'

'So are you on for it?' said William. They were standing

by the rail, and dark clouds were moving from the west, high and majestic. 'For God's sake, Sam, I'm going to go!'

Sam was set to argue, that was obvious. His eyebrows rose comically on his high forehead and his lips began to part.

But he was laughing. He clung on to the rail and hooted, loud and briefly, across the dark water.

'By God, you're mad as well,' he said. 'And to hell with all of it – I'm coming with you!'

Their only hope was Mistress Margery, with perhaps a sweetener in cash. On the way to London they discussed their strategy, but it added up, inevitably, to that alone. Will feared they might have been marked down by his behaviour, and excluded at the door, but Sam hooted at that possibility. Dr Marigold's, he said, existed to take cash, and lack of it was the sole excluder. In any way, some nights there was real mayhem, heads broken, once or twice a death by steel or ball; this was London, after all. A young man in the maidens' parlour was not much cause for panic, as he lived and breathed.

At the door, this assessment seemed exact. It was opened, they were whisked inside as easily as the night before, and as indifferently. No time for meat and ogling, however – they bustled through the throng, across the court, and to the entrance to the 'shagging suite', as Samuel crudely dubbed it. He said it with a sideways glance at William; his intention, nobly, to bring down the flights of fancy about a maid who was a whore. William was too full to notice, naturally. At the doorway as they entered, his mouth was dry, his heart was thumping. Mistress Margery, he feared, would give him short shrift, then throw him out.

Indeed, she did act somewhat surprised to see him, then somewhat cold. But Sam moved immediately to touch her palm with something, and addressed her in a voice of mocking earnestness, its mockery not for her but his companion, who looked a chastened booby in his turn.

'Mistress Putnam,' he began, 'my Margery. Can you forgive me that I bring you such a country stick? Look at him. Young, and innocent, and ashamed. We've rowed up all the way from Woolwich to bring his apology, and could even lose our ship for it. And all because he saw a naked woman!'

'Lord,' said Mrs Putnam. 'It was not so bad a thing he done. Young man, remind me of your name, I have forgot it. You set them shrieking in the kitchen, but you will not hang for it, I think.'

'Will's his name; Midshipman Bentley. He had a shock, that's all. He thought he knew the girl, then he got into confusion.'

Margery's eyes twinkled with amusement.

'With her face wrapped up in covers and her body stark as dawn. Well, not so innocent as he do look and you do claim then, Mister Sam!'

'He was drunk was at the top and bottom of it, and mad with lust,' said Sam. 'Still is, Marge, that's the funny thing. With your permission – well, he wants another shot!'

The woman had a frank and honest face, but her eyes narrowed and hardened. She was seated as usual at her table in the corridor, and she touched her glass of gin, then took a sip of it.

'Well,' she said, at length. 'On account you've got the cash, where's the objection?'

'Oh, we will settle,' Sam said. 'I han't never let you down, have I? The thing is, though—'

Mrs Putnam interrupted.

'Does *he* speak at all? The thing is though is what, though? Why does it need the two of you to row from Woolwich and him to stand there like a dummy just to pay a shilling to dote on a maiden's quim? The rate is up, by the way. It's the demand.'

'And how,' said Samuel, 'if he wished to converse with her alone?'

William felt a complete fool. The woman stared at him,

139

so he lifted his face and met her eyes, as steadily as he could.

'Young man, I told you yesterday. She is not a whore. She is not for solo intercourse. She is exceeding beautiful, and Dr Marigold has designs for her.'

Sam challenged William with a look. They had agreed beforehand that if Cecily had not revealed a connection they would keep it secret. But they both knew what would happen now.

'She is not beautiful,' said William. 'She has had to sell her teeth, like the maiden in the parlour, Cecily. We met them in the country. We gave them some little aid. I must speak with her.'

'You must?' There was a challenge in the woman's voice, but it was not brazen, she was not angry. She somehow seemed amused.

'I would wish it most sincerely,' said Will. 'I will pay the rate, of course.'

The woman chuckled.

'Oh, you would.' She took more gin, as if for thinking time. 'But what rate? There are four places in there, for the looking at her beauty. Each place is reserved for twenty minutes, let us say, although that is my discretion. How long did you expect to talk to her? If indeed she does not call me to have you beaten out, if indeed she will give you audience in the first place? At twelve pence the ogle, twenty minutes would tally something tidy, while the hour would ease your purse of plenty more. And how do you propose to talk to her? Through the spy-trap? Clothed or unclothed, for a shilling naked buys you silence only; for speaking we would have to set another rate. Oh come, sir, look not so down! You said you *must* speak, that was your words!'

'Margery!' put in Samuel, as if to a playful child. 'He wants to talk, not do the deed; by Christ, she has no teeth! Look, the fellow's foolish, but humour him for my sake. Your talk of Marigold and great things is most impressive, but we know the truth of it. Close up the peep-show for a while, and let Will talk with her in a little room, or sit at her feet and worship, if he will! But covered up, for Christ's sake, or I'll never get him back on ship, will I? Yes, we must back on board tonight, betimes, so no harm can come of this, can it? He is not about to spirit her on board with us. He will be assuaged, and you will make five shillings. God, woman, there will be no oglers yet, it is too early. Come on! Five shillings, and a small gratuity in hand.'

'Twenty.'

'Six.'

'Ten. That is the last, Mister Sam. Do not test me into anger.'

'Seven shillings and sixpence, and a whore thrown in for me. I am not a worshipper of gums.'

Mrs Putnam gave in with a smile, and Samuel kissed her on the cheek. She pushed him off, and stood.

'Annette is in the small back room,' she said. 'She likes you, foolish girl. Now come you on, Mister Silence. For God's sake put a smile upon your face, you'll frighten her to death.'

Sam waved a hand in salutation.

'Good luck, Will. When I've done my business, I'll see you in the second drinking parlour, Margery will show you where. Hey! That's your passageway! Second door.'

But Mrs Putnam ushered him another way.

'Not tonight,' she said. 'She has not started yet. Come you to this room.'

'Bah, seven shillings!' said Sam, hitting his forehead with his palm. 'And the maid is still at leisure!'

'And sixpence,' added Mistress Margery. 'Mr Will – is that your name? Stand there a moment while I warn the girl. Are you sure you want this? Are you sure it's wise?' Her face softened, she was motherly, as she'd been the night before. 'It is only a little punk, you know. There is nothing here for you, I warrant you.'

141

Will made a gesture with his hand, and she turned and went abruptly through a door. He stood there in the dark and quiet passageway, alone and in some kind of turmoil. He had thought that this was necessary, that he and Samuel had some duty to this girl and her companion, but Samuel had chosen the softer option of Annette. His stomach hollowed as he stood and thought it through. Deb naked, and as beautiful as life. Deb with a robbed and ravaged jaw, like Cecily. Deb in the rain, excited and exhausted, soaked to the skin. A runaway, a tinker girl, a prostitute, a drab. Deb a toothless, ruined maid.

Mistress Margery emerged with her face mysterious, unreadable. She gestured at the doorway and Will, gulping, propelled himself through it, no chance to change his mind. The room was dim and the young woman in it had her back to him, although her arms were at her sides, she held no cloth up to her face as Cecily had done. There were two candles in the small room, which was not bright, but her dark curls gleamed. There was a table, and a narrow bed, and in the corner a pisspot, that was empty, underneath a straight-back chair.

'Oh Deb,' he said. 'I have come to visit you. To see if you are all right. Deborah?'

She turned then, and faced him rather gravely, but with a small smile that had a query in it. She had a black eye, and a cut upon her cheek with an unsightly scab or crust. But when she spoke he saw her teeth, and her lips were full and sweet, not bruised or broken in the least degree. Deb had her teeth, her mouth remained unrobbed, her cheeks unsunk.

'Well met,' she said. 'But I am not for sale, sir, nor can you take me out of here. I have protection, sir. Pray do not forget it.'

William, for the moment, was bereft of speech. Behind him, very quietly, he heard the door pushed to. Margery, almost inaudible, was chuckling.

13

There were a dozen questions that he had to ask, there were a hundred. But Deborah, in a dark, stuff smock from neck to ankles was an answer, and he drank her in. His relief at her lack of injury was palpable, but he was aware also of great disquiet, a fluttering in his belly that was akin to terror. He had seen her once one might say *in extremis*, one night unclothed, now face to face across a truckle bed. I do not know her, he told himself, I do not know her, she is nothing to me. But she was, apparently she was. Or why this volcano churning up inside him?

'Mistress . . . Mistress Margery said . . .' he faltered. Deb cocked her head, and it was wholly charming to him. 'I understood that you had lost your teeth. Like Cecily.'

'She said,' Deborah replied. 'She likes a jest, does Margery. She said you might not know me with my clothes on, neither. It is not, perhaps, a jest I would enjoy, but no matter, it is necessity. Better I should lie about like that than truly have done what Cecily was forced to do, poor Cec.'

'I saw her. In the kitchen. After I had . . . looked at you, and some fool there had said you'd lost yours, too. I needed to get out and take some air, and I got lost. I was unsure if she knew me, when I barged in the kitchen.'

'She did. It gave us much fear, to begin with. We thought . . . well, there seemed no other explanation for your presence. Perhaps there is not. Sir – if you have been sent to take us back, you cannot have us. You helped us once, which is why we were unsure. But we cannot go back to your uncle's and we will not. We have not told Margery or Mistress Pam we know you – Cec kept it like the grave

143

last night – but Marge said you said you'd met us otherwhere, and she asked me, and I told her we were staying here, and we would not be moved, or forced, or cajoled into anything at all, by you or anyone. Now please, sir, what is it you want?'

And William was stumped. He saw himself from outside himself, for one moment. A young Navy officer, absent from his ship without a leave, on a wild fool's errand. Standing gawping in the bedroom of a maiden whom he hardly knew, but whom he had stared at the privy parts of with an intensity that might have melted lead. Whom he had felt enormous sorrow for, and whose ruined beauty he had had to come and see, despite he knew it would destroy his heart. To find her whole, and strong, and beautiful, and suspicious of his motive for being there. What was his motive? To himself, William could just admit it, barely. He felt he loved her, he felt he knew what love meant, he who had never used the word in all his life, at least of womankind. What did he want, though? He was stumped.

'We were . . . I was; anxious,' he faltered. 'A fellow said . . . that you had sold your teeth, and then I saw Cecily, and knew it must be you . . . lying there.'

'Naked as a new-born babe.' Her voice was harsh, eyes bright with anger. 'I should feel shame, you think? But men will pay and maids must live. You paid, did you not?'

He moved backwards, towards the wall and door, as if an unseen hand were pushing him. But Deborah was not. Although angry, her body was relaxed, her fists unclenched. All the spirit was in her eyes and face, a strong face, dark and lovely. He made a gesture with his hand, and felt ashamed.

Deb said: 'Why did you pay to shame me, though, if your task was to take me for your uncle? When you aided us upon the road you were so kind. You and your friend were.'

She fell to silence. Her eyes were brighter yet, as if bathed in tears, which she was not prepared to shed. He would have blessed the succour, but Deborah was hard on that score.

'He is not my uncle.' Irrelevance, another kind of succour, although it did not ease him much. 'Sir A is Samuel's, well, he has aided him. Samuel, my companion.'

'Who has gone to fuck Annette, says Margery. At least he does not gaze at her through a filthy little peephole, like some loathsome thing!'

It was running from his grasp. He had come in fear, to offer aid, to see if help were needed, and now he was a loathsome thing! William, who had never seen a maiden angry, was almost afraid. The eyes were frankly flashing, the breasts heaving beneath the smock.

'I did not know!' he said. 'What one is meant to do! I have never . . . Indeed, I knew not it was you. How should I, when your face was covered up?'

'But still you paid to look. Oh sir, that is a loathsome thing.'

Her eyes had clouded, and her shoulders slumped. She turned, and sat upon a chair.

'By God,' she muttered. 'What things to say. Margery will hie me out into the gutter. Sir,' she said, loud and clearly to him, 'forgive me for a saucy whore. Pray you, do not tell the mistress what I've done.'

In truth, he almost wept for her, she looked so young and hurt. Fourteen, fifteen, sixteen at the most, and suddenly she was her age, a girl with bruises round her eyes. His voice was thick.

'You are not a whore,' he said. 'And I am sorry I offended you. We have not come to fetch you neither, for we did not know you lodged here. How come you to? Why have you left Sir A's? He did not surely force you into flight?'

She did not answer. She bit the inside of her lower lip, her hands still clenched. But, gradually, they eased. William mastered his emotions likewise.

145

'The mountebank damaged your face,' he said. 'That is why you had it covered. But Mrs Putnam says you ain't a whore, Dr Marigold has better things for you. Dennett, was that his name? That quack that marked you?'

'That's why we run off maybe, me and Cec,' she said, quietly. She glanced at him, then away. 'He would have come for us. He would have tracked us down.'

'But surely not! There are men at Sir Arthur's, even if he had found you out. But how should he do that, in any way? We found you in a wood, and carried you away in darkness. How would he discover you?'

She shrugged. There was a look of doubt, momentarily, almost a sulky look. She was a wayward, stubborn thing, it came to Will. She and her friend had run away before, from home, had tracked two hundred miles or so.

'But you had friends, in any case,' he said, remembering. 'So why run here? You had relatives, was it? You told Mrs Houghton.'

'We thought we did,' said Deb. 'Nay, we looked for them, but we could not find, Cec maybe made them up. London is not Stockport, though, if you take my meaning. It is all a maze.' She met his eye. 'He would have tracked us, Dennett would. He has captured us before, he is a devil, not a man. He is a tight, cruel bastard. London is a maze, and for the moment I go covered, do not I? In the parts that matter, anyway.' A pause. 'We stole an ass. We gave it to some men. Will you tell him?'

No, naturally he would not. Will felt helpless once more, and lost. He sensed a gulf in understanding that he could not cross. This maid was on a chasm's edge, and surely had to fall. And surely, he had to help her, he wanted to, he ached to be of aid. But how?

'Why did you come then?' she asked, suddenly. 'If you did not know? Did you want to tumble with a drab, like your tall friend? It is what sailors do. It is what men do, I suppose. You paid to stare at me.'

He feared she would be angry once again, but her voice

146

had not the ring of it. Her eyes were not challenging, but sad.

'I thought of you,' he said. 'After we had met you, and you had come up on my horse. I could not get you from my mind.'

He was discomfited, but Deborah did smile.

'If you hope to flatter me you go about it strangely, sir,' she said. 'You thought of me so came to make the bent-back beast with anyone you found. Or ogle through a little peephole at their shame.'

'I don't know why I came,' he said. 'You said sailors do, and Sam said sailors do, and I suppose I thought I could, what, clear my mind? You were stuck there, is the truth of it. But afterwards, when I'd seen Cecily – well, you must allow my reasons were more noble! We came back to help you if we could! We—'

'Came back to do it with Annette.'

'No! Sam is just— Deb, what is here for you? What happens when your face is healed? My God, at least Sir Arthur— I want to help you, Deborah!'

'You cannot help me, sir. Dennett would fetch me if I went back there, and I could not stand for that. What would you do? Be my protector! You are not rich, are you? Do you have anything?' Her face was kindly, as if *she* were helping *him*. He had a scant few pounds; less than enough to keep a midshipman on. 'I will be a whore, sir. It is not the worst of fates.'

'But Marigold has a plan for you.' Her mouth twisted, but not bitterly.

'I might be considered beauty enough to pose, and dance, strike attitudes,' she said. 'It depends on what men pay, however. If more cash comes from matching me with tups, then . . . I am not a whore, not yet. So what is your alternative?'

He was still standing, she sitting, with the pisspot peeping out between her ankles. Mad thoughts came and went within his mind, thoughts of a small room somewhere, of paying for her keep while he should be away. It was madness and he knew it, though. For instance, he did not know how much a room might cost, he did not know how much money food would require in a week, he did not know how one would find a place, except a room like Deb already had, which was her quarters and her workplace both. He lived on board the Biter for his duty, and then he would go home to Petersfield. He wondered, fleetingly, what his sisters would say – let alone his mother – if he should turn up with a young woman behind him on his horse. Young woman, whore, wastrel, waif. Deb was no different in her outer aspect from a respectable country maid, but everyone must know, immediately, because she had no trappings of support. At the best they would set her on as a drudge, at worst hurl her out into the night. He did not even bother with consideration on his father; it was unthinkable.

'Then there is Cec,' she said. 'We left the north together, together we will stay. We both must eat, you see.'

'How will they . . . ? Do they use her as a servant wench?'

'She can be a whore like the rest of us, says Mrs Pam. When her mouth is healed up. Some men like that sort of thing, she says, already she has been noticed and written down for when the pain has gone. She was too scrawny for the peephole job, her tits ain't full enough.' She laughed. 'It's a pity you ain't rich, though. I would not mind to be a whore for you.'

Will was in a sort of lather, and a daze. His stomach had dropped into a pit, her words had opened up the ache again. He found her wistful, her bruised face appealing yet boldly challenging, her hair, her neck, her lips cried out to him.

'No, not a whore,' he said.

'Aye then, not a whore. Not yet.' She rose. She seemed quite calm. 'But you may have me, if you want to. It is what Marge expects, intends, but I will deny it, we shall have each other and you shall not pay. You helped me on the road and you came back to help once more. Would you like to be the first?'

He had a vision of her, naked in her silken shroud, and it almost overwhelmed him.

'The first,' he said, but the words caught in his throat. She smiled, not wistful, but possibly amused.

'As a whore I mean. I cannot claim you are the first of all, that's pity but it's true.' Her face lightened. 'The first for pleasure, though. Aye. The first because I wanted to. You do not mind my face?'

'Oh no! I . . .'

She touched her blackened eye, more brown and bluish now, and William wanted to as well, he wanted to caress the hurt. She moved towards him, and, hesitatingly, he approached her, hands lifted from his sides, the bed between them, awkwardly. Then footsteps in the passage-way outside, a carefree laugh, a thunderous knocking on the flimsy door.

'Will! Have you not finished yet! Christ's blood, man, Kaye will have us flogged, do you not realise what o'clock it is?' The handle rattled and the door pushed open, and Sam was grinning with self-satisfaction, like a gargoyle. Behind him Mrs Putnam was peering in.

'Lord,' she said, 'young maidens nowadays. She still has every stitch of clothing on.'

Across the narrow bed, they had only touched a hand.

Will Bentley had been almost angry when Sam burst in, but that did not last for long. His friend was such a humorist, and the sight of Mistress Putnam and her curiosity lanced the boils of both his embarrassment and his confused desires. Deb also – her face was instantly comical in its surprise, then laughter flooded it. She yelped and seized Will's hand to squeeze it, then let it go. Two minutes later, the riots of sensation lost in Holt's jostling, he found himself outside the Marigold establishment, being hustled through the darkness for the Thames.

On the row downstream he kept his silence in the face of questioning, whether playing a sulk or gripped by the real thing he would not have cared to give an answer to. The night had turned out grimmish, with a misty rain blowing from the south and west that kept their necks huddled in their shoulders, so he could think and wonder about what he'd nearly done. Deborah had been going to bed him, no doubt of it, and she said it was because of want, not for the sake of whoring, which was of an importance to him that grew unstoppably. Will could see her face, her eyes, her look, and was relieved but bursting with regret that his friend had ended it. He did not even know for certain that he wanted to, except he knew he did. His feelings for her were confusing and immense.

'Sam,' he said, after a long while. 'You know these matters, I do not. Deborah is beautiful, that's so?'

There were two watermen at the oars, and he sensed their ears prick up. They were old hands with the passengers, however, and their indifference was studied and complete. Sam's eyes flashed with humour, but he played calm and cool.

'Aye,' he responded. 'She's fair enough.'

'She,' William began. 'Well, she takes my breath away. Is that . . . completely normal, do you think?'

'Oh yes, completely,' Sam said, gravely. 'It is known as love, and can be a very dreadful thing. Your cleverness, Will, is to do it with a whore, which renders it inconsequential, and therefore safe. Bravo, as the Frenchmen say.'

He was clearly mocking, and the oarsmen as clearly liked the fun, although all three faces as Will studied them were expressionless as wood. Love, he thought, and suspected it was right, all jesting notwithstanding. Then he cleared that, with a mental shrug. Deb was young and beautiful, that was all, and he had never been that close and open with a maid, nor never had an opportunity to do the beastly thing. She had been ready to, and he had been afraid, but he would by God the next time, yes he would. Next time, if her offer was withdrawn, he would buy her. Then a fantasy came in, and he saw them in a little cosy room, with her long dark curls across her naked shoulder, and his hand upon her breast. He sighed, then jumped as Samuel lightly touched his arm.

'Yes, she's fair,' he said, low and kindly. 'But don't take hurt, there's many of them are. I'll show you a selection as will take your breath away. Don't plump for one before you've even seen the field. Blood! So late as we are, our lord commander will likely cut it off for you!'

But when they climbed the Biter's side ten minutes later – and not unfearfully – it was a surly company who greeted them, and cursed them on account that they were not Slack Dickie. He had not come on board as promised, and when he did they had missed that morning's tide. Will lay in his blanket later, aware of grumbling from forward that was loud and hardly sober. They'd missed their time on shore, they'd missed their fun, they'd missed their ladies of the night.

And what have I missed, Will asked himself interminably. I have missed *her*.

14

The woman who had had the teeth had been a beauty in her time. The women of her household were generous in this consensus, sharing delight in the subtle malice inherent in the position. Their mistress had been a beauty, and had married well an older, solid man. But even before her teeth had begun to fall away to rottenness she had lost the bloom of youth – her time, indeed, had almost passed. If she was old, her man was older, and if she was vain, her husband was yet worse. He had taken her because when young she had been beautiful, and he had agreed to her idea of desperate surgery because his need for female loveliness was greater than her own. The women of the household, watching and waiting since the operation, were gleeful at their own hypocrisy.

At first, it seemed, the teeth had taken well. Milady – Mistress Amella Wimbarton – had suffered bravely in the process of extraction, fortified by far less drink than Cecily but immeasurably more determination. Cecily had been crying even before Marcus Dennett had produced his instruments, and had had a paroxysm of screaming when Mistress Wimbarton had pulled back her lips for one last view of them *in situ*. She had had, indeed, a flash of doubt that so characterless a girl, and one so unattractive in her squawking selfishness should be the donor, as if her teeth might be as inferior as she herself appeared. The other one, the beauty with the hair and figure, was a far more likely maid, but Dennett spoke darkly of problems with her gums (that could, however, be overcome if Cecily's did not take, or broke as he extracted them). What's more – the clincher – the chosen ones were in fact superior in their whiteness and their shape. They also, measured with his callipers, were the perfect size.

The operation was fast, brutal, and extremely bloody. Cecily was tied into a heavy oaken chair, because she just would *not* be still, and Mistress Wimbarton sat beside her, unfettered, and at a three-foot distance. She had only women present, except for the surgeon, because it was not at all the place for men (who would likely faint, as Dorothy, her best woman, rather grimly jested), and least of all for Wimbarton, who claimed he should be there to hold her hand, and whom she suspected most deeply of a black and shameful interest in the sight. The pair had had no children, despite her good wide hips, but she had miscarried once, a long, long time before, and her husband had had a morbid and (she thought) unnatural fascination for the details. That experience, incidentally, had taught her about natural agony. She took only two large glasses of brandy before Dennett set on, and was confident it would be enough. In all twelve minutes that he took, she uttered not a single cry.

It took twelve minutes, and two of the younger women fainted, while the dark-haired girl started a sobbing fit until the surgeon clouted her, then later vomited in a corner and had to be released outside. The surgeon himself went deadly pale at times, and produced so much sweat that it blinded all three of them promiscuously by running off his face, and caused him to put his spike and pliers down quite frequently because he lost his grip. He had pulled teeth before a thousand times, which much was obvious, but no one except himself knew this was his first time at a full extraction. Each time he got a stubborn one, and had to jerk and twist and tug, he found himself wondering what the next step would be, if it refused point blank to leave its home. He heard bone splinter once, and to his horror it was in the buyer's mouth, and he saw small shards drop on her bloody tongue, and he caught her eyes, which were opaque with agony, and she did not so much as groan. Dear Jesus, Marcus Dennett caught himself at thinking:

153

today I *earn* my bread. The smell was evil, also, in the hag's mouth (as he thought her), and he realised he should have charged her husband more.

Twelve minutes of exhausting work, and anxiety in case it all went wrong. The method was tried and tested – although not by him; he'd had instruction of a Scotchman he had beat at cards and who could not pay in cash – with satisfaction far from guaranteed. For best results you did it tooth for tooth, first one from the buyer's mouth to make the hole, then the corresponding one torn from the seller, but torn more carefully so as not to damage it. For the first few, Dennett found this relativity difficult, for speed was of the essence but inflicting greater pain on the buyer by greater haste was not a good idea, and nor was appearing to be more delicate with the seller, despite the fact that fast extraction could end in disaster if a tooth should crack or crumble. The order of attack was crucial, as he had been told not once but several times by his instructor: the front teeth were the easiest to come by, not having the deep and complicated roots of side and back ones, but complications could outweigh advantages. If you took the front ones first it made a passageway, or access, for the rest, and gave you room to lever and to wrench the reluctant biters at the back. But some schools said experience showed the operation could only be successful if the giver's tooth was plugged *immediately* into the socket of the receiver, the very instant that this socket should come clear. Therefore, if one took out teeth and put them to one side for later, the holes would close in the recipient, or would reject the new teeth completely, just never tighten round them for a grip of permanency. Further, one could fail to match them, take the wrong tooth for the wrong hole, or become entirely befuddled.

From his own experience, Dennett knew some of the other problems. Some tooth sockets produced blood in gushes, some mouths filled so full and swiftly one could see no holes at all. Then there was dropping, swallowing, jaw-clenching for the pain, even (so the Scotchman claimed) the fear that one of the surgeon's victims (he used the word, but gave a hoot to soften it) should drown on her own blood. Or his, as some men were vain enough to try it, it appeared; more normally it was a woman, often at her man's insistence. The mountebank, steeped in sweat and fear and gore, had to juggle all this in his mind for this long twelve minutes of his life, buoyed only by the thought that he was making sixty pounds from it, except that only thirty had been paid, with the residue collectable when the new teeth had stayed firm and splendid in Mistress Wimbarton's physog for a week. Oh yes, and ten pounds of the sixty went to the maid for her part in the jollity; although Dennett had his own ideas of that. He'd brought the two maids here by a long arrangement with the gentleman, he'd persuaded them there was no alternative save starve or sell their bodies to some villains that he knew lived locally, and he'd figured that with luck he'd end up with a customer exceeding satisfied, and one undamaged Deb to make a living on her back for him, being a surpassing beauty. Cecily's ten pounds would be paid in drink to ease her pain and pap to pass her gums and serve as food – a neat arrangement he had not even told her of – wherefore her loss soon afterwards from the copse was hardly loss at all, although Deborah had irked him with her going. If Milady's teeth held as they ought to do, no concern – he would collect the second thirty pounds. If they did not, though, he would have to find the spares, or forgo that vastly sum of money. Or run, and lose goodwill from Chester Wimbarton, a magistrate and man of great importance locally. Still, he'd done the operation with great care, he thought, and skill. They should hold.

Mistress Wimbarton had memories of the operation which were as vivid as his were, but different. She remembered great agony, the girl's hysteria, the other maiden's cries and vomiting and running clean away when put outside the door (which she was told about afterwards, and which miffed her dreadfully; today's girls were so dishonest and untrustworthy). Most of all she recalled the aftermath, when Mr Surgeon, without a by-your-leave, had bound her jaw up so that the teeth were clenched one atop the other, leaving her to swallow what blood could not be eased out through her lips, and told her women – as if she herself could not be trusted, or could no longer hear – that she was to remain bound up for one whole day, however great the pain, how much the oozement.

She had lain for one day like that, in a darkened room, then Dorothy and Joan and Sue had taken off the binding bandage but exhorted her, with great fear in their eyes, not to open lips 'as much as for a whistle' and keep her choppers pressed together hard. On the second night she had supped a little broth and sucked a little bread in milk, and on the third had seen her husband, Mr Wimbarton, for whom she had drawn back her lips in semblance of a smile – which he'd returned, an unfeigned show of warmth. By now she was exceeding anxious, because the teeth were wrong, all wrong, they were lumpy and felt – God spare the thought – like someone else's. Unlike her servants, Mistress Wimbarton was confident, as far as any woman can be, that her master loved her (else why take up with her, who had brought nothing to the house except herself?), so his smile was great balm, and she spoke some few painful words assuring him that it had been a fine success and not to mind the bruising and the slurs, for in another day or two she would be herself again; as beautiful and good-tempered and attentive as such a noble man might wish.

She lied, and knew she lied, and one day later three of them fell out, however hard she pushed them back into the screaming sockets. Three fell out, and five or six (or seven? Maybe *all*) began to slip and slide within the holes, some of which were hardening and healing, others of which began to fill with fluid, brown and thin, and one or two with pus. Towards the end of the week her husband came to speak to her, but the women kept him out because, although they did not say it, Milady had begun to smell. Strangely, Milady could not seem to smell herself (no one dared to mention it, or hint, or ask her) but they knew from the way her brow went furrowed, by the horror in her eyes, by the way she was caught on sudden by the bile that tasted on her lips, that Mistress Amella Wimbarton was aware of a great sorrow and a trouble coming on her. Although they did not like her, the women, from Dorothy right to the bottom, felt pity then, as well as admiration for her courage. For she faced it squarely, and called him in, and even ended up by shouting at him, that something must be done.

The women thought the master a cruel man and a selfish rakehell, but conceded that in this they might be wrong. For although he left Milady's room pale in the jowls, and called furiously for his steward Jeremiah, it appeared the target of his wrath was the mountebank, Marcus Dennett. He offered money as an incentive, and for failure he promised blows or worse. The quack, the mountebank, the whoremonger must be found, was his decree. Found quickly, brought to the house, and a cure would be effected on the mistress. Or, by God's blood, someone would pay.

There was no drummer on the Biter, no soldiers, no one at all to beat to quarters or instil a fearful discipline in the crew, while Jem Taylor, boatswain, had an altogether lighter touch than Bentley thought was necessary in that office. At first light, when he and Sam arose, there were men abroad but only two or three, and no smoke was issuing from Geoff Raper's cookstove chimney. Will looked to Sam for a lead, but Sam only spread his hands, then stared downriver to the east, where the sun was rising in a red and livid sky streaked with thin woolly cloud. The rain was gone, but the wind was chill and gusty. As it hit the cordage it raised a throaty hum during the harder gusts; the Biter moved uneasily on her warps.

'Due west,' said Sam. 'High water in six hours, so we'll slip in four is my guess. In the Downs by soon enough, and meet our fate. And here on board? The snores of drunks, and 'tween decks a fug of fart-gas. Hurrah for the King's Navee!'

'Aye, but will we meet it? Is Kaye on board yet, and won't we be too late? He hinted yesterday he knew where and when we'd see some useful action. Won't that have passed us by?'

Sam did not think so. More like, he thought, Lieutenant Kaye had had more intelligence from his spies, or had merely said they'd sail at midnight to keep his people up to snuff. By this time they had reached the rail, and there was the captain's dandy skiff, bearing down on them.

'Likely he'll tell us over breakfast,' Sam added, with a laugh. 'Slack Dickie likes to share his information, don't he?'

They did breakfast with Kaye – a surprise for William, who had forgotten such a thing could happen on this strange and sloppy ship – but he proved Sam's jest in almost every point. He made no comment on the weather, when Sam ventured it would serve their purpose well, he was non-committal when Gunning poked his head in to ask how many of the boats should come on board before they slipped, and he showed emotion only when Black Bob dropped a dish of chops, then not enough to clout him as he clearly wished to. He looked wan and tired, as if he had been drinking nights away, or whoring like a common sailorman, or maybe doing both.

Gunning was not invited to the breakfast, which did seem strange, but Gunning clearly had a certain knowledge of the Biter's plan. Out on the deck they heard the constant yell and clatter as the seamen readied her, and above their heads feet stamped from time to time. The company at table – the fourth man was the tortured 'spy' – sat almost silent for the most of it, riven with embarrassment that passed only the captain by. Kaye ate with a dogged lack of enjoyment though, drinking from a pewter can of wine that Bob replenished frequently. The other three were offered but declined, taking their boldness from Sam Holt, who did not seem to fear to give offence. Will found himself casting back to other breakfasts, other meals, when streams of information would have been forthcoming. His Uncle Daniel would have told them the strategy in every detail, demanding comment and reaction, to be appreciated or dismissed. This man, if he had a strategy, kept it to himself as if his two executives did in no wise need to know, even in the barest outline. William found this despicable.

The 'spy', Lieutenant Kershaw (sick and hurt), did make one attempt for information. This was unexpected, but perhaps, thought Will, he had been briefed by Daniel Swift. Whatever else he was on board for, one task was to aid in pilotage and navigation if it were needed, with the proviso he should do it privily. But Kaye was having none of it at all.

Kershaw said, 'Captain, if I could . . . on the trip downstream . . . These waters, to me, are—'

Kaye, on the instant, snorted like a rutting pig, and dismissed the supernumerary with a scornful wave. His features, pasty and arrogant, turned to him then slid off, and he shouted to Black Bob to bring him bread.

Later, as they moved downriver in the fierce, cold breeze, Kaye took the windward quarterdeck like a proper man, and cast a sulky eye upon proceedings which, however, carried on with little thanks to him. Gunning, at the con, stood heavy and four-square in a great serge coat, with one of his own non-Navy men on the helm. His own men, likewise, were at the sheets and braces, dressed less heavily than their master but equally at their ease, as familiar as bargemen with the crowded narrow water they were slipping down. The traffic coming up was not so heavy, naturally, as most square-rigged vessels could not attempt it with the wind and tide both hard against them, but fore-and-afters were plentiful enough, the ebb not yet running full, to need avoiding action pretty regular. But Biter was not fully canvased, sailing staid and easy under topsails only, so there were no alarms.

The midshipmen, once she had slipped and gone, went to the waist to oversee the Navy men getting ready for the fray ahead. This was not done by order from the captain either, but by custom and practice known to Holt, conveyed to Bentley. The contrast with Swift again struck as acute, for Kaye's method appeared to be to take no active part in anything, whereas his uncle had controlled the smallest particle with a grip of iron. When this complete indifference led the 'proper man' to go below Sam found it funny, but Will was less amused. According to his uncle, he was meant to bring Kaye up; a thought to conjure with indeed, but not, mayhap, to understand or to believe in.

The Navy seamen, all rated able, plus Jem Taylor and his mate Eaton, a ginger shockhead from northern Kent, seemed likewise to operate without the need for supervision from above. They had all been drunk the night before, had fought desultorily with Gunning's crew, but all looked little worse for wear. They needed Sam to produce and turn the keys to the weapons store and powder room, and William to mark down in the ledger the pistols, muskets and cutlasses that were issued, but for nothing more. Taylor and Eaton then took them off, divided them, and set about checks and issues that went off with great efficiency. Before much time elapsed, Will fell to looking out across the estuarial lands and mudbanks of the lower Thames, a flat and boring landscape to his Hampshire eyes, whose villages and stunted townships struck him as chill and sad. The weather did not help, for it was blowing strongly from a sky increasing overcast, which churned the brown waters of the river into dingy whitecaps that piled up on the growing mudflats to make thick rolls and banks of coffee-coloured foam that broke and flew in dirty chunks to every harder gust. Nor was the grass a stark and lovely green like grass at home, but pale and yellowish, sparse near the water's edge, and coarse. And out towards the sea, a long, low grey horizon, isles like Grain and Sheppey, more mud and a choppy vista of grey-brown water, its surface massed with coasting boats and fishermen, dotted with bigger ships anchored or snugged down to wait the tide and possibly a fairer wind.

'God,' he said to Samuel, 'so many sail. It seems impossible we have to tear men off them to fill so few. It seems impossible we cannot just . . .'

'What? Range up alongside of them and ask for any spare? Good chance of that, they fight like tigers to prevent the loss of one drunk cripple. God knows why. Their lordships might not pay so good but the food's a damn sight better and more of it, and we've got twenty men to hand a sail when they've got one or two.' His lips took an ironic turn. 'Maybe it's getting home to hearth and wife more than once in every two years or three, and shore furlough to drink and shag and other soft ideas like that!'

Almost without them noticing, Kershaw had drifted down on them, just forward of the quarterdeck at the weather rail. They had seen him earlier with the lieutenant – near but not with, for he was tentative and totally ignored – but no active movement in their direction had been discerned. Yet here he was, a yard from Samuel, and to add to their surprise, he spoke.

'The master sails her well,' he said, 'and knows the river. I too have some little knowledge which I could impart, of buoys and markers and the shoals.' He looked at Bentley, not exactly boldly, but with an unexpected hardness in his eye. 'I would hesitate to say so, but your uncle might expect it of me, sir.'

Before he answered, William considered. He was back at sea, the die was cast, and if he was to get along, it were better it was quickly. On Welfare he had begun to learn the rudiments, and could take a noon sight as well as any other fourteen-year-old on board, although his theory was deplorable. But fourteen now was many years astern, and he had to learn, and cram, and pass for a lieutenant or his life would be unbearable. He had a vision of more men like Richard Kaye as his commanders, or worse, more men like his uncle. Yet Kershaw was his uncle's placeman, and he despised him still. He should make use of him if possible, but it would be a wrench.

Sam Holt was not so nice, it seemed. He smiled easily at the sick and hurt lieutenant, and pointed to a withy on the larboard bow. It was divided at the top, a short branch and a long.

'I'll listen, Mr Kershaw, and that right happily,' he said. 'I've marked that Gunning goes sometimes to one side of these forked affairs, and sometimes the other. Are they showing middle ground, or do we not hit by luck? I asked him once but he just smirked at me.'

'He knows the bottom hereabouts,' Kershaw replied. 'He knows the state of tide. That forked one's not a middle ground, but it marks a channel that divides. Going down-river as we are, on a falling tide, it should be left to larboard, as he does. If he's left ones like it on the other side I guess it's been high water, or near the top of flood. Withies need special care, though. Without full knowledge, or a pilot, they can lead you hard aground. Now, see that buoy ahead? That is a safer mark, for it tells you which side to pass.'

He taught for near an hour, until the hands were piped to supper. He seemed to tire easy, though, and his exposition went rapidly awry after a certain point. He felt the cold quite oddly, too, for despite his heavy coat he began to shiver long before the younger men were aware of any small discomfort, his one eye watering. It was the end of summer and the breeze was brisk, but it was astern of them and from the western quarter, and hardly freezing. Soon he fell silent, then slunk away – or rather, drifted wraithlike, much as he had joined them earlier. He had quarters near them, a small berth partitioned off, and he collected some biscuit and a pan of coffee from the cook, more like a common seaman than a supernumerary, and went below with it. Lieutenant Kaye was still off the deck, though Gunning had not moved.

'Do we eat alone?' said Will. 'Or is there a standing invite in the cabin? Odds, Sam, this is a pretty ship, indeed!'

'It is,' said Sam. 'Of all the ships I've been in it's the prettiest. I've been in ships where everything was done by calls and drums, and if you missed your dinner by a half a minute you could starve. In Biter if you had a mind you could move Geoff Raper over in the galley and cook your bacon any way you liked. Gunning, going down the river, eats normally at the con, and his best hands at their stations. The Navy men are fast below by now.'

'And us?'

'Well, no standing invite, that I promise you. I've sat at Kaye's table five times or less in twice as many weeks. But Raper's a good man, he'll not forget us. Try patience, and enjoy the sunset. We'll come to killick soon, I guess. Too many ships here to go blundering in the dark. We leave that to the free trade in these parts.'

However, although the sky was darkening, there was other work afoot than dropping hook. Holt and Bentley ate below, in what might have been the gunroom in a bigger ship, but returned on deck within a half an hour. They were beyond the Nore, and it must have been low water for there were high sandbanks visible in all directions. Activity was intense, as vessels that had been still moving brought to in droves to spend the darkness hours safely, but the Biter showed no signs of stopping. Lieutenant Kaye was on the quarterdeck, and he had evidently called Gunning up to him. They were looking off to larboard, across the exposed banks towards the north east, where in the falling light they could discern some distant sails. They were far away, and would not approach the estuary too close at night, but it looked as if Kaye meant to go and meet one of them, at least. At that moment, indeed, he beckoned them across.

'Mr Holt,' he said, briskly. 'We're sailing through the night. I want the men stone sober and full ready, with all arms prepared and dry. I want the four-pounders set, two with roundshot, two with small. And I want every man on watch to keep a lookout. Tell Taylor and his mate I will not have her raised by Mr Gunning's men!'

John Gunning's big slack face formed an easy smile, then he turned back to the con. The wind was still hard from the west, and Biter was plunging into the backs of waves now she'd cleared the shelter of the land a piece. Where once she had been lightly canvased for congested waters, she now had just enough for offshore work. As darkness fell, Gunning would take more in, no doubt. You could not plunge through the coastal blackness like a blind racehorse.

'Aye aye sir,' said Samuel, smartly. 'I see the free trade's out in force, though. Might it not be fun to pick off one or two of them?'

The height of insolence, to make suggestions to a captain unsolicited, but Holt pitched it as a joke, and Kaye harrumphed appreciation. The pair of them gazed off towards the north Kent shore, and William followed suit. While all around were dropping sail, even coasting boats and barges, he saw other vessels, under sail and oar, heading outward from the mudbanks and the beaches. Free trade was smuggling, where he came from, but what this signified he could not imagine.

'We'll leave that to the scum who are paid for it,' Kaye replied. 'Why should we help out the Customs? In any way, you drink brandy, don't you? How much do you suppose you'd pay for it if we stuck our oar in there?'

Dismissed, the two of them went forward to set on the men. When they were barely out of earshot Sam chuckled.

'In any way,' he mimicked, 'how much information do you suppose we'd get about incoming ships stuffed with prime seamen, homeward bound? We see through you, bold Mr Kaye, don't doubt it!'

William did not though, nor could he sort out the implications. But the leading boats from shoreward were ranging alongside the biggest of the anchored ships, and quite clearly anything unloaded to be shipped ashore would be contraband, for the Customs boats were not in evidence this far downriver, nor were the merchants' lighters that were paid to do the job.

'What, are they smugglers?' he said. 'I thought they worked across to France or the Low Countries. It is rather blatant, is it not? What do they deal in?'

'Around here? Why, anything that turns to cash. Prisoners from the Medway hulks or Sheerness, sometimes. Then spices from the Orient or the Carib, sugar, tea, fine silks, playing cards, gin from the Dutch, French brandy, wine. They do long hauls if they have to, but this work is easier, as you may see. Just row or sail out from Seasalter or the foreland beaches, and barter it from overside. Most simple!'

'And can we really not prevent them? Or take them for the Press? It can be done, for I have . . . they have no special privilege, do they, smugglers?'

They were at a hatchway, and this talk had to stop. From the con John Gunning was ordering his men to brace the yards round, as the helmsman hauled his wind. The Biter heeled on the new slant, and the breeze struck colder from the larboard beam, laced with lumps of spray. What light was left was draining fast, and the North Sea lay ahead of them.

'I'd hang them all, not press them,' Samuel said, 'but it is not our job. You heard the captain – we must leave it to what he terms the Customs scum. On some ships it is not unheard of to put the hammer on them, but on this one . . . Ahoy there! Mr Taylor! Hands below! Rouse out on deck there, lively! There is work to do!'

He turned to William with a wry look.

'There are reasons we don't understand, friend, are there not?' he added. 'Not just slackness, neither. Reasons well beyond. Now – let me introduce you to our four-pounders. Unless the moon breaks through, this night will be as dark as pitch. And they are mighty dangerous little things.'

15

It was a farmer's boy who found the corpse of Warren, and it took some days to filter back to Sir Peter Maybold, who had set the searchers on. Before he had been called to Langham Lodge the Surveyor General had been aware he had a mystery on his hands, but after his luncheon with Sir Arthur his minions had come to know with no uncertainty that two men were missing, two important men, two men who must be found. The Customs services in Hampshire and West Sussex, in Portsmouth, Poole, Southampton and the Wight, were galvanised as they had rarely been before, and their networks of informers pitched to a level of extreme activity, with bright gold as stimulus.

The first, and basic, information came in very quickly. Two men of mystery had been noted first at Liphook, then near Horndean, then had been sighted in an Emsworth tavern, on the Sussex border. The collector at Portchester, Adam Price, was told by his best spy that the men were smugglers, who had been travelling the area recruiting oarsmen for a pair of fast galleys being built near Lymington that could cross the Channel into Normandy in eight hours flat, outrunning all pursuit. At Hamble it was a certainty that they were French, but speaking English just like Sussex men, and were seeking passage home for them and eighty others (or eight, or thirty-five), or were setting up a free trade operation and wanted English partners. The Isle of Wight collector, Will Slaughter, had firm reports that they were agents of the Paris government, attempting to recruit pilots from the smuggling fraternity for a proposed invasion force. All reports agreed, though, that some time before, the men had disappeared, shipped out, gone

166

back from whence they came. All reports, similarly, were bare of any names. They had been seen all over, it appeared. But were known by nobody.

In his offices at the Customs House, Sir Peter had studied this intelligence, and felt his choler rise. Although he had ruled it inadmissible for the collectors and their people to let out any hint that the missing men were Customs officers, he guessed that that was known, and was the reason for the silence and their deaths. No – he caught himself at that thought – not necessarily their deaths. They had been gone some weeks, but . . . but what? Sir Peter sat back, and held his paunch, which was uncomfortable from last night's meat and drinking. He had no idea as to who would have found out Charles Warren and Charles Yorke's true professions, or why, once they had done so, they would have spirited them away so utterly completely. Customs officers got killed from time to time, that was the danger of the job, accepted. But dead bodies lay around, and rotted, and got rooted out by dogs – or, more usually, weren't hidden to begin with. Where was the benefit, indeed, in killing these two? If they'd found something that deserved it – and Warren was the man to find things out, no argument to that – well then, what was it that deserved their disappearance?

Sir Peter's mind then wandered off, as it was prone to, to the body of his wife Laetitia, and who was using it. His office window overlooked the Thames, which was dull and busy, a bass note to the drabness of his mood. Impatiently, he clawed back to the subject at his hand, shouting to his clerk to come in and take a letter down that instant. A senior man in Hampshire had suggested that a woman called Ma Foster, a denizen of Liberty Wood, near the hamlet of World's End, might know something, and might be persuadable to tell. Trouble was, she was old and stubborn, the recipient of all sorts of confidences from the local free trade men, for whom she ran a browning factory, known about but not closed down because it was a rendezvous and information source. This senior suggested Adam Price to do the job, because he was held to be more heartless than the generality, and Ma Foster was as tight as any grave. To his annoyance, Sir Peter Maybold had been left to make the last decision, and now he made it. The woman had lived comfortable in illegality for long enough. She would speak, or they would shut her factory down.

Price, a small sly man with a taste for cruelty, had been escorted to the factory by two riding officers, in case the crone had menfolk at her beck. She did not, but the trip was disappointment from the first, and failed. She saw them coming from the forest edge, as she had been forewarned. It was known by all the free trade men by now who Yorke and Warren were, and what had been their fate. Cruel though Price's reputation was, Ma Foster had been told what crueller men would do to her if she should speak too much. Reluctantly – for she thought herself a match for a collector and two riding men – she abandoned her cott and slipped into the Liberty, to watch.

The house – a hovel rather, with turfed-over roof – was empty, naturally. Inside it Adam Price found a pile of skins and rags (her bed), a wooden table, a stool, a water jug. In the shed next door, much better made of planks and thatching, he expected much more, and knew she'd tricked him. At the stone-clad hearth, where Ma Foster burnt the sugar to colour the natural spirit brought in from France at a dozen spots along the coast, there were no pans, measures, tundishes, anything to ply her trade. Similarly, the storage room was empty, not a barrel or a hogshead or a half-cask to be seen. No sugar, either, except in smears across the beat-earth floor. Ma Foster and her customers had thought ahead, and they'd acted. It was not a browning factory, it was a woodland hut.

'Outside,' he ordered tersely, to the riding officers. 'They can't have got it far into the wood. We'll find it if we have to work all day.'

Beside his saddle, Price had lashed a sledgehammer and

some crows, to smash the cooperage and the instruments the old dame would need for browning. There being none, he smashed her door and table, then, as an afterthought, scattered hot ashes from her fire into her bedding pile. Then he blew a brand until it was ready to ignite, gathered a handful of dry grass from beside the doorway, and took it into the factory/storehouse where he piled the combustibles against the inside wooden wall. Lacking spirit by the hogshead, he returned to his saddlebag and got a bottle of his own – also smuggled, but confiscated almost legally – which he splashed freely down the rough wood of the wall. He blew the brand until the smoulder became a glow, then held the grass to it until it took. Then, with a flash, the spirit flickered blue upon the wall, taking hold as real, red fire in the cracks and fissures. Price propped open the door to give it air, and watched the fire roaring up the inner wall. By the time his men returned half an hour later, there was nothing left but blackened stumps of planking, and a pile of turf where the hovel roof was in.

The officers, who did not know the Liberty, had discovered absolutely nothing. Neither they nor Adam Price had any interest left, were hardly even amused by what Ma Foster would discover when she came back to her home. As Price had brought the only bottle, and wasted it as kindling, they needed, anyway, to find themselves an inn or tavern. Price, who had done the hot work, favoured ale.

Ma Foster, who had watched it all from start to end, cursed them mildly as they rode away, and wondered idly if she could perhaps doctor some brandy up for them, and get her fellows to leave it outside the Custom House to be found and drunk, bringing on a slow, unpleasant death. Doubting it, she went to see if she could salvage any turf from her ruined hovel. She would need to build somewhere to sleep, as the nights were getting chilly.

It was two days later that the boy found Charlie Warren, on the day, by chance, that Sir Peter Maybold received the senior man's report from Hampshire that the best efforts of even Adam Price had turned up nothing in the Liberty. The boy was called Joe Simple, and he was thought to be a kind of idiot, from which the name. He belonged to a small tied farmer, who tended a straggle of poor fields that stretched north to south beside a Sussex wood. Joe Simple had been found, not born, but he ate little and his stupidity was not harmful. He had seen the burnt-out hayrick several times, and had even mentioned it to his father, although he did not talk much, in the way of things. Ricks did get burnt sometimes, usually for drunken reasons not malicious, often by drunk wanderers who'd come by some tobacco, so it was not interesting. This day Joe walked close, and smelled a smell he only recognised the half of. Burnt meat, yes, but also putrefaction. Burnt meat? In a hayrick? Perhaps some tramp had smoked himself to death.

So it seemed, when he got closer. The rick was quite burnt down, consisting of a shapeless low pile of black, with one side pulled out and scattered by dogs or foxes, or perhaps vicious brocks, that he had heard men talk of over beer, and which he feared. Certainly he saw a burnt-out boot, with a whitish leg bone sticking out of it into the charry mess. Above the bone a fatter-looking lump, with cloth burned into it, and rags of flesh teased down. This was the part that smelled, and the smell grew stronger when Joe poked at it with his hazel. Soft and hard, some flesh charred, some yielding, almost liquid. He knocked the hay-ash off, uncovering the area of the private parts, nothing natural to be seen there, though. The man had had a leather belt, with a good-sized buckle, which Joe Simple was hoping suddenly might be of silver. Whether of good metal or not, it occurred to him this was no tramp, there were remnants of real cloth there as well, and a waistcoat. It further fell into him that this man was buried in the hayrick, he must have thrust himself deep in its heart before he lit his pipe, which was very thoughtless, not to say— Joe held the thought, a sick feeling creeping over him. This man had been thrust in the hay and murdered by the fire.

Joe Simple stood for some long time before he moved, pondering on what he ought to do. Most likely, if he told people he'd found a murdered man, they would hang him as the murderer. They might ask him first if he had done it, because he was liked well enough, but he knew he would not have the proper words to explain himself. Someone would ask awkward questions, or be tricky with their speed, and he would confess to some guilt and be strung up from the local gibbet. He had seen it done before, and not just once, despite they lived way out of any fair-sized town. The English were a hanging race, his mother said, and who could disagree? Joe thought of this until his mind was flooded with it, which by next day meant that he was gibbering, until his father knocked him over with a lath. It took a kicking to get the whole tale out of him, when to his surprise he was not blamed at all, but told to lead the way. They uncovered the full sad stiffened effigy, which made him cry, but which his father seemed to find not unexpected. Then he was cuffed some more, to make him keep his mouth shut, and the corpse was loosely covered up for time to think.

Later that night he heard his mother and his father talking long and low, and later still two men – he thought, he did not see – came to the house for conference. Joe Simple heard nothing more of the matter after that, and in several days forgot it, almost. Except the black stick bones and purple, bitten bits of stomach that he'd seen and smelt. They stayed with him and never went away.

When dawn came to the Biter, the wind was fierce and bleak. Clear of the Essex coast and blowing truer, it had veered more northerly so their easy reach had given way to a bitter, lumpy plug. Through the dark hours, Gunning had snugged her down to head and close-reefed topsails,

171

and as the east sky lightened there was little reason to increase her speed. There were ships aplenty up ahead of them, mostly hove to in the offing, some bearing off to make the estuary in time to catch the flood, but none of them was large or had the air of a foreign trader, homeward bound.

Sam and Will, on deck alone of all the Navy men, both strained their eyes to equal glum effect.

'Can he have slipped us?' Samuel mused. 'But only if he'd charged by with all sail set.'

'And if he did,' said Will, 'he's likely at the bottom with the ships he hit!'

They both stared harder, up ahead and over the larboard bow. Gunning, they saw, had a spyglass, but Lieutenant Kaye was still below. Awaiting the call, or taking breakfast with his little toy, or maybe still asleep. Will had a flash of anger at Slack Dickie, irrational but sharp. How could his uncle put faith for the future in such a jackanapes?

'No,' said Sam, finally. 'She must be farther off. Oh Christ, it is a mean way to make a living, this. I wonder how far those men have come, just to be met by us? I should rather that we missed them, Will. Oh look, there's Eaton, to pipe the hands to breakfast.'

The hands were as slack as their commander, although they had had naught but beer to drink the night before, and after breakfast Sam Holt made them work at musket drill and sword practice, to put some fire in their looks. Several were seasick, which Will saw as peculiar, although the leaden motion of the old coal ship did not a lot of good to his greasy breakfast, either. He sailed his yawl in any weather, nearly, and his guts were like cast iron in a lively sea, but liveliness was not in Biter's soul. It was with great relief three hours later that he heard the masthead shriek, and guessed that they, at last, had raised their quarry.

To his surprise it was a Navy man and not one of Biter's private people who had done the sighting. Stranger still, he found, was their reaction. Every man jack, from the captain down, seemed stirred by it, and men he had put down as lazy unto death sprang into the shrouds and climbed like squirrels to get a view. Kaye threw his head back, on the quarterdeck, and roared up to the lookout like a veritable deep-sea captain.

'Good man, good man, but where away! What ship is she, does she carry royals?'

It was the size and sort of ship that he wanted an answer on, for mostly from the north came colliers and coasting trade. Sam had already guessed the night before that Kaye's target might have come round the British islands north-about to try and avoid something, most probably the Press. In the southern west approaches, from the Scillies outwards, the tenders hovered almost constantly. His information must have come originally from a northern sighting by a fast ship that had come to shore.

'Aye, she is big, sir,' came the reply from high aloft, then other voices joined in a chorus of happy speculation. Will watched Tom Tilley, a man who never smiled, hang on a backstay like a gigantic inflated sheeptick, whooping and huzzahing as if someone had made him rich. Even John Behar, his long bones folded across the fore topsail yard, had lost his expression of sly affrontedness.

'Blood,' said Will, 'it is like a carnival. I've never seen men change so much.'

Gunning had joined Lieutenant Kaye on the weather side, and both were animated as they talked and pointed. Then Kaye waved a hand at them, imperiously, and they went across. His soft face was beaming.

'Well, Mr Holt, well, Mr Bentley! There's a sight indeed, and now we'll see some hot work at last. Have them recheck all primings and put their swords to hand, then break out a puncheon from the liquor store and give them rum or brandy, whichever comes to hand. Mr Gunning here says an hour, and I want them keen, not drunk, so see to it!'

'If you get your monkeys down off my yards,' said

Gunning drily, 'I'll shake out them reefs. If not it will be longer, or she'll scoot by us on the run.'

'Aye, see to that, an'all,' said Kaye. 'Bob! Come here, black villain! I want a bottle of madeira, and some cake! Holt! Bentley! Skip to it!'

'He's like a bloody potentate,' Sam muttered, as the two of them went about their business and Gunning returned to the con to give his sailing orders. 'No, he's like a bloody pirate captain, he gets them fuddled *before* they do the work and treats them like mere scum, not his only brain. Hey!' he yelled at the red-headed boatswain's mate. 'Get those men out of Gunning's way and down on deck and ready. Brandy is the magic word. There'll be an issue.'

With more canvas set and drawing, the Biter lost her lumpen attitude, which eased the sickness on the decks. She became wetter as she thumped the short steep seas, but the joviality, helped on by fiery liquor, diminished not a whit. Piratical was the word Sam used, with accuracy, Will thought. As they clawed up to the unsuspecting merchantman, both ship and people had a predatory air, while Kaye stood on the quarterdeck in a watchcoat drinking madeira from a bottle that poor Black Bob kept balanced on a silver tray. Balanced expertly, it must be said, for he rode the motion like a natural sailorman.

'This is unexpected,' Will told Sam. 'I knew they liked a fight when we went on the Press ashore, but they seem positively bloodthirsty today. The plan is, though, to catch men, is it not, not kill them?'

'Aye, more than that, to make them volunteer,' Sam laughed. 'But either way, our lads get some tidy cash per head, and all the fun of breaking them to boot. This vessel by the look of her has been at sea a fair long time. Homeward-bound seamen would almost rather die, some of them, than get thrown in the Navy, however big the bribe. Our boys like a rumpus, as you know. This bids fair to be more like a bloody battle, but without the blade or bullet. You see the fun of it? To fight the French is handsome, but you can always catch a belly-opener. This way you can split heads, take a broken nose maybe, then clap the enemy in irons down below to show who's master, and get paid a bonus for pot luck! That's why they're smiling in their brandy, friend.'

At some stage indefinable, the quarry must have realised what kind of ship the Biter was, or suspected her enough to want to sheer away. Although well canvased, she had not been hard-pressed as if racing for the tide. But when she showed more canvas, and trimmed in the rest to push her up to speed, they saw something that explained her slowness. As she eased round a point or so, another vessel detached itself from where it had been obscured from their view, and moved off from the quarry on divergent course. She was a small black lugger, only forty foot or so, with high sides like a West Country fisherman. She was not, though; not a bit of it.

'My Christ,' said Samuel, 'these boys get everywhere, don't they? Kaye will fear they've made away with all his bribes!'

The smuggler unbrailed as she dropped away, and soon was swooping down towards the Kentish coast at a considerable lick, pulling a creamy sternwave two feet high. Will watched almost enviously, so lovely did she look, although Kaye was visibly enraged.

'He'd take a shot at her if he knew he wouldn't fall a half-mile short,' said Sam. 'God, but they've got fine nerve round here, haven't they?'

'But what's the odds to Kaye?' asked William. 'So Parliament loses a bit of revenue, but he shouldn't give a fig for that, surely? He's rich as Croesus, and smugglers aren't his job, he's told us that in no uncertain terms.'

'Aye, true. It's they will have given us away as presters, though, which extra time could make it hotter for us. Some ships take it very hard, you know. We do get fired on at times.'

'What, fired on with . . . You mean they'll fight?'

175

Sam laughed.

'With guns, Will, aye! Not with peashooters or catapults! This ship's come from halfway round the world, maybe, and ships like that go armed. Some captains and some crews don't take kindly to being received by dogs like us who only want to send them out to sea once more. They want the land to walk on, not deck planks, and breasts and bellies underneath them instead of hammocks! You'd fight us, wouldn't you? I would!'

The sad truth, though, was different. When Gunning eased Biter off the wind a mile below them, so that whichever way she steered she could not slip past, the quarry tried no avoiding action nor did her people make a move for any of her guns. Biter did not make a stopping signal, but broke out her colours which was message clear enough. The number of men on the victim's deck was sparse, but after a short while they manned the bunts and clewlines and reduced the working canvas. Then, ponderously, the ship hove to. Kaye eyed her through a spyglass, then told his two midshipmen, whom he had summoned to his side, that she was named the Katharine, and that all three of them would go on board.

As Gunning's people brought her round and hove her to, the Biter's Navy men were almost baying. They shortened up the bowropes of the towing boats, jumping down into them to bail them out and unlash the oars and ship the rudders. Gunning lay half a mile off the Katharine, right downwind in case they had a thought of going for a run, but when the boats were crewed the gap had shortened comfortably. It was not a big sea running despite the briskness of the breeze, so the people discarded their canvas frocks to free them for a sharp hot row then, hopefully, hot work on board. Coxswain Sankey had his men overside the first – the others knew better than to beat Kaye's crew – and the stout lieutenant was discreetly shadowed down in case he slipped and made himself a fool. Sam went with Jem Taylor, Will with the shockhead boatswain's mate, and the strongest oarsmen vied with each other, for once, to do the work.

It was not a race, precisely, but they pulled like hell, with Will thrilling at each surge of power as the men dug in their blades. He took the tiller, to Eaton's surprise, and ducked and wove her round the bigger breaking crests with great dexterity. For reasons he did not care to question both Behar and Tom Tilley had elected for his crew, but although they struck him as both dangerous and intractable, they were also the biggest of the Biter's company, Tilley by some considerable margin. He took the stroke oar, and although he dug his blade in far too deep, his mighty strength compensated for the added difficulty, and indeed he had the ash shaft bending like a hazel switch. His deep-set, piggy eyes gazed piercingly into the distance over Will's head, and the breath rasped through his wet and twisted lips. Although they could have got there first, Will had them ease as they came inside the lee, which earned him a look of naked contempt from out the little eyes. Sam slacked off also, though, so Kaye's could be the first to touch. The Katharine's men, knowing they were fairly beaten, had put ladders overside, and warps to catch. Or maybe left them there, from the accommodation of the free trade lugger. Half Kaye's men swarmed on board, then turned to ease his passage up if needed, then – with him on deck – Sam Holt, Jem Taylor, Eaton and Will Bentley scurried up, in a scrummage with their men. Josh Baines, an idle rat, was told off to watch the painters and stop the boats from coming up too hard against each other or the ship.

Beaten they were, and beaten they appeared, in truth. The decks were worn and dirty, the canvas overhead bleached and sere, and patched in many places. The hold was open, and the well deck strewn with cases the smugglers had not had time to barter for and load, but there seemed hardly crew enough to handle it. There was a man on the quarterdeck who might be the captain, a younger officer abaft of him, a sailor at the helm, and half a dozen others forward, watching warily from the raised fo'c'sle deck. The other thing that struck as odd was that the officers had pistols in their belts, while three seamen carried clubs. The Biter men, some with short cudgels at the belt, some with a cutlass doled out the day before, looked about them eagerly, waiting for a fight. To Will, the chances were invisible.

Even Kaye was nonplussed by the sparseness of the reception. He moved aft slowly, glancing at the clutter from the holds. When he faced the captain he took up his normal stance, of well-fed arrogance. From a pocket inside his tunic he pulled out his warrant.

'I have a paper here, sir,' he said pompously, 'that explains my rights and duties. I am Lieutenant Richard Kaye, commanding HM tender Biter. You are required to present your people to me for the purpose I may select them for the service of the King. Any man with valid passport or protection is, of course, exempt, and I can promise you there will be no irregularity in my choice. Now sir, who are you, sir? Master, captain, owner? I would appreciate the courtesy of a name.'

The captain of the Katharine was an old and tired-looking man. He was tall and thin with stooped shoulders, and his facial skin was pale and papery. He looked ill, as if he had been long afflicted, and his eyes were full of exhaustion, or pain. He did not extend a hand.

'I am the captain. Captain James McEwan. There is nothing for you, sir. In twelve weeks at sea we have lost thirty, from the scurvy.'

It was strange upon the deck, thought William. The Katharine, hove to, had settled in the troughs and taken up a rhythmic roll, while falling down to leeward slow but constantly. Each time her weather side rose high the wind cut off, then as it dropped, the chill blast resumed, sometimes with a spattering of spray. It was two rolls before Kaye continued his questioning.

'So how many seamen do you claim are left, sir? Why do you carry arms? You are not so ill, I notice, that you cannot trade your owner's hard-won goods. Or was that black lugger the undertaker's men?'

Some of the nearer Biters laughed, but their hearts were not in it. They wanted action and it seemed they would not get it, and they were impatient also, because they did not believe.

James McEwan raised a hand as if to remonstrate, but then he dropped it to his side.

'The lugger,' he said. His voice was indistinct. He tried to gather strength, to speak more clearly. 'That's why we carry weapons. For fear they—'

Then another voice cut in, and it was drenched in fury. Everyone was startled, not least Kaye, who jerked his large head back to find its source. It was the younger officer, two yards behind the captain, his face now flushed with anger, his left hand gripped among the mizzen shrouds.

'For fear that they were murderers,' was what he said. His eyes were fixed on Kaye's and he was almost panting. 'We have lost our men, we are helpless. How did we know they only wanted contraband? How did we know they were not on for piracy, their ship looked like a pirate, they looked like blackguards, to a man. What should we do? Give up?'

The old man made a gesture meant to calm. The officer's lips were a grim line, breath hissing through his nostrils. Kaye was languid.

'Pirates? Off the Essex coast, this day and age? Pah.' He turned to Holt and Bentley. 'We do not believe them,' he said, almost grandly. 'Take your men and do a search. The hold, the fo'c'sle, don't overlook the lazaret. Sankey, round up those men up forward. If any claim exemption, bring them to me with papers. No papers, no escape.'

'They are all I have!' Captain McEwan's voice was high and harsh, then cracked. He began to cough. Bentley and Holt, matching the reaction of their men, ignored it, on the run. Sam took the stern accommodation, Will the main hatchway, while the boatswain led a party forward to where the Katharine's men would have their quarters. As Will went below, he saw that Kaye had drawn a pistol from his pocket, short but of a heavy bore. He also saw the younger officer move forward, and for a moment held himself from dropping down the ladder to the hold.

'You should not do this!' he was shouting. 'How can you pick on us when there is the enemy to fight! It is those blackguards in their lugger you should catch and take! We have been away a year or more! We have been decimated! Men! Do not let them touch you! Fight them off or you will go to sea again, but in the bloody Navy! Think of your women and your children, men!'

William, transfixed, felt strong fingers grip his ankle. Tom Tilley's mean eyes met his as he glanced down, the twisted lips expressing, maybe, humour.

'Dost need a hand, sir?' It was bitter humour, that suggested he needed help on steep ladders like a landman or, implied, like Richard Kaye. Will brushed the hand off pettishly, and clattered down until he reached the deck. Outside the spill of light from the half-lifted cargo hatches ahead of him, his men, like shadows, moved off to disappear.

There was shouting down below as well as up on deck, and he hurried forward fast but carefully for fear of losing touch and getting lost. The Biter men were greatly expert at his game, and frisked about like rats where he could only blunder in the dark. On one great beam he found a dim horn lamp, lashed hard for fear of fire, and cut it free with his pocket knife. This gave him some security from falling ten or twenty feet among the massed cargo that he had to walk across, but threw a glow ahead that scarcely helped at all. There were smells he did not recognise, except the smell of filthy bilges overall, and rustlings and groans among the close-packed bales and cases.

Then, close, came shouts and screams, and the noise of

beatings with fist and stick. A high yell, from a young voice, then a voice he recognised as John Behar's, mouthing imprecations, corrupt and hard. Will, discouragingly, had a sudden memory of another man, an officer called Matthews who had died on Welfare after illegal impressment by his uncle, Daniel Swift. He remembered Jesse Broad, and Thomas Fox. Of a sudden, the dark oppressed him horribly, he had to catch his breath. Of a sudden, he needed air, and light, an end to beastliness and screaming. As he picked hurriedly towards the hatch again, two Biter men, Tom Hugg and Silas Ayling, emerged from between some cargo stacks, their faces beaming, while behind them came three bloodied seamen and behind them in their turn Tennison and Mann, who had a pistol, cocked and dangerous in such a space.

'All sick, eh sir!' said Ayling. 'They nowt but lying buggers, be they then!'

By the time they reached the ladders they had eight lurkers rounded up, and up on the deck there were already seven more possibles. Two of them had been on the foredeck when the Biter boys had come on board, and to tell the truth they looked pretty sick, while the other four rounded up by Sankey had been let go again, two whitefaced and yonderly, one aged sixty if a day, the last one with one arm and a twisted leg. They stood to one side, out of it, as the boatswain, Jem Taylor, demanded to know which of his five from their fo'c'sle hideyholes claimed to have passports, and if so could he see them. Sam Holt had not yet reappeared, but down below, Will had heard shouting from the dark aft section, possibly the lazaret.

The captain of the Katharine was leaning on the binnacle, as if only the power of his mind was keeping him upright, and his mate and Richard Kaye could not be seen. There was a skylight, though, set in the quarterdeck abaft the mizzenmast, and suddenly an enormous row issued from its open wings. One voice, thick with fury, was the young officer's, who was repeating his arguments of earlier

181

with tremendous force. William heard the words 'and you are in their pockets, that is why!' quite clearly, so loud it was practically screamed. He also heard 'fight the French', and 'cowardice to take men off a ship like ours'. Then Kaye's voice, which was as loud but without a cutting note, and choked with rage. Then there was a crash, another roar, and then, amazingly – a report.

On deck, all human noise ceased instantly. Men had been listening, but others shouting, and one pale young sailor had been in noisy tears. They stopped, staring at each other, then round about. Then the captain, James McEwan, let out a ghastly croak.

William, after a split instant, went for the aft accommodation ladder at a pelting run. As he dropped down towards the cabin he saw that Sam was halfway through the door, but had stopped himself from plunging through by catching at the jamb. Will hurtled into him, and both of them half fell in. They saw the young merchant officer stretched out on the deck back by the transom settle, with Kaye bent over him. One of the young man's legs was shaking violently, but as they stood, it stopped.

'Sir!' said Sam. 'Sir! What?'

'He shot at me,' said Kaye. He had turned towards them, but did not appear to see. His eyes were milky in his big, bland face, his lips in a kind of puzzled frown. 'He shot at me. I think I've killed him.'

As he moved back, the young sea officer was revealed, flat out and gazing upwards to the deckhead. His eyes were open but unseeing, and his chest was an enormous mass of blood from the heavy ball that Kaye had fired into him. Kaye had his pistol in his hand still, but in his left one. In his right was the long, old-fashioned weapon that both Sam and Will had seen earlier at the dead man's waist. Kaye had his hands together, his left, hampered by his gun, covering the action of the other. There had only been one shot.

'But sir,' said Holt. 'We only heard one shot.'

Kaye's eyes cleared slowly, then he looked down at the pistols in his hands.

'Aye,' he said. 'He was primed for shooting, but I got there first. Look. Look, his gun is cocked.'

He pulled his hands apart, one pistol in each of them. He held the dead man's in his right, forward of the action, showing the cocked hammer and uncovered priming pan.

'Poor man,' he said. 'He called it on himself, but we must pity him. He was in such a choler, then he aimed to murder me. His pistol's cocked, d'you see?'

Holt first, then Bentley, moved slowly into the cabin. Outside, through the large stern windows, Will caught sight of the North Sea, grey and rolling, with white crests. Numbly, he studied it for a moment, then Kaye's face, full of odd anxiety, then the poor dead man, lying there. His face was drained of blood, quite white, his mouth was open, he was very young, not twenty-two or -three. He was my countryman, thought Will. He was not the enemy, we were not fighting him. Oh, this is horrible.

With a shock, he noticed men at the cabin door, Jem Taylor, Wilmott, Behar and Tilley to the fore. Only Tilley wore a grin, showing broken teeth as if it were a festive or a jolly sight. Not being officers, they did not come in.

Then, with a sigh, Lieutenant Kaye turned from his officers, to his men, and dropped the unfired pistol on to the stomach of the bloody corpse.

'Well come on, boys,' he said. 'Enough of this. What is the tally, Taylor? There is still much to be done.'

Then, before they left, he bent and picked the pistol up, and carefully uncocked it, and blew out the pan. Then he thrust it somewhere inside his thick blue coat.

16

There were seventeen prime seamen to put in chains when they got back to Biter, because not a single one of the Katharine's sailors would volunteer, despite that their refusal cost them cash. 'Prime seamen' was a cruel jest used by the Biter people, for most of them were anything but prime. They had suffered much illness in the East, and even those who had not died were weakened and demoralised, wanting more than anything in the world to get ashore, and home to those they loved or who would look after them. Geoff Raper gave them fresh food and good bread, and not just because he was a kindly sort. It had been found on many an occasion that homeward-bound men could be induced to volunteer if the food was good and plentiful. For the moment, the Katharines showed no sign of falling for this dodge.

The leaving of the merchant ship had been as unpleasant as the time on board of her. Kaye had spoken to the captain when they had emerged on to the quarterdeck, even expressing a type of peremptory regret. James McEwan had been more stunned than anything, looking horribly to Will Bentley as if he might die himself, so grey and vague did he become. But when Kaye had suggested that he might perform a simple burial there and then, with aid from the Biter men, the old captain had refused with vehemence approaching rage, and screamed at Kaye to go, and take his 'villains, worse than pirates, villains!' with him. Moments later he had changed again, and almost pleaded with the Navy man not to take all the seamen he had rounded up.

'We are not enough,' he cried. 'Sir, I beg of you, we are

not enough to get this ship to port! I must have men to hand the sails, to anchor!'

All told, he had fifteen – unless more able hands were hidden below, which was eminently likely. Certainly Lieutenant Kaye thought so. He glanced round the crew – the aged, the infirm, the crestfallen, the hangdog – and let out a well-bred snort.

'But you have enough to undertake your own burying,' he said. 'Sir, my patience is worn out with you. You can square your yards with this fine lot, you can drop your anchor in the offing, you can signal for the pilot that you must engage. Hold! I will be generous with you. Mr Bentley, a commission! Keep Tilley there and, ah, Behar is it? Two fine strong lads, and – oh, have Mr Eaton, too. There you are, sir! One officer, one warrant, and two of my strongest men. Now are you satisfied? You will not come to grief like that, will you?'

William saw through the ruse, even if the merchantman did not. If he kept all the Katharines on deck and got her under way, who knew what might not creep out of the woodwork, thinking the coast was clear? He wondered at the illegality of undermanning a ship so drastically, but then Kaye's attitude to law was wondrous in any way. A picture of the young man's corpse came to his mind, and he thought he heard Kaye say again, 'He aimed to murder me.' Oh how I wish, thought Bentley, that I had asked him, 'Why?'

It took ten minutes to reorganise the boats' crews, and another fifteen to get the pressed men all on board. Tilley and Behar were pleased at first to see their shipmates go, then furious that Bentley had guessed their plan to go below and search out liquor, and got Eaton to scotch it. Between them they must have been three times his weight, but Eaton had a firearm, while they had only cudgels. Not only that, but the stocky, wild-haired man had gained his warrant, it appeared, as much through his way with men as through sea ability. He faced them at the after scuttle and there ensued a silent battle that Will guessed the content of, but did not know. Then Eaton told them off to man the braces as the Katharine's men were shaping up to do.

Bentley joined the captain at the con and watched with little passion as the yards were hauled round to fill and take her off the wind and sailing. A cable's length to leeward Biter rode, still hove to, with the first boat already back and hooking on. By the time the Katharine, slow and unwieldy, was under way, Gunning had got his ship paying off, increasing sail, and the small boats strung out astern of her for the tow. Will imagined Richard Kaye climbing up the tender's steep, dark side, and hoped, absurdly, that he had fallen down and drowned. His mind wrestled with the problem of the man below, lying abandoned in a pool of blood, and wondered what could, should, *would* happen to Lieutenant Kaye for it. Nothing; the word kept ringing in his head, a knell. Nothing, and why not? Kaye had killed someone, and said it was in self-defence, and left him with a complex knot inside his skull. I do not believe you, Richard Kaye, he told himself. I do not believe you. But in this life, in this Navy life in England, who will find you out?

The wind was strong, but not so strong, and Biter soon creamed away from them under a full press. The Katharine still had much canvas stifled, and her captain was determined he should not shake it out to push her up to speed. He consulted Bentley, as if he were the commander and Katharine his prize, but Bentley replied frostily that such matters were naught to do with him; he was there to render aid if necessary, as were his 'men in lieu'. Over half an hour the sails were snugged, and the tired ship lumped along towards the north Kent coast, with Biter dwindling into the ruck of boats and ships converging on the estuary. It was Will's assumption that Kaye would ply the Impress trade with any hopeful-looking vessel, then come back to pick them up when McEwan had dropped hook and signalled for a pilot.

After about two hours, when the shore was clearer in the falling light, and Behar and Tilley extremely bored and frisky, William consulted with the boatswain's mate and decided they should be allowed below, ostensibly to see if they could flush out any more lurking hands. Eaton went with them though, and Bentley made it very clear they should avoid the cabin, and the corpse, under every circumstance. The merchant captain, watching the three men disappearing, asked stiffly for permission to view the dead officer himself, a request Will could see no way of refusing. He would not let the seamen leave the deck, however, and took a large pistol into his hand to emphasise the point. These men, who were huddled into any lee that they could find, sat stoically in silence. The oddity overcame him yet again. A British ship, a British crew, and him a British officer. To them, it must appear they had been overwhelmed by an enemy. He was alone beside the helmsman, and pondering, when he saw a sail he thought he recognised, making up for them, hard on the wind. No certainty, but he would bet on it: the free trade lugger.

Wishing for a glass, he moved unhurriedly towards the larboard rail. Most of the ships on that side were moving parallel with the Kentish coast, with a few beating up towards him to gain the open sea. As Katharine neared the Thames mouth she was getting into heavy traffic, but in that direction little could be made out against the glare of the westering sun reflecting from the surface. The lugger, though, as she beat closer, he was certain was the one. Black hull, high topsides, her two big lugsails making her look almost overcanvased. William considered the cargo still scattered about the deck. It was unfinished business, surely. She had been interrupted by the Press, the Press had gone, so she was coming back to get the rest.

Watching her, he realised he was ambivalent in what he felt. She was a beauty of a boat, extremely fast and weatherly, and he remembered Jesse Broad's strictures on the trade as harming no one in any great essential. The rich needed their brandy, the poor their gin, and everyone should pay less for tobacco and for tea. Even in his own house he knew they bought illicit goods, and in truth the trade had led to little violence he knew of in their locality, despite what chapbook men and village gossip sometimes said. The lugger went about, her men dipping the yards fast and handily, and he wondered what would happen as she got nearer. His duty must be to await them, to entice them if possible to come on board, and arrest them for the service, although he had no warrant on his person. This made him smile. Himself, Eaton, two men with sticks. Against a lugger crew of half a dozen, maybe more, plus the Katharines, who might welcome some revenge. It occurred to him that he should call his people up to consider a defence, and that right quickly. Maybe check one of the vessel's swivel guns for firing, at the very least.

At that moment the red hair of Eaton emerged from a scuttle, in a commotion. Will assumed that they had found more seamen down below, but the boatswain's mate was shouting over his shoulder and two men were shouting back – Behar and Tilley, who had found and taken drink, he feared. But as they made the level of the deck Behar – not drunk by any means – saw something away to starboard in the dying sunlight, shielded his eyes, then gave a whoop.

'To weather there! It's the cutter! Now we can get off from this, at last!'

Will moved back to the starboard side to get a better sight, and saw clearly what he had missed, as a cloud cut down the glare for him. The cutter, under sail, was racing down on them just off the wind, much closer than the free trader he had been studying. As she came bowling down he saw Sam Holt was at the tiller with, apparently, only one other man on board, small and huddled at the bow. Baines, he'd know that rat-look anywhere, already.

Eaton, beside him, nodded to the lee.

'Them free trade men, sir. Did you see? Will they run

on board of us, dost think? Tom!' he then snapped. 'Take a line in off the cutter. Oh, handsome, handsome, sir!'

Sam, who did not hear the praise, no doubt deserved it. He had run the small boat at them perpendicularly then shot the tiller up, let fly, and brought her stern to wind along the big ship's side. As she had lost her way, he'd unjammed the halliard from its pin, lowering the mainsail fast into the boat where Baines – to avoid a split head – had grabbed the yard and doused the canvas. Sam then skipped forward across the thwarts and threw a coiled bow-line up to the waist of Katharine, where Tilley caught it like an angel and turned it on a pin. Down came the flapping headsail, and Holt was up the side like a monkey. Baines, useless and unwanted, fended off.

'Ho, Will!' hailed Samuel, as he came across the deck. 'You're not the only man can handle small boats, see! Mr Kaye says— By God, man, that's surely him, I was not sure from down there in the cutter. You've seen the lugger?'

'Have they seen you, sir, that's the question,' said Eaton, rather forwardly. 'I fear they're coming for a fight with us.'

'They won't have done is my guess,' Will said. 'We hardly did, the sun is well aglare from their position. Where is Biter? If she is near enough she could try her with a cannon.'

'Hah!' went Sam. 'Not that near, even if our man could shoot! Even if our captain was—' He caught Eaton's eager face, and changed that statement to a laugh. He gestured out across the starboard bow. 'See those two pinks? Shore-side of them but coming down for us. We struck lucky with a Baltic timberman, and I set off with Baines to try a little schooner – drew a blank – then down to pick you up and save Gunning some time. This old sow's close in, they can drop the bower and wait for a pilot, can't they? Where is the captain? That poor old walking ghost.'

When he heard that Bentley had let him go below, Sam was concerned. Will said stiffly that it was out of courtesy,

189

to see the dead unfortunate, and he considered it unlikely they would be fired on with secreted muskets or attacked by sword. Eaton and the other two had made a search, but come across no hidden men at all. He thought, he added, that they should prepare a hot reception in case the lugger could be lulled to come and grapple them.

Sam was not put out by his touchiness, and strode down to leeward to check the free trade man. The lugger had not seen his cutter – unless they were happy to make a fight of it with an unknown quantity of Navy men, which was unlikely – and one more short board would bring them up to the Katharine. He turned back to Bentley with a wide and friendly grin.

'God knows what Slack Dickie would make of it if we did go back with a band of smugglers for the hold,' he said. 'But he can hardly argue, can he, as it clearly is our duty! Eaton! I take it you and those ruffians are pleased to die for His Britannic Majesty!'

The words were not completely out before a flat, hard report cut over them, and rendered them absurd. None of the men knew what had happened, then a blue cloud swirled along the ship's lee side, bringing the friendly stench of gunpowder.

'Oh *bastardy*!' yelled Sam, raising two clenched hands to heaven – but Bentley was charging for the aft companion-way, with Behar close behind. The great cabin was filled with smoke, and at the quarter light stood Captain McEwan, staring out beside the swivel gun that he had fired as a warning. Behar leapt at him and knocked him down before William could prevent it, and would have kicked him in the head had not the midshipman gone mad with anger.

'No!' he shouted. 'No, sir! Get back on deck this instant! Back!'

The young man's corpse was covered by a blanket, while the old captain lay and watched, quite unafraid. Then up above they heard a pistol shot, and Behar leapt for the door and disappeared.

'You may kill me if you wish,' said the captain, dully. 'Or arrest me. I do not mind.'

'Oh, to hell! To hell!' said Will, almost desperate. 'Just do not fire any more. Your word of honour!' And left without expecting a reply.

On deck, things were happening at breakneck speed. Eaton had leapt into the lower rigging with a pistol in his hand, presumably the one they'd heard below. He was waving it at the lugger as if in threat, and on her deck, at half a cable's length, men were enjoying this immensely, waving and jeering as at a baiting show. John Behar was balanced on the weather bulwarks, ready to jump or scramble down into the cutter, while Tom Tilley was tearing at the painter, which he'd belayed at the pin-rail a short while before. Sam was running to the weather, shouting for Eaton to join them or be left behind. He saw Will with obvious relief.

'Good man! Come quick! How is the old chap, have you spiked his guns? If we're quick we'll have them! We'll lay the swine on board!'

In short order they were in the boat and gone. Tilley dropped down last, with the painter, then it was fend off until they cleared the stern, up sails and away. Downwind of them the lugger had squared off, not intending, it appeared, to stay and fight. Will eyed the cutter's mainsail critically, telling Josh Baines to ease the sheet. Tilley had set the mizzen, on a long bumkin over the stern, and Behar was at the foresheet. They were going well, but he feared not well enough.

'I doubt we'll catch them, Sam,' he said. 'They cannot care much for what they've left on board the Katharine now they've seen how few we are.'

'The fact we're here is what will count, I guess,' said Sam. 'If the Biter left us she won't be far away is how they'll see it. Indeed, they're right, for is that not the tub herself? Look, there to starboard. No, there.'

Bentley saw her, although pretty far away. However,

she was on a course towards them, which for the luggermen would be enough. To tackle Navy men would be
to risk a halter anyway; to take on a full-armed tender
would be self-destruction.

'What, then?' asked Will. 'Do we abandon our free
traders and head for Kaye? He will not thank us if we run
ashore merely to get our heads broke, will he? More serious, she is showing us her heels, and when she hits the
shore she'll disappear like that' – he clicked his thumb and
finger with a snap. 'The tide must be not far from bottom.
We don't know these runs and creeks and swashes, do
we?'

Surprisingly, red-haired Eaton, on the tiller, gave a nod.

'I do, sirs,' he said. 'This is where I come from, int it?
She'll run out of water in twenty minutes will that lugger,
'cept in the main channels. I bet I know where she's
headed for.'

The sun was going down and it would soon be dark.
The wind was falling with the light and the sea had flat-
tened out considerably. Biter, not above a mile or two
away, would not come up with them, so Kaye could not
complain. Most likely, having seen where they were
headed, he would anchor off and wait for them. A soft
elation rose in William. Small boat, warm air, good breeze,
and fun ahead. If the luggermen thought they were pursuing her, they could never guess they had a pilot. When
darkness fell they could be on them like shadows.

The midshipmen exchanged a smile. Ahead, the land
was flat and featureless, a swathe of gleaming mud with
grass beyond it, a few low trees, some clumps of houses.
Up the creeklets there would be landing points, and villages, and inns, while Kaye and reinforcements would
never be far off if they had to cut and run. However, Will
considered, if Eaton thought it feasible, and him a native
of the area, it could not be too dangerous an undertaking,
else why suggest it? Eaton, from his expression as he sur-
veyed the land, was rather keen to get there and begin.

It took another hour to come to land, by which time it was dark. Not completely, for the clouds had mainly rolled away and the moon, though on the wane, was good. They had seen the lugger go down a long but narrow water that ended, Eaton said, at an old ramshackle shed among the coarse marsh grass, where she would dry out in half an hour so the men could carry the Katharine's goods ashore. He directed them down another, smaller creek – they having dropped the sails and masts some time before – where they found a small lagoon to tie up in, with a hundred feet of shallow mud to wade through till they hit the hard. They left 'the Rat' – Josh Baines – to mind the boat and keep her floating by whatever means, in case they had to pull out in a hurry.

To the surprise of Will and Samuel, there was a small town not far away – they saw its outskirts as Eaton led them along the marshy tracks he said would take them to the smugglers' landing den. Tom Tilley and Behar looked hungrily towards the outlined buildings, asking if there were taverns they could get a glass at, and showing unafraid when Samuel faced them down. As they got nearer to the shore again all talking died away, and they found themselves an elder clump from which to spy the men who toiled from the building to the lugger and back. Within five minutes they had counted eleven.

'Well, here's a bastard,' Sam whispered, cheerily. 'That's two to one and extra, and only three of us with guns. Thank God John Behar can use a cutlass and Tom's a giant! I say we pen them in their shelter and let off a shot or two, to make them think we are an army of dragoons. Then Will or me can cover them while you boys tie 'em up. What say you, Mr Eaton?'

'I say let's give it up,' muttered Tilley, through his twisted mouth. 'Get to an alehouse and drown out the world. What difference?'

The cunning look on Behar's face got more pronounced, but Will, without a thought, had taken out his pistol. He

193

checked the pan. The boatswain's mate shook his head.

'No shots, sir.' A slight grin creased his face. 'Whether it's to fear the traders or Behar and Tilley here it would be the end. They go armed for a certainty, and we're much too near the village. One report would be enough if we're unlucky. They're all in it, hereabout, and they're always on the watch. Not only menfolk; the maidens, wives, the children, all. If we can't pen them in without a shot, I say we'd best forget it.'

'Hah!' went Tom Tilley, and suddenly stood up, a great grey shape against the moon. As he lumbered forward, driven by his impatience or his thirst, they could see the last man of a line go into the wooden hut, with no one left outside. Sam leapt up to follow, casting a look of exhilaration back across his shoulder.

'Good man!' he hissed. 'Will, Behar, Mr Eaton! Quick – we have them caught like rats in traps! But fast!'

They did go fast, but as they neared the hut a young lad who'd been on watch quitted his bush much faster. He swerved like a frightened dog, shouted once, and darted off into the reeds. Behar without a word went after him, his lanky frame crashing through the bushes, his heavy club balanced like a projectile set to be thrown. One of the smugglers appeared in the doorway, but before he could raise the blunderbuss full to his shoulder, the form of Tilley hit him like a ram. The gun went off with an enormous bang and flash, but when the rest of them reached the door Tilley was scrambling to his feet while clawing off the gunman's clinging arms. Two more men leapt at him, while another two with pistols raised them to face off the intruders and a third scrambled through an opening in the rear wall to get into the night.

'Hold in the name of the King!' Sam shouted, levelling his pistol, and a gun in front of them threw a jet of smoke and fire at his face. Just behind him, William was aware that Shockhead Eaton had spun on his feet, assuming with a shock that he'd been hit. Sam had not and nor had he, and before the other man could fire, Tilley was interposed between them, with one of his assailants swinging through the air gripped by the upper arm in an enormous paw. What part of him hit the threatener they could not see, but his long horse-piece flipped above Tilley's head into a corner.

'Tilley! Leave them be!' Will shouted. 'They're beaten, man. I have them in my sights!'

'Look out!' roared Holt and thrust him to one side, hard enough to knock him over. As he did so there was a flash and bang in front of Will, at the back window, and he heard a thud behind his head as the ball hit wood. On the instant Sam fired, then dragged his cutlass out while running for the door.

'Eaton should have cleared that up,' he said. 'Cover them, Will, I'll not be long.'

More a case of saving them, at that moment. Tilley had been breaking arms it seemed, for the hut was filled with screaming of an agonising kind. The blunderbuss attacker had definitely been done, his right arm was snapped and angled horribly. The others had been backed into a corner, one crouched over on his knees and keening, the others trying to shield their heads. Tilley had picked up a horse pistol by the barrel and was using it as a hammer. One of the victims had a smashed and bloody face.

'Christ man, stop!' shrieked William, but Tilley did not. Oh Christ, thought Will, I'll have to kill him, too! He had seen this thing before, men blinded with their own rage, or power, or drunkenness of blood. Then the gun in Tilley's hand discharged itself and he hopped backwards like a giant frog with a shout of astonished fright that was almost comical, spinning the hot barrel away from him as if it were alive. He had picked up the wrong one, for a club, and the ball had missed him by a miracle. Not that, in later times, it made him noticeably more devout.

Sam was in the doorway, in the smoke, but he'd missed the comic act. His face was anxious, tight.

'There are horsemen coming. Eaton's disappeared, Behar ditto, and I missed the fellow out the back.'

'Eaton? But he's shot.'

'He's run. I didn't have him for a coward, neither. Listen. What to do? We haven't any time.'

'But who's on horseback? It may be the militia.'

'Aye shit, and so it may!' It was Tom Tilley, apparently in anger. 'Well I'm off, then! Shockhead said we'd get a drink, the bastard!'

In the time it took to reach the door, he'd gone. Will looked after him with an open mouth, amazed.

'Muzzle up,' said Sam, almost gently, touching Will's firearm. 'If you hit the floor, we're both dead men.'

The free traders, in the hiatus, had seized the opportunity to edge apart. Even the bloody one had a sardonic face.

'You'd better shoot one,' Sam said, not meaning it, Will guessed. But no, thought Will, not in cold blood. I never, ever, will do that.

'Should we go?' he said.

Samuel shook his head. They could hear hooves drumming. They could feel them through the earth. The smugglers who weren't in agony were almost smiling.

'We'd better take pot luck,' he said.

17

Unlike young Cecily, whose mouth healed rapidly, Mistress Wimbarton suffered a putrefaction that – starting slowly – seemed set to reach a gallop. Throughout the time her features, unlike Cecily's, were full and uncollapsed, but the very fullness became a horror to her as soft tissue swelled and brightened to a smarting glossy red. By the sixth day after her operation, when she called her husband in, she was in constant pain (beyond the agony of mind), and stank of dying flesh. When he had gone, to set the hunters on for Marcus Dennett, she called for water and a bowl from Dorothy, and spat out seven teeth, all pretence forgotten.

'Oh God, I hope they find him soon,' she said. 'If the other doxy's teeth aren't pushed in quick, I'll end up with gums as hard as yours are, Dot. Oh pshaa, bring me some brandy to wash this taste away.'

By the arrangement, Marcus Dennett was due to be back at the house that night or next morning to collect his second thirty pounds. Despite the condition of Milady was the darkest household secret, no one expected him to come, because household secrets had a way of getting out. In theory Dennett would bring back the other young maid if the first teeth had not taken, but village men who knew him knew he had lost the black-haired beauty (to their disappointment, as they all had hoped to buy some time on top of her), while his attempts at seducing a slow-wit milking girl two miles away to provide a substitute had been rebuffed by her three brothers, who (anyone could have told him if he'd asked) used her themselves.

Quite usually for a man who had failed to make a fortune

many times, though, Dennett was an optimist, and rather stupider than he should have been. With Deb gone he should have known his chances of replacement teeth were drastically curtailed, while his lack of experience as a tooth-replacer should have made him at least more wary of expecting simple success. Within four days his drinking friends started the rumours of something going wrong, and Dennett disregarded them as based on jealousy. On the fifth night it was reported by a thatcher who was seducing Sue, Milady's dressing maid, that 'the mistress had a gobsmell like a charnel house', but he would not concede a worry. In two days' time, he said, he would prove them wrong, and pick up his money into the bargain. He did not say how much, in case they robbed him in the woods. But everybody roughly knew, from Dot, and Sue and Joan.

One thing Dennett did not lack was courage, for he was a fiery, peppy little man. But he awoke before dawn on the sixth morning, lying on his pallet in his wagon in the woods, in something of a cold sweat. The rain was lashing at the canvas, and his straw and clothes were wet, and he sorely felt the lack of a young woman at his side, both as a comfort and to earn. He still had cash in plenty from the first half of the teeth transaction, but if the gossip over Mistress Wimbarton was right, what would the likely outcome be? Deborah was gone, the dim-wit milker had almost cost him a broken head or worse, and rumour had him marked down as a failure, not a rake. If he cut off this very morning it would cost him thirty pounds, but he could go to pastures new, where he would find more girls to seduce, or prostitute, or spirit to the Colonies; or even sell their teeth. Too late for corpse-breath Wimbarton, but that was her bad chance – the cash would still accrue. Ah – he would not lose all the thirty either, for he owed more than four from cards and dice, which if he cut he need not ever pay. Some of the local men were hard with it, but they would not follow far, they would not waste their time. The most he owed to any one was thirteen shillings.

No sooner thought than done, for Dennett knew he was at a disadvantage in the running stakes. The wagon was the main problem, for it was slow and obvious. Even if he took the posters off it, even the canvas cover, people would see him for a traveller, a seller, quack, musician or a mountebank, but if he left it and just took the nag, he gave up his home, his bed, and all his trade trickery. More, when he captured a new young woman or two, even a young lad (some customers were not fussy), he would have got shut of his rolling whorehouse. He cooked up some water for his coffee, kicked out the fire, ate some bread, but did not tarry long over his thinking. It was early, he knew the back roads well (that was a special skill he always exercised), and in twenty-four hours or thirty-six, when the magistrate began to wonder at his absence, he would be far away. He had a mind for heading west, Aldershot, Basingstoke, Andover maybe. He ran not from fear, but from intelligence. He liked that in himself. He much approved.

Unknown to him, seven hours later, Mr Chester Wimbarton unleashed his human dogs. At first it was only Jeremiah who was sent to make reconnaissance by horseback, but he returned within the hour to set up a company. Jeremiah was entitled steward on the estate, a name that fitted ill with his history and mien. His master, as a magistrate, had tried him once and might have hanged him if he had wished so. But he recognised in the lean and craggy highway robber – alleged! – the sort of fellow he could buy protection from, and loyalty as well quite possibly. Instead of hanging him he had struck a quiet deal beneath the court, and the man had walked free from there and, discreetly three weeks later, into service. He ran a gang of ruffians of his own choice as stablemen and household guards, whose reputation alone ensured the Wimbarton estate was not plagued, as some were locally, by livestock theft and burglary.

Dennett, to give him his due, had chosen empty roads,

avoided settlements however small, and travelled fast. The Portsmouth–London road was busy, so it was established quickly that he had not been seen thereon, unless he had abandoned his cart, which Jeremiah deemed unlikely, knowing as he did the breed that travelled as naturally as they breathed. He then sent scouts down every likely by-road, and himself made a wide circle with the quack's last-known camp its centre, crossing all the roads and tracks, checking passengers, and shepherd boys, and houses, huts or hovels on every one. His best assistant, Fiske, who was a fast and skilful rider, was the co-ordinator, bringing him the latest informations at predetermined rendezvous. The master had offered threats for failure, which Jeremiah had curled his lip at. Success meant gold, and both he and Wimbarton expected him to gain it.

In his wagon, next morning, Dennett was awoken by the nervous stamping of his horse. The trees were hissing in the wind, and rain spattered unevenly on the cover, but it was the horse's unaccustomed movement that disturbed him. For a moment he was content to listen, then remembered the situation he was in. After his experience with the two young men who'd stolen Deb and Cecily he had dug out his heavy pistol with a bell-shaped end for scattering loose shot, and he dragged it from underneath a tarry cloth in case. He tried to open the end of his cover with one hand, then put the gun down to jerk the sides apart. As he emerged, head bent inside to see his pistol, two strong hands gripped each of his upper arms, jerking him bodily out of the wagon and landing him upright between the shafts on the soggy ground. He had no boots on, although fully dressed, and the mud forced up between his toes unpleasantly. Beyond the two who had dragged him out there was a tall man on a horse, a man he'd seen at Wimbarton's before. Dennett sighed.

'I was on my way to your master's house this very day,' he said. 'He owes me thirty pound. 'Tis good of you to come to guide me, Jeremiah. How fares it with Milady?'

'Hah!' said Jeremiah. He almost smiled. 'Very well, except she has no teeth. Aye, very well!'

You're capable of killing me, thought Dennett. Quite capable. Ah well.

At first, when the horsemen had arrived, Will Bentley had had a rush of wild relief. There were eight of them, and they had the look of a militia or a local watch. Best of all, the man who led them was attired as a gentleman, with the authoritative air of a justice or a wealthy landowner. The two midshipmen had moved to just outside the open door, which Will covered with their only pistol to forestall a rush attack. The gentleman was not armed, but his out-riders had swords and pistols. William lowered his gun ostentatiously.

'Well met!' said Holt, as they reined in. 'We are the Impress Service, sir, our tender's lying off. We have caught a crew of villains here.'

The men inside the hut were surging forward, and Bentley eyed them nervously. When they were close enough to threaten, he raised his pistol.

'You, sir!' snapped the leading rider. 'Put up that arm immediately! How dare you threaten those poor men! Is it you caused them these injuries?'

The light inside was feeble and outside rather worse, but the blood and broken arm were clear enough. The smugglers were very close to Will and pressing harder, with smiles upon the nearest faces.

'But sir! They are smugglers! We caught them at it!'

There was a baying of denial from the men in front of him. One, large, black-haired with a deep cut on his cheek, reached out for the barrel of his gun. He had to shoot, or raise it clear. He could not shoot.

Beside him, with a lightning movement, Sam swished his cutlass point across and upwards, as if to prod the big man's neck.

'Call them off,' he shouted. 'If they press us we must kill them, we are officers of the King. Call them off, as they are clearly yours!'

'How dare you! I am here to see the law upheld! These men are injured, have you attacked them? You slander them with talk of smuggling, where is your evidence? You say you are the Impress, where are your warrants? If you have warrants, which local justice backed them? Not I, for certain! Anybody?'

There was a tendency to jeering in the smuggling gang, but well suppressed. Samuel, if not Bentley, knew quite clearly what had happened to them and his main aim was to get out of it unscathed. The militiamen had got down off their horses, and several pieces were levelled at point blank.

'Our warrant is with our captain,' he said quietly. 'I grant that in the heat of things . . .'

A louder jeer. The big man reached again for Bentley's pistol, so he thrust it fiercely into his belt.

' 'Tis not uncocked,' the man said, in a delighted voice. 'But you soon will be, won't you, sir! Unbollocked, also!'

'Make it safe,' the justice said, peremptorily. 'Then give it to Saunders there. You, sir' – to Samuel – 'that man will take your cutlass. You must come to the village, where we have a secure room for such as you. It looks that charges will be laid.'

'Aye, attempted murder!' came one voice from out of the hut. 'Look at Peter's arm! John's face is broken in!'

Sam raised his cutlass furiously, but not in threat. Immediately gun muzzles were thrust at him.

'We are Navy officers!' he shouted. 'These men are thieves!'

Will yelled: 'They have a lugger in the creek, full of contraband. All you have to do, sir—'

'Disarm them,' the magistrate curtly ordered. 'Young man, be careful that your pistol does not go off. Saunders, take it out. Aye, so. Now you, sir, your cutlass if you please.

Where are the others of your gang? What ship are you? I suggest you call them out if they're in hiding or it will be the worse for them.'

Will, feeling naked and confused, looked to Holt for guidance, but he was deep in rage. A smuggler and two militiamen made as if to jostle or strike at them, but Sam launched himself, unarmed, towards them, baring his teeth as if he might bite chunks. The men dropped back, and the magistrate gestured them away.

'No beatings, boys,' he said. 'The law will deal with these two in due time. Is anybody killed? Have they done murder? Where is your boat? What is your tender called?'

Neither Sam nor Will replied, nor would they answer any more questions of any sort. In a few minutes their wrists were bound, and each was led off by a horseman with a saddle line at a none too gentle pace, the justice staying behind, they guessed, to confer with the free trade men. The walk was not above a mile, and when they reached a dark, empty building on a marshy edge, lamps were lit and they were bundled in short order down cellar stairs into a small cramped room. It was damp and silent with a small, dirty window half below ground level, but their jailers did, at least, untie their wrists and leave them with a stump of candle when they locked them in; about two hours' worth. They listened in silence to the footsteps on the stair, then across bare wooden boards above them.

'Well,' said Sam at last. 'Here's a tale to tell the parish priest! I'd not have come ashore with you an' I'd known you were a criminal! Do you have a way to get us out?'

There was amusement in it almost, but Will could not respond. He was crushed by the weight of it, he was astonished more than anything. They had caught smugglers red-handed, been shot at, might have died. And they were locked up in a dungeon, with a magistrate claiming they had transgressed the law.

'Oh come on, Will,' said Sam, seeing his face. 'It could be worse, you know.'

'But how? Good God, Sam, I . . . well, speak up, then: but how?'

Sam walked to the window, which was stoutly built and would not open however hard he shook. Presumably it had outside bars as well, although it was too dirty to be seen through.

'Oh I forgot,' he said. 'You like the free trade gentlemen, don't you? And they did not kill us it is true, and they did not toss us headfirst in the mud or beat us senseless, so mayhap you're right, they're gentlefolk. That is one way we got off scot-free, my friend – we are still breathing. If we'd been Customs we might not have done so well. Or not been protected by that magistrate.'

Will turned this over in his mind. Without the justice, he could not deny, things could have gone much harder for them. But here they were, imprisoned, and who knew what next day might bring?

'They won't be hanging us and that's another thing,' said Sam, as if he'd read the thought. 'Lucky that mad bastard Tilley did not have time to kill the one whose face he smashed. I tell you, if they find him, no justice on a horse will keep him from hanging from a tree, but all we've done is overstep the mark. It could be weeks in prison though, less Kaye should buy us out. Months.'

'But did we break the law? The warrant thing—'

'We did not have "the warrant thing",' Holt interrupted. 'That's against the letter of the law, and it means everything if the courts down here should say so, which they will. Then the backing of the warrant, which we also did not have: another big transgression if they should care to deem it so. Then protections. We did not ask to see them of the free trade men, and free trade men have protections of the best in my experience. If ours did not last night they will tomorrow, you may depend on it – our magistrate will draw them up, let's say. Of course we're lucky, Will. They won't be hanging us.'

There were no chairs or benches in the room, but there

204

were steps up to the door. Sam sat first, and Bentley got beside him. They were silent, but the only sound outside was of a wind, moaning across the marshland wastes.

'Why do you say I like the smugglers?' he said finally. 'That is mad. I dislike all who break the law. Did I hang back tonight, in your opinion? Surely not?'

Sam did not reply. Will tried to remember if he had ever expressed sympathy with smugglers, but could not recall he had. His difficulty was, that in certain areas, and certain men he'd known . . .

'There was a man who saved my life,' he said. 'It sounds a stupid thing but . . .' He paused. Perhaps he should not be so open with Sam Holt. 'He called it a necessary trade,' he went on. 'He said it was condoned. And then they hanged him.'

Sam kept his silence, while Will remembered Jesse Broad. Another thought dropped in, a much more recent one.

'You said you'd hang them all. You said you hate them. Remember, as we came downriver? But Richard Kaye tended to my opinion, did he not?'

This elicited a brief laugh, as Will had hoped it might.

'You've made my case,' Sam said. 'If Kaye agrees with you, you must be wrong. Maybe it is a question of who you know and where you come from. Your man sounds fine, and so God keep his soul. To me it is a vile trade, and where I lived and grew, so it was applied. They work as families in my part, except such families could only live in hell. I've seen two hundred men run stuff ashore, nay three hundred with the batmen and musketeers, and I've seen them murder, burn and beat. My father, who believed the good in man, refused to stand for some of them in court after a bloody incident on the Adur, and it ruined him in many ways. They did not offer violence in his case, the backers were a very subtle crew. All other lawyers in the area, all judges, magistrates, even clerks, refused to deal with him, they cut him and ignored him, froze him out.'

'Judges?' said William. 'But surely . . .'

He stopped. There was a silence. Sam scratched the stubble on his chin, quite noisily. He had a fierce black whisker growth, and it was many hours since they had shaved.

'A necessary trade,' he said, musingly. 'Aye, there's truth in that if not merit, I suppose. Yes judges, Will, and merchants, bishops, Navy officers. Kaye gives smugglers the clearest of clear berths, and it's not just because he likes to drink cheap tea, I fear. This eastern part's too close, too near the Lowlands and the enemy, the trade is ruthless, dangerous, it's protected by the great. If that is not the case in Hampshire, then God preserve it so!'

Will did not know, that was the truth of it. In the part of Hampshire where he lived smugglers had been hanged, but the tales of violence chapmen told, or balladeers, tended to come from farther east. He could recall one Customs rider murdered in a churchyard by the sea, but that was a song from long ago, when he had been a child. Broad had not been a violent man, far from it, but surely, if he'd been set upon by officers on land he would have fought, and killed to get away.

'He had a wife and baby child,' he said. It was sudden, he had not intended it. Sam cocked his head, no expression on his face, and waited. The opportunity was made for Will to stop. Will sighed.

'I went there once. After Broad was hanged, long afterwards. That was his name,' he said. 'I went to the place he came from, he and his friend Hardman, who also died. It is a little place, a hamlet at the head of Langstone Haven, I sail the waters in my yawl. I beached there once to mend my rigging.'

'By God,' said Sam. 'What happened? Would not the men have set on you, alone, a Navy officer?'

'No men,' said Will. 'Just women and small ones. I thought I saw his wife, but I could only guess at that. Fair, and in her twenties, with a boy. The men were . . . out fishing, maybe? Or maybe decimated. It was very poor.'

'Or out upon the trade!' said Sam, jocularly. 'Well, I think you're brave, or else foolhardy. You did not speak? Make yourself known? Perish the thought, I guess, an officer from off the Welfare.'

Perish the thought indeed. He had not been an officer by then, at least an active one, for many many months. He did not even know if Broad's existence on the Welfare or his fate as mutineer had been brought to the knowledge of his wife and home. But if any rumours had filtered from the prison hulks he had no doubt they would have blackened him, to hell and further. No one had spoken out for Broad at the court martial, not him, not anyone. That was still in him; deep hidden, but a burning, bitter shame.

'They would not have known me as an officer,' was all he said. 'I sail not dressed even as a gentleman, I was just a youth. But I did not speak to them.'

'And was she very fair?' asked Sam, shifting on the stone step they sat on. 'Christ, my bum is sore! Too fair to be a blackguard, is that the root of it! I'll say this, Will, for a chap with such a not-melt-butter look, you have a great eye for the sex! I'd drink to Deborah right now!'

There was nothing Holt would not jest about, however inappropriate, but to Will's surprise this one struck a target in him. He saw Deb in his mind, clear as a picture, first naked then – as if he'd censored it – dressed in her simple bedroom garb. The pang was fresh and sharp as ever, he ached for her. God, days only but it felt like a year. He'd had his chance and missed it, when might it come again, if ever? They were in a dungeon now, and very far from the Biter, London never mind. To Will, she seemed to fade away, still beckoning. But the hurt was vivid as a knife.

'Talking of blackguards,' he said, as if to tear his mind away from her, 'what of Mr Eaton and our gallant boys? That old man on the Katharine called us worse than smugglers, and true it is that lot stood firm together when

207

the game was on. I expected nothing of Tilley and Behar, I suppose, but Eaton is a warrant officer. I thought he had been shot, but he was running! If we had died, it would have been his fault.'

The candle end was guttering, but neither of them had thought to put it out. Seeing it flutter to a close made them wistful. Sam's attempt at heart came rather hollow.

'You cannot blame them, when there was a drink about. Blood, Will, they are British seamen! As to Eaton, I'm as lost as you are, I confess it. I've always known him as a fiery little beast. Tom Tilley mentioned drink though, and Shockhead as a part of the same gabble, so maybe Mr Boatswain's Mate's a slave to it and something was set up. That candle's going soon. Feared of the dark, are you?'

When it was dark, they both lay on the earthen floor to ease their bones, having eased their bladders, reluctantly, into a corner of their not-extensive quarters. Sam talked of drink and maidens for some while, but William made few replies, despite he examined Deborah from every angle in his head for many minutes. He decided, sensibly but with reluctance, that he would never see her again, and convinced himself that he would learn to live with it, it being, after all, an outcome that would greatly please his mother if she ever got to hear of it. Then, deciding he was half delirious or mad, he turned to much more earthy things, like what if Sam were wrong, and they were hanged as would-be murderers? From there to that young officer, shot dead on Katharine by Slack Dickie Kaye. He would have liked to ask Sam's thoughts on that, and if there was likely any chance the law would question their captain on that act, unexplained and inexplicable. But he knew the answer anyway, and Sam might be asleep. He saw Kaye with the pistol's action covered with his hand, and saw his look and heard his voice. The Press was hated worse than any smugglers. He knew the reason why.

* * *

He must have slept, because he was awoken with a shock. He was in a black hole, the deck not planks but earth, the smell not— He was awake! There was a spill of light at the edge of the door, a man's face peering round. Beside him Sam jerked upright with a gasp, twisted his head, then blinked in a flash of lantern light. A voice then, rough and jovial. A voice they recognised.

'Rouse out, rouse out, sirs! Soon be cock-crow and we've far to go!'

'Bastard!' said Samuel, in complete surprise. 'Mr Eaton, what do you here? We've marked you for a rogue, a bastard, a coward and a poltroon!'

The face beneath the red mop creased in smiles.

'The others would have left you, sirs,' he said. 'I had to knock Tilley down, which I trust you will remember if my pension's in dispute! Thank God he'd drunk three bottles or he'd've broke my bleeding back. Come on quick, before they kill some bugger else.'

'What?' said Sam. 'Are they here? Jesus, I'll never have the measure of these men. Did they not run, then? And you? What happened?'

There were noises up above them, some crashes, then a door slamming. Eaton turned, glanced back, then led them off across the outer cellar.

'Oh they ran,' he said, 'but not for badness, just for drink, I guess. No, Behar chased the guarding boy then lost him, then Tilley heard you say I'd gone, he says.'

'I did,' said Sam. 'You had, for Christ's sake! Come on, Shockhead, admit it was a ruse!'

Eaton did not deny it, but his face was jovial in the lantern light. He hushed them when they reached the stairhead, and all three peered down along the passage to the front door. It was hanging open, despite they'd heard it slam seconds before.

'We split the lock,' he said. 'Tom Tilley did it with an issue cutlass, and smashed that too. I doubt the Navy Board will charge it to him, eh! I did not run exactly, sir, but I had to hide my face. When we dashed in the hut, I knew the men and they'd have recognised me, my village is three mile away, that's all. Bad enough I joined the Navy, but if they knew I was an Impress man, and hunting down the night-time gents to boot, well! I ran to save myself, in hope of saving you two later. I'd said to John and Tilley, merely, that I'd lead them to a water hole when we'd done our business. But they were thirstier than me.'

His voice was low, but as they approached a side doorway he touched his lip for silence. He was not a large man, but powerful and full of sense, so they let themselves be guided without demur. Will remembered he had thought him stolid when they'd met, silent and unwilling. He had rather changed his mind.

'I will not go in, an't please you,' Eaton breathed. 'I left it to the shipmates who aren't known. Please God they haven't murdered them.'

Will went in first, in trepidation, but no one was dead. Eaton need not have feared recognition, either, for the three men there, tied back to back, legs thrust out in star pattern, had their shirts pulled up and over their faces and their heads and knotted. They were wriggling and thrashing violently, but sailors' knots – even drunken sailors' knots – were more than a match for that. The sailors, though, were gone.

After a look, both Will and Sam went out again to Eaton, who was standing at the broken entrance door. It was still dark, but the light of morning was rising in the sky.

'They've gone,' said Will. 'Did you give them more instructions?'

Eaton's laugh was short and harsh.

'Instructions is it, sir? I said I had to fight to get them here. I found them in a barn with drink they'd stole, so maybe they've gone back, or more like they've gone to meet Rat Baines down at the creek. We'd better leg it, sirs, and lively.'

'Will Baines be there?' said Sam. 'He's a sorry coward, ain't he?'

Eaton, not asking their opinion, was pushing down the lane at cracking pace. Sam's legs were man enough, but Will was forced to jog to stay with them.

'If he's good at anything it's staying alive,' said Eaton. 'He'll have hauled offshore and hidden in case anyone was looking, but he knows not to have left them two in the lurch. It's us I'm worried over. Be quick, or they'll have gone without us, if they 'ant already.'

He skirted dark houses on the edge of the town, and led through marsh and wood without hesitation or a doubt. When they reached the lagoon, though, it was dark and still as death. All three listened, when their breath had eased, but the only sounds were air and water, and a distant, peaceful barking. The tide was about full, all mud covered, last evening's wind quite gone. But even in the stillness they could hear no oars or voices.

'Should we call?' asked Will.

No one replied. They strained their ears. Sam made a small note of disgust.

'They'd not call back is my guess. What think you, Mr Eaton?'

'Less noise the better, sir. Dawn's not far off and they may find you missing anytime. London's your best chance, ain't it? If you've got money you could get horses, you could do it in two days. Sooner if you're quick and lucky.'

'But Lieutenant Kaye,' said William. 'Do you not think he'll come in for us? At least they'll tell him what has happened, and that we're out of jail.'

'Aye, and there's a justice and militia after us,' Sam said. 'Attempted murder, was it? Assaulting protected citizens for the Press? No warrant for a start-off? Some captains might care to start a civil war for two bloody midshipmen, but Mr Kaye ain't that man, or am I wrong?'

'Any road,' said Eaton, 'Slack Dickie's caught some men

this time out. Beg pardon, sirs, I mean Lieutenant Kaye. He'll likely want to go and spend the profit.' He showed them a frank challenge with his eyes, alive with humour. 'Piss it up against the wall, or shag some top-notch doxies. Begging it again, if you think me forward.' He gave a grunt of mirth. 'No room to call him, really, have I? I'll stay down here a day or three myself, though Maggie would not thank me to hear me dub her whore.'

'A village maid?' said Sam. 'So that was where you run to, was it? Afraid of being recognised, my arse!'

Eaton denied it, but without any heat. Will found this joking, officer and man, extraordinary. And was the boatswain's mate, in theory sadly missed by Biter, planning to take a few days' furlough, for some tumbles with a wench?

'By God,' he said. 'I know captains who would flog a man for less. Running's a hanging matter, come to that.'

'Aye, but you'd stand up for me,' Eaton replied, chuckling. 'Didn't I just spring you from the choke? In any way, Slack Dickie don't flog, he can't be bothered. Sir,' he then said, 'we must none of us be found round here so go, for mercy's sake. I'll show you the best ways to cut inland to where you can lie up as long as you think fit. Flaxton's the place to get a horse if you've the wherewithal, I have a kinsman who will set you right. He might even take your Navy clothes off you, for safety's sake. God's eyes, though – let's be off.'

In twenty minutes it was light, and Sam and Will were alone in a narrow country road. They had a long hard way ahead of them, but figured on safety once they'd cleared off the coastal parts. They did not look like gentlemen; indeed, either one of them could have gone apprentice to a tramp. It was too cold to throw away their blue, though, and replacements were too costly. In these parts any sight of them could mean danger, quick and deadly. They thought to spend a lot of time in ditches.

18

They laid Charles Warren's body – what was left of it – in the parlour of a small inn at the village near Joe Simple's father's house. Joe had found it on a Friday, but it was Monday night before the local justice and the coroner were told. When they arrived, with a constable and the undertaker's men, the corpse was in a sorry state, there having been, it seemed, some attempts at dismemberment. Joe's father insisted that he'd found the man that very day, and had not touched his poor remains in any way. In fact, the men he'd called in to his house had wanted it reburied, gone for good, but could not bring themselves to help him move it. When he had tried, an arm had pulled clear off, while the leg he'd dragged on had broken at the charred knee joint. Sickened, he had told them his boy Joe would never keep a secret such as this – which turned out not so, although it was believed – and who could track them by discovering a cadaver in a field? In the end they'd ridden off, telling him to keep it secret for as long as he thought fit, in hope the dogs would scatter it.

The inn was thronged with gawping Johns and Jills, and the landlord, despite the foul smell, did a most satisfactory trade. The justice had knowledge of the Customs search for missing men, although they were quite far from any sea, so despatched a man to Portsmouth on a reasonable horse and told him to seek out the collector at the Customs House on Point. Within half a day the little inn was bursting at the seams with officers near as lathered as the horses being tended in the yard, and their fury and upset at the dreadful state of their dead colleague meant an increase in the already roaring trade. More villagers poured in because of the commotion and reports of gruesome sights, the news spreading like a fire in dry grass. By early evening it was riotous. Three landlords from houses within five miles brought extra beer in hired carts, and got a handsome price from their lucky colleague, despite the ale was churned up and undrinkable by normal standards (not prevailing). Charles Warren, in his latter life an undercover man, became in death a wild celebrity.

Sir Peter Maybold got the news at an hour not far from midnight. He had gone to see an opera, and by arrangement, meet his wife Laetitia there. She had not turned up, despite he had a family box, with wine, and food, and friends to share the pleasure with them, so he had a miserable evening listening to warblings about unrequited love and cuckoldry. He could not leave as he was playing host, his disaffection fed continuously by the veiled amusement he detected in his companions' glances. When he did get home he found a riding officer, half dead with road-dust and exhaustion, and Laetitia with shiny eyes and an elevated mood, despite she said she'd spent the hours alone and not quite well in her darkened boudoir – having foolishly given the footmen an evening's liberty and making do with just a maid or so. The officer, who forty minutes earlier had watched a rider leave as he had reached the lane up to the mansion, said nothing, but knew he had another tale to add to the collection.

This man was Sunfield, of Portsea Island, and he had not known Warren. But as he told the news, the sadness of it all came home to him, very strong. As a Customs officer he had been filled with fury, naturally, because any injury or hurt to one was by proxy meant for all. But telling this fat personage the grisly details, and seeing that Sir Peter's hurt was to his office and his standing, not to his heart, the loneliness of Warren's life and death came in on him. He had died and been thrust inside a hayrick and set fire to, and mutilated. And Sir Cuckold hoped it was a step upon a road.

'Ah horrible!' he cried. 'Ah horrible! That the poor man should have suffered such a thing! However, it is good we've found the corporeal remains at last. I only wish it had been an officer who could have had the fortune. A farmer, you say? Was he of quality?'

Sunfield shook his head, his features set.

'I'm sorry, sir, I know nothing of the discovery. We Portsmouth officers were called out by the coroner, whose name I do not know. We have searched up hill and down. Poor Warren was well hidden, and then burnt.'

Sir Peter tutted, pulling at his wig. He had a horrid feeling that they were nowhere further on.

'So many men, so little achieved,' he muttered. Then, catching Sunfield's face, he added: 'Nay, but it is not their faults, nor yours, I'm certain all have done their best. It's only that . . . God damn it, where is the other man!? Charles Yorke! They are laughing at us, they are making play!'

Most likely dead as well, thought Sunfield. He had seen the rotting effigy of Warren, and he saw and smelled it yet. Sir Peter would not risk his nostrils on such corruption. Oh Christ, poor Warren; and poor Yorke. He had known neither, but felt he knew them at this moment.

'Who is in charge down there?' asked Maybold. 'Is your collector gathering the strands, or is it someone else? Price is the man, Adam Price of Portchester, he is the man for me.' He jerked, bodily, as if hearing what he'd said. A flush spread across his jowls. 'Nay, I'm speaking out of turn. That will go no further, do you understand? Pocock, is it? Do you understand?'

'Sunfield. Aye, sir,' said Sunfield, 'you may depend on it.' I do not say on what, he added, to himself. You cuckold bastard. That swine Price is just your sort, and all.

'Aye. Well,' said Maybold, tiredly. 'You must forgive me, Mr Sunfield, this is very hard, is't not? Poor Charlie, I knew him, I knew him many years. I wish to Christ I knew how to catch them, what? To run them down and string them up. So very, very infamous.'

Both of them, for a moment, were close to tears, with Sunfield, exhausted, the more surprised by it. Suddenly he'd seen through Maybold's mask of privilege, realising that he could suffer for these two poor lost officers as well as he could. They stood for a while, their eyes holding, their bodies awkward. Then Maybold shrugged.

'Fine men,' he said. 'We must catch the perpetrators, and I'm sure we will. You know the place, don't you? Why is it so hard? Why is there so little information? Every officer I have is on the search, every avenue has been explored. So very, very hard.'

Sunfield, sadly, had nothing to offer that he thought might help, and shortly Sir Peter called a man to find him a bed behind the stables. Alone, the Surveyor General poured himself a brandy and sat disconsolate, wondering, to the bottom of his soul, what other they could do. If the officers at the heart of the matter were flummoxed, what use was any order from the top?

Worst of all, he thought – with a familiar twinge of pity for himself – was the next step, unavoidable. Tomorrow, first thing in the morning, he would have his carriage readied to set out for Langham Lodge to tell Sir Arthur Fisher. Good, in one way, that the body found was Warren and not his nephew, but . . . No – Sir Arthur would still hope, and so must he. These men, he told himself, were taken for a reason and Yorke, not Warren, was the senior and could still against the odds turn up. Sir Peter had no warmth for Arthur Fisher in particular, finding him a little acerbic and puritanical for his taste, but strangely, over this, he felt he recognised the kind of pain that was involved. Maybold had no sons nor other young close relatives, but he had a wife, who tortured him. Gazing into the dying embers of the parlour fire, inhaling brandy fumes from his cupped glass, he saw Laetitia as a wayward child who was similarly lost to him. Beloved, lost, but the focus of eternal hope.

Tomorrow morning – *this* morning, it was after one

o'clock – he would go and tell Sir Arthur he must not give up the fight.

The journey back to London cost Will Bentley and Sam Holt quite dear in time and money. They had only been walking for about an hour after parting from Shockhead Eaton when they guessed an alarm had been raised, for the sound of horsemen galloping, on such roads at such an hour, was a thing to be remarked on. They took immediately to a ditch, getting wet about it as it was shallow with a dire lack of cover. Neither could raise his head enough to see for certain, but they agreed four horsemen clattered by, and they were riding hard. Out of the mud, they looked comical, but were not inclined to laugh.

'Bastardy,' said Sam, in a conversational voice. 'I had hoped for longer before they found us out. They weren't looking though, they were going too fast for that. I guess they're gathering, then dividing into posses.'

Will was wringing water from a sleeve. The flat landscape was not made for hiding in, and his nerves were fluttering.

'Eaton said this road was hardly used,' he said. 'Do you think we ought to trust him?'

'Oh no,' said Sam. 'The man's a liar. Let's take any road except the ones he recommended. You choose.'

'But there is no—' William broke off, as Sam shot a grin at him. 'You jest too much,' he added, rather sourly. 'And what if we go to Flaxton and his kinsman is waiting not with mounts but magistrates? Why did he not come with us? We should have ordered him.'

Sam had started off along the road again, but faster than before.

'Aye,' he said. 'And he'd have quaked. Whatever else he is though, Shockhead ain't magic, is he? When we get to his cousin's we'll be the first. Come on, play the man, there!'

They strode at their best pace (it damn near killed Will,

with his normal legs compared with Holt's lanky ones), which led them fairly quickly to some better cover, and another road the boatswain's mate had mentioned. This was deep and narrow, hardly suitable for mounted men at speed, so they felt more confident, although they saw too many people out in the fields for comfort. At a cross-roads in about two hours they came upon a positive gang of roughheads who may – who knew? – have been on the keevee for them, and they went to ground until the way was clear. It was mid-afternoon before they got to Flaxton, a distance, Eaton had said, of only about ten miles, which they recognised by the broken steeple on the church that he had told them of. On the outskirts they had to hide for ages because some horsemen rode in ahead of them. Even without their blue coats, which they'd bundled up when heated by the walking, they'd have stood out from the local country sorts like broken thumbs.

Worse was to follow when they reached the cousin's farm. The dogs were called off quick enough, although Sam got a bitten hand, but the woman who had control of them was as suspicious as anybody could have been. Eaton's name was acknowledged only grudgingly, their claim to be officers of the King was greeted with a sort of grumpy hauteur, and she suggested anyone could have picked up a pair of Navy coats in any gutter. What's more, she said, news was abroad of two criminals who'd escaped, and probably there would be rewards. Sam, who had retained an extraordinary good humour throughout all this, smiled very broad and then produced his purse. Things began to change.

Even when the husband returned, however, negoti-ations dragged slowly. This man, less miserable than his wife but just as mercenary, could sympathise with their problem, so he said, if they would sympathise with his. He could see his way to hiring out two horses, but how would he ever get them back? If they rode to London then clearly he would lose the beasts for ever (he spoke of London as of some hell of vile and foreign dreadfulness), and if they went to Chatham and from thence picked up the stage, what then? He would have to trust them to leave them at an inn, he would have to trust the innkeeper not to sell them on but hack them back, and if the two gentlemen (said with remarkable disdain) were apprehended when they reached the town or on the road before, would he not be held responsible for aiding and abetting? Thus it was that they became the owners of two broken-winded nags, with blankets but no saddles, at a price a gipsy would have blushed to ask. A knockdown price, he told them earnestly, because they had been recommended by his kin. Nobody else would have had them for that money . . .

They left in full dark, on a dire, moonless night with enough rain, at least, to wash their outer garments, and their progress was desperately slow. The wife had sold them supper the night before, and sold them bread and cold bacon and some beer for their sustenance, but by the time they saw the dawn they both felt starving. They figured out they were well to the west of Chatham, but they were still avoiding all but the smallest roads, so they could not be sure. After discussions they decided they might breakfast at an inn, but as they approached one, two men in army coats hove into sight the other side of it, and turned into the yard. Probably coincidence, almost certainly they were not seeking them, but neither was keen to risk it. They found a shepherd's hut beside a stream, hobbled the horses, washed, and slept a bit. Later that morning, six miles further on, they bought a breakfast off a farmer's wife, then slept an hour more.

By now one horse was lame, but both of them were determined that they must press on. While they had slept, the wife had sent a lad to seek her man, and Sam awoke to find him examining the crippled horse. He was a big man, ill-favoured, but a different proposition than they feared. As Sam shook Will awake a smile transformed his hairy face, and he greeted them right heartily. They'd sounded out the woman, who had heard of nothing suspicious on the road, and nor had he, apparently. Navy men en route to join a ship, they said, and he asked no questions, save where did they get so poor a horse and would they like a trade for her?

'If she's so poor, why trade?' asked Sam. 'She's lame and damn near worthless.'

The farmer nodded happily.

'I have a worse,' he said. 'She's due for knackering, but she'll last a day or two, by which I mean she'll walk to London easy, for what she is ain't lame. Your horse will soon find its feet given a day or two of rest, then'll suit me champion for a light job I've got on. And me wife'll throw another meal into the bargain, this one free. What say you?'

'Have you got a razor?' Will asked. Food sounded good, but some luxuries were even pleasanter to contemplate. The farmer, who was bearded, stroked his chin.

'Oh aye,' he said, 'I do. I have the steel, but not the application and I like my nose. We have a bit of soap though, and hot water, an' you want it?'

The deal was struck.

For logic's sake, and the sake of duty, both Will and Sam knew fine well what they should have done. With two horses that could achieve a reasonable pace, and no longer afraid to use the high road out of Kent, they should have struck out for the south Thames bank as near to London as the nags would take them without collapsing, then hired watermen to pull them up to town. Biter, most probably, would be moored by the receiving hulk, and they could lay along her and present themselves as fit for work or punishment, as Kaye should deem appropriate. Neither of them could frankly contemplate such action.

'Sam,' said Will, as they jogged along the muddy road near nightfall, 'if I said Dr Marigold's – what would you say?'

He knew Sam now, and they were friends. It fell into Will that he had never been so comfortable with one his own age. He trusted him to laugh, to mock at the suggestion; but he trusted him.

Sam mocked.

'Deborah!' he said. 'My God, Will, one sight of that maid's quim and you were lost for ever! How will it sound at the court martial, do you think? "I realised on the London road I had to get a look of it. I knew my good commander would fully understand." It seems not fair *I* have to hang as well, just for friendship's sake!'

'There is Annette,' said William. 'You've paid more for the horses than I have, so I could treat you.'

The rain had stopped but the road was like a bog. The heavy traffic of earlier had died away so the going was easier, but both men were exhausted. Light-headedness brought its own rewards.

'Aye, true,' said Sam. 'That is a fine prospect. You've not seen Annette yet, have you? Not "had the pleasure", so to speak. She is not plump and gorgeous like your one, more a whippet, muscle and lean flesh. Like this poor old horse was, maybe ten year ago: a very splendid, brisk, and noble ride! A treat indeed Annette would be. But talking of them – will these old nags make it that far?'

'We could take a boat still,' Will responded. 'Abandon them at the ferry steps, or sell them, trade them for the passage, maybe. And I doubt we'll hang, Sam. Only Shockhead knows where we got to, and that was days ago. Or was it yesterday? And when will Shockhead bother to return?'

'Another one mad for the doxies,' laughed Sam Holt. 'Well, it is shame on us, for sure!'

Will did not argue, but for him it was not shame. It had wrenched his heart to leave her, and his heart was craving, now they were on the road to London, to take up with her where they had left it off. Her face was plain before his eyes, and her black eye was faded to pale brown, which meant, she'd said, she'd soon be put to whoredom if she

221

weren't lucky; but even that was not what hurt him, it was just her absence. He had tried to sort it out in the days and nights since he had seen her, whether it was her beauty he was mad for or something else he did not understand, but it was questions still, not answers. All he knew with certainty was that he had to go to Marigold's and not the Biter, and that was all about it.

'On the other hand,' he said, 'if we take a boat and see the Biter, might we not tend to stop? Out of sight is out of mind they say, but pulling past her when we ought to be on board . . . Just possible someone might even see us.'

Sam snorted.

'If you believe in miracles,' he said. 'There's a better reason for not using the watermen, though. The tide's against us, isn't it? It will be running hard out for hours yet, as I compute it, which will add to the expense. We've got the horses, they are paid for, so why not ride 'em? Although a hull beneath would ease my aching arsebones, to be sure. I've rowed against the Thames ebb in my time, for longer hours than I've sat this blasted horse, but my bum's never been in half the state it's in today!'

Sometimes they talked, sometimes they rode in the silence of companionship, once they stopped at an inn and took some beer and bread and cheese. As they approached the outlying villages the roads grew busier again, and in places they wished they had not lost their weapons to the law, although they did in truth appear too dusty and unkempt to be prime targets for the robbing bands. By the time they reached London itself the pace had grown funereal, both horses limping and in urgent need of rest. They entered the road of Dr Marigold's with great relief, but did not try to urge the horses on. When they dismounted stiffly in the yard, both beasts dropped heads immediately, one almost staggering as it balanced on three hoofs. An ostler sauntered up to them.

'Christ, sirs! Come far, have we? Them nags is bollocksed, beg your pardon!'

He had taken them for some sort of scruffs and neither of them, for the moment, cared. They wanted beer, hot water, food. And, for Will Bentley, Deb.

'Look after them,' said Samuel, roughly. 'Treat 'em like the King's own, they've done very well. Old Marge is in, is she? My friend here needs her, quick.'

The way he spoke, the cut of his blue coat maybe, asserting through the highway filth of miles, made the ostler more aware of what they were, or might be. He stooped to pick up reins.

'Aye, she's in the usual place, I think. She may go armed though, isn't it, after last night's shenanigans. Go easy, sirs, is my advice.'

His expression was expectant, his gay speech a question, scarcely veiled. From their blankness, he knew they did not know.

'Why, you have been away a pace!' he said. 'Oh, such excitements as we've had, sirs! Indeed, some people think we all should carry guns, only Marigold won't pay, will he?'

Will had an odd sensation, of creeping flesh, of weird anticipation, though God alone knew why. Sam similarly, it would seem. Without a hint of warning he shot out his hand to seize the ostler's tunic, just beneath his adam's apple. Suddenly his face was pressed up to the man's, his expression intense.

'What excitements?' he demanded, low but sharply. 'What's happened here? Tell quick.'

The man pulled back, frightened, and Sam let him go.

'Pardon,' he said. 'There was an armed band, sirs, last night. There was shooting, and they took a maid. One of Mrs Putnam's, he said he owned her, he said she'd run away. The leader of the villains, sirs, there was seven of them, our men were overwhelmed.'

The cold in William's gut was horrible. No point in asking who it was, he knew. Sam, much more experienced, who knew such things were not uncommon where men used maids as earning things and would fight to save their property, thought he also knew, but asked.

'Deb? Was it the dark one, Deborah?'

The ostler nodded.

'And was she hurt?' said Will. 'Was anybody shot?'

'Aye, sir,' said the ostler, almost frightened by the intensity of the question. 'One maid has died. Not that one, though, not the buxom one, she was just took away. A poor maid that was her friend and lost her teeth. She tried to stop it, sir, and she got bulleted in the face. Some might say—'

'Oh God,' said Will. 'Oh God, oh God, Sam.'

'Marge thought it were relief,' the ostler mumbled. 'But if you knew her, like . . .'

'Come on, Will,' said Sam, taking his elbow, gripping firm. 'We'd best go in and talk to Margery.'

19

Mrs Putnam, that most jovial of women, no longer had a smile upon her face. They found her in her corridor at her table, from a distance looking as if nothing had changed. But when she saw tall Sam she rose, and when she recognised his companion she raised her arms then dropped them to her sides, a hopeless gesture.

'Mr Sam,' she said. 'And Mr Silence. Now here's a pretty turn-up for the books.'

Will stood in front of her, but saw no comfort in her face. He tried to speak but had nothing to say.

'She is all right,' she said. She put a hand towards him. 'Not Cec, poor thing, but your one, Deborah. It was she they came for, but they wanted she alive. She will be back again, she might, you never know.'

'What?' said Sam, Will staying wordless. 'Margery, what can you mean? Why will she come back, is not she kidnapped by the little rogue?'

'What, do you know him?' Her face cleared slightly. 'Why then, there must be hope! I only meant she's run away before, and could again.' To Will she said, as if explaining, 'When maids run off to London to earn a crust they don't go home again, do they? She'll turn up in some vile house or other when this man's sick of her or she gets free, and Marigold has spies aplenty, he'll find her out. Dr Marigold thinks highly of Deb, as I've told you. You did not believe me though, I guess.'

Some vile house, thought Will, horrified. Then thought, no, it's not so bad as that, because it must be Dennett who had got her.

'He'll have taken her back to that villain's near Sir A's!'

he said to Sam excitedly. 'Mistress, when did this occur? A small, ill-favoured man with dirty hair? No wig, pockmarks? Sam, it is Dennett for a thousand pound!'

'It was five or six of them or more,' said Margery. 'In cloaks and hats and such. The one who got her was exceeding small I think. I did not see to notice. Poor Cecily, you see. A ball—'

Sam cut across her.

'But it means he wants her teeth!' he said to Will. 'Else why come for her and risk Marigold's heavy boys? Christ, Will, that woman's teeth must not have took, and Deb was second string! Dennett's done like Margery says they do, he's combed the houses till he got wind of her. She'll be back in Surrey long—' He broke off. Will's face was sick. Sam continued carefully. 'If it was last night, Will, she's likely been at the magistrate's some good long time, all afternoon at least. Of course, there's no saying he'll have done the operation. There's no saying they could hold her down to even try. She's a good strong fighting girl.'

'She's a devil for the running, too,' Margery put in. 'Whatever,' she said, abruptly and direct to Will. 'She's only a poor whore, ain't she? What matter if she an't got teeth, so long as she can eat? Some men like whores to have no teeth, some toothless maids find better ways to earn their bread than whoring. She is a good tough girl, I liked her and it's a crying shame. Poor Cecily is dead though, and that's far worse.'

Will was distracted, he could not take it in. His bones ached, and his heart and head, he was exhausted, he was thirsty. Mistress Putnam, having said her piece, stood foursquare in the passageway, uncompromising.

'Well,' said Sam Holt, mildly, 'it is a crying shame, Margery, that is a fact. What o'clock is it, dost think? Midnight or later? We have had a long and bitter ride. Is there a bed that we can purchase for the night?'

'A bed?' said Will, bemused.

'With or without a trollop in it?' laughed Margery. 'Annette is busy for the moment, but she'll likely strike a deal. What, both of you at once, for all the night? It is a narrow bed as you well know, Captain Sam!'

'Now stop!' said Will. 'Sam, what are you saying? Stop.'

There was real concern on Margery's plump face, but only for the state she saw him in. She reached out to touch him, but he almost flinched. Sam made a noise of sympathy.

'It seems a better way than going back on board, that's all,' he said. 'What if Slack Dickie wants a fight? I'd rather face that in the morning, wouldn't you?'

'What morning? When?' Will shook his head. 'Sam, we have to ride to Surrey, to Sir A's! If we are quick, who knows, we might save her! Good God, man, Dennett is a murderer this time, you do not think to leave her to her fate?'

Both Sam and Mrs Putnam were uneasy. To Sam it looked like crystal that whatever was intended on Deborah would by long ago have been achieved. Margery, more cynical, thought the younger of the two men must be drunk, or slightly mad. Whatever – as she told it later – he was living proof that love existed, being so distracted he could hardly walk straight; although maybe, she conceded, he was merely saddle-sore. She could also see a customer at the end door to her corridor, and needed them away.

'La, sir!' she said to Sam. 'Go down to the stable and see Rich. If you've rid so far you'll need new horses, and he'll find a patch of straw for you, no doubt. If I was you I'd go and have a drink instead. Now shoo away. There is a gentleman.'

She indicated a door beside her and almost pushed them through it to a stair. On the second or third tread Will stumbled, which Sam seized on for his argument. They needed sleep, they needed rest, to go on was absurd.

'If it's done it's done,' he said, trying not to sound

227

unkindly. 'If it ain't we'll get there just as soon tomorrow if we've had a rest. We don't know where this justice lives, if that's where Dennett's taken her, but Sir Arthur's Tony might have found it out, and we can't arrive at Langham in the middle of the night, can we? It's help we need, not getting shot.'

'But will you come?' asked William. 'What of Kaye? What will he do to us?'

This cheered Sam up, apparently. The thought of thwarting Kaye appealed.

'There are more important things than Captain Kaye,' he said. 'Anyway, he don't know where we are unless Eaton's back, which I severely doubt, and the journey could have took us longer, couldn't it? Let's get our heads down in the straw, get two hacks, and be away first light. Whatever way it goes, we'll be back on Biter by tomorrow night or so. Let him call us liars if he dares!'

From Rich they got makeshift beds, some bread and cheese, and a trade-off for their nags which suited all of them. Will did not think to sleep, his mind was filled with Deb and awful possibilities. But he slept, and did not even dream.

Amella Wimbarton, wife of a justice, a learning lady, not long ago a beauty, had only this to hold on to now: her husband loved her, oh yes he did indeed. When she found out it was not true, the effect it had was terrible. For the while at least, however, it did save Deborah's teeth.

Deb reached the house unconscious in Marcus Dennett's cart, because finally it was the only means by which he could transport her. He had tracked her down without enormous difficulty, although it had cost him dearly and risked him meeting several men he would have avoided at all costs, one reason for steering clear of London as he did with assiduity in the normal way. He had hired locally for the raid on Dr Marigold's, as Jeremiah had his own reasons for avoiding certain parts and Dennett his for keeping dark his destination. He gave the steward gold as a collateral – an arrangement Jeremiah forced on him – to keep him waiting with the cart south of the river while the mountebank and his hired posse went by horse. One of the men was badly cut, and Dennett himself had to shoot poor Cecily when she ran screaming at him, but the expedition was a quick enough success, with Deborah clubbed nearly senseless early on, so quiet as they came across the bridge.

It was afterwards, when the London men had got their pay and gone, that she came round sufficiently to give them trouble. They had decanted her from off a horse into the wagon before setting out for south, and Jeremiah and Dennett, having settled the cash questions, were talking almost amicably. Fiske, Jeremiah's deputy, had stopped off at some bushes luckily, and as he rode to catch them up he saw the girl – bound but not inactive – slip-sliding off the tailgate of the cart. She hit the ground heavily but with little sound, and was struggling to climb on to her feet when the horseman made himself known to her, grinning fit to crack his face. Deborah, in pain and furious, let out a shriek and tried – he swore – to bite his leg before the horse's shoulder knocked her flat into the mud. Then, hobbled like a grazing mare but her determination not a whit diminished, she bounced up once more and tried to jog and hop away towards the roadside and some cover. Retaken, she set up a screeching and a bellowing that could not be borne, busy as the road was at this time of evening. Despite her face had earlier been battered, but thinking she would no longer need her beauty anyway, Dennett clubbed her harder than before. Which saved her in one way, for Fiske had been so taken with her wild spirit, he had half a plan to creep in with her at some later stage for business underneath her skirt, but was put off by the quantity of blood and bruises.

Madly, though, Chester Wimbarton was not – which led Mistress Wimbarton to a despair far greater than the one she suffered from her rotting mouth. She *was* rotten by this time, in a state of self-disgust and pain that a weaker vessel, man or woman, could simply not have borne. When she had demanded of her husband that he track down the mountebank and get the second teeth, she had been able to face him. His love was her only touchstone, and – dressed in black – she had thought to impress him with her bravery, to achieve some transcendental beauty through her naked suffering. She had seen him flinch, his eyes slide sideways, the muscles round his mouth go rigid, but he had recovered, he had set the search in hand and would succeed, he promised it – and quickly. By the time Jeremiah returned home with the prize and hope, however, Mistress Wimbarton could not face even Dorothy and the other women with her face uncovered. She was in her room, fully clothed before the fire, a bowl of water by her for her weeping gums, a pomander and some burning cloves beside. She did not hear the horsemen coming home.

The wagon, by arrangement, was taken to the carriage house, where it could be kept from general eyes. This was not the only reason, for above it was a suite where the girl could be safely kept until everything was ready for the operation, and where Dennett could stay with her to get all set. While he and Jeremiah carried her upstairs, Fiske went to see if the master was astir and wished to come and see. He was, and did. Before he went, he crept to his wife's door and listened, where he heard no sound.

Deb, laid on the bed, was not a lovely vision, but the master found himself dry-mouthed. She was dressed in a shift and cloak as they had picked her up and wrapped her at Dr Marigold's, she was shoeless, and she was caked in mud and dirt. Her face was pale as death, with dark patches round her eyes and darker bruises where the mountebank had struck her senseless. Dried blood caked her hair and ear and neck, and she was scarcely breathing. Chester Wimbarton, magistrate and man of standing in the parish, had a wild idea.

'How is Milady?' asked Dennett, at last. He had stood ignored for moments while the man had stared, and he had noticed Jeremiah's look of sly contempt. The master turned his eyes reluctantly to him, then flapped his hand impatiently to dismiss the steward. Dennett, with an inkling of what was going on, also had a need to lick his lips. He smelled money.

'You see,' he said, 'if she is too ... far gone, it could turn out a little ... difficult. Will you permit I ... ?'

Wimbarton did not reply, but his eyes were hard and pitiless. Dennett, checking that Jeremiah had closed the door, went to the bed. Deb was breathing shallowly, and for an instant he was afraid that she might die. Hurrying, he turned the simple knot in the neck cord of her cloak into a mess of hard twists and loops, but hardly dared to bring a knife to bear. The smile he cast across his shoulder was rather sickly.

'My wife fears it is too late, they will no longer take,' said Wimbarton, levelly. 'I told her that can not be so, I have your bond.'

And thirty pounds, in both their minds but left unsaid. Dennett tried harder at the knotted cord.

'Indeed you do!' Said heartily. 'Nay, it is not so easy, but ... never say ... die.'

The knot parted, and he hid his face by getting closer. Say die, indeed. Christ, had he gone mad?

'You said this maiden's teeth were not so good,' said Wimbarton. 'That's why you chose the other one's for my wife. I do not believe that, Mr Mountebank. I believe you saved her for her beauty, for the profit you might get from that. I believe you cheated me.'

Poor Dennett's face was like a rigid mask of ease and humour. He scrabbled at the cloak, to pull it open and away.

'She's not so beautiful,' he said miserably. 'Indeed, sir, she looks a very fright.'

He had one breast out of the shift, held like an orange

231

or a pomegranate, carelessly. The skin was soft, translucent, but he was gripped by fear, his stomach tense and knotted. Wimbarton's eyes were blank.

'You lie about this operation also,' he said. 'My wife's gums are black and foul, her breath is like a butcher's cesspit. Drag this maid's teeth out all you like, they will not take. You know it, I know it, the blindest halfwit knows it.'

'No!' cried Dennett. 'On my mother's grave, that is a lie! The thin girl's teeth I thought were best but they were too – too narrow, possibly. Now this maid's teeth—'

He stepped back smartly at this point, pulling the shift and ripping it, exposing Deborah from the neck to the thighs, all perfection save some bruises and her bloody head. He was sure he knew the man's intention, he would stake his all on it. What all he would have left if this evening's business went wrong, he thought ruefully.

Outside there was a noise on the stair, then a loud cough. The catch lifted as Jeremiah's voice said urgently: 'Master, it is I! Milady comes, they cannot deny her!'

'Stay!' shouted the magistrate, but it was too late. Jeremiah stood in the doorway, and his eyes were fixed. As Wimbarton came towards him he moved backwards in caution, but his eyes were merry.

'You operate, I see!' he said to Dennett, who was scrambling to cover the naked woman. And, more quietly, 'How well he knows the master.'

There was hysteria in Dennett's movements, and hysteria clattering up the wooden stairs, Mistress Wimbarton and Dorothy and Joan. Jeremiah tried – not over-hard – to keep the door against them and was barged aside, while Wimbarton, having first moved to the bed, dropped back towards the wall a fair good distance, and watched as coolly as could be, his dark, thin face saturnine. Milady was majestic, eyes blazing above her veil, wafting in a heady mix of spices and corruption. Deborah was covered, just, but Joan, like a little country thing, let out a squeak.

Mistress Wimbarton, if she had had the power, would have shouted. Instead her voice came throaty-hoarse, not much above a whisper.

'Operate? Do you need her naked, then? What operate?'

She moved towards the bed like an attacker, staring at the girl. Dennett had a hand upon the cloth, but he let go, moving carefully away.

'My dear,' said Wimbarton. 'Dennett is checking her condition, as there is urgency involved. The news is bad.'

'What news? She has still teeth! I see them! What news?'

She leaned across the bed and pulled at Deborah's mouth, brutally.

'See?' she said. 'My teeth. You have paid for them.'

'She would die,' said Wimbarton. 'She has been bleeding, she is weakened, we must—'

'No!' The sound she made was horrible, halfway between screech and croak. Above the veil her eyes were bright and furious.

'My dear—'

'So if she dies, what difference? What care I, or you? Yes, husband. What care *you*?'

The steward, Jeremiah, had seen the signs and eased out from the room, not waiting for an order or an onslaught. He plucked Joan's sleeve and she followed, reluctantly. Dennett, who had nowhere to go, decreased in size, sought invisibility.

But Wimbarton only shrugged, then moved towards his wife with open palms, exuding gentleness and sympathy.

'You are right, my love,' he said. 'It is only it would be embarrassment, and me a justice of the peace, if we were to end up with the body of a whore about the place. Dennett says we ought to wait a day, when everything will be safer. The teeth are healthy, he has confirmed it. Everything will proceed to satisfaction.'

Dennett's face had cleared, till Mistress Wimbarton, with her great directness, tore aside her veil. He saw her lips were tinged with black and yellow, her eyes alive with terror.

'But will it be too late for me?' she croaked, and the breath of mortality took him fully in the face. 'Doctor. Look at me.'

Doctor! The mountebank moved up to her, and eased aside the dying lips to see inside the putrefying mouth, hoping the miasma she was exhaling did not bear the plague or bloody flux. Instead of gums with sockets she had . . . well, he could not see.

Marcus Dennett coughed.

'Nay, excellent,' he said. His eyes, above her head, met those of her husband, who was faintly smiling. 'Tomorrow will be excellent to do the deed.'

Ye gods, he told himself, and was ashamed. Ye gods.

Sir Peter Maybold, the Surveyor General, had done his duty by Sir Arthur Fisher only the day before Holt and Bentley rode up the long drive to Langham Lodge. They arrived well after breakfast time, but Sir A still had not emerged. Mrs Houghton had taken breakfast to him in his bedroom, and stayed to watch in silence as he picked at it. She was the only person in the house to whom he had told the awful news. Warren had been discovered, abused and dead, his nephew Charles Yorke was missing still. Sir Arthur, who had grown old and frail with the passing days, had grown frailer before her anxious eyes.

The two Navy men were greeted at the stable door by Tony, who marvelled at their villainous appearances, but buttoned his lips on any comment. He had watched the fat man turn up in his official coach the afternoon before, and seen him depart, all powdered wig and sombreness. He had his own ideas as to what the visit meant, and noted afterwards the continued absence of the master. Rumour did the rounds, unhelped by him, and the arrival of these two – and fairly well unkempt – could hardly be coincidence, he guessed. Indeed the younger, blond one, was pretty agitated.

Few words were passed though, save for greetings, and

they went to a side door Tony indicated, where an underling of Mrs Houghton sat them down and went to find her out. Two minutes later the housekeeper arrived, scolded the women for not preparing coffee, and said the master would see them in his parlour on the instant. Something in her manner jarred with Samuel, and he asked outright if anything were wrong. Mrs Houghton eyed him, unsmiling.

'Aye,' she said. 'I fear there is. But wait a moment and Sir A will tell. It is not appropriate that I should.'

So early in the morning, but there was a fire blazing in the grate. The great windows had not been opened, and after the fresh outdoors they did not relish the building fug. They sat, declined a drink or breakfast yet, and waited silent for a while. Will's mind was full of Deborah, and the time he felt as draining rapidly away. Sam's disquiet was growing by the moment, and he arose convulsively when they heard a tread outside.

Sir A stood in the doorway, for the moment like a shadow of the man he'd been. His face was sallow, his collar awry, and he had no wig upon his thin and grizzled hair. He glanced at Will, turned his eyes to Sam, and almost stumbled as he moved towards him. To Will's surprise the men embraced, and the clasp seemed set to last for ever. It was not embarrassing, precisely, but he had a vague sense of loss that was discomfiting. And overlaid with a horrified awareness that the search for Deborah was being overtaken by events they'd find far weightier.

The embrace ended, but Sir A and Sam did not move far apart. Hands touching, they moved into the front part of the room where, suddenly, the old man detached himself, sitting heavily in an upright chair.

'Sam,' he said. 'Mr Bentley. You have heard somehow? How glad I am you've come.'

Sam spread his hands.

'Sir, we have not heard. I guess, though, it is Charles. Has he . . . ? Is . . . ?'

'Pray sit! Pray sit!' said Sir A, distractedly. 'Nay, my Charles, our Charles . . . well, he is as yet unfound, so we may still have hope. But the other Charles, good Charlie Warren. Oh God, Sam. The evil that men do.'

They waited, for Sir Arthur had covered his face, may even have been weeping. They avoided each other's faces, but Will noticed Sam run a finger round inside his collar, clearing sweat. He found himself gazing longingly through the glass at the garden grass, scythed short at summer's end.

'They found him stuffed into a hayrick,' said Sir Arthur, not distinctly. 'Cut, mutilated, picked over by dogs. Not the work of men, of Christians, but of beasts. And in the name of what they call the free trade, may they rot in hell for that damned lie; they'd fired the rick to try and burn him. And where, and how, and when did my Charles die?'

Sam, eventually, cleared his throat.

'He may not . . . until they find his body, sir. There is always hope. There must be.'

Sir A raised his head. For a moment he seemed blind and deaf.

'Aye,' he said at last. 'There must be hope, or what else is there? But you two. Sam, if you had not heard of this, what do you here, and so early in the day? You have been riding, you have been living roughly. Surely you do not seek men out down here for pressing? For that other wicked trade?' He stopped. He touched his brow, eyes dropped. 'Nay, forgive me, all trade is wicked to a degree, I do not mean to be gratuitous. What has happened?'

Deb rose in William's throat, but he crushed her back. Deb was his sorrow, and her own. Sam stood up and, with tacit permission, attended to the windows. From the grass outside a cooling, welcome breeze blew in.

'We got left ashore,' he said. He almost made a jest of it. 'Marooned by the King's most gallant commander on the seven seas. We went to take some of those very men, those smugglers, but they had allies on shore of the most

236

useful kind. A justice of the peace, and what we took to be the yeomanry. We were jailed, set free by our boatswain's mate, bought horses, and we ran. William here was most displaced by it, head over heels – for the Hampshire men, he says, are almost honest!'

He must not have realised what he'd said, for Yorke and Warren had been in Hampshire, and disappeared there. Will dared not speak, but Sir A, eventually, broke the silence.

'Charles Warren was killed not far from Petersfield,' he said. 'Do you not hail from Petersfield, young man?'

Will nodded.

'Not far from there, sir. Two miles.'

'And you know smuggling men? How would that be? You do not deal with them, surely?'

Sam, having got him in the mess, tried to pull him out. He explained about the Welfare and her mixed people. Smugglers had aided Will, in the troubles, a smuggler had saved his life. Will added that he knew their villages, their haunts, he sailed his own boat in their waters, often. He did not think them honest, but he had assumed they might be honourable men. He had not heard they had a brutal reputation. But now, of course . . .

Sir Arthur Fisher sighed. The room was quiet for some little while, save for a hissing log and the breeze outside. Clouds were blowing across a fine blue sky, and Will thought of Deb, and desolation.

'So why here in Surrey, Samuel?' asked Sir A. 'When you say you've run, you mean from your captivity, not your ship, I trust. Kaye is a foolish man, and venal I have heard, but he is not that bad, I will not allow it. Is he still out in the estuary, or the Downs, or what goes on? If he is back in London, should you not have gone back to the ship?'

Sam glanced at Will, read hopelessness, and bit the bullet. He knew it would sound tawdry, but he would do it for his friend, who could not.

'Sir,' he said. 'It is that young maid we brought here. Deborah.'

'Hah!' said Sir A. 'Young men and their humours, like flies around a honeypot! But she is gone, sir. She and her poor companion of the teeth. The very night we took them in they fled, and stole an ass. I do not blame them, for they lived in fear, although we'd not have harmed them for the world. Good God, though. To risk your neck for a young doxy, Sam. Lieutenant Kaye would slaughter you!'

'Not Mr Holt,' said Will. ''Tis I, Sir Arthur. But there is more than that. We know they ran away, for we met them in London in, I beg your pardon, sir, in a sort of gay house.'

'Hah,' said Sir A once more. 'Poor things, poor things, but what else could they do? But the smaller one, the little mouse thing, I can't recall her name, she had no teeth. Surely, even in a London bawdy house . . . ?'

'Cecily is dead, sir,' Samuel said. It came out harsh, and Sir Arthur bit his lip. Sam made a gesture to his friend, a helpless sign, that they should not go on. He finished lamely, 'We think the mountebank has stole her back, the other one, so we followed here. And now we find you with this dreadful news and worry on your mind. We are truly sorry for it, sir, both of us.'

There was another moment's silence, while Sir Arthur took all in, and pondered it. Then he raised his eyes.

'Why here, though?' he asked. 'The villain is a travelling man. You found them in a wagon in a wood, I thought?'

'They said a magistrate had bought the teeth,' said Sam. 'We thought perhaps . . . well, if the first set did not take . . . so Deborah . . .'

'Please, sir,' said William, 'we wondered, I wondered, if perhaps you'd found him out? The man who made the purchase in the first place.'

'On suspicion only,' said Sir Arthur. 'Suspicion only. There are tales, but with the maidens gone, well, what could one do, in any way? Tony named a man, but he is

238

of great respect, whatever one's opinion. And powerful, whose house is like a castle, almost fortified. Forgive me, but your story sounds like slander not like fact, like romance not firm sense. I'll wager that the maiden is not there, you have no proof, do you, of any kind? And if she were, and had been carried back, surely it is far too late by now, even if one could gain entrance?' He stopped, but neither of them spoke. He moved a hand, the fingers long and bony, in a gesture of regret. 'Oh young man,' he said, 'I'm sorry for it, but you'd best forget her, hadn't you? We live in troubled times, but some cases are less terrible than others. Hers may be hopeless, or it may be not, but at least we have no inkling that she'll die for it. Be brave, sir, and forget her.'

From Tony, later on that day, they did get more information, but it was as depressing in its details as Sir A's had been. He named Wimbarton as an almost certainty, and confirmed that tales had flown around the parishes that Mistress Amella, or Milady as she madly styled herself, had got new teeth, then rotted, and was in her dying days. No hints had emanated that the mountebank was back, although there had been some activity in the past few days with Jeremiah leading horsemen in a search. It was Jeremiah, his man Fiske, and their band of ruffians he was most strong about. They were unhung desperadoes to a man, and kept the house impregnable. If the maiden was there, he said, she was there until it suited them, and no one else.

The interview with Sir A had terminated abruptly when Mrs Houghton had bustled in uncalled, tutted at her master's state, and driven Sam and William to have a wash then breakfast. They had gone over both aspects of their trouble at length, but reached no conclusion as to what they should or could do, or attempt. Behind it all, and brooding, was the question of the Biter and Lieutenant Kaye. If he chose to, he could make life extremely hot for them for this action, and sometime soon, whatever, they must return on board and face it.

Sir Arthur had made it known that he would see them later, and try as they might they could get little information that might lead them to believe they could help Deborah. The nearest was the exact location of the Wimbarton estate, which Sam wheedled from a younger girl by a combination of charm and browbeating which left him not exactly proud. Even she, though, reported on the house as if it were a fortress, and probably haunted into the bargain. When called to luncheon they were clean, depressed, and not seeing at all which way the day would go.

It was a long affair, with their host in brooding mode, discoursing at length on Charles Yorke's past, the possibility that he might be saved, and his helplessness at what to do immediately. Although Sam and William added little to the conversation, they both sensed that it was heading somewhere, as if Sir Arthur had been thinking something through, searching for a fixed direction. However, it was not until the maids had cleared away, and hot chocolate and biscuits had been brought, that he revealed his hand.

'Young man,' he said to William. 'Or Will, I must learn to call you Will now you and Sam are friends. I have been thinking, and I have a thing to ask. First though; correct me if I have it wrong. You know Hampshire well, do you? Especially round where you live, you know the wood paths and the secret ways?'

Will felt his stomach hollowing, but he nodded, dumbly. The old man's face was so stricken, so torn with anxious hope.

'Ah, you do, you do, of course. And you know the smugglers of thereabouts, and their ways. And you are an honest man, and brave.'

His voice had dropped to just above inaudible. Will wet his lips.

'I shall not beat about the bush,' said Sir Arthur, more normally. 'Charles Yorke is missing and I am quite prepared, almost prepared, to think him dead. Now he was going under cover, for the Customs House in London, and it has taken all his colleagues, all those men, this time to find poor Warren's corpse. In a word, there is no chance in hell that they will find a culprit, because I have it on authority of the highest that it was fortune alone that led them to Warren, he was stumbled over by a farmer's boy. No information, no hints, no intelligence either bought or gathered. Wherever my own Charles is, sir – he will remain there. Unfound, unsaved, unshriven or unburied. That cannot, shall not, be.'

He looked at both of them, and both bravely kept his eyes. The hollowness inside Will Bentley's stomach grew.

'You can guess what I am driving at, I think,' Sir Arthur said. 'I know both of you hate this trade, these men, as much as I do and Sam, at least, knows Yorke. What I would ask of you is that you become my spy, or spies, and follow in their footsteps for a while. If Charles lives you may find him for me, if he is dead, knowledge brings its own relief of sorts. I wish you to divest yourselves of Navy personality, and become my spies. Only for a little while, for if you discover nothing, what's the point? Just a few days, enquiring of the people that you know, searching out the secret ways. Please, Will. Will you do it for me?'

Both, in some ways, were aghast, but both could see the attraction it must hold. At best a long, long shot, at worst probably fatal. Each knew they could not refuse.

'But the Biter?' said Holt. 'You said yourself, sir, Lieutenant Kaye would slaughter us. It may not be entirely a jest, I fear.'

He pooh-poohed it. There were ways and means, he said, there were people in the Admiralty and the Office. Lieutenant Kaye was – his lip curled in contempt – a booby and a fool from what he'd heard, despite his father was a duke. In any case, how long would it be before they were truly missed? In the end, checking the clock with great impatience, he called for quills and ink and paper.

'We will have it on a proper footing, after all. Kaye might be troublesome but I have greater power in a fight like this. How long to London, if I give you good horses? Not many hours. You can go to Deptford if that is where she lies and give him letters to his hand. First to the Admiralty Office, where all shall be made good. I'll write to Bobby Beaumont, and if Kaye cares to defy him we should have some capital fun, capital in the hanging sense, mayhap! Then, when you have cleared it all, back here and sleep, and off betimes tomorrow. Does that meet expectations?'

Sam, for Will's sake, mentioned Deborah. Was there a possibility, he asked, that they might ride that way?

'Deborah?' asked Sir A, blankly. 'What way?'

'The magistrate's,' said Sam. 'Wimbarton's. It could be that . . . well, just to—'

Sir Arthur's eyes cleared with sudden anger.

'Are you mad?' he snapped. 'Just what, to rescue her? I have told you, there is nothing we can do. Who mentioned Wimbarton? Not Tony, surely? Charlie lies bleeding somewhere, in an unknown place, and all you think about is—'

He stopped, and touched his forehead and his eyes.

'I am sorry, Sam,' he said. 'Mr Bentley, my humblest apologies, that was uncalled for. But believe me, if she is at Wimbarton's, there is noth— Look, maybe tomorrow. Maybe I could ride over. You must away now, it is getting late. Please ring the bell again. Where are my ink and paper?'

They left a half an hour after that, and, by the young maid's directions, went via the 'fortress house' of Chester Wimbarton, just to see. The nearest they could get was to a road lodge, at a gate, with three men outside it who indeed were armed. They did not stop, or reveal their faces for too long, but passed along the way to London. William was in a kind of agony.

In the coachhouse, about a mile away, Deb's agony was just beginning.

20

The night before, when Wimbarton had won his point, thus saving Deborah her teeth, she had been awake already but was shamming. Through part-closed eyes she took in some of the scene, and thought she knew the thoughts that all were having. Wimbarton, a whip-like, sharp-like man, had changed his mind about the operation, and wanted her instead. More, he wanted his wife to leave them on the instant so he could have her now, and never mind the blood and bruises. The wife, she saw, had read this in his mind, and would not have it. Despite his exhortations, despite his wheedling, she was hard as adamant, and prepared to scream if need be, as well as argue. The mountebank, that evil fox she hated, was watching and pondering which way to make the greatest profit from her body, and to save his skin.

Deborah's hurt was terrible but she knew that Cec was dead and that was worse. The kidnap had been fierce from the start, but the moment she had realised it was Dennett the dread had almost overwhelmed her. Cec had become an ugly, bitter thing, laughed at by the harlots and ill-used by the men about the place, which filled Deb with a guilt she did not understand. Even the knowledge of her death was guilty, for she feared that in some obscure way she'd caused it; and worse, Cec had died attacking Marcus Dennett to defend her. The real dread though, was that she would have her teeth torn out in turn, so her death would surely follow, and so what? To end like Cecily would be a death itself.

The argument the magistrate was deploying went like this: the maid was at death's door and needed attention from the mountebank, immediate. The wife could do no good by being there, but could upset herself, exhaust herself, exacerbate her already weak condition. She needed rest, as much as possible, and the physician (ho, a promotion, noted Deborah) could give her a gentle potion, could he not? Deb almost opened her eyes full out at this audacity, but Milady's snort erupted from the depths unprompted. The only potion Deb had got from him came in a wooden bottle labelled club, but at deadly poison Dennett was equally a dab. Wimbarton's last try was that she needed sleep to make her fit before the morrow's operation, while he needed to talk to Mr Dennett of business things. Mistress Wimbarton, looking like death on legs and smelling worse, had kept her spirit.

'Sir,' she'd said, 'we leave this room together or not at all. I have never had an ordeal yet I could not get through with brandy, and the maid is in far worse a state than I. Let Mr Dennett stay with her, and give her pills and potions until they pop out of her ears for all I care, and use her body in the way men do if that's his bent. You shall not, sir, or I swear I'll kill you. Just let him call us if she dies is all, so that he may pull her teeth then and seal them in my gums. If she recovers it shall be done tomorrow, I will not wait another day. And now, sir – go to bed.'

Deborah, who knew a strong woman when she met one, knew also that the justice could not win, be his power never so great in theory. He was a horrible man, who looked very cruel and evil, and she took some strange comfort from that fact. The fight would go on until it reached an end, and all the time it did she had her teeth. She might run, she had proved good at getting out of scrapes by grabbing chances in her time, or something else might happen. She had a thought, a fleeting thought, of a young man on a charger. Last time she had been in these parts William had come, the knight in shining armour. She did not think this time he'd come again.

In the end, with great bad grace, Chester Wimbarton

bowed to the storm and took his canvas in. He threw a look back into the room, Deb noted through her lids, that told Dennett to keep her well and safe, and distinctly unmolested. The mountebank, who had always exercised great caution in that field with her, on the grounds that maids with child were little use to him after four months or so and precautions however keenly made could not be trusted, appeared to be in two minds whether to change his tack this time alone. Quite clearly she was bound to die in short order, or otherwise be concubine to the justice and therefore prone to falling pregnant, no blame attached to Marcus Dennett. He stood in front of her for some short while, then sprang his club out from his breeches' slit. So Deborah – miraculously! – came back to consciousness, and made it clear she'd scream the household and the master instantly back around his ears if he so much as put a hand on her. To Dennett, discretion had always been the better part of lust, he made his living at it, so he put his prick away for later. He smiled rather friendly, and sat down on the bedside for a conversation, but Deb would not respond, only groaned and wriggled in discomfort, and put her back to him. Two difficult and most stubborn women in one night, the mountebank considered darkly. Then took himself to his pallet in the corner with his dreams.

Next morning when she woke, Deborah felt herself all over and decided she would live. Her face all down one side was swollen, her right eye almost closed, and her whole head was tender to each probing finger. On her body, which Dennett must have covered with a blanket while she slept, there were areas of scrape and bruise, both hands were stiff and full of aches, while one knee would bend only by a gritting of the teeth. The teeth. She clicked them together, almost ground them, somehow to reassure herself. They are there, they are mine, please God I do not lose them. She thought of God a little while. Teeth were so important, the most basic of necessity especially for every woman, yet they were prone to rot, and damage, and disaster and He had willed it so. Why? She decided swiftly that she was bordering on blasphemy, so thought of her bowels and her bladder instead, both of which were full. She tried a groan or two – she must keep up her one defensive line – and Dennett was instantly awake. No use of privies in the outer world, as they were bolted in, so he showed her through a doorway to a cupboard-room, then made her use the leathern bucket after him, so he'd not have to bear her morning smells. She bore his own with stoicism, then washed with a pail of water that was there, unsurprised that Dennett had not bothered.

When she returned his club was out again, and the sly smile was back upon his face, the foxy grin she'd grown to know and hate in the months since she and Cecily had sadly lighted on him. It was a small and ugly one, to her, but when she'd used that line to deflate his drunken lust once in the past, she'd got a beating for it. This time she eyed it in an almost friendly way, as if it were sad she'd have to turn him down. She did not think it likely under any circumstance, but there just might come a time she'd need his aid.

'Oh Mr Dennett, is there no end to men's desire? My face is like I'd fallen off a horse and then he'd kicked me!'

'But I won't be looking at your face. Quickly, girl, just pull your shift up and lie back. I will not be long.'

A tired jest rose in her mind but she did not express it. Dennett with his pocky face and dirty hands and filthy lust revolted her. She wondered why she bothered, but she did. If not him now, Wimbarton soon, or possibly no teeth and welcome lepers for a short, unhappy life. But she saw him there and bothered, horribly.

'No sir,' she said, incisively. Then tried to soften it. 'Please, Mr Dennett, think of your own safety. It is breakfast time and everyone is abroad. The master warned you, I saw his look to kill. And Milady is watching like a hawk. Put it away, sir, before somebody enters.'

Dennett had it in his hand and it was very eager, but he appreciated sense. He squeezed it, hard, as if to teach it manners, letting out a small, regretful noise.

'Hah, Deb,' he said. 'You have a brain as well as beauty. I know you're right but I would love to have you, just the once for old times' sake. If you refuse me, and I take your teeth out, I might hurt you worse, you know.'

His small eyes glittered, despite the amicality she'd engendered, and she knew he might, that he was capable. Then they heard a noise on the stair outside, and he cursed, and pushed it out of sight, and she breathed a little breath out, of relief. It was Fiske, with bread and milk and cheese, and he eyed them curiously, but said little except to comment on the weather and tell the mountebank the master wished a word with him when he had eaten.

While Dennett was away for half an hour, Deb explored her dungeon with increasing gloom. Three small airing windows high enough for bats and owls but too high for her, nothing in the privy cupboard, rough walls of enormous thickness, a robust wooden door. There was a table big enough to lie her and missus on side by side if need be, and if the thing was to be done here she could not imagine how she might escape. Her only chance had been the master's lust, when it came down to tacks. But the mistress, quite definitely, had worked that one out herself. And foreclosed on it.

Marcus Dennett, though, was very thoughtful on his return. Fiske closed the door on them and bolted it as usual, but the mountebank no longer looked on her with lustful eyes. He sat on a chair indifferently, so Deb, who had been standing, perched on the bed, it being comfortable at least. He did not speak for such a long time that it was she who felt the need to break the ice.

'Well? Is he set to dig them out yet? Or has Milady cut his cock off with a saw?'

For moments longer he did not reply. He hissed air out quietly through his nostrils at her humour, but he was

247

still thinking. When he spoke his tone was tentative.

'You're sharp, our Deb, you're passing sharp,' he said. 'What he'd like to do is get you on your back, as any man with red blood would. If he did, and if you played your hand right, you could marry him, I reckon, with him a magistrate and that. It seems to me most like that's how he got the first Milady, who is young enough to be his daughter after all. His trouble is – and yours – she fell in love with him, and he with her, he told her, so Fiske says. So any settlement of the hole and corner kind is definitely not possible, because she'd kill you like a bug. Which leaves . . .'

'My teeth,' said Deborah. As if in sympathy they hurt, inside her mouth. Milady's desperation came to her vividly for an instant, that she would risk all this to try and keep that love, or that awful, snake-like man at least. 'Oh God,' she said. 'Mr Dennett.'

'Nay,' said Dennett, 'but he's a single-minded man, and a ruthless one himself. He hinted at a potion, although he did not come straight out with it, he left the work to me. I know his type too well, don't I? He'd take the liquid, kill the wife, and I would end up hanged, so I played blind and dumb. I said —' He stopped, arrested by her face. 'What?' he asked.

'A potion?' Deborah was aghast. 'You mean he'd poison her?'

He smiled, and carried on.

'I did not ask, I'm telling you. I played it like a mute. I said I thought that there would be no point in medication, if that was what he meant. I said I thought she'd die, she was too far gone for saving.' His eyes narrowed. 'I should think I might be right, at that. I told him he should talk to her, say you were still too weak, and neither I nor he could kill you just to get your teeth out of your head. I told him to persuade her I could help her with some soothing stuff which would cure her gums, and I would share it with her to show it wasn't poison. Coloured water as we call it in the mystery, but it would buy some time she might expire in with luck. A sixpence gets two pints.'

He fell to silence, watching. A small hope stirred in her, but not significant. God, even if this justice was the sort of man who took up pretty doxies and married them, he'd kill her when she lost her looks! Deb's head had begun to ache.

'He'll try,' said Dennett, 'but she'll have none of it, I'd wager all I have on that. There is another way that came to me. Fiske might be open to a bribe, or one of the lesser men, more like. We could fly from here in the extra time I've talked us into. You are fair and know the ropes and have a ready wit. I thought together we might make a living, pretty good. Partners, not pimp and whore nor anything like that, although there are worse ways if we select good customers. I've known whores of twenty years and more who've never parted thigh! What say you?'

Come live with me and be my love, thought Deb, the old line from the song. She knew men married doxies – rich men like Wimbarton, poor crooked men like this mountebank – and it was possible to make a life that way. Not today though, not like this, not with either of this pretty pair. It occurred to her that, as life was so hard and men so stupid for her body, she should aim her sights far higher. Maybe Marigold did have a scheme for her in reality and not in jest. For the moment, even her viewing room and cushion seemed worth pining after.

'Dr Marigold said—' she started, then broke off. 'We could go there, I suppose, to start off from. A safe place in London. Oh no, Jeremiah knows it, I suppose. When you came for me.'

'I came alone,' said Dennett. 'One does not throw away good secrets on such as him.' He did not voice his own dislike and fear of London, though. Or say he would hardly entrust her to another pimp to put her in safekeeping! Enough to get her out of this.

'What say you then?' he asked her brusquely. 'If you

are agreeable I must go about it quickly, for there will not be much time. If she agrees to wait she won't wait long. Well, come on. Do we run?'

You are a spirit, thought Deborah. You will use me as a common whore till I no longer suit, then you will sell me to the Colonies as a slave or servant. And the alternative is to stay here for my teeth to be ripped out, then die of the infection or end up a drab without good looks. For even if Milady did die it would be too late, he'd hardly trade one gumhag for another. She nodded her assent.

'Well, good!' said Dennett, in delight. 'Now, I do not say that I can bring it off, but by God I'll try! First of all I'll go speak to the master and see how he fares with keeping her at bay. I have a little sleeping draught would do the trick most excellent, if only she would take it! Then I'll try to ease some cash about, into some useful palms.'

He crossed to the door and rapped on it. Before they heard a step he cocked his head at her. His foxy face was sly.

'One thing, Deb,' he said. 'I'll try to stop it but I fear it is inevitable. Before the teeth come out – because he still thinks they will – the master will have your body, he will go to any lengths. If he comes through that doorway, with me or without, that is his intention. For God's sake, for the sake of everything, do not resist.'

Deb saw it all. You've sold me, haven't you, she thought. The bolt was drawn back noisily, on the outside. You've sold me, he will have me, then you'll take my teeth. She turned away as the mountebank went out.

It was not the master who came through the door an hour later though, it was Amella Wimbarton. Deb had heard the noises on the stairway, quiet noises, and had stiffened as she lay upon the bed. Before she'd stood, and smoothed her shift down, she had forced her mind to say to her once more, and to mean it, that she would endure this thing, this raping by the master, then – if the mountebank did betray her – she would fight them to the death rather than lose her teeth, she would rend and tear and battle until they would have to beat her beyond saving. As the door had opened she had bitten her lips, and braced herself.

The mistress, who had come in so quietly, must have gained her entry through force of personality or through cash. She closed the door behind her, and her eyes were wide and staring, with enormous pupils, wild. She had taken off her veil, and her face was still impossible to look at. Deb's eyes lit on her eyes, slid downwards till she caught the nose, and careered upwards as she gasped, involuntarily. And the stench. From across the room, immediate, horrifying. Deb might have had a flood of sympathy, but she knew she was to die.

The pistol, small and bright, appeared from underneath a drapery at her right side. Deb gasped once more, almost choking as her throat went tight with fear. She raised her hands in front of her, fingers crooked.

'No,' she said. 'I—'

'Be mine, that's what he said,' said Mistress Wimbarton. Her voice was thick and slurry, but the thought incisive, like a knife. 'Be mine and live happy ever after, happily and rich. We will marry for love, he said, and hang the Doubting Thomases. I would do anything to please him, which is why I bought your teeth.'

The thoughts were incisive, but they were completely mad. The smell was overwhelming Deborah, she was becoming faint. She tried to speak, to plead, but nothing came.

'You'll be better dead,' said Mistress Wimbarton. 'The pain is awful, to lose your teeth, and what comes afterward is worse. I agreed to go on pleasing him, do you understand, for he loves me and your teeth would please him in my head but now it's you he wants, it's you. He's on his way here, with that filthy man. One to hold you, one to . . . oh Jesus, Jesus, I was beautiful.'

She walked towards Deb, and as she did so Dennett

came through the door, and Wimbarton. Dennett had a cudgel in his hand, and a rope, but for a moment both men stood amazed. As the barrel of the pistol rose towards her, Deb made a small and breathy noise, not a scream but saturated in fear, and Wimbarton let out a squawk, propelling the mountebank across the room with an almighty shove. Dennett, yelling, struck out wildly with the club, the end of which caught Milady in her awful face as she tried to turn. As she went down the gun went off with a flash that closed Deb's eyes, and a shattering, ringing bang. Falling in her turn, she saw Dennett fold up like a clasp, as the master ran into the thick, blue, acrid smoke that bade fair to fill the room. Outside, women screaming, on the stair.

Oh God, she thought, Dennett is dead. They came to have me, then to tie me down. Oh God, my teeth are saved.

The ride to London, although long, went without a hitch. They took the letters first to Bobby Beaumont – Lord Wodderley, as he turned out to be – whose house was just off Seething Lane and who greeted them as valued messengers from a valued friend. While he read he snorted, then called for tea and pikelets to restore them while he scratched out some missives of his own. The Biter, his servants ascertained, was back by the receiving hulk, and Lieutenant Kaye could be with her, or at the Lamb, or 'any bloody where, how should I know? Heh? Heh!' If they found him, good, if not no matter any bloody way, the order was specific. Five days' leave of absence on a special mission, 'no questions asked or answered!' It occurred to him, he said, that they should not even bother to seek Kaye out, but let a man take the orders down, as 'old Sir Arthur says despatch is of the essence'. But this would not be courteous, he agreed with Will – who felt daring just to hint at contrary opinions to a lord – and offered them one of his pinnaces and a crew, which Sam accepted with alacrity.

Kaye was not on board the dark and silent ship, nor her owner/master Gunning, nor any of her people, at first sight. She lay to piles not far from the hulk, with only one small boat tethered to her boom. They left the pinnace crew to wait, and climbed quickly overside. There was a watchman – one leg, one arm, one eye, but very fierce! – and when they'd told him who they were, he gave tit-for-tat with information that there was an officer somewhere aft. This turned out to be Kershaw, whom they found sitting reading by a lamp, hunched far forward, they supposed, to bring his eye to bear. He greeted them with his usual nervousness, then asked if he should have a bottle brought.

'By whom?' said Samuel. 'Do you have servants now?'

Kershaw almost smiled – not quite – and said Black Bob was in the captain's berth, but would do things for him if asked. But Sam and Will, obscurely, wished to be away. The Biter empty was a bonus they did not wish to risk by hanging on. They showed the sealed missive from Lord Wodderley, with the letter from Sir Arthur Fisher to explain his need, and told Kershaw he must pass on their apologies as well. An explanation, Bentley said, would have to wait until they should return.

'It is in the best of causes, that is certain,' he added. 'I confide that he will understand entirely.'

'I am sure,' said Kershaw, drily. 'Aiding the Customs will please him. As it would your Uncle Daniel Swift.'

There was something in his voice beyond the distaste for the other service that was expected of a Navy man, but nothing in his expression that William could read. Sam was prepared to probe.

'You don't think Lieutenant Kaye will appreciate our mission, then? Why so? Come, spit it out, sir!'

As well ask this odd, crippled man to dance a jig. He shrugged the shoulder he had movement in.

'He was . . . aggrieved, a little. By the manner of your parting, and your failure to return. He questioned Behar and Tilley closely on the matter.'

'Those two,' said Sam. 'No sign of Shockhead, then? Eaton, boatswain's mate?'

Kershaw shook his head.

'Those two and the ratty one. They waited for you on the shore, they said. You did not return.'

'The buggers split and left us,' Sam said bitterly. 'Did not return, indeed!'

'However,' Will said, 'Kaye knows from them three that we got away, and now we're off again, without a by-your-leave. Mr Kershaw's right, Sam. Aggrieved won't be the half of it.'

'And to aid the Customs once again into the bargain! Then good!' said Sam. And then, remembering maybe this man was there to watch over William, even to inform, he coughed, to fudge it. 'Nay, apologies to the good lieutenant of the very humblest, an' you please,' he added. 'Tell him we shall return with all despatch.'

Dropped back by the pinnace at stairs near where they'd liveried their horses, Sam wondered if they should take some food and drink themselves before their ride to Surrey and Sir A's. The thought of his distress, however, the fate of Yorke, weighed on them both so much they paid their charge and rode. Their conversation as they went through Southwark and out into the country blackness was stilted, but by an hour's time they were back on the comfort of the general, ranging over Tilley and Behar's behaviour, the fate of Eaton, the whereabouts of the good captain and the drunken Gunning, and that 'infernal oddfish' his Uncle Swift had foisted on them, the ghost-like Kershaw. Will ventured that he had begun to like the man, or see some value in him rather, most difficult to put a finger on, and to his relief Holt agreed. They mused on what had crippled him, what he made of the Navy's 'most outrageous ship and overlord' (Sam's phrase), what he made of the uncle's nephew if it was indeed his place to make some comment in the future. They both admitted there was more to him than they had guessed.

The time passed easily enough, with the weather chill but far from unpleasant to be abroad in, without alarms from passers-by or lurking ne'er-do-wells. It was gone midnight by the time they approached the gate lodge, by which time William had fallen into an introspection once more. They had not made a detour to go past Chester Wimbarton's, although the urge to do so had been strong on him, but his mind was back to Deb and raw regret. He was pulled round by a note of surprise from his companion, who pointed at the lodge.

'Lights,' he said. 'What's afoot? Sir A don't normally keep it manned these times, at night.'

As they came closer, men emerged, and they were armed. Tony was in the centre of them, looking tired.

'Well met, Tony,' said Sam. 'What's all the pother? Have the Frogs invaded us at last?'

The steward took his bridle for a while.

'Men abroad,' he said. 'Not seen them for some hours, but not the sort you'd wish to share a dark street with, sir. Sir Arthur thought they might be troublesome to us, although there appears no reason they should think she's here that I can fathom.'

Will Bentley's heart rose straight into his throat and almost strangled him.

'What?' he choked out. 'Who?'

A knowing grin lit across Tony's broad face.

'Why, the maid,' he answered, disingenuously. 'She came running here this afternoon. A maiden in distress. She's battered, sir – but has got all her ivories!'

But Will had not waited for the end; and his friend was in a very hot pursuit.

255

21

The tale Deborah told Sir Arthur was harrowing, but it was not entire truth. When she had arrived at Langham Lodge she had been in a state of terror and exhaustion, having found it more by luck than memory and in mortal fear that Jeremiah and his men would have set out in pursuit. She had no connection with Sir Arthur that they knew about, she hoped, but a general hue and cry might pick her up on roads, so she kept to fields and woods and by-ways. The mountebank had been very good at picking across country, and had taught both her and Cecily how to spot and memorise, for which she had been grateful on at least one flight before. The thought of gratitude and Marcus Dennett was an odd congruence though, so she decided she was grateful he was dead.

Her main fear when she skirted the gatehouse and flitted up beside the tree-lined avenue was of what the lord might say when she arrived. He had been a kindly man, but she and Cec, assured that they were safe and would be kept so, had stolen an ass and some food, and would have taken money if they'd known where to lay their hands on any. The house had offered them the milk of human kindness, and they'd spit in it. She was trembling and hungry, with her bare feet ragged from the woodland paths, and she caught herself hoping she was an object of sufficient pathos to be forgiven for her trespasses. Blasphemy again, she thought, oh help me, help me God, and please forgive me, I know not what I do. In her light-headed state, she felt like Mary Magdalene, whom her Stockport parson had told them was a blessèd whore. I'm in a shift, thought

Deborah, and it's so torn parts of me hang out. Oh please forgive me though, Sir Arthur. Please.

She'd walked out in the confusion as if it had been the most natural thing in the world. The smoke that gushed out from Milady's gun had been prodigious, and one of the men who'd stormed in from the stairs, by accident was all she could assume, had set off another piece with a charge in it that all but deafened everybody, as well as doubling the smoke and bringing down parts of the ceiling. The screaming on the stairs redoubled, more bodies were crammed in, and everyone was shouting, with the master worst in bellowing at his wife, whom Deb saw cowering on her knees with blood flowing from beneath her hands. Blood and bodies, that was her impression, as she glimpsed Dennett still folded like a knife, with his erstwhile patient curtaining his body with her sadly lustrous hair. In the choking mist groups crammed and surged and coughed, and on one surge, almost without thinking how to do it, Deborah slipped out. Almost without thinking, but not quite. Outside the dogs were too excited to be troublesome, and in thirty seconds she was away into the wider grounds. Deb, despite her injured leg, could run. If I had had them both cut off, she told herself through gritted teeth – I'd do it still.

It was Elizabeth, a maid she thought she recognised at the Lodge, that she let see her first. She stepped out from behind an outhouse on the home farm, stood there, and Liza screamed and almost dropped a basket.

'Oh hush,' said Deb in anguish, and the maid stared at her injured face and caught the next yell in her throat.

'Hide me,' said Deb, but Liza walked right up to her and touched her arm, and said she'd be all right. Deborah, losing control, then stood and cried. They were soon surrounded, they were quickly in the kitchen, and to her amazement and alarm, fat Mrs Houghton washed her face for her, with unaffected tenderness. Deborah cried as if she'd never stop, as if she were a little girl again. She sobbed.

Later, when she'd been fed and given clothes to dress herself more modestly, Mrs Houghton told her that the master wished to see her in his parlour, and she would take her there. Deborah, whose courage had been sapped by kindness, cried once more, so the housekeeper agreed that she would stay with her for the interview if Sir A allowed it, which he did. There was a fire in the grate, the coal-oil lamps were low and smelling very friendly, and he let her sit so far from him that he could hardly see the bruises on her face. It was a world that she had never known. It made her lonely.

Sir Arthur made it clear right from the outset that kindness and sympathy were the emotions that were ruling him, that he did not feel insulted, spurned, or robbed. She, falteringly, brought up the ass, at which Mistress Houghton and the master made it a jest, as if the subject had been rehearsed. Of all the asses they had on the estate, it seemed, she had chosen the most stubborn, with a marked propensity to bite. They waxed apologetic, hoping it had served the trick and eased her journey, and assuring her that it would have found a good home for itself when it had run away. It had not done, but she did not argue. It had been given to the men who helped her and Cec to London, in payment for their kindness. With similar delicacy, Sir A and Mrs Houghton never mentioned Cecily. The ass might exist still, so had existed. Cecily was a different case.

He tried to draw her on the life she'd led since going, but here reticence was Deb's choice. It had not been long but it had been a lifetime, and this warm, lovely room and cosy chat beside the hissing logs were an interlude that would end in more unpleasantness, and soon. To her, neither this ageing gentleman nor straitlaced dame seemed really fit to bear tales of lust and prostitution, even to associate the goings-on at Dr Marigold's with the sort of fine young men they knew. It had been unlooked for, and unpleasant, and at times there had been fun. If she was lucky, Deb thought, she would go back to it, there was plenty that was worse. But she did not want to burden these good sorts with it.

So it was when they got up to today. In her mind the scene was vividly confused, a fine mixture of impressions, so she felt. Most vividly she smelled the gunpowder, and the way it had wiped out the stench of Madam Wimbarton. Then Dennett, bloody on the ground, then the master, mad with rage and panic, roaring at his wife.

'There was a ruff,' she said. 'Part of the roof fell in, the ceiling. Servants all rushed in the room and . . . well, I sneaked off down the stairway, no one saw.'

'But what did you there to start with?' asked Sir A. 'In the stable, you say? How came you there, and why?'

She'd told him that. She thought she had.

'I told you, sir, beg pardon. That mountebank, quack doctor, Marcus Dennett. He'd come to London where me and Cecily was hid and brought me back. The teeth, sir. Cecily got shot by him.'

Mrs Houghton tutted quietly. Maybe I han't told it, thought Deborah. The loneliness came back, it was strong in her.

'It was for the teeth, that's all. Cec's hadn't took, Milady's gums went off like meat in summer, so he come up for me in London to take mine out instead. Then . . . and then the roof came down a bit, and then I run away.'

'Poor thing, poor thing,' Sir Arthur muttered. 'They were going to prise your teeth out, were they? On the spot! Well, it's providence, I suppose. God has His ways.'

'Making the roof fall in,' put in Mrs Houghton, at Deb's blank look. This struck Deb as funny, and she noted Mrs Houghton took some small amusement in it, too. 'But you sneaked away, you found your way back here, which is provident, my lass. Provident enough, we hope, to make you feel safe this time. You must not go again.'

'No, mistress,' Deb said, humbly. 'Please you, I am truly grateful for your kindnesses.'

'Were you pursued?' Sir A leaned forward keenly to peer at her. 'Do you not fear it if you were, because we have a good crew here. But were you followed or sought after, that you know?'

She shook her head, hoping she was right.

'No sign, sir, that I noticed. And I've racked my brains, but not even Dennett knew I ended here the night the young men rescued us. Dennett could find me, I suppose, Dennett could ferret anything. But Dennett's dead, God rot him.'

'God rest him,' Mrs Houghton amended, again with humour, surely?

'Yes, the young men,' mused Sir A. 'Well, Deborah, those young fellows will . . .'

He tailed off, and Deb saw a look, or signal, pass between the two of them. She made her face most open and aware, but the sentence stayed unfinished. Those young men, it occurred to her, would find her gone if they went looking, ever, back to Dr Marigold's. Well, Will might. Will had been about to— God, she'd been prepared to do the thing with him, she'd been surprised by feeling that she *wanted* to; some women, if not the maids, said jestingly it could be even sweet. Ah well. If he did come back he'd find her gone and that was that. Nothing more certain than that he'd soon forget her. It simply did not occur to her that she might see him here, although she knew Sam was somehow related to the house. Deborah saw this warm room, this kindness, this promise of release from vicissitude, as a tiny break from her real life and destiny. It would not be long enough to make a lasting change.

Deb was asleep when Bentley and Sam Holt arrived, as were most people in the house. Sir A was in his parlour still, alone, and there was a footman posted to tell him when the men came back from London. Sir A had thought it through most carefully when Deb had left with Mrs Houghton earlier, and had determined there was no point in telling her of the imminent arrivals. The whole thing was a fever in Will's brain most probably, he'd likely used the girl a time or two and had romantic madnesses on her. Whatever, he and Sam were pledged to try and find his nephew, and would be away from Langham Lodge as soon as they'd turned up, and slept, and ate, and made all ready.

In any way, Sir Arthur told himself, the maid was safe, her teeth were safe, and that was all that mattered, was it not? He could tell them that before they left, maybe, to give them something joyful for their joyless journey. And when they returned – why, she would be still here, and everything might turn up capital. His mind, despite himself, turned then to darker things. His nephew Charles. The fear that Samuel could die seeking him, and William. Indeed, the maiden was a horrible irrelevance. It was right he had not told her, and he would not tell them neither, not at first.

He knew the instant they came in that he'd been pre-empted. The footman knocked, but that was the only nod to procedure that there was. Sam came first, and had a concerned expression plastered to his face, but the life and curiosity in their tread was all he needed. In the saddle many hours, long trips by river, hard interviews – and they were lively as small boys. Sir Arthur felt quite old and tired.

'My dears,' he said. 'I am glad to see you home so quick and well.'

'And we have permission,' said Samuel. 'We've had letters off Lord Wodderley and one of them's on board the Biter for Slack Dickie. Forgive us, sir – but the maid? Tony says she has not lost her teeth! How did she come to be here? It is a marvel!'

'Aye, it is a marvel, it is a marvel, but—' Oh boys, he thought, so full of life, so full. And my poor Charlie Yorke. Will bowed.

'Forgive us, please, sir. It is only the surprise. The morning will do well enough, now she is safe. We will be leaving early as you know, but a minute before we go would be most excellent. Our journey was successful. I suppose there is no further news?'

Sir Arthur Fisher rang then for the man, and ordered him to bring the cold collations from the pantry, and hot tea, then some wine. He dismissed the subject of his missing nephew because, he said, it was now all in their hands and he could only wait, and was prepared to. He raised a twinkle in his eye for William, and told him all he knew of Deb's recapture and her flight. William affected cool and common human interest – one of the King's subjects who had had some local problems but had overcome by luck and fortitude was his attitude – but his reaction when Sir A mentioned her awful cuts and bruising gave him quite away.

The subject of Charles Yorke came up before they went to bed. There were horses ready, said their host, with saddlebags containing blankets, some basic iron rations, two pistols each, with shot and powder. In each a wallet, with both coin and notes, a not inconsiderable sum. Both demurred at this, but he flapped his hands at them and would not argue. It was theirs to spend on whatever need arose, he said. Food, shelter, buying information, bribes – the money was of supreme unimportance to him, its existence was solely to facilitate the achieving of an end.

'If you can do it without spending a groat, all well and good,' he said. 'If it costs me every groat I have, the case is just the same. Now to bed. And William – the maid will wait!'

But Deborah did not wait. She slept fitfully, and woke up with a start of terror when she heard the sound of horses in the yard, and woke another girl who had been put in with her to keep her company. The second maid was heavy with sleep and tiredness, and most uninterested in supposed marauders, which was 'not the way in master's house', she said. Then she told Deb casually – having no idea of its significance to her listener – that perhaps the two young Navy men were back, who'd gone off that day but no one had known where. Her irritation at being further questioned had gone away when she remembered Deb had been first brought to Langham Lodge by Mr Samuel and his friend, and she confirmed that these were the two who had been seeing master earlier, having ridden in 'all in a sweat'. The girl had wanted more talk on the subject then, but Deb, a little sore that Sir A and Mrs Houghton had kept so mum, pretended no further interest or knowledge of them. But she lay there with her brain positively seething, straining her ears and all her other senses. If they were here, if Will was here, she was going to find him out. She knew it.

Another half an hour to be sure her bed companion slept, and Deborah, without a candle, with almost no light throughout the women's quarters, began her quest. Last time she'd gone from here she'd had Cec with her, clumsy and whimpering with pain, an awful liability. This time it was almost easy, she almost knew the place, she knew at least the doors she should avoid and where the stairways were. Clear of the quarters, on a lower floor, she needed luck, some sort of clue. Dressed all in white, and drifting into proper people's chambers, she might be taken for a ghost. More likely she would find Sir Arthur Fisher or (if her rooms were not on some servants' floor) the house-keeper, both of whom clearly wanted her to know her place and keep it. They would not take her for an unquiet walker of the night, but they would surely exorcise her, and double quick.

She had the luck. As she stood hovering at the end of a long, forbidding corridor, a latch clicked, and a door opened as she stepped into shadow, and Sam Holt emerged with a candle in his hand. He was fully dressed, and before he closed it, he said clearly through the door, 'Till morrow,

Will. God rest,' then turned his back to her and took another door a good way further on. The passage dark once more, Deb stood stock-still for just one brief instant, afraid that she might change her mind, then almost ran, touched the latch, lifted it, and entered.

William was standing by the bed, a big one with a canopy, but he had his back to her.

'Back soon,' he said, not turning. 'What ha' you forgot?'

Deb opened her mouth, but found she could not speak. Will bent to fiddle with a boot, and grunted.

'Be useful, then. Give me a pull with this— Ah, Christ! Deborah! Oh, Deb!'

They made a picture standing there, the maid in shadow but her nightgown glaring in the candlelight, the young man all agape. He was in breeches and an open shirt, and momentarily, he had balanced on one leg. He put his foot down to the floor, he opened out his hands, then dropped them to his sides.

'I'm sorry, sir,' she said. 'It was just— They did not tell me. Am I allowed?'

''Fore God, Deb! Jesus, have you seen your face? God, what have the villains done to you?'

He stepped towards her, and for a moment she tried to hide herself. Then she decided, and stepped forward strongly, lifted back her head. He flinched.

'Yes, I have seen it, it is mine,' she said. 'I am sorry if it offends you, but it's the only one I have. Look—' she bared her teeth, and snapped them like a dog. 'I still have all my teeth.'

They needed laughter, but neither one could laugh. But suddenly they could move together, and they were touching hands. Will gazed upon her face extremely closely, and neither of them shrank.

'Well, I am glad for that,' he said, at last. 'Deb, you are a walking wonder, how come you to be here? Sir A has told a tale indeed! Sam and me went to see the house, we wanted to break in but it's a fortress. I thought we were too late, that they would— Oh Deb, you are a lovely sight!'

'Hah!' This was a shout of laughter, short but merry. 'You only ever see me with a broken face, sir! This time a broken knee an' all, I had to hop off from them, and some pretty bruises underneath the gown! Dennett came for me, sir, the one you had to save us from before, he stole me out of Dr Marigold's and killed poor Cec. But . . . but you say you went there, sir. What, to the magistrate's? How can that be? How come you here, for that? I thought it was Navy business you were on.'

'Aye,' said Will. 'But afterwards. We looked to save you, Deb; we talked to Mrs Margery, and came on hot-foot. The work downriver was sooner over than we thought, is all. We thought . . . I thought . . . well, instead of going to our duty we went to Marigold's.'

He was looking fairly at her, and he blushed. The odd sensation that she'd felt before caught her strongly and – extremely bold – she put her arms around him. She did not believe they'd come to try and save her, run from London and their duty, that could not be true, but for now it mattered not at all. There was a warm and giving feeling in her, and when their faces met, not all the tenderness was forced on them by her bruises. Their faces met, and their mouths were joined, and moved and rested on each other as though their souls were flowing through. For both of them, it was amazing sweet.

Will knew little of these things, and Deb but little more, but they both began to undress him, half clumsily but with a pleasure that was intensely keen. He fell across the bed to drag one boot off, while Deborah, on her knees, dealt with the other, which was not so tight. She then leaned on to him, between his legs, and helped him to unfasten at the waist, which made him squirm, and gasp, and grit his teeth for fear that he would spend. Deb, as deftly as she'd done it in the past to little brothers, eased his breeches down his legs and off him in a movement, then in another, seeing what was happening to him, untied the ribbons at her neck to let her nightgown rumple to the floor.

'Sir,' she said, 'look now. And it is free!'

Perhaps it was the humour, perhaps his crisis passed, but Will opened his eyes, rolled on to his side, and got his passion under rein. Perhaps it was her saying 'sir' which saved it for him. He stared at her great beauty, her bruised and abraded body, the red and livid patches on the milky white, and he was swept by awe and gratitude. He reached his hand out, she hers, and they touched at fingertips.

'Don't call me that,' he said. 'Deb, my name is Will. You cannot call me sir.'

Then she moved on to the bed beside him, by his plucking at her fingers, and they rolled together among the softness of the downy coverings, and he slipped into her and they held each other hard but gently until he ceased to throb. For a moment it was wonderful for Deb, a comfort and sensation she had never known the like of, then she thought of what was happening in her life, and she thought that she might get with child and what would happen then, and she, briefly, thought of home. Then she looked down Will's slight body, the curving of his back, and smelled the sweet smell of his neck and musty hair and it began another, double ache, of gladness and regret. The young man, she noted with an affection almost motherly, was asleep.

But Will was not, just drowning in sensations and confusions of his own. Mainly was the continued sense of awe, the happiness of being with this maid like this, the sense of lightness that was spiritual and physical as well, the sense of unexpected purity. Will knew whores, they'd been a presence in ships and streets and taverns in his life, and he'd known what sailors did with them. Whatever it was meant to feel or be like, in his imaginings, it was not like this, there was not a remote conjunction. Opening his eyes, he was overwhelmed anew by the tenderness she aroused in him, the love with which he beheld her face. Her eyes, to him, were grave and clear and honest, her face a model of perfection, her body beautiful in a most astonishing way, as if it spoke to him, existing for him only. And then she kissed him on the mouth, and very soon they were making love more slowly, but with very little movement, as though their bodies breathed together, they were one. When he spent this time, Will made a low crying sound, as if he were distressed, and Deb's eyes, afterwards, were filled with tears.

When they talked, she told him all the truth about what had happened at the magistrate's, including how she had watched Dennett killed and how she'd revelled in the fact. He had come to help the master rape her, that was her certainty, he had brought a rope to tie her up if necessary, and a cloth to gag her with, and he would provide the strength to hold her down. Then, afterwards – had Milady not come in to kill her first – he would have torn her gums bare as per contract, then let her meet her fate. Will could believe Wimbarton would rather have had her as a replacement than have stuck with his blighted wife (although he found it hard to bear the thought, and hugged her tighter underneath the sheets), and told her she was mad to harbour guilt about the mountebank and his fate, which he deserved most richly. He soothed her fears as best he could about Wimbarton finding her. What was the point, now his quack-surgeon was dead; who else would try the operation? And in any way, would Mistress Wimbarton let her near the house again? Never in this world.

He would prevent it, was what he wanted to say, he would look after her. But cold fingers of reality kept worming through his guts, and he was an honest man, and intended that he always would be. Sir A, he said, knew all her troubles, and would treat her like a seeker after sanctuary, one of his household. Deb's own fingers of misery moved within her then, and she cried out silently, 'But I'm a whore, I am just a whore, and no one will protect me because I am not worth it.' This time the tears did spill from her eyes.

I will never leave you, thought Will, I will protect you always; but he said: 'Sir Arthur is a good man, Deb, why are you weeping? He will keep you from all harm, I'm sure of it.'

'But I han't even told him all the truth,' sobbed Deb. 'I said the roof fell in, which is true, but I han't said that a musket brought it down, or that Milady was going to kill me or that Dennett's shot to death, or that the master aimed to fuck me. Oh sir, oh Will, I would have let him, and become his doxy too if it would ha' saved my teeth! Oh sir, I am a liar, I'm a liar!'

This stabbed him with a vicious pain, although he knew she must have done, she would have done, she had no choice, but there was a small mad fear that she might, somehow, not have minded. This horrified him also, the fact he'd harboured such a venal thought, so he forced himself to say it did not matter, why should it matter that she'd not disclosed the details? It was not a question for an answer, but Deb treated it as such.

'Because it is a piece,' she said, voice low and not quite steady. 'I've stole from him, and now I've lied to him, and all the time I'm just a little slut that run away from home and family and has become a whore. Oh sir. Do you think I could tell him in the morning? Do you think that you might be in the room, or tell him I have got to say something? Or something of the sort, sir? Please?'

But I won't be there, he thought. Then: she must stop saying 'sir', she is my lover. Oh Christ, is there no end to pain?

'But Deb, it is impossible. I am not your . . . it is not my place to say such things to Sir Arthur Fisher. You tell him, do; he will not mind. Or tell Mrs Houghton, it is an understanding woman. In any way, by this morning I will be gone. Sam Holt and me. We have a duty to perform. And please; don't call me sir.'

Deb had rolled away, was propped up on one elbow, her clear brown eyes regarding him. Will felt he could detect contempt, indeed he was ashamed. But maybe he was wrong, for Deb smiled at him, and reached her free hand out to touch his cheek.

'Duty,' she said. 'You men and duty. I sometimes wish that I'd been born a man. Oh well, as you say, he is a good man, and I suppose the details are no great moment to him. A rat shot down is still just one rat less, however much I found it shocking. Dennett deserved it, that is one thing. And I've seen worse at home!'

He was tired. There was no denying it, an ache was growing behind his eyes. Her breasts were soft and wonderful, and he touched one, but she merely smiled more broad, and covered them. She leaned across and kissed his cheek and patted him as if she were older than he was, and much wiser, then slipped out of the bed despite he tried to stop her when he realised. Leaning across, all glorious dark hair and injured beauty, naked, she was more like a dream than real, and he let his hand drop down on to the coverings.

'But you must not go,' he said. 'Please stay.'

'And who will do explaining in the morn? A doxy in a master's bed, an empty one, the master gone! Sir, don't look so cut, I'm jesting, but it is the truth. Forgive me, I mean . . . Will.'

She bent to pick her nightgown off the floor, and wriggled into it as lithe as any snake. It startled Will to see it happen, it was the first time in his life. One moment this warm thing that was somehow his, it filled his eyes and made him fearful with regret that it was parting, and then, as if instantaneously, it was gone. He remembered the breasts, the pale brown nipples, the mass of jet black curls that marked her Venus mound, but abruptly and irrevocably, they were no longer his, or concrete. Deb's face reappeared, and there was no alteration in the way she gazed at him, but William was bereft, forlorn.

'I will be back, Deb,' he said. 'Not long away, I promise you. And then we'll . . . we will . . .'

She did not wait to hear him end the sentence, if he ever could. The women's quarters, as quick as legs could carry her. Perhaps the scullery to seek out vinegar, but in any case a very thorough wash. Deb tried to keep the good parts in her mind, and true it was he was a very lovely man. When he returned, who knew? There were worse ways to conduct a life.

22

Even in the morning, even in the lashing rain as they picked slowly down the London road, William could not clear his mind of Deb and what they'd done together. At first it was a warm euphoria; he awoke to it, snug in the bed they'd made love in, regretful only that she was not there still. He lay on his back, aware of noises in the house and rain upon the window glass, and touched himself, and felt sensations, and re-envisioned things. For the moment, all seemed marvellous, except perhaps the rain. He saw himself riding off with Sam, and doing things vaguely heroic, then coming back to Deb. Then what? Well, going back to bed with her. Then what? He tried to claw back to euphoric memories.

The rain was terrible, it had set in with a vengeance, as if it had been away too long but now was back for good. It was not so heavy as insistent, driven by a one-reef wind from the south west, the progeny of clouds low and dark and dense. Sam and Will got kitted in the house, with footmen helping them lugubriously, then completed their protection in the stables, with tarpaulin capes and three-cornered hats that would gutter excess water well off their necks on to their backs and shoulders. It was a point that they should not look like shipping men, or Customs officers, which filled both with some unease because they were not actors. 'All I know's the sea,' said Sam. 'It was my father who could wear a wig as if he meant it. What shall we do if someone talks of business? Play deaf-mutes?'

The farewells were not aided by it, either. Sir A had tried for false brightness in the house, but outside the stable he ignored the umbrella Tony brought for him, and let his own wig saturate, the powder running down his face and neck. He clasped both firmly by the hand for just an instant, wishing them God-speed, then bade them turn away, and quickly. But when they reached the first bend in the way and Sam glanced backwards, he was still standing there, although Tony had managed to put the umbrella above his head. By the time they reached the gatehouse, where a keeper with a firearm acknowledged them through the open window, Will had water trickling down his neck and felt one foot was getting soggy. Yet thoughts of Deborah still kept him warm . . .

For the first part of the journey they said little. They knew they had to work out a strategy, but they'd agreed the first thing was to get along the road. In normal conditions they might have come to Petersfield in half a day or so, but progress in this murk and wet was going to be painful. There was not much traffic, but in almost every dip there was a quagmire, and in almost every quag there was a wagon or a cart or coach, either bogged down singly or in contention with another one, or two, or three, or four. Sometimes they could ease their way by going off the road, but more usually the fields were bogs, or the roadside densely wooded. And almost every hamlet was a bottleneck.

Why Petersfield, in any way? They were not going to the Bentley house, because one never knew who servants might be attached to, but they saw it as a point of no return, from where they could strike for the Hampshire coast or the West Sussex one, whichever they decided on. It was the point, also, where goods were gathered in – 'free trade' as well as more legitimate – for despatch to London up the high road. A busy town, where William should not be recognised, except by extreme ill-luck. That was in both their minds. In the event, they guessed they'd find somewhere not far away, a country inn not on the beaten track, to do their planning in.

From time to time, when the road was good enough, they would fall in side by side and try some conversation, just to pass the time. Sam marvelled that people should choose a life ashore, when going was so much easier in a boat in general terms, and the food and drink went with you. He by now was wet from neck to navel-hole, as he put it, and cold as charity. On board, unless there was some emergency, he could have gone below at some set point, and took a glass or so.

It was just chatter, and Will paid little heed to it. As they moved further off from Langham Lodge the memories of the physical delight did fade under the onslaught of the dedicated rain, but his mind gnawed and worried at the larger elements of his time with Deb. The feelings that seemed to fill his stomach – yes, he found them physical, quite definite – were not for denying any more. Delight remembered, loss, pain, fear for the present and the future; it was a jumble and a whirl. And what was she? Some little maiden they had rescued from a mountebank, a traveller, a runaway, a whore. Before God, how could he think he loved her – or whatever it was that burned inside his head? He had seen her naked, kissed her, done the thing with her. And she had said, she had acknowledged, she would have gladly gone to Wimbarton, to be his mistress, just to save her teeth. Which thought was followed on the instant, and drowned out, by shame he'd let it form.

'Sam,' he said, in the third hour of their way. 'Do you believe in love?'

He supposed that Sam would roar, or curl his lip, which – with eyes averted – he took care he would not see. But Sam did not answer for a while, squelching on beside him with his shoulders hunched, head bowed. Will wondered if he should repeat the words, or some words like it, or let it fade into the mist with gratitude. Then came an answer, but without contempt.

'Ah,' said Sam. 'So that's it then. *La belle* Deb's got her teeth in you that deep, has she? Forgive me, Deb,' he added, to the air, 'for mentioning a painful subject like your teeth. Well, what d'you mean, by love?'

Great help, thought Will. So fine, that gets me off those horns. Why should Sam know, in any way? I guess he's near as green as me, although he's not so virginal. I will speak no more.

'Well, I don't know,' he said. 'That is the problem, isn't it? Last night I . . . well, when we found her there at Sir Arthur's house. Well, I knew I'd be relieved, well, both of us. The poor girl's suffering . . . But . . .'

'Aye, you looked relieved,' said Sam sardonically. 'You dug your heels in that poor horse the way I thought he'd stand you on your head. I don't know how you kept yourself from blurting out to Sir A, neither, but he saw through you soon enough.'

'Nay! He thought 'twas you!' said Will. 'I did not show myself at all!'

'He was playing with you, of course he knew, you fool. I'm surprised you did not ask him where she slept. I would have done.'

A glow of pride swept over Will at this. He had not needed to. He licked rain off his lips, uncomfortable. And what if Deb had not found him out? Appalling thought.

'So,' he said, after a brief, stiff pause. 'You think it only lust, do you? Not serious emotion? Or a worthy one?'

'Hah! Three questions all in one! You should not link "lust" with "only" in the first place, whatever I think, though – what's wrong with good old lust? And is it serious? Oh well, it can be, believe me. And what's more worthy than to do the act by which we're made? You sound like some old knock-kneed vicar, or a puritan. It may be lust, I suppose, but only time will tell. You've not done anything to test it yet, have you?'

Will did not reply to that, and his silence must have pricked Sam's conscience.

'You're serious,' he said, after a little while. 'But Will, you cannot really think you love the maid, surely? She is one of Dr Marigold's! And yes, if you want me to answer, I do believe in love. I think maybe, once, I was almost touched by it. And I have seen it, certainly. I've seen maids torn to bits and men made fools by it. That's why people marry, isn't it, to avoid the traps and pitfalls? With love we'd all be destitute.'

A cloud swept down low then, and for a while the dogged horses stumbled on, heads bowed, while Sam and William hunched into their cloaks to try and guide them through the most unpleasant bits. The traps and pitfalls, Sam had said. Will's mother and his father had wed like every other pair he knew, for family, land, inheritance. It had not occurred to think of them and love.

When the squall had eased, Sam reined in and turned his horse so that he could face him. His hat was like a triple waterfall, his face pale and streaming, the tip of his nose bone-white and pinched.

'Look, love is not for us,' he told Will, seriously. 'Maybe it is lust, and it's run you mad, or maybe it's lack of sleep or something simpler than that. We're under orders, man, we're always under orders. Sent here, sent there, sent one day to our deaths. Look at us now. If we don't drown on horseback we'll get shot, how can you think of love? Think of the maiden, if you love her – and have pity!'

Will tried to smile, appreciating that Sam was lapsing into jest only to soften it. As he picked past, he tried to joke himself.

'At least she's poor,' he said. 'If a maid depended on me for wealth and luxury, it would be terrible. She's used to poverty.'

'Aye, but it's *us* who are dependent,' replied Sam, following. 'I don't want poverty, friend, I've had my fill of it. It is us who must find rich ones, and damn quick. Do you want Slack Dickie lording you around? You do not! Do you want to spend your life with sixpenny harlots, with or without the scars and bruises? Indeed you don't! There are two ways in the world for us, boy – rich wives or prizes.

Deb's breasts are passing beautiful, but you could suck 'em till the cows came home if you had money in your pocket. I do believe in love, and you ain't got it, it's not for you, you can't afford it, do you catch the way I'm drifting? When we get back to Sir A's, for God's sake slip her five shillings for a shag. You'll be amazed how quickly you forget her, then, or at least get over thoughts of love. I tell you – if you're that besotted, go up to a sovereign, or a guinea, that will clear your mind. Rich wives do it just as well for nothing, and they bring their father's wealth into the bargain! The ugly ones are the most generous of all I'm told, and you can always blow the light out first, or close your eyes! For God's sake, Will, it is not sensible. She's a *whore*.'

Ahead of them, a small house was emerging from the sweeping mist, with a stream of smoke blowing almost horizontal from its stack. Will nodded dumbly when Sam indicated they might stop and sup, assuming it was some kind of tavern, glad that this conversation should lapse. It had a walled yard, with men to take and feed the horses and get them in the dry and warm, and soon they were inside, beside a good wood fire, being divested of their outer clothes and never mind the splashing on the flags. Hot gin was brought, and towels, and the smell of roasting meat was strong, and for a while their talk was all domestic. That Sam pitied him for Deb was not in doubt, and he said no more that might upset him. Will brooded though, and sometimes had a flash of memory and delight. He supposed his friend was right, in all the details; he was a second son, no expectations, and Deb was a . . . a victim of ill circumstance. He thought maybe he ought to welcome the fact a gentleman like Wimbarton could want her for her beauty, that she carried in her loveliness the seeds of an advancement. But it made him rather sick, was all. Sam, after some tries, insisted they must talk about their mission, and as they supped they did. But oh, Will thought from time to time, such pain, such joy, such misery.

They travelled all the afternoon, but this time with a purpose. After long discussion they had both agreed the best way, and the quickest, would be to try for information from the source, exploiting Will's own past as well as his knowledge of terrain. Neither was confident that it would work, and if it did not they knew it would be dangerous, although – as Samuel said – they had the benefits of Sir Arthur's guns, and cash, and two good horses, if they did not die of chill! They made for Chichester, a busy, lively town with men of business in the streets, and merchants, traders, solid citizens of every sort. They went into an inn, paid in advance for lodging there, and let themselves be seen at backgammon in the parlour, with not a care save a steamy dampness around the shoulders of their coats. They talked about the filthy weather with their fellow guests, and reckoned winter to be earlier each year. But they asked no questions, none of any sort.

The ride to Langstone in the morning was a hard and anxious one, but they did it boldly and their bravery paid off. At breakfast they had wondered if their plan was wrong, but Sam was an impatient man, so set a time for them of two full minutes to come up with another one. They failed – although Will suggested they might get his boat from Port Creek and go by sea – so the subject was foreclosed. They ate a solid meal, checked their saddlebags and strapped them to their waiting horses, and clopped out beneath the arch into the clean, fresh, sunny air. The main streets of Chichester were paved, and had been cleared and washed down in the night. A mile away, however, the westward road was a canal of liquid mud.

It was crisp this morning, with white clouds blowing across a pale blue sky, but Will and Sam were sweating before much time had passed. The way was very busy, the bog-downs innumerable, and the labour to keep their horses out of the worst parts hard. Sam laughed at one stage that a boat trip would be fine indeed – except that

Will's yawl was moored two miles beyond their destination. However, by sea they would have turned up like honest men, and not like two scarecrows made of mud and dung. Will further pointed out they had no idea of the state of tide, and that his yawl was in the mud eight hours out of twelve. Also, on horseback, they possibly had more chance of escape if the men they sought turned villainous. Smugglers, whatever else, were the very ace at seamanship.

They passed through Emsworth beyond midday, which even Sam, from distant parts, knew as a haunt of the free trade. It was time to eat and wash and rest the mounts, so Will suggested Havant, a small market town just farther on, close to Langstone but not on the sea so less likely as a point of trouble. They chose a small inn in the shadow of the church, where they took a room to stow their saddle-bags so they could travel light. It seemed they both still favoured going in, walking abroad, and seeing what might happen, and, strangely, it excited them, this dreadful inexperience as spies. Now it was close they relished the thought of action, any action.

'I tell you what,' said Samuel, 'I'm glad I joined the sea service, ain't you? Much more of bouncing on a bloody leather saddle and my backside would explode. How far is it to Langstone? Why don't we walk?'

They did not, in case they needed to escape, but when they'd reached the outskirts they decided on the foreshore as the tide was low, tethered their horses, and mingled with the crowds around the Hayling Island causeway. The smell of mud from off the creek was keen, and Will snuffed at it with deep appreciation, although Sam was less enamoured. The village was a scattered one, so they strolled towards the mill and the cottages beyond, where Will had come ashore once and thought the fisherfolk – and smugglers – most likely lived. On the shingle, in fact, above high-water mark, there were some women working on nets, and one or two small children.

Making contact, it came into them, making the first move, was going to be the hardest trick of all. The sun was out despite the cutting wind, so to begin the job they found a shingle bank above the beach, and sat. The women – three young, two older, one a matriarch – glanced at them uninterested, then ignored them, bending to their task. The children ran around about their business, and it occurred to Will that the robuster of the two young wives, aged somewhere not too far off twenty-five if he could judge, could well be Mary Broad, as he had guessed at that earlier time he'd come. What should he say or do, then? 'Hallo, mistress, I knew Jesse Broad. Not only knew him but I watched him die'? In the bottom of the creek, between the island and the mainland mud, the water ruffled to a gust of breeze, and Will was cold. It was hard, so hard.

The children did it for them in the end. They ran near them, a girl, two boys, in a wild and frantic chase, and one boy sprawled headlong almost at Sam's feet. Before his screeches came, while he drew in a monstrous breath, Sam lifted him, and he did not struggle, but looked astonished for a moment, until the wail burst out for his mamma. All the women stopped as both men stood, and the boy kicked and pumped with legs and arms until the one that Will had noted walked across, not hurrying, but calm and purposeful. She had an open face, fiercely tanned from wind and weather, clear eyes and full kindly mouth. She put her hands out for the child, and he wriggled into them and bawled.

'Thank you, sir,' she said. 'Now Jem, my Jem, my little love. Come on, Mamma's got you, where does it hurt? Your knee?'

Jem. The name struck into Will, the memory of Jesse Broad stabbed home. He'd talked of Jem, sometimes, to soothe Will in his fevers. He'd talked of Jem, and goodwife Mary, and of home.

'Mistress,' he said. He almost stumbled. 'I think I know

279

you, I think you're Mistress Broad. I knew your husband. My name is Bentley. William.'

She did not start, she did not shriek or drop the child, but stared at him. She was a little taller than he was, and more robust, in dark grey wool and a dull red skirt. She held the child, and patted him and cooed, until the squall of tears passed by. The tension in the air, for Will and Sam, was extraordinary, but she was oblivious. Pats, and coos, and cuddles, and a level, daunting gaze.

'I know your name, sir. I am pleased to meet you, after all these years. I never did expect to see you here.'

'Mary!' called the youngest woman. 'How does it with Jem? Peter wants his playmate back, he says.'

It was a check to see she was not needful, and Mary glanced across her shoulder, smiling.

'I must return my little boy,' she said. 'Jesse's little boy, poor mite. What do you here, sir? An accident, a passing-by, a social call? You have left the Navy, I suppose, they said that was the strongest rumour. Do you have business hereabout?'

'Peter! Peter!' cried the little boy. 'Mamma, I want to play with Peter!'

She slipped him down on to the shingle and he scampered off. The other women were still watching, halfway to suspicious. She waved to reassure them, but was in no hurry to return. Sam, visibly, was relaxing, but William blushed furious. In all his life before he had never known women so prepared to talk out loud to men, and now it was a day-to-day occurrence. Except she called him sir, this one could have been his equal, it would seem. Yet Sam was grinning, and suddenly sprawled down to sit on the bank again, without a by-your-leave. Scandalous.

'Mistress,' he said. 'My name is Samuel Holt and I'll level with you while Will here tries to get his knots untied. I may die for saying this because we don't know you, but what the hell's life for if not to take risks? Despite our togs, despite the crazy headgear, we're in the Navy still and we sought you for a reason not your company, however excellent that has proved to be, pardon my boldness. Will knew your husband – nay, I may tell you that he loved him – and you seem well disposed to Will. We need some information, madam. Pray say you'll talk to us.'

Mary's eyes were glistening, perhaps with tears. She turned to William. Who had the need for honesty, however deadly.

'Your husband . . . Jesse . . . was a smuggler,' he said, to those unflinching eyes. 'We know this, Mistress Broad, he told me, and he made me understand. We are seeking smu— We are seeking men who've murdered a Customs officer, and may have murdered two. It is a matter for a friend, Sam's unc— A friend who suffers badly from this case. Please: we need your help.'

'The men are fishing,' said Mary, carefully. 'Off the island, all of them.' Behind her the old woman was moving towards them, stooped but purposeful. Mary was aware of it. 'Yes,' she said. 'I have heard of what you did, sir. We do get messages from off the hulks sometimes, from those poor prisoners. I know the case, as well; the officers you're talking of. Our men are all at sea, sir. We shall talk.'

The old matriarch was up beside her, watching them through washed-out eyes that were as hard as pebbles.

'These are seamen,' she said, in a voice both harsh and breathless. 'What do they tell you, Mary? Their clothes are wrong. They're Customs, or the Navy. They're of the sea.'

Samuel, who had stood at her approach, removed his hat and bowed.

'Aye,' he said. 'Well spotted, mother. Sam Holt's my name, midshipman. My friend is Will, Will Bentley.'

She uttered a harsh sound, that might have been a laugh almost. She gripped her stick and forced her head back so she could see him better.

'God's blood,' she said, 'God's blood and bones. We were

going to have you killed, young man, one day. Well, here's a fine one to come calling, isn't it?'

The talking took three days, by the end of which Will felt that they had scratched the surface and Samuel that they had got much farther. The first evening they talked solely to the women, and rode the long road back to Chichester to sleep in safety, but by the second they were confident enough to stay in Havant, at the inn. They did some local travelling from the second day, escorted by men of the fraternity to visit other men, but it was all by water, and over short distances. The man who seemed the leader of the Langstone crew – although leadership was not a notion they would allow in their secret trade – was called Isa Bartram, and was the husband of Mary's friend and neighbour Kate. He was a lean and dour sort, with beetle's eyebrows, who was not disposed to openness with them, or to trusting anyone outside the tight-knit fellowship of men who used the twin havens joined by the drying creek he lived on. Two of the meetings indeed, so great was his suspicion of the landbound, were held on a fishing lugger off the East Winner shoals. And fishing did go on, too authentically to be just done as cover. William almost lost two fingers to a skate, and Sam was seasick.

The first talk, soon after the introductions on the beach, was in some way a false dawn. Mary, it appeared, was as strong a person as Jesse Broad had been, who handled the old woman with grace and firmness. She introduced her as Seth Hardman's mother, Hardman having died, she said, with her eyes on William, the night the Welfare's men had pressed her husband. Murdered, she then added, another intelligence that had come from the incarcerees inside the prison hulks in Fareham creek. In the nature of a rebuke it was sufficient to satisfy the old woman, then Mary rebuked Samuel openly – but with equal kindness – for using words like 'midshipman', and Will Bentley's name, in front of people he did not know. Even in a village as small as

Langstone, she pointed out, not everyone was to be trusted, and Widow Hardman – said with delightful humour – could have been a spy.

Within five minutes the old one was back on the foreshore overseeing, while Mary, Kate and a young woman introduced as Sally, dark-complexioned with a tendency to silence, conducted the men into a nearby house. There was a kettle on the hob in the small, lightless kitchen-parlour, and very soon all were drinking tea. A turn-up for the books, thought William, and wondered idly if it would be of the finest sort, supped on by smugglers as normal perquisites, no duty paid. But it was dark and bitter, well below the leaf drunk in his father's house, although Samuel relished it and smacked his lips for more, low swine.

Mary was exceeding open with them, not overawed one whit by their presence and proximity, and she set out by explaining what Widow Hardman had meant by her earliest remarks. First news when Welfare had returned to England, long before the court martial on the Admiral's flagship, had indicated Will Bentley as one of the chief villains, nephew and henchman to the unconscionable Daniel Swift. There had indeed been talk of assassination in the first months afterwards, and not just of him. But it was mainly wildness, was her opinion, engendered by frustration, drink, and anger that the Navy saw no ill in any but the common sailor, nor brooked suggestion that ills could be wider spread.

'The thought of you lying in your sickbed, helpless in your father's house near Petersfield, pretty undefended, struck some hotheads as enticing,' she said. 'Not a worthy thought for men despising tyranny, but not unnatural, I suppose. There are such hotheads, we have some even in the local band.' She and Kate shared a smile. 'John Hardman, let us say; who you will meet.'

'Hardman?' said Sam. 'What, the old dame's son, is it?'

'Her third,' said Kate. 'The youngest. Seth died at the

Navy's hands, and Joseph, who was oldest, was lost at sea. John is not twenty years yet, Ma Hardman had but three but spread them out.' The amusement shared with Mary grew. 'John came beyond a natural age, people round here insist. She's a witch, no question of it.'

'Did not even bother with a man to help her get him,' said Mary. 'Now there's proof! There's an old chap down Bedhampton way who's very fond of widows, but that don't come into it, except with spoilsports! Want more tea?'

Sam did, Will did not. When the fun had died down, Mary carried on.

'In any way,' she told Will, 'it was not long beyond that when better stories began to come out of the hulks. There was a man called Tobin, and a man called Harry Wilson, do you remember them? They told first how you were a friend of my Jesse, and fought with him and Mr Matthews at the end. Then that you refused to testify against the rebels, and others told us why. Wilson and Tobin, they got life, and Tobin later died of fever. But they've helped you, haven't they? For folks round here will talk to you. If you had come alone, sir, on such a mission' – this to Samuel – 'you'd likely have been killed. There's no one more hated round these parts than Customs men, or those who give them aid.'

Dark Sally gave a little chuckle, in her corner.

'Unless it be the Press,' she said.

Will was brooding on the fact he did not remember the two men who'd spoken up for him, or possibly had never even heard their names in all the crush of sailors on his uncle's ship, either way a cause for shame. But Sam had picked up on Sally's voice.

'Ah, the Press,' he said. 'A necessary evil some would say, but hated wherever seamen go, I'll not deny. Your accent, maid. Or should I call you mistress? You're not from here, I guess?'

'Nor am I married, sir. Your ear is quick. I come from

Guernsey. I lived there till some years ago. French influence on my voice. Most people do not hear it.'

'Least of all in so few words,' said Kate, gaily. She stood and walked across the kitchen, blocking Sally's corner from their view, almost as if on purpose. She opened a small window, leaning out to listen, then stooped back.

'Just play,' she said. 'I thought I heard Jane bawl. My little one. But sirs, you've only hinted so far, Mary's only sketched us in. My husband's in the trade, I may be frank with you she says, but what exactly do you here? She says it is the matter of those spies. Can not you tell us more? I fear you must.'

Sam, with his nerve of iron, plunged in to tell them briefly and succinctly about Sir A and his lost nephew, and his agony of unknowing now Charles Warren had been found. There were so many mysteries to the case, he said, it was so unlike any normal run of war between the Customs and the so-called free trade, that Sir A was fearful he might never know the truth.

'"So-called"?' said Mary, mildly. 'You might take care with words like that in certain quarters, I should say.'

'Madam,' Sam answered, 'I am a Navy officer, so everybody knows my public duty. I take your point though, and thank you for it. I suppose what I was hoping to convey was the most unusual level of violence involved, the barbaric depths these people went to. Charles Warren's body, I am told, was burnt, abused, dismembered. Pray God that is not normal in such cases in these parts.'

From outside came the sound of children, and the higher screams of gulls. Inside, no one stirred.

'Sir,' said Mary, finally. 'It is not. I cannot go into details with you, you must understand our difficulties here. We live in fear of death ourselves, either from a bullet from a riding officer or the rope, and one man or woman cannot talk for all the others, least of all to officers of the Crown. Our menfolk will not get to shore until the early hours, or may decide to fish another tide. Until we've spoke to

them we can go no further. Except to say, in part way if
not all, we do agree with you. We know of it, we are not
party to it, and it is a most dreadful case, inhuman, horrible. There. I have spoken. You must return tomorrow
after we have conferred.'

'You are the leader, aren't you?'

Sam let it out as an expostulation, which made Will
jump. But Mary shook her head, unflustered. To Will she
said: 'I'd take him home now, Mr Bentley, his mouth is
far too big for safety. Come back tomorrow when the men,
I hope, will be here. It has been, I promise you, some sort
of pleasure to me to have made your acquaintance at last.
My Jesse was a fine man, and I mourn him still.'

She stood, they all stood save for Sally, and Kate said,
mildly but with purpose: 'But realise the details of this
talking will be passed on the instant you are gone, and
will reach the men if . . . well, if by some sad chance you
were acting to a purpose we know not.'

Will nodded gravely.

'You may trust in me,' he said, 'if nothing else, to do
nothing underhand. In both of us. You have my word.'

Sam nodded, and threw a glance at Sally, who ignored
it. Shortly, they were trotting back to Havant.

Mary was not the leader, they found out, although she
was deep inside the counsels of the band. Next day they
met Kate's husband Isa Bartram, who was no man's second
fiddle, nor woman's either. In the village there were three
men they were introduced to – they knew them by their
first names only, Bob, George and Joe – and also John
Hardman, the nearest neighbour, who was a thin, intense
young man with burning eyes and an air of impatience
bordering on violent. At first he seemed the most against
them, more deep in his suspicion even than Isa Bartram,
but in a day or so he formed a strange alliance with Sam
Holt, they shared a boldness and outspokenness that set
them quite apart, and they often huddled off together, and

286

swore and laughed in a dialogue of their own. Sam told him he should go for a Navy officer (Sam revealed to Will one night, in their lodging) and Hardman, far from thinking it a jest or kind of insult, became thoughtful. The outlaw life and fishing, he allowed, had some attraction, but he was a man who loved his country, and would like to fight the French, not trade with them. There were, he added darkly, many of his fellow countrymen who filled his heart with shame, and not just common men like him. Sam said he liked him and (more mysterious but he would not expand on it) that he had high hopes.

Their simple hopes, though, that the men would take their cue in trust from Mary and the other women and quickly give them information about Charles Yorke, dwindled as the talks went forward. Bartram said several times that he was pleased to trust their story in as far as it went, that their purpose was discovery of information which would not lead to general wreaking of revenge against the local free trade, however innocent they were of blacker crimes. But Yorke and Warren had not been just Customs men, there was more to them than met the eye and everybody knew it. If they had died, why was that abnormal anyway? These things happened. So what next?

This struck Will as sophistry, but he could not clearly see the way to beat it.

'But Mary said—' He nearly choked on his frustration. 'It was a dreadful case, sir! She said inhuman, horrible, that—'

Bartram interrupted.

'And Mary had no right! We tell you things, you go away, what happens next? More spies, with harsher purpose? We are known as traders, naturally we are, but unless we're caught red-handed, the Customs cannot act against us. Will this be seen as evidence, if it carries on? Will this lead to destruction of our band?'

'But Mary says that it was not your band!' Sam shouted, and Isa slammed his hand to the table, hard.

'It is enough! No more! There are things here that we cannot say! Go now, this meeting's over. Now go away.'

'Isa!' snapped John Hardman. 'Why can't we tell these men? Why can't—'

Isa stood up, a big man, face dark with anger, and his chair went down with a crash. Upstairs a baby cried, and Mary also stood, quelling them with her calm. Later that evening, at the inn, Sam suggested using money, but Will was horrified and told him he was mad. Money was not the problem, he insisted, money would insult them, money was not their need. It was trust they had to reach for from the traders, and they were on their way. What's more, when they had left the house, Mary had smiled at him, and he thought a change was coming, if they were only patient. Samuel, who was drinking brandy to ease his bitterness, was inclined to laugh.

Next day though, it turned out Will was right. They went to Langstone in the morning, to be confronted by an empty beach – no boats, no men, no women working either, except for Widow Hardman. She greeted them perfunctorily, and said the men were fishing and the wives and young had walked along the shore to Warblington or Emsworth. Sam's bitterness, not helped perhaps by a brandy headache, increased, until shortly Will found himself alone. The day was fair, so he mooched about along the foreshore for a while, then took a glass of ale and bread and cheese in the Royal Oak. In early afternoon he saw Mary and Kate, with children, coming back along the shore and went to meet them. Kate took off the little ones, while he and Mary sat to watch the water creeping up to meet across, then drown, the Hayling Island causeway.

'We have been to Emsworth,' she said, when they had sat awhile. 'Seeing Sally off on to a coach. Where is your friend today?'

Will shrugged.

'We've fallen out a little. He has a head from drinking. Where has she gone?'

'Oh, east some way. On her usual business. Drinking, you say? Does he do a lot of that?'

Will would rather have asked what Sally's normal business was, but he had a strong idea she would not answer. She was tense, as if anticipating.

'No, not a lot, we are not the usual Navy soaks. It is Isa Bartram, if I might be frank. Sam felt we were going to be told something we really need to hear, and then Isa . . . well, you were there.'

She nodded.

'Sam does not fully understand our difficulties,' she said. She paused, as if assessing. 'May be that you don't neither, but I think you do. You do believe me, don't you, Mr Bentley? That the men round here were not a part of it?'

'Oh yes,' said Will. 'Oh yes. But we have problems of our own. There is poor Sir Arthur. Sam is beholden to him in the most basic way. It is very hard for him. Not to know.'

There was a long pause. Tentatively, a mule was stepping through the watersplash, lifting its front feet high. The woman on it appeared indifferent whether they would get across, be drowned, or no.

'He is dead,' said Mary. Her voice was low. 'Charles Yorke. I am sorry to be the bearer of the news, but we decided we should tell you. He was taken with his companion, the same night, and both were killed, although there is some doubt in Charles Yorke's case as to if it was . . . intended. It was many, many days ago. I'm sorry.'

The mule was in the middle of the causeway, the water flowing just beneath its belly. The rider, still indifferent, had lifted her feet clear rather delicately.

'Who?' asked William. 'Are you permitted? Why?'

'It was . . . no, not an accident, but . . . it was unforeseen. They ran into a band of out-of-towners, some hired men who had, well been too free with broaching half-casks, who did not know the . . . I cannot say rules, but I reckon you take my meaning. It was not done the way our people would have done it. Or any people hereabout that I have ever heard of. It was the act of beasts. These things happen, these . . . killings, on both sides. Last year we had two fine men . . . and one riding officer, fine too, I suppose, to his wife and family.'

'But do you know the men?' said Will. 'The perpetrators? I suppose you cannot tell me that.'

Her face was sad.

'You will never find that out round here,' she said. 'Your colleagues – no, the Customs men, from Dorset, Hampshire, West Sussex, London, they have done everything, searched everywhere, but they will never find that out. Nor where his body lies buried, neither.'

'Buried? What, is he in a grave? The other man, Charles Warren, was he "buried", too? They found him in a haystack, burned and desecrated. Do they call that "buried", these beastly rogues?'

There was a small silence. Her face was stricken.

'Buried, that is our understanding,' Mary said. 'We do not know where, we were not told. The men who did it are a desperate crew, the rumour is that they did grievous wrong. But he is . . . you may tell Sir Arthur, he is buried. That must be enough. You, Sir Arthur, nobody . . . you will never see him more.'

But that night, by half a moon through broken clouds, in a depression called the Devil's Punchbowl, Will Bentley looked upon the sad remains of poor Charles Yorke, and wept.

23

The body, which was like no other Will had ever seen, was still half covered when Samuel brought him to it, which he found an everlasting mercy. He had been warned, as they got nearer, that it would be a sight he would find horrifying, but to steel himself. When Sam had come on it earlier that afternoon, he said, there had been too much light for necessary avoidance. John Hardman, who had brought him there, had told him some of what had happened, and suggested he should keep his distance and make do with hearsay. That, said Samuel drily, had been impossible. Hardman had started moving rocks at the entrance to a kind of cave, and Sam, impatiently, had had to help. From four feet or so, he had seen the awful sight.

'They had buried him alive,' he said simply. 'They gave him bread and water – blind stupidity, or cruelty, even good intentions, John Hardman did not know. However many days it took to die, Yorke spent clawing at rocks too big for one man to move. His head is squeezed between two stones, and . . . oh Christ, Will. How shall we tell Sir A of this?'

In the darkness, with a soughing wind, there was a stench that came and went, and mingled with the sweet scent of the Punchbowl. William knew the place, not many miles from home, and had wandered there on horse and foot. A fine place to be buried, but not like this.

'Hardman,' he said. 'And . . . and did he take the money that you offered? Christ, that is horrible.'

'Yes. I thought he would, Will. I thought he was our man, I observed him yesterday, when that big bugger Bartram was obstructing us. Don't blame him too hard. He wants to get away from this, I think he's had enough. He is thinking, seriously, he is hoping, to buy himself into a safer trade, less horrible, that Navy talk I told you of is not a joke. But he has friends and obligations. To leave would not be easy. And not safe.'

Will tried to think that through, but his craw was full of bitterness and hatred. So Sam had gone to Hardman and made a bribe, and the bait had been snapped up. A shaft of moonlight shone down into the tunnel that they stood over, and before he could avert his gaze he saw a face, a skull half stripped of flesh, at least one eye pecked or rotted out. God, no excuse. The devil, no excuse!

'He was not part of it himself,' said Sam, carefully. 'You might not believe that, but I do. The local crew, John's crew, were ... well, there is something going on that I can't get out of him, could not get out of him for any money. This murder, and that of Warren, was the work of some other men, some men from farther east, I think. Some Hampshire men took part in it in some way, but not John Hardman nor, I guess, any of the ones we've spoke to. But a friend of his, maybe. Yes, a friend of John's did, which is how he could take me to the grave. This lad showed it to him and now he's gone, John says. He says he fears he's killed himself. Aye, I see your face, Will. 'Tis hard to swallow, I ain't sure myself. I'm pretty sure John is, though. I think he's had enough of it, and that is why he told me.'

'Aye!' said Will, with passion. 'And you paid him for the telling! Oh hell, Sam, hell! Poor Yorke is lying there! Mary said it was the work of beasts, but they are part of it! All of them. And Jesse Broad was, too!'

He stood there, panting and in sudden tears, and Sam was silent for a while.

'We ought to bury him, whatever,' he said at last. 'I asked John why they'd done this to him, and why they'd stuffed Warren into a burning rick as if a decent Christian burial was a thing they could not have, but got no answer

I'd call sensible or straight. He said it was not the normal way, that nothing like this had ever been done that he knew of, that there was food and drink, he was not meant to die. Will, I believed him. Except it did not seem like all the truth. He took the money, true, but he was sweating on it, as if ashamed almost to death. I truly do not think we'll see him any more, nor will his companions. Maybe they are evil, and not him. Will, he *tried* to tell the truth, I do believe that.'

'But surely Mary—'

The cry, half a question half a statement, crumbled in his mouth and turned to ash. Out-of-towners, she had said, and called Yorke 'buried', but surely she must have known? He agreed with Sam on this point, that Mary Broad was a high officer in the Langstone crew, if not their leader-captain. Surely she must have known as much as the Widow Hardman's son?

'What did she tell you?' said Sam, his voice low. 'That Sally is not a Guernsey maid but French? That her real name is Céline, and she smuggles prisoners? Did Mary tell you that?'

'Prisoners? What do you mean?'

'French prisoners of war,' said Sam. 'They have a net, to get them off the hulks in the Medway and the Thames. They closet them in farms in Kent, then ship 'em out in bulk. John says the signs are there's a shipment soon. Soon now, Céline will disappear. She does it regular. Now – is that what Mary told you, honest Mary?'

But honest Mary had told him Sally was gone east, that very morning. 'On her usual business.' A breath arose from the grave-hole, vileness mixed with a zephyr of the autumn, and Will gagged. Had Mary lied? Had Hardman? The body down beneath them was all that they'd discovered that was concrete and visible. The body crying out for decent Christian rest.

'Sam,' he said. 'We cannot bury him. Sir A would not forgive that. What, just cover him with stones? Leave him

293

unmarked and unspoken over? Sir Arthur, when he knew, would—'

'He must not know!' Sam interrupted. 'God, know what? Should we tell him this? This man was his flesh and kin! What, tell him they walled him up and let him starve to death?'

For some long time they neither of them spoke. The breeze was gentle, blowing now a sweet breath, now a foul. Sam put his hand on Will's upper arm and squeezed it.

'We cannot bury him, you're right,' he said. 'How can we tell him in a way that he can bear, though? He will bring the body home to Langham, or maybe do a service here. No, he will take him home to rest. There is a chapel in the grounds. A memorial to his wife and children. He would have had the boys back from Batavia if he could have done. Let's cover him against the beasts, though. Would that there had been some way to protect him from the human beasts.'

As they toiled, piling stones on stones, Sam mused aloud on why it should have happened, and if this was the end. It seemed to both of them the murderers had wanted it a deadly secret – unless it could be true they'd meant to save him at a later time, which they deemed a fairy story – so who knew what they might not do when the tale was out? But they could see no actual reason why Yorke's resting place should draw them any more, or why it should be desecrated before Sir A had chance to send a party. As their final act, they made a cairn of stone, and blazed every third tree on a direct way to the road. With instruction, other men could find it now.

The journey back was long and arduous, taking them the most part of the night. Although it was not cold there were rain flurries, and the road was difficult with mud in places, which all cut down the opportunity for talk or tracking side by side. This suited both of them, as each had hard and lonely thoughts to ponder on about their expedition, and what they'd found. Will did have thoughts of Deb as they got nearer, but he found it easy to dismiss them, or push them sideways with thoughts of other things. Other women indeed, for Mary and Sally (or Céline) kept buzzing round and round his head like rats in a wire trap. Deb might betray him with Wimbarton (the mad thoughts went), or he might betray her by denying what he felt was love, but Jesse's widow had betrayed him already with her lies, and Sally might be a spy. This was grist to wrestle with, and then he'd realise that as he rode along towards the Lodge, he saw Deb lying there in front of him, naked and with arms stretched wide in welcome, and he would be ashamed.

Dawn was breaking, fair and mild, when the gatehouse hove into view, and both their minds were full only of the buried man and how they would tell it to his uncle. This time there were no guards in the building, which was shuttered, so they trotted up to the house wondering if they should drift in quietly to the stable yard and find some straw to sleep on. But dogs barked, as they were bred to do, and quickly an ostler with a musket stepped through a door to check them. Within five minutes Tony joined them, to tell them his orders were to wake Sir A whatever hour they returned. He took them to the parlour straight away, where there was food and beer laid out in case, and the thick embers still gave out unneeded heat. It occurred to both of them that the poor old man's anticipation was a constant state, and he had geared his house to their return. In the short time that they waited they were tongue-tied and hopeless, with a picture built in both their minds of tragedy.

Sir Arthur Fisher entered silently, and for a long moment all three of them kept the silence up. At first it was appropriate, because whatever news they had, the situation was solemn, but rapidly it became an embarrassment, a pain. Will saw hope in the old man's face, hope fighting with despair. After some seconds he felt a wild desire to scream out, 'It's all right, your nephew's found!', and the madness of it gave him a stabbing in his stomach. Sam raised both arms as if he also could not speak, and Sir A's face was like a landscape in a summer gale, with clouds and sunshine racing over it. Finally, a tortured release, Sam let out a groan. A noise followed from Sir Arthur like a sob, and the two moved together into each other's arms, their faces buried in each other's shoulders. Will turned away his eyes.

When Sir A drew back, his face was stricken but controlled. He nodded formally to Will, he pushed Sam gently towards a chair, and turned his back on them and stared into the dying fireglow.

'Tell me,' he said. 'You've found his body, have you not? Tell me where, and how he died.'

It was swiftly, simply told by Samuel, who included Will and praised his knowledge and his history as the keys to their success. He started at the beginning, when they'd ridden off from Langham Lodge, and he emphasised the civility and humanity of the smugglers they had met. These, he told Sir Arthur, had blamed it on a lawless gang – lawless by the terms of the fraternity – probably young, probably drunk, who had behaved in a way none of their fellows would descend to, and whose bestial behaviour had put them 'in free trade terms, beyond the Pale'. Charles Yorke, he said, had been buried, roughly and without compunction of observance, in a country place that had been discovered to them by a young man 'eaten up by shame'. At the end of that, he faltered to a halt. In the rising light blazing through the enormous windows, Sir A, unblinkingly, studied him.

'Roughly, you say. Buried roughly, and without compunction. He was abused, then? Abused like Warren? Worse? Tell me, Samuel, I have to know. Poor Charles is dead. You must tell me the circumstances, however unbearable. I shall bear them.'

When Sam had finished, the old man had shed a tear

or two, but he did not avert his eyes or lower them at all. He was in his wig, despite the hour of the morning, and was fully dressed, despite he'd been in bed, so they assumed. For his own part, Will had a headache across the temples, the ache of lack of sleep, although he was anything but sleepy. For his life, he could not see how this would end. Now there was another silence, longer than the first, and not embarrassing in any way. Sir Arthur Fisher thought, and Will and Sam sat with him, waiting. Will sat, and waited, and his head hurt. That was all.

'I do not believe it,' said Sir Arthur, in the end. 'I do not believe your simple tale at all. You must go back for me. Will you?'

As a bombshell going off, it had a strange, delayed effect. They heard the words, but did not seem to understand. They had told a simple tale, and he did not believe it. They were dislocated. For moments more they did not speak. Sam broke the silence.

'Do not believe what aspect of it, sir? But surely . . . ?'

'It is too pat, too simple. Outsiders, young and drunk? So why were Yorke and Warren mistreated so abominably, why were their bodies hidden and abused? Most Customs men die in the heat of confrontation, you must know that, they meet a band who are too well armed and desperate and they lose the sudden battle. Most of all, their bodies are not hid. They are abandoned where they fall, they are casualties in a war that is as open as it is long-standing. This is not the normal run, it is of a different quality. Our two men disappeared, entirely. With not a word of anything going on at all, least of all a sudden bloody skirmish. Do drunk hotheads go to such strange lengths? I do not believe it.'

'But,' Samuel began. He faltered. 'Perhaps it is not the whole tale, but . . .'

'There is a reason,' said Sir A. His voice, despite it all, was strong and clear, his presence suddenly commanding. 'My nephew and Warren were put to death and hidden for some reason, and not by drunken layabouts. Nay, drunk they may have been, I hope for reasons of humanity that they were, as drunk as fiddlers' bitches. But the thing was planned, and executed, for a reason. Either something had been discovered, or . . . or I do not know. But I will, I must. You both must go back for me, I . . . require it. Request it. Humbly.'

'But the Biter, sir,' said Will. 'Our release from duty was for five days only. Lord Wodderley—'

'Aye,' cut in Sir A, as if distracted. 'Aye, Kaye will expect you, certainly. Well, you must go and fight it out with him, and I will make more representation to Bobby Beaumont, by express. Now you have found my nephew so cruelly murdered more time will be allowed, no question of it. Can you go today? Oh no, you are exhausted, what am I saying, you must have sleep.'

The authority was gone again, and he looked old and tired, an old, saddened man. But both of them knew, horribly, that he was right about the nature of the deaths, and they had been somehow duped. Both said they would go immediately to London, but Sir Arthur would have none of it, and called his man. The details they must leave, he said, the way to find Charles Yorke. Then a meal, a wash, sleep, they could even have a coach if they preferred it, which enabled them to do some young man's bantering on the theme of luxury, to ease the mood. With this in mind, also, Sam dropped in Deb. A shock for Sir A, he realised, but 'Will here's took a shine to her. Perhaps a small hallo before we go away?'

Sir Arthur, drawn and grey, turned eyes from one to other of them as if they themselves were ghosts, or spoke a foreign language. Will blushed at his friend's crassness, and moved his hands dismissively.

'Sir,' he said. 'A jest. The maid is nothing to me, naturally.'

'Aye,' muttered Sir A. 'The maid is nothing, that's a fact.'

His voice got stronger. 'The slut has gone,' he said. 'And this time, good riddance. It is a little whore.'

'Gone!' said Sam, although William was struck speechless by the shock. 'What? Run away, sir, like the last time? Well, glory be!'

'Nay,' said Sir Arthur, 'not run away. Wimbarton came for her, oh, yesterday. She's gone back with him to be his concubine, for all I know or care. As far as I can see he's saved her from the gallows, for the time at least. Mistress Wimbarton is dead, killed by the accomplice, that mountebank, and he's the one that's run this time. William, I can't believe you've took a shine to her, your friend here has a senseless sense of fun. But if you have done, rid yourself, I beg of you. The woman is, to all intents and purposes, a murderess.'

Will, head splitting with exhaustion, tried hard to catch his thoughts and ask a question. But the door opened then, and Tony came in. Before Sir A had finished his instructions Mistress Houghton had arrived, guessed it all from the expressions, and took control. She bustled round Sir A like Mother Hen, and drove them out – after hurried greetings, and thank-yous, and condolences – to the tender care of Tony and the women of the kitchen. In the passage just outside the door though, Sam turned to Tony fiercely.

'What?' he demanded. 'About the maid? You heard him call her murderess. This Deborah, this little pretty thing. 'Fore God, Tony, spit it out! And sense!'

There was little sense to be had so easily. All Tony knew was that last morning, Chester Wimbarton had turned up with an entourage led by such types of danger as Fiske and Jeremiah, and they had all come armed. Deb, known to be slippery, had been guarded instantly, while the magistrate and Sir A had been closeted some time. No shouts, no arguments, until they had emerged in twenty minutes and Deborah had been brought and told to go with them.

Then there had been screaming, Tony allowed, for she had been hysterical as any wildcat, and screeched that Wimbarton was a liar and Sir A a fool or worse. In the end, with Sir A unmoved, she had been bundled up on to a horse – no carriage had been bothered with – tied across it like a bale of wool, and carried off. This last, he added, seeing Will's white face, had been considered pretty vile by all of them, and shaming that Sir A had allowed it. Although, by then, he'd gone inside and closed the door.

'But what is thought?' asked Samuel. 'Tony, your opinion. You run the house. You must have an opinion.'

'I do not run the house, sir. Mistress Houghton does, I would ask her. But the story as we have gleaned it, right or wrong, is that Mistress Wimbarton was struck at by the mountebank with some kind of club, from which she later died. Both the man and Deborah then ran away, she here and he to God knows anywhere, and the magistrate has raised a hue and cry and offered a reward for him. His servants later picked up on the grapevine – probably from within this house, I'd guess – that she at least was here.' He looked at William, expression neutral, and added drily: 'Wimbarton wanted her for her teeth, but when his wife's face rotted would have taken her for other purposes, I'm told. Maybe his wife died from her vile reaction to her tattered mouth, that is another story we are told, aided by the beating from the stick. Whichever way, the magistrate had paid for her, so she was his. If she refuses to be his concubine, he can always have her hanged. As an argument in favour of a little whoring, it is not unpowerful.'

'But it is the mountebank that's dead,' said William, at last. 'The woman killed him, not he her. It is the mountebank that's dead.'

The steward, large, implacable and calm, eyed him thoughtfully.

'That's what Deborah kept screaming,' he said. 'The master shouted once, just once in all the time he kept the yard. She screamed that, not for the first time or the tenth, and Sir Arthur shouted that she was a liar, else why not mention it before? She screamed the mountebank was dead, and the servants must have buried him, she'd seen Milady shoot him in the head. She screamed Wimbarton must have murdered her. That's when Sir Arthur went inside and Jeremiah dragged her across his pommel. In truth, sir, it sounded—'

Mistress Houghton came along the passageway, and Tony stopped. At a sign, the steward left them, and she took them into a room they had not seen before, a sitting room with a small bright fire and a sewing box and contents scattered casually on the rug. She bade them sit, and told them Sir Arthur was in a tired state, but grateful for the things they'd found out for him, however horrible. She had heard the tail-end of the former conversation, she added, and had heard Will's name – 'young Mr Bentley's' – from the maid herself, while the magistrate and master had held their confabs. She looked at Will not unkindly, but in a manner of reserve.

'She said that she had told you that the mountebank was killed,' she said. 'She insisted on it. But earlier she had told a different tale, so as not to ... ah, *upset* the master. I'm afraid I ... well, I did not believe a word of it, her latest version, I thought she would say anything to avoid Wimbarton having her. Sir, forgive me if I insult her as a friend of yours, but ... Do you believe her story could be true?'

There was only one time and circumstance in which Will and Deborah could have spoken in this intimacy, and all three of them now knew it. Impossible, of course, that it should be acknowledged. Will nodded.

'Madam,' he said, 'I believe it to be true. I believe, as Tony said, the magistrate's men have buried Dennett and the hue and cry is but a blind, to obviate a risk that Wimbarton be suspected for his disappearance. As to the wife, I do not know. Deb said she was in a dreadful way of health, quite putrefying; she might just have died. It is a way to frighten Deb to silence, saying the mountebank killed her, also. Deb was, in general eyes, the mountebank's accomplice.'

'A way to get her as a useful pretty whore into the bargain,' Sam added coarsely. 'Beg pardon, Mrs Houghton, that was not nice.' He did not apologise to Will, despite his jealous sensitivity.

'Aye,' said Mistress Houghton. 'There was the money, too. Wimbarton said the mountebank stole money, and Deborah as well, he guessed. Another piece of stuff to shut her mouth.'

'Hell, hell!' said Will, passionately. 'When was the time for all this to be done!? There was a shooting, a bursting in of servants, and Deb's escape! How was she accomplice? How steal? If they escaped both, why is she now with the magistrate, and Marcus Dennett clean away!? It is blackmail, plain and simple! Play ball with him or she may hang, it is her choice. It's horrible! She saw Dennett fall, she saw him bleed and die! Is there no way that we can get her off from this? You do believe me, Mistress Houghton? You do believe her now?'

She nodded.

'I'm inclined to say I do, young man, I do. But sadly my belief is an irrelevance. The magistrate has witnesses who will swear to every detail of his case, and in any way he is a magistrate. Who would believe her story contra his? Or ours, or yours? So Deborah must be . . .' She sighed. 'Perhaps he'll be a kindly master to her,' she added. 'Stranger things have happened, when all's said.'

'And Sir A?' asked Sam. 'If you told him this? Or Will did? If he believed it?'

Mistress Houghton shook her head.

'I cannot tell him at the present moment. He could not stand it, I promise you. But when I do, when the opportunity is right . . . then, what? The fact remains, sirs. She is the magistrate's, he probably owns her even if she would deny it. And how could she deny it? She would hang, you know that's true. Mr Bentley. Sir. There is nothing to be done.'

'But you will tell him?' Sam said. What else was there to say?

'I will tell him,' she responded. 'When the time is right. But sirs, you know the news that he has suffered, because you brought it. Have pity on his age, have pity.' She stood, and came to touch Will on the arm.

'We all need pity, sir,' she said.

Although they ate, and slept for some few hours, William and Samuel left Langham Lodge both miserable and exhausted. The thought of detouring to pass by Wimbarton's estate occurred to them, but neither expressed it. They set out at an almost gentle pace, to conserve their dwindled energy and because the prospect of arrival was not a happy one. William in particular felt lost and powerless, not only for himself. Deborah, not far from where he rode, was a prisoner, facing legal rape and worse. Short of storming Wimbarton's house and dying, probably, in the attempt, there was nothing he could do. His death, in such a case, would be legal, equally. They had not any rights.

'You are right,' he said to Samuel later, as they moved through heavy rain. 'They send us here, they send us there, we are not free in any sense at all. The world rules us and tosses us about, there is nothing but constraints for us. And here we go again to face that fat hog Kaye and battle with his whim, to try and persuade him to let us go and do something with honour in it. Sam, I must aid Deb! And cannot. Oh, it is intolerable.'

Sam could not reply to that, for he feared a difference of opinion inherent in the thought of honour might put a wedge between them. Sir Arthur's reading of the thing had shaken him, but he could not get it from his mind. Most men in Customs battles died in the heat, most Customs men did not work in deepest secrecy, but Yorke and Warren had disappeared without a trace, with not a word of any kind of something going on. There was something up, Sir A thought, something afoot, and Sam feared Céline or Sally was the key, and Jesse Broad's widow and her crew were not the bystanders – almost innocent – that his friend took them to be. Sam saw Will's pain because of Deborah as doubly unfortunate in this – because it made his thinking cloudy on the other issue. Sam thought that Kaye would let them go – he thought he'd have to, if Lord Wodderley would act on the express – but he feared what they might uncover on a return to Hampshire would make things for William seem ten times worse.

'Aye,' he said, after some contemplation. 'It is intolerable. The wicked crew of smugglers and what they've done to Yorke and Warren, the thought that Sally might be springing our enemies back to France, Wimbarton and that pretty little girl he has no right to, Slack Dickie and his power over us, poor Charlie in the Devil's Punchbowl. Lord, friend, how lovely it would be to be just rich!'

They were not rich, they were as poor as dirt, though not without their horses and their privilege. When they arrived, Slack Dickie exercised his power ruthlessly, and overrode all arguments and claims. At dawn next morning the Biter slipped downriver, with Gunning – drunk and hardly capable – at the con. Kaye's agents had reported juicy pickings in the offing, the remnants of a storm-tossed convoy from the East, crammed with fine sailors for the taking. Kershaw implied some pressure had been on from their lordships, for this lieutenant of the Press to do some pressing; there was a war on, after all. Slack Dickie, on the quarterdeck in the fine bright morning, his fat face and plum-pudding eyes a picture of unwonted keenness and efficiency, was off to make a killing.

24

When Deborah awoke, that same bright shining morn, she knew her time had come, with no escape. She was in a high room, more like an attic in the house than her prison of earlier, and from the open window she could hear only country silence – birdsong, breeze, some cattle lowing. It made her think of her home, on the Cheshire edge of Stockport near the River Goyt of a summer Sunday, and she had a strong wrench of dread and misery that she would never see it, or any of her people, ever again. Well, she told herself, you left them without farewell or by-your-leave, so home-sickness is no one's fault but yours. Then she wept at her own hard-heartedness; for she missed her mother, terribly.

Two days before, after she had sprung at him, the master, her new lord and master Wimbarton, had withdrawn from her presence apparently unaffected by her attempt to rip his face. This was in the coachhouse, a large, bare, bottom chamber, which Jeremiah had pushed her into after she'd been dropped down from the horse. Deb had been almost broken by the journey, bent across the backbone belly-downward, and when she'd hit the ground she'd had spots before her eyes and could not stand unaided. Fiske had cleared the others off with brisk brutality, slamming a door on her and Jeremiah and the master, then she'd been left swaying like a baited bull. Her stomach pained her, she had an urgent need to piss, but her heart was filled with only hatred and mistrust. She had a feeling this would be a little sport, to show her in what respect he held her, what she might expect if she did not co-operate. Wimbarton and Jeremiah watched, like farmers at a market, as she stood her ground. By Mary and the saints, she thought, I'd rather die than let him play with me.

Wimbarton, perhaps, had more shame than Dennett had done, God rot his soul. He did not pull his club out, but moved in on her like a thin and feeble wrestler, in anticipatory crouch. Jeremiah, far better able to give a maid this sort of paying out by the look of him, merely leaned back against the wall with a half-smile on his lips as Wimbarton approached. Deb, from her aching bladder to her aching limbs, was the breathing antithesis of submission, crouched also, but hers a feral crouch, a pre-explosive bunching led by glaring eyes. She had all her clothes on also, her skirts were long and full, winter ones borrowed from one of Mrs Houghton's maids. If he should try for me, she thought, I'll make it half an hour till he finds the spot, by which time I'll have blinded him.

Wimbarton could read minds, perhaps. Anyway, he straightened up, and turned away from her, and said to Jeremiah, 'Take that gown from off her, will you? I am too old for all this teasing, strip her to the buff.' At which moment Deb sprang at him, claws out, and Jeremiah moved like lightning to smack her a heavy blow between the eyes, placed nicely so as not to crush her nose, and Deb sprawled out in the coachhouse dust and lay and pissed herself. Her skirts had risen up as she had skidded, so they knew what was happening, there was a puddle and the hot wet smell. Jeremiah had looked angry, but Wimbarton had laughed, which Deb found much more frightening. But it ended the attempt. Before he left her, he told his man to lay off her or else, and get the women to look after her.

'Next time I'll have you clean,' he said. 'Next time I'll have you civil.'

Jeremiah, if he resented not getting at least a sight of shagging, amused himself with a feel or two, taken in good grace, when he could easily have hurt her badly and never have been blamed. But the urine put him off, for which

Deb was grateful (she'd heard in Dr Marigold's of men who would pay more for things like that), so pretty soon she ended up with Joan and Sue, whose job turned out to be to strip her down and scrub her, which they did as viciously as possible until they saw the scars and bruises her body bore already, when they seemed dampened, if not ashamed. When they decided they would talk, not sneer at her for her immoral life and strange outlandish accent, she decided she would answer, and confirmed that Dennett and their master, between the two of them, had done the injuries, and she would presumably get worse until she ran away again. At which they told her one man had had his leg broken by Fiske and Jeremiah for letting her escape and Dorothy, chief woman to Milady, had been whipped naked in the yard for getting her mistress past the guard to start with and causing all the mayhem. Deb was amused to hear them beg her to stay put in future, for fear of punishment *they* might have to suffer if she ran.

'But you will not,' said Sue, a simple girl. 'The place is like a fortress now, and we're locked in even washing you, and the place where you're to have your room is right up yonder in the roof, with no way down but one, and guards, and locks, and I don't know what all else. And Fiske and Jeremiah will shoot you like a rat, or cut you down like wheat. That surgeon man of yours got his payment in the throat, and Milady's dead and gone, an'all. There's no compunction killing in this place, believe you me!'

There was no compunction either, it appeared, in Wimbarton's search for sex. Milady – lord, the graces of that woman, who was just a slut from gutterland in their opinion! – Milady had come as a replacement for an earlier, and Dorothy (much older than her girls) remembered other ones before. Milady, though, had ruled him with a rod of iron, and told them, and all and sundry, how he'd fell in love with her, and she was different. More impressive that would have been, they started, if the master had not— Then giggled, and rolled their eyes. She could end

307

up as a wife, Joan finished it unkindly, but most whores he'd had there ended up as whores.

'And such a ratty little bugger,' crowed Sue. 'Like a bloody scarecrow that couldn't lift a skirt. Well let me tell you, lover, he's got a prick on him you could stir a pudding with. I know, I've had some, and I'm bloody ugly, ain't I? So don't give yourself no fancy airs round here. You're nothing special, are you?'

But for all that they were friends, as women in these situations went, and Deb knew that she was close enough in spirit to them not to be as quickly hated as the one they called, so sneeringly, Milady or Mistress Corpse. She could not really see herself ending up a wife to Chester Wimbarton, or so-called wife or consort, because just at that moment she thought she'd rather die. He must know by this time also, that maids young enough to be his granddaughter had nothing to offer except quick poking and a smirk (or pained expression) hid behind a hand or handkerchief. If he'd moved so far beyond the law as to murder wives and passing mountebanks without the slightest fear, he must know similarly, that young maids could be bought in quick succession, used, and turned on to the road. As for that, she hoped it might be soon.

They fed her, then they took her to her room and locked her in. It was a pleasant place enough, with a bed adequate for the business, some chairs, a cupboard and a table, but the dormer was too high to get a view out of, except of sky, and had been nailed or jammed to open only its fixed amount. Like the room she'd shared with Dennett, it had a closet off, where she found a pail and a jug of water and some soap. For clothes, Sue and Joan left only shifts and a flimsy gown for keeping off the draughts, and nothing for her feet. If she was to run, she would run naked in the world. Deborah sat down to wait.

Her fate, if coming, took a good long time. On the first day, when the women washed and left her, she spoke to no one else for many hours. Dorothy brought her supper, but it was a Dorothy much changed. Remembered as Milady's confidante, a robust country type brimming with life and vigour, she was cowed, enfeebled, with welts upon her face and one closed eye. She hardly spoke, but Deb got the message plain enough: this was how women ended up who defied the magistrate, the justice of the peace. Later, when they brought food next morning, Joan and Sue crowed at her reduction. She'd thought, they chirruped contentedly, that she was Lady Muck. One more false step and she could join her mistress, in the grave.

'How did her mistress die?' asked Deborah, bluntly. 'Did he kill her, to make way for me?'

But, 'Good heavens, no!' they twittered, she just 'stunk herself away'. Her head blew up to twice its natural size, until it burst one morning 'in a storm of pus'. They pitched it horribly, but they were shifty all the while, and quickly left when she pursued the subject. Joan, going, warned her almost sternly to be 'careful what she put abroad, or asked'. Deb lay on the bed, stared at the ceiling, and guessed the truth but knew she'd never know.

That day she spent many hours lying on her back and staring, for nobody returned to talk, or feed her, or to rape her or seduce her come to that, nor even to propose her as the lady of the manor and Wimbarton's wife. She thought of many things and wished that she could read, because there was a Bible, and became frantic with both thirst and boredom. She slaked her thirst with water from her washing jug, which she'd made soapy earlier, but the boredom would not go away. She found it quite peculiar that she could be bored, in such a situation, when her recent life had had so many turns and twists and upsets, but it was so. She thought of Will, and the fun they'd had, and found it funny and a little sad he thought he loved her, maybe did. Much good it would do the both of them, fine chance of that! Which led her on to Wimbarton. He would come and have her, and if he liked it and the fates were right she might last a month or two until she was thrown out, or became an under kitchen maid to Joan or Sue or Cook or whoever superseded Dorothy. Or she might fall pregnant or get killed, who knew? She remembered Will again then, and the beauty of his small, slim body, pale but muscular, and hoped the magistrate, unclothed, would not be completely vile. As she went asleep she thought of Cecily, but only briefly. At least she, Deborah, still had her life.

Next morning she was right, her time had come and no escape. Joan and Sue brought breakfast, warm water, even a towel, and they were full of merriment at the morning fun planned out for her. They gave advice, pretended to, which boiled down to smile but not to laugh, *never* to laugh! Then made that hard for her by referring, archly, to the birthmark on his inner thigh, and his twisted knee, and the fact his prick would rise from a nest of hair all grey and sparse and straggled. It *would* rise though, Joan averred, which was more than some old pigs could manage, so at least she would enjoy herself. They made the whole thing sound like a circus, or a theatre show.

When he came in, the magistrate was not so jovial. He had a bitter face, and he did not disguise his purpose or let her think he might find pleasure in it. Once more she thought of bulls, remembering watching fascinated as they'd doggedly tramped from cow to cow to do their duty, as if all they wanted was to get it over with. He did not speak, excepting for a greeting grunt, nor did he take time to get ready. He was dressed in a loose smock tucked into breeches, which when he released them allowed the smock to drop so that he was still covered to the knees. The famous grey mare's nest and pudding stirrer were thus obscured, except for a bulge in the smock material that rose and fell in a slight rhythm, as if there were an animal in there, and breathing. He stepped out of the ankled breeches, and his pair of soft slip-shoes, and advanced towards her with intent, so that Deb could only drop back

310

to the bed. In his right hand – for fear she planned to claw at him, perhaps – he held a short, sharp knife.

Deb, as she sank back on the bed, realised she still had not formed a stratagem for dealing with this situation. She did not want this man – although he was not half so old or vile as Sue and Joan made out – she did not want, above all else, to lie with him, she was rendered hollow by her staring lack of choice. But as he forced on her, she lifted up her shift, and rolled her backbone into the yielding stuff, and moved her knees apart, for him to widen with his advancing thighs. As he hauled up his smock she glimpsed the club – quite long and massive, much bigger than her lover Will's – thrusting, indeed, from a bed of grey-white curls. Then her head was back, her knees jerked up, and he pushed into her, his feet firmly on the ground, a forceful, painful, stab. Her eyes stayed open, his did not, but she kept her face composed politely, just in case he peeked. Four times he stabbed at her, five, six, seven, eight, with his upright leg bones pushing out her yielding ones, his hands clamped on her knees, the handle of the dagger digging in. Then he grunted, stopped, and stood more upright, eyes still shut, pumping in his stuff. Then blew air out of his closed lips, jerked backwards and his smock dropped down, and the dagger clattered to the floorboards as he took his hands away. He wiped his brow, his doxy smiling up at him, as if content.

'Good,' he said. 'You're a pretty little piece. Next time I'll look at you all over.'

And he left.

Gunning was drunk, but not so drunk that Lieutenant Kaye could notice. Gunning could keep his feet like any seaman, and the act of pilotage down the Thames on a racing ebb came to him as second nature, so it appeared. The dangerous manifestations of his state, a refusal to give way to other ships however tight their situation until it was a hair's-breadth off too late, and a wild aggression that

311

moved him to seize the wheel when the helmsman made a move that he thought lily-livered, were mainly done when Slack Dickie was not looking, or were disregarded with an approving eye. Kaye was in a hurry, and Biter was moving fast. When one enraged captain shouted imprecations at them of the very vilest, his quarterdeck only fifteen feet from theirs, he only nodded at him insolently, lifting a rope's-end as if offering a tow, the deepest insult in the sailor's canon.

At breakfast time, however, he was not half so jolly. His two midshipmen were invited not for the pleasure of their company, but for a roasting. Black Bob served them, but he was sadder and more obsequious than ever, and was clouted when he raised a smile. Kershaw was also called, but hardly spoke a word, as if he'd been forewarned. Kaye was in the mood for hectoring.

First, their lateness of return. They had been released for five days, they had taken six (which was almost true). Second, their infernal insolence, to greet him on arrival not with apologies but with demands for further leave of absence. Third, the reason for their going, to aid the Customs House, as if those idle villains needed aid, as if those ingrates ever did a thing for Navy men except to harass them for trifles that officers, at least, brought in of right. And what had they discovered, he demanded, what had they achieved to justify his loss of them (not that they were any loss, damn sure they weren't!)? This, when Sam answered stiffly and evasively, put him in a greater passion, because he knew from Wodderley's first letter that their task concerned some missing officers and that the matter could in no wise be discussed. Did they find them, he demanded to be told, had they found the dogs, and if not why not, and if so why did they want more time for gallivanting? It occurred to William at about this time that Gunning was not the only member of the afterguard that had been sluicing brandy.

Later, while Will stood working on the foredeck with

the men, Kaye called Sam Holt across to his point high to windward, and quizzed him harder. When Sam demurred the captain raised his voice, then led him off below to carry on discussing in the cabin. He said, as Will learned later, that Lord Wodderley's second missive – received too late for him to act upon and let them go again, he claimed – had been extremely dubious about the value of their jaunting, and demanded yet again to know what interest they had in catching smugglers, and precisely what the outcome of their search had been. Sam, anxious to get the blustrous fool off the subject, hit on the Frenchmen-smuggling as a safe bet, and told how he and Mr Bentley had met a 'woman spy' (he did not name her) who had come to England to aid prisoners to escape, and how they'd gleaned there was an operation being set in motion at about this very time – which was why, he hinted, they had been told off to go down and search some more.

Kaye's hazel eyes grew keener at this point, less congested with undirected anger. What woman, how a spy, was what he wanted in more detail, but Sam began to hedge as if this were part of the secret too. For himself he felt sure the Céline link needed hard looking at, but he wanted nothing less than that Kaye should take a special interest. Enough the line should wean him off his probing into Sir A's affair.

'It is nothing yet, sir,' he said, circumspectly. 'Apparently the villains plan to spring them from a prison hulk and transport them back to France, but it is just a rumour till we stick our noses in it. As you can see though, it is the sort of thing their lordships play very close to chest; it's more important than the running of some tea! In all likelihood it won't add up to much though, will it, so if anyone's to end up looking gulled, Will Bentley and myself will be the men!'

Kaye considered it, his transparent face incapable of much guile.

'Aye,' he said, almost to himself. 'But interesting though,

for all that. It's not just trade for profit, is it, which some people think is not so . . . Nay, there's treachery and stuff involved, there's King and country.' He tailed off, his eyes refocusing on Sam's. 'Hah!' he exclaimed. 'You're right, there's nothing in it. But I'll be silent as the grave, so you may freely speak, if any further . . . Perhaps you'd be so good . . . ?'

'Oh indeed, sir,' Sam said, heartily. Congratulations, man, he told himself, a sticky situation brought into dock. Next he'll be giving brandy!

'In any way,' snapped Kaye, remembering his mood, 'you owe me favours, you and Bentley, so don't expect to get away too light. There is the matter of your jaunt in Kent, an'all. The boatswain's mate damn near got flogged for it, that saucy devil Eaton. Turned up as bold as brass and said the two young gents would vouch for him. I'd a damn good mind to knock him back to landman. I need a drink. Bob! Black Bob! Where is the bastard boy? And you – may go about your business, sir.'

The confrontation with the homeward-bounders, when it finally occurred, had all the makings of a Navy knockabout, hallmarked Richard Kaye. Indeed, the two midshipmen might have found it funny except that it cost one sailor's life, that of Shockhead Eaton, whom they valued rather highly. They took only seven men, three of whom were later released because of their protections, and it was several days after the engagement before they limped back to London under jury rig.

The first day out they made good time, and by nightfall were skating down the Kentish coast, from north to south. They took in sail when it was dark, as there was traffic as always in the Downs, and in any way they did not want to miss their target, whose position they knew only vaguely. Four ships was Kaye's word, although it seemed to Kershaw impossible they would stay bunched so close to home, so close to ranging Press tenders. He stood with

Sam and Will as Gunning gave the orders to snug down, all three of them marvelling at the level of his inebriation.

'It's his second day,' the strange spy told them, in his quiet voice. 'They last from three to five, they tell me, then he lies down like a corpse till he's recovered, and doesn't touch another glug for days or weeks. Worst is, it's catching. We'll see some sailors dropping from the yards I shouldn't wonder.'

It was catching with the Navy men as well, not just the owner/master's crew. There was an element of competition as to who could hold their liquor best, and a greater one as to how they should obtain it, well beyond the daily ration. Even on his uncle's ship, where things were tightly regulated, Will had been aware that that ration was enough to knock out weaker-headed men, while others hoarded it for use as bribes or currency. On Slack Dickie's ship, with men often ashore, or rummaging and stealing from vessels stopped and searched, there was rarely any shortage. Tonight it was apparent that there was a general spree.

'Should we warn Lieutenant Kaye?' said Will, but tentatively, for fear that they would mock at him. The captain had remained below since dinner, when he too had been drinking heavy. But they did not mock, they shared in his concern.

'No point,' said Kershaw, with unusual brusqueness. 'I think Black Bob's the target of his thoughts tonight, he'll not brook interruption. Thank God it is a quiet night, that's all. By morning maybe, most will have sobered up sufficiently. I'll do first turn on watch, shall I?'

The wind had died down, as it often did at nightfall with high glass, and the air grew very chill. The stars were showing in an almost cloudless sky, and the sea was velvet black, rolling but unbroken. Soon the moon was due to rise, almost full.

'I'm not for my bed yet,' said Sam. 'Jesu, what a rum life, this life upon the sea. Silence, beauty, and a drunken rabble. And over there, not much above ten or fifteen leagues or so, the enemy. I wonder if they conduct things so, or different. Have you had many dealings with them, Mr Kershaw?'

The three of them stood on the quarterdeck alone. Gunning had overseen the lashing of the wheel, then wandered forward with the erstwhile helmsman towards the noise of revelling. He had thrown a glance at them, a type of challenge, that they should care, or dare, to question his shipkeeping. But they were happier alone, in charge of her. For some time, Kershaw was disinclined to answer.

'I lost my eye to Frenchmen in a fair battle.' His voice remained low, but it was firm. 'A little privateer, sailed very well, shot very well. The rest of me was spoiled by the Spaniards, on land, in prison. I am not so keen on them.'

'Ah,' said Sam.

A small cry came from beneath them, escaping through a port, or cabin skylight. A small, low cry, full of unhappiness and pain.

'Less inclined to drunkenness than us, though,' went on Kershaw, his voice only slightly changed. 'More amenable to being told to keep the peace.' He paused. 'Some men are very bestial, you know. They are very much like beasts.'

'Well,' said Sam, 'I suppose we'll meet 'em some day, me and Will. In the meantime, we are off to fight the English, there's a thought. I wonder what Slack Dickie would do if threatened with a hardnose merchant broadside. What think you, William?'

William was silent and it had been noticed. His thoughts were with the black child down below, the sad child and the fleshy man who owned him. He knew in theory what might be going on, but could not understand it. His experience was small, and Lieutenant Kaye was keen on whores, or any woman.

'Beg pardon? I am miles away.'

'Hah!' said Sam, but nothing more.

'They go well armed, some Indiamen,' said Kershaw, keeping up the conversation. 'Better than a tender anyhow. Better than that Katharine we stopped.' They were all uncomfortable about the noises from the cabin. When something splashed to windward, a jumping fish or porpoise maybe, they sauntered over there, the captain's holy spot, when he was not busy down below. 'There was a case some years ago with one, pitched battle with the Press and one or two men killed. The judge took sides against the Navy, I believe, but nobody was hanged.'

They stayed conversing for the best part of the night, usually a pair on deck and one below to snatch a sleep, and for Will and Sam the time passed most pleasantly. Sam raised the business of him tutoring them in navigation at one stage, with the implication he was there to spy on them put up so clearly that Kershaw, an honest man it seemed, could not pretend he'd missed it. His crippled features altered to amused acknowledgement, but he did not make some startling admission.

'I think you'll find that Daniel Swift has another man in mind than you,' he answered. 'He implied to me, or so I read it, that in Mr Bentley he reposed his trust. I assumed that you, sir, might be engaged to spy on me!'

'No!' said Will. 'But . . . I don't know, the other man is Kaye, is that correct? I don't think it's a secret to say he thought Kaye needed smartening? But . . .'

'But Christ!' said Sam. 'No man could call him wrong on that score, could they? So Mr Kershaw, did Captain Swift put no charge on you at all, concerning us? I can scarce believe that!'

Unfortunately though, the talk of Swift, the tone of rising banter, was affecting the nervous man adversely. His face was clouded, and his stoop was more pronounced, as if he was withdrawing from the conversation, while standing still. They saw him so infrequently that they'd almost forgotten their first impression, that he was as timid as a ghost. It was clear he wished he had not spoke so freely.

In the east the dawn was rising rapidly, and Gunning, against all expectation, chose this moment to burst back into life, and take the Biter with him. Lurched might have been a better word, for he came into their vision from out the forward scuttle like an unfolding knife, shouting loud orders back across his shoulder. He had a bottle in his hand, and the object of his wrath was Jem Taylor, the stolid boatswain, who was not a jot put out. Taylor, if drunk, did not show any signs, and before too long had passed there was a man to helm, hands were tailing halliards and braces, and Geoff Raper's galley stovepipe was belching smoke. Straight up, to be sure, for the windlessness continued, but not a man jack expected that to last for long. Kershaw, without another word, had disappeared below, leaving Will and Sam to watch the strange activity almost disconsolate, so divorced it seemed to be from them. But as the light grew so did a breeze, and out of the fading darkness ships appeared, first few and close, then farther off and many, mainly fishermen or trading barges, but with taller masts, white sails, dotted here and there. Soon Kent was visible, three leagues or so, and the Biter was leaning to a good north-easterly and throwing foam. After an hour, even the captain deigned to come on deck.

They plugged south all that day, moving across to check out larger vessels beating up, enjoying the wind advantage that made their task so easy, and by mid-afternoon were pretty sure they'd found one of their reported fleet. She was a good-sized merchanter, laden deep, with fronds of greenery they could spot through glasses from considerable distance. Weatherbeaten too, with the sails bleached by weeks or months of southern sun. From the ports they counted she had at least eight guns, and as Biter bore down close on her, they could see that knots of men had gathered round the pieces, almost as if they meant to clear away for action.

Will and Sam, leeside of the quarterdeck, watched Kaye watching her from his windward point, wiping his brow occasionally. His face was pale and blotchy from the night's debauching, and he was in the mood for trouble and unpleasantness. No shared breakfast today; he'd nodded curtly in acknowledgement of their polite good mornings and then ignored them. One thing about him, Sam said laconically – he did not need advisers to help him make his bad decisions, he was his own fool in entirety.

'Do you think they'd go so far as firing?' Will asked. 'It must be bluff?'

'They have a good excuse,' said Sam. 'They're clearing just in case we turn out to be a private Frenchman. Our colours count for naught in these waters, everyone flies false on principle. Did you not hear about the French frigate, oh not so long ago? Engaged a Netherlander off the South Foreland, brought down her mizzenmast, lost her fore and half her bowsprit, went in hand-to-hand and called it off when the first lieutenants met in the chains and knew each other, went to school together, Canterbury I think. They were both English, like their ships. Big to-do!'

Will laughed, unsure if it were true or not. But he could see the trader's point. The Biter was not armed much more than adequate, and might sheer off if shook at with a heavy stick enough. Kaye, to give him benefit for some sense, had made no move to order his guns readied. But there was still time in plenty. Despite the good wind Biter was slow, and the East Indies man was moving upwind slower yet.

'Mark you,' Sam added, 'you'd have to be a bloody pessimist indeed to think this sad old tub was really a French privateer. Built for lugging coal and the hold rigged out to make good sailors think they've gone to hell in handcuffs. Slack Dickie's glancing at us, hoping to catch us shirking off our duty. Time to break the swords and pistols out, I think.'

The action, when it came, was more a mess than glorious. In the last half-hour, as the two ships closed, the Biter signalled her intentions exceeding clearly, and the Noble

Goring, as the trader was bizarrely named, ignored them with plodding insouciance. Kaye's guns were manned, although not shotted, but his colour rose as the gap grew smaller and the trader's captain, quite visible at the con, made not a move to bring her to, or ease a sheet, or deviate in any way at all from either his course or his intention. Kaye's colour rose, but John Gunning, at the Biter's con, almost on the helmsman's back indeed, showed signs of gibbering.

'Give her a shot!' he shouted, when his breaking point was reached. He turned to Kaye, his face congested, both hands clenched beside his cheekbones. 'If he goes past, how will we claw back up to him again!'

Kaye turned large eyes on him as calmly as you please, expression supercilious. He was intent on asserting his command, that had become quite plain. He was as near as damn it sneering.

'You will cut across her bow and give the fool a fright,' he said icily. 'Then round up handsomely and lay her alongside. I suppose I can trust you to do that, Mr Gunning?'

'Well,' said Sam, for Will's ears only, 'you're a wizard in a boat. Could you do it?'

Will's stomach was knotted with excitement. The ships were careering down like two mad bulls. Two madmen in command, no one was giving way. He drew his breath in sharply.

'Aye, with a handy ship and handy crew,' he said. 'Not drunk, though; never in the world while drunk. Christ, Sam, he don't believe we'll do it! Look at him!'

The captain of the Noble Goring, as if waking from a peaceful sleep and finding it a nightmare, was rushing towards his helmsman to tear the wheel out of his hands. He was shouting things they could not hear, and men were scurrying to sheets and braces. Instead of hauling hard up, as the race demanded and the Biter men expected, he spun the wheel to put her head to windward while his crew –

good, fast men despite their worn appearances – braced main and foreyards round at such a speed they went aback instantly, with a battery of explosive cracks. Tacks were not raised, so presumably the old man – and close-to he was old, maybe sixty – had decided belatedly to stop dead in his tracks, not go about on to the other tack, in case the Navy mad dogs sent vessels, men, and all his precious cargo to the bottom.

'Fuck,' said Sam. 'And one gun shot across his bow would have done it like a dilly. Now watch out, Mr Gunning! Avoid him if you can.'

That was the only option, sensibly – to jig past if possible, and slip away downwind and then regroup. The Noble Goring lay in an amazing carpet of green weed that waved out from all sides as she stood ashake, the seamen attempting to brace yards round to heave her to before she smashed her gear. But Gunning, so drunk smoke from his ears and nostrils would not have been surprising, still thought that he could fling his ship about, turn on a half a guinea, douse sails and lie along her side as neat as in a dockyard.

'Hard down!' he bellowed, pushing the man aside and spinning spokes himself. 'Brace all to weather! Raise tacks and sheets! Prepare to grapple him!'

Far too late, his people far too fuddled to respond in time, not possible to begin with, maybe. The Biter slid past the Noble Goring's bowsprit almost close enough for it to catch her weather shrouds, then she rounded up more like a floating hayrick than the swagger yacht Jack Gunning seemed to think he had control of. By the time they'd reached the waist they were not pointing bow to bow as he'd intended, but lay at right angles, with Biter moving in, not fast but with implacability. Men frantically tried bracing yards aback to stop her, but the wind was wrong, her set was wrong, and Noble Goring, inevitably, began to fall off from her upwind position, sideways into the Biter's bow. Bentley caught sight of Kaye, mouth wider than his eyes, his hand gripping the weather rail which now was at the lee, not capable of moving.

Had it not been at the waist they hit, the bowsprit sliding almost neatly in between the fore and mainmasts, their damage must have been much worse. As it was, the substantial sides and bulwark of the eastern trader absorbed their stemhead thrust with little more than a grinding judder, moving slowly as the Biter was by now. The sound of crunching, splitting timber and tearing sail went on interminably, accompanied by screams and shouting like a riot at a country fair. Then, in a sudden quiet, just as the Biter stopped her forward movement and began to disengage herself and slide astern, the fore topsail yard, bumped and pulled and jostled in its parrels, broke at the truss. The starboard arm came slicing down like nemesis, and smashed Eaton's ginger head into a bloody pulp between his shoulders, then covered him with canvas in an instant shroud.

Gunning responded to his great humiliation by lashing out at everyone and everything, while Kaye, of sterner stuff, came steaming across the deck at Sam and William near foaming at the mouth with rage.

'Get men on board, on board!' he shouted. 'Draw cutlasses, they will attack for certain! By God, I'll string them up, not offer them the bounty, the bloody fools! Away now, do your duty! I want men!'

Already some of Biter's people had spilled from off the foredeck on to the Goring, with the bony form of Behar in the van. Jem Taylor was not far after him, with a wooden club, and the bulk of Tilley swept other men along to join the boarders. There were drunken shouts and howling, but the Noble Goring's people, sober and fleet of foot, were disappearing like chaff before a wind. The captain, grey-haired and angry, was on his quarterdeck, staring down into the Biter's waist, and he did indeed have a pistol in his hand, although he made no sign that he would ever use it. The midshipmen, when they reached a point where they could jump, saw great confusion, and a growing gap. Biter, her sails untended, was easing back from off the bigger ship, with only the bowsprit ropes and furniture to keep her. The jib-boom was broke and hanging down, and that had snagged the bulwarks of the 'prize', but it would not hold them on for long.

'Ayling!' shouted Samuel, over his shoulder. 'Hey, Tennison, Hugg! Come over quick, we need you! Get some more!'

But Tennison was cradling Shockhead Eaton, and the instruction was ignored. There were four or five friends of the boatswain's mate to hand, with others – sobered by the awful shock – standing about and watching. Above, the canvas thrashed like thunder, yards swung about, blocks swooped like deadly vultures looking for another skull to smash. This was work for Gunning and his hirelings, but that society was worse collapsed than Kaye's. Until Will strode aft to take it, there was not even a sailor at the wheel.

'She's falling off, sir!' he shouted to Kaye. 'Where is Mr Gunning? If we're not careful we will leave our men on board!'

Kaye went storming off up forward, where the Navy company were now almost all gathered round Eaton, but he gave them a wide berth. Will saw him talk to Samuel, then found Kershaw at his hand. Kershaw, with anxious face but shoulders back and braced, indicated that he would take the wheel, and Will set off like a dervish to force some men to work. Even Gunning's lot, who were not paid to take his orders, jumped to his harsh commands, and the men round Eaton, when yards began to swing intentionally, went to their positions to give a hand. Sails were backed and filled, canvas was quieted, the ships began to move apart and disentangle. Kaye gesticulated furiously on the prow, and shortly men began to climb off of the windward ship to get on board their own. They brought seven of the Noble Goring's men with them, some bloody in the face and mouth. Throughout the whole manoeuvre, John Gunning never reappeared.

It was not the end exactly, but they were almost there. The Biter, fallen off, could only go downwind in her condition, but home was to the north, against the breeze. First thing was to get the canvas off, as she did not possess the necessary sails to heave her to. But as they busied themselves at that, Kaye made it plain to Will and Samuel he wanted more seamen from the Noble Goring, and he would have them. Boats' crews was his word, to cross the growing gap and press at pistol point. The Indiaman, apparently undamaged, was already under way, hauling her wind for London River, but she was slow and weedy while their boats were fast. His juniors thought him crazy, but they did not argue. Neither did the people, when he bellowed his intentions – but continued their allotted tasks with great stolidity, taking care to keep their faces turned away. Some were engaged in carrying Eaton's body down below. Like the others, they did not argue, but did not respond. Lieutenant Kaye stood in a rage, forsaken.

The light was falling, but the wind stayed sharp and strong. At his first tour of assessment, Will figured they would keep the bowsprit, if not the outer clutter, but had better bring both the topgallant and the topmast down because they could not stay them safely. The topsail yard and sail, in falling, had destroyed the forecourse and maybe sprung the yard, which would be some hours' work to check and rectify, if it were possible. Abaft of that the main topgallant mast had got a wrench, and the main topsail was badly ripped. All headsails and their stays were down or ruined. The carpenter was good, Sam told him, so was Watkins, sailmaker, except he was in love.

'But that does not stop a man from working does it, friend?' he added, with affection. 'Of course it don't! We'll have her under way again tomorrow.'

The Noble Goring, being the closest ship, was the last to fade into the encroaching night. She did not go well, or fast, but everyone who watched her knew she'd beat them into London however good the makeshift rig they managed in the day or days ahead. It was five nights later, in fact, that Will and Sam saw the ship again, after Biter had limped to the Nore and then been towed by dockyard pullboats up to Deptford. She was lying at a quay near Pickleherring Stairs as a wherry shot them past up to the bridge, yards canted, holds open, in the hands of wharfingers. Unlike the Biter, way down the river, she looked very peaceful lying there.

25

They buried Shockhead Eaton's body within sight of his home coast, with little ceremony but enough emotion. Lieutenant Kaye conducted, having decided as was his right not to transport the man's remains to land, there being little point. As far as anybody knew he had no people waiting on him, he'd never talked of home or family. Sam and William remembered the maid he'd stayed to be with, but knew neither name nor place by which to trace her. Or indeed, if she were wed to someone else, which would make a welcome for the sorry corpse a shade unlikely. They did not even bother to heave the Biter to, just handed spokes to bring her to the shake, so cranky was she under bodged-up headsails, a jury staysail instead of forecourse, and her brigsail. Shockhead was popular but men died, that was the general attitude: he should have kept his eyes aloft, and not sailed with such a drunken crew. By the time they buried him the spree was long past, and the company were very far from liveliness.

In Surrey that same day they buried Charles Yorke at Sir Arthur Fisher's house. This too was done with deep emotion but no great pomp, except that all the women of the household were swathed in black, and Sir Peter Maybold, the Surveyor General, was invited to represent the Customs House. He did arrive by splendid coach, but respected his friend's request for simple dignity, although his periwig, chosen by his wife Laetitia, was rather full and lustrous, and a touch archaic. Laetitia, who enjoyed a funeral for the dressing up, had been persuaded to stay in town and make some other amusement for herself. She had pouted, thought for three seconds, and announced that she had hit on 'just the thing'. Maybold, sombre eyes across the rolling green of Fisher's land, had looked the very picture of well-bred misery. It was no act.

The decision to retrieve the body from the Devil's Punchbowl had been forced on Sir A by the fact that, heavy with the knowledge brought by the two midshipmen, he could no longer bear to wait to see the right thing done. It had become apparent within a day that they were not coming back as planned, which was confirmed by a letter the day after that from Bobby Beaumont at the Admiralty. Kaye had slipped his moorings without a by-your-leave, it said, and 'for all his papa is a bloody duke, I'll roast the bugger's buttocks'. That same morning Tony and some trusted men had set off with a light closed cart, and muskets, cutlasses, and picks and shovels. They had found the marked trees, then the cairn and body, and had met no opposition. The undertaker had begged Sir Arthur not to view the corpse before he'd coffined it, but Sir Arthur had insisted.

Kaye's buttocks were not roasted when the Biter was lodged finally alongside a quay at Deptford, but there was a reception for him that all on board found immensely shocking. The last minutes were a monument to chaos in any case, as Gunning's men, within a sniff of shore, behaved as private seamen always did – and ran. As the dockyard pullmen manoeuvred her the last few complex yards, unmanageable in a falling tide, they dropped all vestiges of obedience, ignored orders from Gunning or the Navy officers, and perched themselves on the bulwarks and in the chains to get first jump for shore. Before the Biter's side was six feet from the staging the first men had launched themselves above the swirling water, and when they hit the ground they scampered off like rabbits. Gunning did not even watch them as they went. Within two minutes of the mooring lines being secured, he had also gone.

But on the shore, watching this performance, was a post

captain with severe eyes like an owl's staring out from underneath his wig, a pair of Navy Office clerks, and an old, thin man who Sam said could only be a lawyer, for any odds. In moments he was proved right, as the party came on board and spoke to Lieutenant Kaye, the thin old chap wagging a furled parchment like a judge's gavel. As Kaye heard them out his mien changed from its normal bored superiority, his insouciance seemed lost. As he led them aft to the cabin's privacy, Sam swore Slack Dickie's eyes had flashed alarm. He guessed the Noble Goring's captain had lodged complaints, and had the pull with someone to back them up. When Black Bob was ejected, to stand disconsolate and watch the Deptford shore, they asked him what was up below, but he would not reply, and ran off forward where he disappeared.

The truth, when they came to it, was stranger yet. They busied themselves for half an hour with their people and the Deptford men in snugging the Biter for her dockyard work, until one of the clerks sought them out and bade them aft. When they pointed to unfinished work he told them it was orders, not of Lieutenant Kaye, but Captain Oxforde from the Admiralty. There were no more answers to their questions, but soon they stood in front of this august man, who was at a table flanked by the other clerk and the aged legal type. Kaye sat to one side, his self-satisfaction overlaid by a glower, and stared intensely at them in a way William took as threatening.

The post captain had a voice to match his looks, and he outlined what he was there for with crystalline acidity. The owner of a ship called Katharine, on information from her master James McEwan, had raised a yeoman posse that had come to London from the depths of Hertfordshire to effect an arrest on the person of their own commanding officer, Lieutenant Richard Herbert Kaye, for the alleged murder of one Peter Morris, Katharine's first mate, by discharge of a pistol. Their lordships, he added, viewed the allegations with the utmost seriousness, reflecting as they did on the honour and integrity of the service. Naturally, Lieutenant Kaye was scandalised by the accusation, which he denied in its entirety. However —

'However,' interrupted Kaye. 'As you fellows damn well know —'

'Lieutenant Kaye,' said Oxforde. 'You stand across me, sir.'

'But —'

'You interrupt me. I will not put up with it. You deny this charge, that is understood. The posse is disarmed and waiting. They have a warrant, signed by a magistrate, but we have lawyers also. I am here to give them ammunition. You do not help by blustering.'

The lawyer cleared his throat.

'The Impress is not a favourite service with the layman,' he said. His voice was soft but clear. 'Before I can have that warrant set aside I must have facts that will make even a country justice see there is no case. That, gentlemen, is what I hope from you.'

'Within the truth, of course,' said Captain Oxforde. 'That is understood, I hope.'

William could see it with an awful clarity. He could see the Katharine's great cabin, he could smell the burning powder, remember what that young man looked like, chest torn open in a bloody hole. He could see Kaye with the first mate's pistol, pawing at its action. His stomach sank inside him in disgust.

'I heard a row, sir,' he started. 'We heard —'

'You were not asked to speak.' Oxforde's voice was cutting. His finger moved up from the table, to point at Sam. 'You. Tell me what you saw.'

Sam wet his mouth.

'As Mr Bentley says, sir, we heard a —'

The captain's hand slammed down, a loud, sharp bang. Sam stopped.

'It is an easy language,' said Captain Oxforde, almost pleasantly. 'Speak it with me. I said tell me what you saw.

The incident was in the cabin, was it not? So we are in the cabin, aren't we? You, sir, and Lieutenant Kaye, and your friend Mr Bentley. And the ... ah ... Lieutenant Kaye's attacker. What did you see?'

There was a pause. Will saw it still, but the clarity was of a different kind. Sam wet his lips more noisily. Will smelled sweat.

'But sir,' said Sam. Hopeless, and he knew it. Oxforde quelled him with a look. 'The officer was on the deck,' he said. 'His leg was twitching, he had been shot. Lieutenant Kaye was standing over him, with his pistol. He had fired it.'

Lieutenant Kaye's mouth moved as though he was going to open it, but he changed his mind.

'Whose pistol? Who had fired it?'

'Lieutenant Kaye had them both,' said Sam. 'He had fired one, his own, short barrel and a heavy calibre, a Leyden Callender I think. He had the other pistol also. Big, horse pistol type of animal. It had not been fired.'

By the crashing on the decks, the sound of tramping feet, the shore gang were unrigging her. Inside the cabin a long silence fell.

'You are an expert then, I see.' Oxforde's voice was pleasant. 'Who says it was not fired? You were not there to see if the man was on the deck already, were you?'

'Lieutenant Kaye said it had not been, sir. He said he had shot his gun. He said the man was primed and cocked, but ...'

'But what? Do you say he's lying?'

This was so direct that Bentley's stomach clenched. Kaye had had the action covered when Sam and he had gone into the cabin. He could have cocked it himself, then showed it cocked before he spoke of it. 'See, it is cocked,' he'd said.

'Well?' asked Captain Oxforde. 'Was it primed and cocked, midshipman? You have eyes, did you not see it?

Was it primed and cocked? You are the expert, you know guns. The truth, sir; now!'

The smug look in Kaye's eyes was back, Will saw that in a glance. The tilted nose spoke of confidence restored. Sam was being challenged to say the unsayable, and damn himself to hell. He could not do it.

'Aye, sir,' he said. 'It was cocked. I later saw Lieutenant Kaye blow the pan out.'

'So it was primed?'

The slightest hesitation.

'It was primed, sir.'

'With your permission, sir?' said Kaye. 'Thank you. Now Holt, now Bentley; did I not say this? That the villain drew a sight on me, and made to fire? That I lifted my gun first – as Holt says, sir, small, fast and powerful, a masterpiece of Mr Callender's – and shot him down? Is that not correct in every detail? Would he not have killed me, had I not? Mr Bentley? You have not deigned to speak, I see.'

The captain raised a hand, as if amused. But he made no rebuke to Kaye, just smiled at Bentley.

'Well, sir? Have you aught to add? Or do you agree with Mr Holt in every detail? You both seem circumspect, somehow, I might say, *overawed*. We are not so grand as all that, we old fighting men!'

To Will, the heartiness rang false as hell. The smell of sweat from Sam was powerfully bitter, and his own cheeks and teeth were clenched. He was surer than he'd ever been that Kaye had cocked the pistol to prove a threat that in life had not existed – but he did not *know*. He did not know, and he could not voice suspicions. To call a man a liar was an awful thing, and to do so without hope of any proof was at the very least stupidity. Fact was, he *did* not know. Kaye, to him, was a charlatan, whom he would not trust for anything. But did he really think he was a murderer in cold blood?

'Sir,' he said. 'When I saw the action, it was . . .' All eyes bored into him. He had seen the action covered first, and he did not trust Kaye. It came to him with bright clarity that he should not say this, as he could not add to it. He gestured feebly. 'It was cocked. Later, like Mr Holt, I saw him blow the pan. Lieutenant Kaye told us he'd been threatened.'

He caught the eyes of the post captain for a moment, and thought he saw a flash of understanding there. But probably it was illusion. Oxforde then nodded, satisfied.

'Good,' he said. 'Well, Mr Kaye, 'tis as you said in every detail. You went into the cabin, you were attacked, and shot the man in self-defence. Mr Palmer? Have you any questions more?'

The lawyer, scratching underneath his wig, paused to shake his head in negative. The clerks made play with horns and pen, Slack Dickie beamed in satisfaction. Sam Holt and Bentley looked for a sign, of dismissal or invitation to the higher company, but – ignored – soon cleared their throats significantly, then slid away. An hour afterwards, as the only officers or gentlemen left save Kershaw, and the ship a swarm of dockyard men who judging by the flares and preparations were due to work all night, they packed small bags and hailed a waterman. Even the slack-tide stench of the foul Thames struck William, poetically, as sweeter than the air had been in Biter's cabin.

It was the lateness of the hour Sam gave as his excuse for seeking Dr Marigold's rather than getting hacks for Langham Lodge, but William needed neither excuse nor much persuading. He knew that by the time they had reached London the yeomen from Hertfordshire would have got their weapons back and been sent home, and that the Navy's ranks were closed for ever against any suggestion the first mate's death had been improper. He and Sam, between them, had had the only chance of setting up a doubt, and both of them had felt they could not do it. They sat in the sternsheets of the wherry, silent for the most part, and both felt guilt and hopelessness. No one, because of them, would be able to point a finger at Richard Kaye on this incident, ever again.

'We would not get to Langham Lodge till the early hours,' said Sam, at one point. 'We've been away for a week and more, so half a day won't make no difference. Quite honestly, Will, I ain't sure I could face . . .'

He did not finish, but Will was there with him. Events were like a grindstone, crushing them, wearing them down. Will looked across the dark roofs and buildings pressing to the river and longed, strangely, for the open sea. He recalled that when he'd started, as a boy, the Navy life had been such a fresh and open one, with him and his fellow officers dedicated to a fine and noble calling, to Englishness, Englishmen and England, the jewel of all the world. Now he felt dirtier than the Thames itself.

They paid the rivermen and walked up towards the Fleet and Dr Marigold's, but even alone they did not talk much of what they'd seen and how it fell to them. Sam made it clear as soon as he crossed the threshold that he had Annette in mind as his best drug, but Will, left alone with Mrs Margery, could not be tempted by her tales of bright new maids, nor yet of 'coddling' by those of more experience. She had judged his mood exactly though, because he was deep in need of comfort divorced completely from the world of men. They did not mention Deb by name, but she talked of girls who did not whore, but came to live at Marigold's out of necessity to find a place, maybe of refuge, maybe just to string their lives together, to earn enough in services unspecified to see them through a time of hardship that they could some day end. Young men like Sam, she said, wanted one thing only from a maid – and none the worse for that – but 'we can succour too, both maids and bloods. Look at yourself. I have work to do, always there's work, but I have time to talk to you, and here I am. No charge, free, gratis, and I'm glad of it.'

Will almost told her about Deb's disaster, but feared it would upset them both, for nothing. He almost told her about the Katharine's first mate, asked 'if you saw a young man killed, and knew that it was wrong, then what?' But as the words formed in his mind he knew it was impossible, so stopped. When more men came for custom Will backed off into shadow, then she led him to a bedroom and left him, with a glass of port. He stripped completely, splashing himself with water from a jug, then lay in the bed and blew the candle out, hoping for sleep. It did not quickly come, and he thought afterwards he'd stared upwards to the ceiling until dawn or so. But it was Sam who woke him, a Sam refreshed and in a better spirit, who forced him to a very early breakfast and then to the yard, where he had horses saddled up and waiting. Not long after first light, they were gone.

Chester Wimbarton, as he had promised, 'looked Deb over' next time he came to her, and many times thereafter and very frequently, as he was as wiry and insatiable as an upland tup. The first few times he brought his knife, but soon he left it far away from them, and then he dared to face her unprotected. He always wore a long white shirt, he always stood between her thighs while she was pressed back on the bed, and apart from muttered greetings and farewells, he hardly spoke. On the second time he said she should be naked, and when she moved too slow he hit her. After that, when he entered the room, Deb pulled her shift off to be ready, and only put it on when he had gone.

She talked to Sue and Joan, and sometimes Dorothy, and counted them as her only friends. Her greatest fear was falling pregnant – although all three of the household women recommended it as a hope, for poor Milady had failed in that department and had cried about it to them in the depths of her despair – but they brought her vinegar in plenty, and more soap than most poor maids saw in a lifetime to undo the damage in the bud if possible, and hang expense. When his wife was still alive, she figured, he might have found a little baby welcome, but a bastard fathered on a locked-up slut would strike the neighbours very different, especially for a justice of the peace. Deb no longer knew what she expected of the future, or wanted even. But to be thrown back on a most uncaring world great with child, or snuffed out quietly as an embarrassment, was not on her agenda. She had her body, which seemed to drive him mad with lust, and it was meat and drink to her, if not contentment.

Contentment, in a way, would have been a walk outside. This came on Deborah as a realisation slowly, and it amused her when she thought how much her world had been reduced. At first she'd craved for freedom, mainly from the sight or sound or thought of Wimbarton and his stabbing thing, then she'd craved for company or friends, or maids who – unlike Wimbarton's – were not moved (as they were at first) by envy or suspicion. She'd craved for Dr Marigold's, its comforts and its jollity, she'd craved good food and drink, variety. She'd sometimes, weepily, craved her shining prince, neat William, although she knew that was a fairy tale, nothing more. In the end, it boiled down to four drab walls and one high, obscure window, and the smell, the sound, the memory of a world outside. She tried to talk to the master, to make him think she liked him so that some day she could hint she'd appreciate a stroll, but the master, whatever he thought of her, did not like her 'prattling' (as he once called her twelve words, she counted them up after the rebuke). She did get out once, the first Sunday, when she was allowed to go to church, discreetly hobbled underneath one of Sue's skirts so that she could not run far before Jeremiah or Fiske could skip after her to knock her down. She saw Milady's grave, and very nearly wept.

It was a drab life, but she guessed she'd stand it, as being better than no life at all. She wondered if she would or could escape, and how, but all in all it was beyond imagination. She very rarely fantasised, these days, about Wimbarton falling for her for her looks and making her the new

Milady, nor did she want it, under any circumstance. But she remembered, ruefully, she'd had the fantasy common to her trade, that some rich, handsome, noble man would lose his heart and soul to her, and make her great in happiness. Not Wimbarton now, though. No, not anyone.

They talked of cases as they rode along for Langham Lodge, and they got near expressing the thing that nagged at both of them, the odd notion that the times were out of joint somehow. Slack Dickie Kaye and his venality were ill enough, but the urbane post captain had shaken them more deeply. He'd brought a lawyer and two clerks all the way to Deptford not to hunt and find the truth (and shame the devil, even if his father was a 'bloody duke'!), but to make certain that it would not get out. What the truth was did not come into it, he'd made that all too plain; what mattered was the Navy's reputation, and that anyone's indiscretion, however violent, should not mar it.

'My father was a lawyer, and he said the country was gone wrong,' said Sam. 'He said there was a cancer had got in, a creeping corruption in our public life. But by God, Will, the Navy is an honourable service. We fight these evils, not go in for 'em.'

'In Navy terms, though,' Will started. But he broke it off. His Navy terms were blighted by his past. He'd seen too many means justified by uncertain ends. 'No,' he said. 'Kaye is not general, Sam, he's not of normal quality for a Navy officer. I guess they just worked out that one man dead was more than enough, and where's the point in breaking Dickie down? The Press itself is hated and reviled by many, but are we to blame ourselves for being part of it? Without the Press we should not have men to work our ships. It has been proved.'

'Aye, that's true enough, I can't gainsay it. And you mean Slack Dickie's worse than most of them, but still we must have men like him? One thing – he takes far less than most! In terms of sailors craving for their homes,

Richard's a benefactor, almost!' He sobered rapidly. 'But still, Will, there's a man was murdered, and—'

'Maybe,' said Will. 'Sam, I would have said an' I'd been sure, and so would you. Slack Dickie said the man attacked him, and the gun was cocked. I think – we think . . . But we can't be sure. And let's say Oxforde had worked that out, and all. What do? Admit Lieutenant Kaye's a murderer? Have him strung up? It feels dirty, Sam, God knows it does. But . . . Sam, we'll never know.'

'So many things we'll never know,' Holt muttered. 'Blood, Will, in the past two months the teeth of my blind faith, my faith in honesty and reason . . . well, even Annette called me tedious in her bed last night, she stopped my mouth to stop me droning on. But look at where we're going now, and why, and what we must find out. God, even gentle smuggling, that you at least think no worse than usury, is— Will? What's going on up yonder?'

Ahead of them, as they followed round a curve, there was a group of people, some on horseback, some on foot. It was a road they knew, not above a mile from Langham, the crossroads marked by an ancient turkey-oak with huge, spread branches. There was something dangling from a limb, an awful, characteristic shape that twisted on itself as the group milled round about it. It was a makeshift gibbet, with a hanging man, and they both stopped involuntarily, disquiet rising in them.

'It's Tony!' said Sam, suddenly. 'Look, he's seen us!'

Not the corpse, but a man on horseback, Will realised with surging relief. Sir A's steward wheeled, and spurred towards them. There were others of the baronet's retainers also there, he recognised.

'Sirs,' said Tony. 'There's some poor fellow here's been strung up like a scarecrow. Not above three hours since. I fear you know him.'

'What?' said Will, incredulous. 'But—'

But Sam had dug his heels, with Tony twisting his horse to follow him. As Will came up on them Sam had stopped, but he did not dismount. Despite the congestion of the face, eyes bulging out in blackened cheeks, a tip of tongue jammed out from the strained mouth, Will knew the man immediately. His wrists were tied in front of him, his breeches soiled. It was John Hardman, who'd revealed the body of Charles Yorke to Sam.

26

Sir Arthur, when they got to him, was overwhelmed to see them, he was flooded with relief. While Mrs Houghton tried to calm things down and give them food and drink and organise hot water 'for a wash at least', he fussed around them, mood swooping from delight that they were safe to relived horror at what they'd seen and what it meant. A message had alerted the household to the murder, brought by a labourer who had been paid (and threatened) by two armed horsemen not long after dawn. On their journey back with Tony he had revealed the message to them, but now Sir A needed explanation and reassurance.

'It mentioned you by name,' Tony had said. '"The tall one, called Sam." The labourer said you'd interfered in other folks' affairs and must desist, or else you would be killed. Oh Mr Sam, did you know this poor unfortunate? What means it all, for Jesus' sake?'

Sir A had not been told that they had found Yorke's body through a bribe, nor many of the details. Sam said now that the murdered man had been an informant, and guessed the other smugglers must have found it out. Both he and Will also guessed, but they did not say, that the men who'd killed Hardman must have had a damn good idea that they'd be coming down the London road this morning, or else their choice of place and timing was an amazing stroke of luck. The thought chilled both of them; they did not feel it wise to share it.

'But you were going back down there again!' Sir Arthur said in anguish. 'If Kaye had not sailed off against Beaumont's orders, the villains would have strung you up, not

339

him! You must not go now, you must call it off! Indeed, you shall not go!'

It was cold outside these days, with a definite feel of autumn. As always, the parlour had a fine bright fire, but Sir A seemed to have died somehow himself, or shrunk in and aged since Bentley had first seen him, not so very long ago. He was sitting close, hands folded on the knob of a walking cane, the fingers thin and bony. They worked against each other, constantly.

'Sir,' said Sam, choosing words with care. 'I do not say you overestimate the danger, that is a sort of thing a fool would say. Both Will and myself are conscious there are ruthless men in this, but we are confident we have the measure of them, to some degree. We are also confident, I think, that we are close to getting at the core of it. After what you said last time we thought long and deep about what we'd done, and who we'd seen and spoken to. Sir, Charles Yorke and Warren died, and we will never rest until we've brought their memories justice. I beg you. We beg you. Let us go.'

Bentley stood there feeling as if he were in another world. John Hardman's death had numbed him to the point where his thoughts seemed barely to connect with one another. Sam's speech had made no sense to him, although he got the gist and did, indeed, agree with the apparent sentiments. Hardman dead, Yorke and Warren dead, an enemy somewhere that was to all intents invisible and formless. Sam's face came into focus, eager, upset, passionate. They would go and find and fight a monster, he was saying, and they would win where other men had failed. Why? Will wondered it, but there came no answer. He heard his own voice speak.

'We've thought of nothing else,' he said. 'All the while on Biter, as we wasted time. Sir A, we are desperate to get the chance to do the world some good for once! We are Navy men, we are sick of pressing helpless sailors, of illegality, or sordid pettiness! Oh God, sir, we must go!'

He was panting through his nostrils, chest heaving up and down. Sir Arthur rose and came to them, took each by a hand. As he smiled, his eyes were glistening with tears.

'Lord Wodderley has allowed it, and has cleared it with the Customs House,' he said. 'For the King's Navy to volunteer its men to help, and for the Revenue to grant permission of acceptance, is no light achievement from anybody's side. If we unpicked it now . . . Mark you,' he added, 'nobody knew then about this latest outrage. Sam. William. I do not want you killed, my boys, I cannot stand you killed.'

'Uncle,' said Sam. He did not use the word in the normal way to Fisher, Will had never heard it said. They held each other's eyes, the old man and the young. 'Uncle,' he repeated. 'We will not be.'

There was further talk, but both of them, now the die was cast, wanted to get out of Sir Arthur's presence, and his house, and go to meet their fate head-on. He told them they could call on Customs men as reinforcements when they got to Hampshire – Sir Peter Maybold's bond – and that certain Navy men had been informed 'something was up'. Did this include Kaye? On that, Sir A was ambiguous: but certain he would not obstruct them any more, or try to override their higher orders. Best way with him though, all agreed, was to keep well out of range. They left mid-afternoon, well fed and watered, well provided for with money and small arms. Will watched Sam and his benefactor embrace, with a tiny twinge of envy. Then Sir Arthur gripped him by the hand, and looked into his eyes.

'My boy,' he said, 'I thank you for all this, from the bottom of my heart. Please return safe, and we will all have better times.' He faltered, then he cleared his throat. 'Return safe with Samuel,' he said. 'Take care of each, the both of you.'

*   *   *

341

The death of Hardman made their plan for them, because whatever else, they knew he had been loved. They set their course for Chichester, to give them one good clear night of sleep, but talk it as they might could not improve upon their first idea – to go to Langstone in the morning and plunge into the lion's den. Sam had an idea fixed that the Frenchmen were the key, or one Frenchwoman rather, as their agent, but Will kept what he saw as a more open mind. That the depths they had to plumb were deep and serious they had no cause to argue over. If Céline were at the centre of the spider's web so be it, thought Will; but it was Englishmen who'd died so far, and not by foreign hands, he guessed.

They both slept long and hard, sharing a bed for safety's sake, for they were pretty sure the gibbet at the crossroads had been set to chime with their arrival, and it was possible they had been followed on their way from Surrey. Possible but not likely, as the journey had been clear and in clear weather, and they had done some detours and some watching stops without surprising anyone. Further, they had not told anyone their destination – not even Sir A himself – on the principle that walls have ears, and even fine and loyal men like Tony was, in outward aspect, might be possessed of a black and secret heart. They breakfasted on lamb and kidneys, washed down with Sussex ale, and kept their conversation light and general. Back in the saddle, they japed each other for the care they'd taken to be like 'top-nick spies'.

As they passed through Emsworth, though, each felt the weight of expectation pressing down on him. The wind was keen and off the sea, which meant they could go muffled and their hats pulled low, but eyes seemed to linger on their faces, and to probe. There was a lot of traffic and the narrow way congested, and the fear of challenge grew in both their chests. By afternoon they were in Havant, which was jam-pack full, it being cattle mart, and they sat down in a crowded tap confident for the while that they were anonymous and safe. Until they saw Isa Bartram watching them, quiet in a corner of the room. When he knew they had seen and recognised, he emptied the pot in front of him and gestured towards the door. By it were three others that they knew, remembered as George, Bob and Joe, although Will could not put names to faces certainly. None had knives or pistols visible – that was frowned on heavily in a town – but there was no doubt that they were armed. And they were waiting.

Sam smiled at Will.

'It's do or die,' he said. 'Blood, but they have good intelligence. Here's to your very best of health.'

He drained his pot.

William, meeting Isa at the door, had a certain feeling that he and Sam were very soon to die. The man was lean and bitter-looking, his eyes on them unflinching, hard.

'We have your horses,' he said. 'We were expecting you. You will come with us.'

'Ah,' said Sam. 'Expecting us' – as if it were significant. Will said: 'Mr Bartram. John Hardman's death. We are truly sorry.'

There was no reply to that, and as they rode sedately down the road to Langstone and the causeway, no other words were spoken. Sam and Will stayed together side by side and made no move to show their weapons, although Bartram and his fellows did, not ostentatiously. At his saddle, on a thong, Bob had a scattergun, short and deadly. Had they run, he could have slaughtered them.

As they approached the houses, Will began to be aware, quite slowly, of the devastation Hardman's hanging must have brought to the community. The Widow Hardman, he recalled, had lost two sons already in most awful circumstances, two of her three, and now the last was dead, hanged at a crossroads like a most vicious criminal. Most ironically, he'd been trying to escape the chosen life. The Hardman house, he saw before they all dismounted, was closed and shuttered up. Perhaps the poor old dame had died as well, from grief and shock.

It was Mary's house they made for, not Bartram's own. As they got near the door – them leading, with pistols at their backs – it opened to let Kate emerge, a child in arms and others at her skirt. She eyed them almost fearfully, no hint of any greeting, and hurried to her own front door, and through it. Then Mary Broad appeared to watch and let them in. Her eyes met Bentley's levelly, cool but not antagonistic, and he had a sudden surge of hope.

'Mistress Broad,' he said. 'Mary. We found John Hardman at a crossroads. We were coming here in any way. We have to stop this dreadful spiral. We have to know the truth.'

Then, with Bartram glowering, she stepped forward and embraced him, arms strong, her bosom and her body warm.

'Poor John,' she said. 'Poor John. He talked to you, we know that. He told you things he had no right to tell. It was not us though, if you were meant to think that, maybe. We heard last night. The warning was for us as well.'

'Mary!'

Bartram's voice was harsh, but she was not intimidated. She pulled back from Will, but kept her hand on his upper arm.

'There are disputes within our company,' she said, mildly. 'Come you in, and let us talk about it.'

Sam said, as they began to cross the threshold: 'It was not Will, mistress, that John Hardman spoke to, it was I. Will did not want me to, he is in no way to blame.'

'No matter now,' said Bartram, gruffly. 'Let us discuss inside. Bob, George. We must be guarded. Be discreet.'

Inside the house was dark, and warm and still, with little light from the windows and no lamps or candles. Mary moved to make a light, then changed her mind. For all of them, the dim was preferable. They sat, but then seemed lost for words. Finally Will spoke, the oppression weighing heavily on him.

'The Widow Hardman,' he began. 'John's mother. Is she . . . ?'

'We had her brother come for her,' said Mary. 'She was . . . she would not allow us to look after her. It is . . . . John was her third.'

'She would not have let us talk to you,' said Bartram, quietly. 'She did not know, but guessed what he had done. She would not understand that, ever.'

'But you do?' Sam asked quickly. Then, getting no reply, he added: 'I remember, you would not let John tell us something that he wanted to.'

'He told you later,' said Mary.

'For cash!' came Bartram's voice. 'He sold us out for cash, and now he's dead! That's why I would not let him tell you. Was I wrong?'

After a few long moments, Mary sighed.

'Isa,' she said. 'These men, these Navy officers. They must be told, we have agreed it. They are not Customs, they came for private reasons at the start. I told them we were not behind the other deaths, and I suppose young John confirmed it. I said the other deaths were wicked and that's proved, also, by his own. William; and Sam. What we do to get our living, as you know, is a hanging matter, if caught we're killed, and sometimes kill preventing it. But not like this, for any reason, never. Will knew my husband. Could you see Jesse doing it? To stop the mouths of people? To burn them? To stuff them headfirst down a cave to starve? Could you see my Jesse doing that?'

She covered her face, and the men stirred, uncomfortably.

'You lied to him,' said Samuel, unexpectedly. Mary's head jerked up, she was astonished. 'To Will, about the French maid,' he added quickly. 'Sally, or Céline. She smuggles Frenchmen. Is that the cause of this? I think so.'

345

Isa let out an explosive Hah!, while Mary shook her head from side to side, dismissively.

'Céline is nothing,' she said, '*nothing*. I said she'd gone to business off down east, did not I, Will? She had, as usual, but that has naught to do with us, or this. Indeed, I did not lie.'

'But—'

'You said Charles Yorke was buried,' Will interrupted. 'You said hotheads from out of town. Charles Yorke was trapped, hurt, incarcerated, he was not buried. He was not even dead. Was that the truth?'

There was a longer silence. Mary's voice, when she broke it, was lower than before.

'It was almost what I knew,' she said. 'It was much of what I hoped. Forgive me, for it was not all the truth. They were not local men, the most of them, they were not of our people nor any of the bands we know and work with. Gentlemen; sirs. All this is why we have to speak with you, to put it on the level, or things will get much worse. Something is happening down this way, something we do not want. There are families moving in on us, from the east, and coercing us. Yorke and Warren found out names and plans, and they were killed so horribly to be a lesson to us, and a warning not to resist. John Hardman was more determined and more foolhardy than most, and looked to you for help, maybe. He was gibbeted to discourage you, I guess, but us as well. He was a wild boy, but we loved him well.'

Bartram stood, and went to place a log on the fire. He stirred it, as if thinking, then faced out into the room.

'These families Mary mentions,' he said. 'That is not proper families, understand, it is just a word describing how we organise. In Langstone, on part of Hayling, Warblington, along the Emsworth shore, we have a family, linking in with others round this stretch of coast. Down Kent way they have much bigger gangs, and go about things much more ruthlessly. In years past these families have joined, and in the past five years or so have joined with other teams in East Sussex, Brighton, Worthing way. Now they're horning in on us. They run bigger cargoes, much more frequently, they use much more force and far less stealthiness. Two hundred men with guns and clubs to guard the tubmen coming off the beach, luggers big enough to fight a Navy cutter, pack horses, mules, carts provided by the local population out of fear. Death and brute behaviour is the norm for them. Those are the out-of-towners Mary spoke of, that is what she meant. They cut up Yorke and Warren because they found them out. They strung up John because he went prating truth.'

Sam's face was dubious, he was unconvinced; still sore, Will hazarded, at the dismissal of his Sally theory. Mary and Isa watched him narrowly, to see how he would jump. After a moment, Mary pre-empted.

'We do not say we are good,' she told him gently, 'only that we are better, or at least we do not use force unless it's forced upon us. Behind us, of course, behind us workers in the boats and on the shore, there are other men, of much more power, of wealth and influence. Do you not see? Our market is in London mainly, the centre of the world, for distribution anyway. In France the stuff is not ours for free, it must be bought and paid for in advance, made somewhere in the south maybe, then put in casks, if liquid, transported hundreds of miles, stored, lightered out to our expensive ships – which must be built and owned and paid for – then brought to England, landed, stored, coloured with burnt sugar, maybe recasked or even bottled, then up the road to London as I said, guarded, bribed for, and protection paid to any Tom or Harry who might have a safe conduit to betray us through, when he's had the goods and benefits. Some of them,' she ended, on a bitter note, 'some of them Customs men, and some Navy officers. And above us all those rich men, shadows, who provide the money in advance that makes it happen. Those rich men without names who want to join up with the men of Kent and East Sussex and will maim and murder anyone who dares to say them nay.'

The nub was, when they'd talked it round and round, that a movement started many months before, resisted 'on the lower deck' and fought and argued over passionately, was getting close to being clinched irrevocably. The Kent and East Sussexers would no longer be gainsaid, and the local venturers and shadows had decided to go in. There was money in the question, a mint; thirty, forty, fifty thousand pounds perhaps. In a week or two – Isa and Mary were vague on this – there was to be a meeting of the sides, possibly with a brandy run as a diversion, an enormous show of arms to discourage interference and, perhaps, to mark it as a special time. Behind the beach though, in a house they used beside the River Adur mouth, would be the highest-level business, a shaking of hands and meeting of minds among the greatest of the shadow-guard, the venturers. It was this rendezvous, and the local names behind it, that Charles Warren and Charles Yorke had uncovered or been on the point of doing, and had therefore had to die. After the rendezvous, said Mary, such sort of action, such beastliness, would spread along the coast like cancer.

Outside, people were calling as they crossed the causeway, cows were lowing. It only served to emphasise the quietness within.

'These men,' asked William, at last. 'These local men. They are not working people, like yourselves. What kind of men are they? If we were to, somehow, get to this rendezvous . . . how would we know . . . ?'

He let the question tail, because he had a growing sense inside, a vague foreboding. But Isa Bartram, impatient, interrupted him.

'What mean you? Get to the rendezvous? Lord, sir, there will be the wildest men to guard it in three counties, men of blood and iron. We told you, a show of force unprecedented. We did not tell you this to have you murdered out of hand! An' you went near it you would be torn to pieces!'

'Then what,' asked Sam, 'have you in mind? You've told us for a reason, we are not bumpkins, are we? What is it that you hope we'll do? And why?'

'The "why" is simple!' said Mary, passionately. 'John Hardman, and Mr Yorke, and Warren! We are free traders, we earn a living, not a great one neither, and everybody knows the law is mad and breaks it at their will and buys their necessary luxuries from us! We are not savages, nor murderers, nor rich! The "what" we have no real idea of, except you're of the Navy Royal and we have trusted you. You could have us hanged, the lot of us, the moment that you go away from here. Or you can find a way to help us, if you can. Us and our country, that needs it sorely. These new ways; this greed for money. It is growing out of conscience, it is wrong!'

Bartram, whose lean and bitter features were not prone to warmness, looked at Mary with pity and affection, and leaned to touch her arm.

'You see,' he said, 'we are not common criminals. John died for honesty, despite he took some cash for it. If you don't have us hanged and we're found out by the great ones we want to thwart – well then, we'll all end up butchered too, I guess. Mary is fearful for the future of her little Jem. I too have children. I wonder who would take them in?'

'But we are midshipmen,' said Sam. 'We are the lowest of the low in some respects. If we had times and dates and places, well, perhaps we could set up a Customs force. We have been told they should co-operate, but we are Navy men, as you so rightly say, and the rivalry is bitter. Likewise if we tried to get the Navy in, what would the Customs say? In any way, we need times and places, something firm, or we will be laughed out of court. You say next week, or later. How can we work on that?'

Bartram nodded.

'I see your troubles, but . . . Look, I can try to find out more, although we are in suspicion, because of John. Can you not go away and try yourselves? Not to find out the detail, but if you can get a force? The Navy would be better because we know the Customs too damn well. Some would be bought off, some would blab your secrets to the families, and if they made the beach and the force was strong or odds too great, they'd run. Warren and Yorke, among their other annoyances, were not bribeable. The way they died will make all lesser men think hard before they copy them, I promise you. Whatever else I've heard about the Navy, courage is not a doubt, is it?'

He did not need an answer, although Will's mind, and Sam's, slipped on to Kaye and his absurdities. But they took the point about the Customs House. This operation, if it should come, would be a facer even for the bravest men. They could call in dragoons perhaps, more like militia or the mounted yeomanry, but then again . . . It was not so very long ago that they'd been hunted by that sort of gallant band, and jailed. For what? For catching smugglers.

'We will go,' said Will decisively. 'We will try. If we had names, you understand; if we could name men and say that they'd killed Warren and Yorke?' He sighed. 'No, it would be too easy. And even if you knew, and told, you would be done to death. But without names we can only stick our necks out and make promises, predictions. It may go hard with us to drum up a response.'

'We do not know the names,' said Mary. 'Believe us, Will. We were thorns in their side in this right from the start, and you're right, they'd kill us. They'd kill us if they knew about your being here, if they knew the half of what we'd told you. It's growing dark. You must wait until it's truly black before you do set off. Isa and the friends will look out for you and set you on your way. Look, there is bread and cheese and I will mash some tea. Isa, go next door and bring your Kate and the children in, let's have a little normality round here. And let me say that when we have a date, a fair idea, you will know of it. But we will need a go-between to get the news to you, or one of you will have to ride again. We must work that out.'

She went and checked the kettle as it bubbled, and stirred the fire under it.

'Now, tea,' she said.

Before they left, three hours later when it was pitchy dark, Mary took some trouble to speak to Will alone. Sam had gone outside to see the horses and talk to Isa and the others, with whom he was much easier now all the cards were out. Will would have gone, but Mary held him with a look.

'A word,' she said. 'I hope we meet again, but if we don't, I wish to say farewell, and properly. I need to thank you face to face for trusting me. And say sorry if I've used deceit.'

Will protested, but she shook her head.

'Céline,' she said. 'Young Sally, who we told you was a Guernsey maiden. She's not as you now know, and her usual job, that I so gulled you on, is to get Frenchmen back to France, man-smuggling, under the Customs' very noses. And yours, I suppose, the Navy's. I'm sorry.'

Sorry for what, he wondered. For deceiving him? But what about her patriotic duty, the treachery involved? He caught her gaze and found his mouth was open. He had been about to speak, but no words had come.

'You take it very light,' he said. He faltered. 'But Mistress Broad; our countries are at war!'

She hastened to explain then, and he tried hard to take it in. Firstly, she said, Céline brought Englishmen across the Channel too, it was a both-ways trade. She was French, yes, and they were the enemy, but not many years ago they had been allies against the Dutch or Spanish, and would doubtless be again. Sometimes she worked with Englishmen, on the same boats, sometimes exchanging prisoners in mid-sea. Sometimes it turned out that the

Frenchmen she took back were English in reality, going to be spies she guessed, and she it was who had been tricked – except that Englishmen she brought were sometimes French.

'It is a job like any other for a smuggler,' she said. 'Frowned on by authority, deep against the law, but there to make the wheels go round. Céline would tell you, if she were here, she would explain to you. *Vive la commerce* would be her motto – long live business.'

Will wrestled with it, but sensibly he was shocked. Later, as they picked slowly through benighted countryside, he wondered if he should bring it up with Sam but decided, on the whole, it would be better left unsaid. When his friend raised the subject on his own account, as they sheltered under trees during a heavy downfall, he was noncommittal, but not surprised by Holt's vehemence. Of all the parts of the free traders' story, Sam averred, it was the one he hated most. But when he'd raised it with Isa on the Langstone foreshore, the dour smuggler had only laughed.

'They don't take it serious at all,' he added. 'He says it's part of normal intercourse between countries at war, else all the jails would burst. He says she's working now, down at the Medway, there's a ship expected, a rendezvous set up, he was as open as a drunkard's cellar door. The only trouble is, he might be joking me, it might be another strand he's laying up to tie us with. Dear God, I wish we had the picture laid out straight, don't you?'

William felt the chill rain dripping down his neck, but could not reply. He was tired, rather lonely, getting cold. They had only been abroad two hours, and there were many hours more. He thought of bed and thought, inevitably, of Deborah. Beneath him, his horse blew through its nostrils, noisily.

'They're using us,' Sam said. 'They're using us unmercifully, you understand that much, don't you, my friend? My feeling is the French maid may be the real heart of it, but my trouble is I can't be sure. I can't make up my mind if we should be aiding them at all, I only know they're using us, unmerciful.'

Will wrestled with that too, but had to ask, at last. How using them, did Samuel not believe there was a meeting coming off, that a force to shatter it might not bring off a fairly mighty coup? But yes, Sam did believe it, but then again he thought it half the story, half or even less.

'We're being used to save the locals' bacon, that's what I think,' he said. 'They talk of rich shadows and a ruthless gang, but what it boils down to is they're being took over by a bigger "family", God spare the word and me for using it. They want to stay small and masters of themselves, don't they? To do mayhem, to murder, and to thieve. While Sally/Céline sells our country down the river.'

'But don't you believe they're sickened by the last few weeks? By Yorke and Warren's deaths? By John? Hell, Sam, I can't think Mary's acting it! Nor Isa for that matter. He seems an honest man.'

'Aye! For a smuggler! For a merchant in cold steel and instant death! Nay, Will, don't look so glum, my opinion's not so far from yours, in actual. They're using us, I guess, because there is no other way, and who knows, we might even bring it off. I wish they'd tell us who the "shadows" were, though. Not the murderers, I believe them when they say they do not know. But these rich venturers, around Hampshire and West Sussex and so on. It is the way they looked at us when they did not give us names. Ah well, a different kind of power, I suppose. The sort of respected gentlemen who threw us into jail in Kent. It is a murky bloody game they play, when all is said.'

At any rate, they both agreed, as they shook rain from off their hats and cloaks and prepared to set out along the sodden track now the worst of the storm was done, there was no fault in breaking up a smuggling gang, even if by doing so they helped another thrive. Their first move, after going to Sir A to tell the latest, should be to tempt Slack Dickie with it as a plan, which neither of them guessed as easy. Helping the Customs would not appeal at all, except there was a clear chance to beat them at their own work and show them as incompetents, and a battle on a beach would be a hard and bloody venture, with long odds. Sir A had said keep clear of him as well, advice they both agreed was only good. But with the dearth of concrete facts they knew, with a venture based on speculation only, they could hardly dare to try for other Navy aid. Lord Wodderley had issued firmer orders now, Sir A had promised, and Kaye could not refuse them, despite he'd scorned instructions once. They could but go and try, in any case. If he spurned them, they would have to think again.

'I know the Adur well where it goes into the Channel,' said Sam, 'it is my patch. There are not many houses it could be, I have a fair hazard already as to which. If all else fails we could go down there on our own account and watch it happening. We might even recognise some of the perpetrators! The sort of men like Chester Wimbarton, no doubt. Somehow, we might even spot the murderers.'

This sounded ludicrous beyond belief, but Sam insisted it could be done if need be. The ideal thing, he said, would be to use a small Press gang as cover, a band with horses searching for seafarers as they were supposed to do, not hunting or expecting to have stumbled on a free trade game. If they saw crowds but played dumb and accosted no one, no one would accost them probably, and they could run at need. At very least, he added, seeing Will's dubiety, he ought perhaps to spy out the land himself alone beforehand, or any band they brought or ship that landed men would face a rout. With stealth and his local knowledge that should be quite possible.

They were close to Langham Lodge by this time, and looking forward to their beds, when ahead of them in a lucky shaft of moonlight they saw three men on horseback. They both reined in precipitately, but even before the flash of light was gone they knew it was an ambush. 'Left!'

bellowed Sam, then kicked out to steer him to the right. As they left the track and got on to the soft, in pitch dark once more mercifully, there came a smaller, redder flash ahead of them, followed by a loud report, a scattergun or blunderbuss with heavy charge. Shortly there was another gun let off, a musket crack this one, then they heard shouts and imprecations. The ground beneath their horses quickly became too soft for speed or safety, so they got back on the road, though very fearful. Within two minutes they were under threat, and going at top speed, and praying there were not more villains waiting up ahead.

The chase went on, on highway and down by-ways that Sam knew, for more than twenty minutes, although none of the shots that they heard fired came close. They had come from Emsworth at a slack pace, stopping to watch for followers and to shelter frequently, and Sir Arthur's horses were of the best. After an hour – miles past Langham Lodge – they drew in rein behind thick under-growth, and watched and waited for another hour. Then it was a case of finding the London road once more, and keeping out a constant weather eye. To east the sky was lightening, and market traffic from farm and dairy soon started to build up. By the time they reached the London Bridge, full dawn was wanting half an hour. Hungry and tired as they were, they did not use the Bear's Paw at Southwark. Whoever their attackers had been – just high-way rogues or part of some conspiracy – they knew where Sir Arthur Fisher lived, it seemed, and might know more. It was Will's idea to try the rendezvous, not take a boat so far downriver as the Biter, because it was unlikely Lieu-tenant Kaye would deign to share quarters with a dockyard crew. He'd be asleep and snoring at the Lamb; and there would be a better breakfast there.

27

The great surprise, when they faced Kaye across a table, was the change in his demeanour and his attitude towards them. They had slept a while, after some bread and bacon, but left instruction that they must be called when the lieutenant rose. They approached in trepidation as he sat with meat and coffee in the best parlour room, feeling and looking like two rather weary tramps. They had thought and talked themselves to stalemate before sleep had come to them, they had assessed their chances with increasing gloom. On appearances alone he could have turned them out, let alone when they broached their thorny subject. He could have turned them out, he could have shouted, he could have used them with his customary contempt. Instead a broad grin stretched his face, and he gestured them to sit.

'Lord, lord,' he said. 'So we've quit the service, have we? Two proper long-togs, who could use a wash and wigs. By the walks, you've got sore arses, too. Have you ridden far?'

As they sat he called a boy across, for coffee cups and plates and irons. He was beaming, in a fine good humour. They mumbled pleasantries, but he brushed off their apologetics.

'I did not thank you, friends, before you left the other night,' he said. 'Rude oversight but you will bear with me I hope. It is not every day one lands to be arrested! That gallows lawyer, and Oxforde who strikes as a cadaver! You stood up to the questions like a pair of Trojans, and you saw them off most capitally. My deep appreciation, sirs.'

That was not as they remembered it, but never mind.

For whatever reason – and there would be reason, surely – it appeared their task might not be so hard at all, least-ways not in the broaching and the explication. Their cups were filled, and the waiter brought an enormous plate of new hot rolls, with butter. Will took his cue from Sam, whose actions matched his landsman clothes – legs stretched, back arched outwards to ease the aches, and crunching like a lawyer's clerk. If Kaye intended to be pleasant for a change, then hallelujah, let's have some of that!

He told them, in the next few minutes, that he'd had more information about their 'strange activities' and knew, at least while Biter stayed in the dockyard, he was at liberty to let them have their heads. He did not wish to pry, but might he know if they had 'further jaunts' in view, and if he might be, somehow, of any small assistance?

Considering the trepidation they had lived with, they found this almost laughable in a heady sort of way – but not an opportunity that they should overlook. They did not know how much of the secret business of Yorke and Warren he'd been told, but could see no harm at all in outlining in general terms the problems and opportunities they must soon be facing on an East Sussex beach, with the implication that they must have help to be successful, and he was perhaps the man to give it them. Sam laid it on quite thick, with Will adding some telling points, but afterwards they both agreed that someone, most likely Bobby Beaumont through a messenger, had laid it thicker that Kaye could bear a hand in anything they could convince him on. Straight orders to this effect, they deemed, were rank impossible – backs must be covered, the niceties of rank and custom faithfully observed – but he had clearly been opened to persuasion that the game could be a worth-while one. Indeed, Sam's exposition of the kudos to be gained by breaking up not one but two notorious free trade bands – and underneath the noses of the Customs House – made the slightly bulging eyes go positively bright.

'Well,' he said, when they had finished. 'This is most fascinating, it makes me positively hungry! You say the Customs lords have given you their blessing? You may tread on corns with gay abandon and impunity? Well, capital indeed!'

'But not just us,' Bentley interjected. 'The agreement is between them and Lord Wodderley, the Customs and the Royal Navy. We may cross boundaries for the . . . ah, the common good. For you, sir, as the captain of the Biter, it could be a splendid opportunity. It is not just the common smuggler we could take and destroy, that's the gallantest! The men behind them, the men of capital, the most *un*-common rogues! We could strike a blow against the trade along the South Coast from which they might not recover; ever!'

Something moved behind Kaye's eyes at this point, but Sam's hearty laughter made the moment light.

'Don't tear the arse out, Will!' he said. 'We are not demi-gods, success we get is like to be more commonplace. But sir, Lieutenant Kaye, almost sure some good would come of it. Men taken – and some of them for pressing, surely – illicit trade disrupted, goods recovered, maybe some pay-off cash. To play the cynic, the part their lordships will thank us for the most they won't make public, but they won't forget it in the future, I'd make bold to hope: our friends the Customs shown up for fools, missing an opportunity. Which,' he added, chuckling, 'we shannot offer them to start with, poor unfortunates!'

'We'd need a damn good force, I reckon,' said Kaye, when the amusement had been let to fade. 'And arms in plenty. God, it would be more a landing party on a foreign fort. We could anchor off, and land in boats, and go in with cutlasses and muskets blazing. Perhaps a few rounds of grape before we hit the beach, to show them we meant business. Ach, we're running on too fast! We do not even know exactly where or when yet, do we? No, I thought not. And the ship is stuck in Deptford, one mast stripped.

We're running on like foolish boys. You know that yard, or Mr Holt does at any rate. A two-day job could take them months.'

He was blowing cool, before their eyes. Sam dropped forward in his chair, more businesslike, and raised a hand.

'Urgency would give you extra clout, sir, down at Deptford. Perhaps a mention of Lord Wodderley? If they knew he had an interest?'

'Aye, I know how to suck eggs, sir.' Kaye waved a hand. 'More importantly is times and places. I cannot say I will or nay until I know the business to the bottom, can I? How quickly can I have these things? How certain can I gauge the opposition? It is a story only at the minute; you must convince me, must you not? Great heavens, if it was true in black and white just as you tell it, you'd go to Wodderley out of hand and ask him for a line o' battleship. I need information; hard.'

'You shall have it, sir,' said Sam. 'My word on that. Mr Bentley rides this very morning to get exact locations and the day and hour. I go to the East Sussex coast to reconnoitre, if you'll excuse the French.' Significantly he added, 'We are well supplied with cash and helpers, sir. But we do, of course, need your permission.'

He granted it immediately – so much for the imagined difficulties – although in truth Will hardly heard the words. So, he went this very forenoon, did he? Thanks indeed, Sam Holt! Jesu, he was weary, but never mind. Slack Dickie, for once, was fired up, and such an opportunity must not be missed. He would set out for Hampshire as soon as he could get a proper shave and change his horse. The shore-base clothes, though draggled, would serve him for another trip if need be; in any way he could go and see Sir A, nay, absolutely must. He thought of the attackers of the night before and had a flutter in his guts, of apprehension. No reason, though, for them to lurk outside Langham Lodge for ever.

The words 'French woman' caught his ear, snapping him back to the parlour room. Sam was being questioned, but was being circumspect. On the smuggling of prisoners and its supposed importance they had had their differences, and they'd agreed to leave the matter out of conversation, at least until they'd done the job in hand. Kaye had neither the scruples nor, to be fair to him, the knowledge that it was a thorny point.

'Well then? D'st think the move is imminent? Have you heard aught of her again? Have you a name? Surely she is of the party you have known?'

Sam was fiddling with a butter knife.

'We've heard no more than I've told already, sir. Quite honestly, it does not seem of interest to the band. They see it as another branch of commerce, no better and no worse.'

'Pshaw!' went Kaye. 'That is the measure of them, truly! God, such filthy scum, to sell their nation like a poacher's coney! Look, I charge you: while on your travels on the Sussex coast, wherever. Find out about this ill venture, if you can. You also, Mr Bentley, can you do that for me? You'll be nearer to the "source", perhaps?'

Will nodded gravely.

'What Mr Holt has said is true, sir, they do not take it as serious as we. But if I hear I'll tell you, naturally.'

'You will ask, sir. That is the way to find out information, is it not? So you will ask.' He frowned, and touched his temple with his hand. 'And hereabouts,' he said, but almost to himself. 'There must be knowledge hereabouts. Old Coppiner should—'

They were watching; he was aware of it. He pushed his chair back, stood up with a laugh. He was dismissing them.

'It's better than trudging the streets and bawdy shops, eh friends?' he said. 'Heads to be broken on a beach no less, guts to be pricked! Come on, come on – there's information to be got, instanter!'

*   *   *

Before they left to go their separate ways, Sam and Bentley took time alone to plan their future moves and meetings. They marvelled for a while at the ease with which they'd turned the trick, and when Sam apologised for 'striking while the iron glowed' (in sending him off to Hampshire straight that morning, without a by-your-leave), Will agreed it was the only way to keep Slack Dickie bubbling. As they washed and tidied in the dressing room they'd hired, they computed on a three-day minimum for Will to gather vital information and return, by which time it was surely likely Biter would be free of Deptford's clutches. The ideal would be for both of them to meet in London and join the ship together with their final intelligences, to set up Kaye and go with no backsliding; although they knew it was the nature of such businesses that something would go wrong, or change in detail. Most like, said Sam, he'd find he could do best by staying put down near the Adur mouth, and *in extremis* could express a message to Dr Marigold's, where privacy could be guaranteed. Will, although he hoped such measures would not be necessary, suggested Mistress Margery to mind a letter, but Sam plumped for Annette, his favourite.

'She's like a whip,' he said, 'so I know she's safe with you. Your fancy was a rather padded thing, too much to squeeze for my taste!'

Will felt the stab of Sam's insensitivity, despite it was nothing new to him by now. He pushed them from his mind, that 'fancy' and that 'was', and pointed out he did not know the girl Annette. But other men knew Margery, said Sam, and she was there to earn, while Annette and he were friends, and very intimate. What's more – she could not read!

'I'd put a note to Margery upon the packet,' he added, 'to make her tell Annette to hide it within the bosom of her dress. There! You cannot say that I'm ungenerous, although it's you who'd have to pay her a gratuity! Just don't fall in love; I know your weaknesses.'

'If all goes well, in any way,' said Will, 'we'll join up at the receiving hulk, shall we? Biter might be moored near it by then, or it's not so far by boat to Deptford. I can't see how I could need to leave a message with Annette, but you'll check her if you have the time, you could not keep yourself away, I know!'

'Pah! If you think I'd manufacture troubles just to see Annette – you have my word on it! If worst comes worst, though, and messages cannot get through by any means, I'll meet you on the bloody beach as planned. Then when we've smashed the gangs we'll deserve some furlough, for Kaye will be the Navy's hero. I'll go to bed with her for days, and you can do the other thing!'

Their parting was quite sorrowful, although they laughed it off. Both faced dangers that would have eased with company, but both were buoyed with hope. The sight of Yorke and Hardman lived with them quite fresh enough to make them determined that some sort of justice should be done, and would most likely be through their actions, even if the hidden men, as was so normal, got away with it. Will felt much for Sir Arthur by this time, and longed to tell him of their prospects. He also longed for news of Deb, despite the fact it was unlikely to be ever good. Even passing some way close to her was a pain he would not care to miss.

The road, once clear of London, was quite easy and he made good time. It was light throughout his journey, he had a heavy pistol across his saddle, but saw nothing that gave him much alarm. Past Chester Wimbarton's, by act of will, he did not go, clattering into the yard at Langham Lodge where Tony greeted him. Master was in his parlour as per usual waiting for intelligence, he said – but where is Mister Holt? His anxiety touched William, so he set his mind at rest, and hurried himself to the house to reassure the baronet, who might have seen his lone arrival. Mistress Houghton, before he had sat down in front of the fire, had bustled in, her keen eyes full of fear.

'No terror, Mrs H!' said Sir Arthur, gaily. 'Young Will's come here alone and Sam's on other business! He tells me it is going swimmingly!'

Will, half down, stood up again to bow, and nodded all the while. In three minutes the housekeeper was satisfied and gone.

'Now,' said Sir A. 'The details, sir. Sit down and give the details. From the start.'

Will told it briefly, leaving little out except that they'd been chased not far from Langham Lodge, and the details of man-smuggling and Céline. They were certain now, he said, that the deaths of Yorke and Warren were part of an internecine war and – backed by himself and Lord Wodderley – were hopeful that great damage could be inflicted on all the smugglers, which would go some way to avenging them. Lieutenant Kaye, put in the picture, was prepared to play a part, providing the Biter and a naval force to disrupt a landing and – possibly – apprehend some of the leading men. Sir A, throughout, was thinking deeply.

'Hhm,' he said, at length. 'Words like "hope" and "possible". Is the business not clear cut? I suppose that's not in the nature of this game.'

He looked very old and tired sitting there. Since Will had first met him, he had aged quite visibly. But Will could not pretend.

'We can only go on trust,' he said. 'Unfortunately, sir. The names of the actual men who killed poor Yorke and Warren, aye, and John Hardman too, I fear we'll never know. But the Hampshire folk appear to hate the eastern men because of it, although behind the Hampshires there are some rich men they deplore. Best thing would be if the whole damn lot fell out, and shot and stabbed and clubbed themselves to death upon a Sussex beach. Helped by us and the Biter men, of course. It could occur, if luck went with us.'

Sir Arthur's smile was pale and ghostly.

'Please God for luck then. These . . . ah, richer men? Do

you have a clue who they might be? I'm not sure that I understand.'

Will laughed briefly.

'Nor us, sir, neither, that's the truth. No, it is all boxes within boxes, ad infinitum. Our people down in Langstone talk of "shadows", outwardly men of great respect, but hypocrites and villains.' He paused, momentarily. 'Sam and I suppose . . . well, men like Mr Wimbarton, for instance. That well-known justice of the peace. They seem to say we'd know them if we met them, or the type, that is to say. In the Adur secret house, for instance.'

'So. As you say it, all on trust. It is good that Mr Kaye is showing backbone at long last, it would be very hard to persuade authority to put up an official force. Worst possibly, I suppose, you could storm up to the beach and find nobody there. A dream, a tale. Chimera.'

'Yes,' said Will. 'But hopeful is the watchword, is it not? The people that we've spoken with seem truly on our side, they have put themselves in danger for it. I'm going down there now, with your permission, and I hope to get a place and time, exact. Samuel, as I said, is heading for his own old stamping grounds by the Adur mouth, to see what he can see. On the night in question, if all goes well, we might do shrewd damage, and apprehend some "shadows" into the bargain. One day, Sir Arthur, you might yet see men swing for those two gallant friends.'

The old man nodded, but seemed hardly reassured. He asked who was known down that way, and if Sam was likely to be safe. Will made light of the danger, claiming jocularly to be in tighter straits himself in Hampshire, viz. poor John Hardman at the oak-tree crossroads – but realised quickly that Sir A feared equally for both of them, so tried to bite it off. In the midst of the embarrassment, Sir A came to a decision – as if unconsciously to render it complete – and brought up Deborah.

'Sir,' he said. 'There is something I must tell you. It was in my mind when you and Samuel left, I hoped you would

. . . well, never mind for that. That maiden, sir. That Deborah. I have some news of her.'

His face was tortured, and Will had a reflection of it, in his guts. He caught his breath, waited, as if on tenterhooks. For a long while, Sir A did not go on.

'Yes?' said Will. 'Please, sir?'

'She is . . . she has left the magistrate's— No, all I can say for certain, is that she is well. She . . .'

'Left?' cried William, in a burst of hope. 'How mean you, sir? Run away? Blood, but she's— She is not *here*, Sir A!? No. But – where is she, sir?'

Sir Arthur's face was a picture of regret, so clearly did he wish he had not spoken. William, ashamed of his reaction, had stood, fists clenched at his sides, and now stood with his face towards the window. Across the park, the trees bowed to the wind.

'Will,' said Sir Arthur, quietly. 'I should not raise these hopes in you. I had forgot how much affection you had invested in this maid. In honesty I cannot tell you where she's gone, save that it is to a place of safety and she has protection. For the moment, do not ask me any more.'

'But Sir A!' Will fought to keep the anguish from his voice. Good God, if only *nothing* had been said! 'How safe? How did she get away? I need to— I feel I—' He ended in confusion. But I am helpless, he thought passionately, just like her. Men guide our actions, push us, never give an explanation. Where is she now? Where *is* she?

Sir Arthur, flustered, stood to ring a bell. He muttered, 'She is safe, I give my word on that,' but would not be further drawn. When Mrs Houghton entered Will pulled himself together to give a smile, and dragged his mind back to the task in hand. The woman, realising they were both upset, was motherly, and touched Will gently on the hand. However, from then until he left an hour later, the atmosphere was strained. Sir A sat with him at table, then came with him to his fresh horse, and watched while Tony adjusted straps and stirrups. When Will was set, he raised one hand in salutation.

'Farewell, my boy. God will be with you I am sure, for you deserve it more than my words can say. On that other matter ... well, try to return here on your way back to London, if you have time. I will try ... I will endeavour to have some proper news for you. Some explanation.'

By riding hard, despite soreness and exhaustion, William was on the top of Portsdown Hill two hours before midnight, on a clear full-moonlit night. He paused for a long two minutes at the vista, which still took his breath away however many times he saw it. The Solent was glowing like silver plate, the Wight behind it, brooding and crouched. High water springs, with Portsmouth harbour and its lakes joined in one expanse, with moored craft, royal and merchant, clustered down the Portsea side, at Portchester, and down the Forton and Gosport shores. From his vantage point, the hill dropped sharply to the heath and marshland, with villages and hamlets like small herds of waiting animals. Will breathed in deeply, through his open mouth, and loved it all. Then he peeled off left to trot through Stakes and down the hill to Bedhampton. In twenty minutes he could make Langstone.

At what o'clock? He was not certain. But as he walked up to Mary's door he knew that he could knock and not be unexpected, at whatever hour. He had dismounted at the hamlet's edge, tethered his horse, long rein, on a grassy patch quite hidden from the road, and walked the last two hundred yards extremely cautiously, shying at every noise and shadow. But all was still, the causeway being under many feet of sea. Few of the cottages had lights on, either. It was like the grave.

Within two knocks the door had opened and he was drawn inside. Mary, all alone save for sleeping Jem upstairs, embraced him as she had before, and bade him truly welcome. He looked so pale and drained, she laughed, that he could haunt churchyards for a living, but she was pleased to see him well, and pleased to see him come so very timely. If he would sit – if he *could* sit! – she would make him tea, or would he prefer a brandy? Duty free . . .

She was elated, it emerged, because had he not turned up this night, it is likely that the day would have been missed. Isa's confirmation, obtained not far after dark, was shocking close – not six days or more, but four. There had been a conference as to what to do, how to contact them, but finally, at Kate's insistence, two boats had gone to make a rendezvous of long standing way off St Catherine's with French 'colleagues'. Kate had had two reasons, she added, both good: had Isa tried to get to London to track them down his chance of failure would have been enormous; and had the crews not sailed to meet the Cherbourgers, spies might have noted it, and shadows wondered why.

But Will, still standing, could hardly take it in. In four days' time, four *days*? His back ached horribly, every bone and muscle could be counted, his head buzzed with fatigue. He could not remember when he'd last slept a proper night, or had his clothes off and scrubbed himself with soap and water, all the cracks and crevices. He was sore, and tired to his marrow. A plume of steam burst from the kettle spout, and he wanted hot sweet tea.

'But I must ride,' he said. 'Mary, four days? I must ride. Our ship is scarcely ready, and even if she were . . . Heavens, is this for definite?'

It was, and Mary did not try to stay him, or suggest his anxiousness was in any way misplaced. This was a one-chance thing, the only opportunity, and both had an equal longing it would be carried off. As she explained exact locations and a time, with tide details and a hand-drawn chart and map, Will drank tea and ate cold ham and cheese, and then – as he was forcing his mind to quit the house – he fell asleep beside the fireplace. Mary considered waking him, but then brought a blanket to drape him with. She sat for two hours opposite, and watched his grey, strained face but would not sleep herself. At some time after three o'clock she gently woke him, and he had more tea, a wash, and went out to the privy. She did not make him up a saddlebag of food, because at some stage he would have to stop for another horse most likely, and would eat there. The night was cold and clear the hour that he left; the moon had set.

'God speed you, Will,' said Mary. 'And . . . and let us meet again.'

Biter was still at Deptford, Will discovered at the receiving hulk, and when he got to her was positively aswarm with dockyard hands. Both masts, from a distance, were well set up, but as his watermen hauled nearer he could make out tasks still to do with fore topmast rigging and the bowsprit furniture. Alongside was a variety of yard tenders, but astern of them, rather to his surprise, was the captain's skiff. Anxious though he was to see him, Will had half expected him to be away in London's fleshpots. In half a day or less, as he computed, the vessel would be fit to sail. All she needed was a captain and a master.

Gunning was present, too. Will paid the wherrymen and scrambled overside to see the bulky form – quite clearly stone-cold sober – working at the binnacle with a Deptford man in overseer's beaver hat. Gunning gave a double look at the pale-faced landsman in the much-travelled clothes, but did not stoop to smiling when he recognised him. Some of the men did though, and let out jovial shouts, which Will ignored. He headed for the cabin. Despite the chill breeze down the river, its door was ajar. Will rapped, heard the command, went in.

For Kaye, it was a scene of rare activity. He was at a table spread with charts, with the stooping supernumerary, Kershaw, pointing with a bony finger. Even upside down Will recognised the outer estuary of the Thames, with the Kent shore up to the North Foreland. Oddly, he had a premonition. Why these charts, this area? Surely this was not a navigation lesson?

'Hah!' said Kaye. 'At long last, Mr Bentley. We are sailing in the morning, I had started to give up hope of you. Mr Kershaw, you had better go.'

Kershaw straightened, then bowed briefly. As he passed Will he nodded a small greeting but did not speak. Will's mind was in a turmoil.

'In the morning, sir? Well sir, that is excellent. I have the times, exact, I have a chart that shows the spot the landing's due at, and the meeting in the house. It is three days hence, but if the weather holds—'

Kaye interrupted him. He set his soft face into hardness, made the petulant soft mouth firm. His voice was touched with righteous anger.

'No sir!' he said. 'It is not three days hence, but the day beyond tomorrow. I have my own charts, here, and here. I have intelligence received – no thanks to you – and the plan is set for all contingencies. You talk of rich men and corruption but you have no detail. You talk of common smugglers as if they were a worthy prize. I talk of black-hearted traitors who give succour to our enemy. We will take a hundred of them, sir, and slam them back in jail where they belong. No thanks to you.'

It fell in to Will that Sam must have betrayed him, though inadvertently for sure. The target was to be Céline's Frenchmen, there could be no doubt of it. Kaye had got intelligence somehow, and had reneged on the East Sussex operation. In his exhaustion, Will found it all quite dizzying.

'But sir! Our friends are— There will be important—' His head was buzzing. There was a look like triumph in Kaye's eyes. 'It is a golden chance,' he ended, lamely. 'An opportunity. I understood that you—'

Kaye spoke incisively.

'I weighed it up and found it wanting, that is the fact of

it,' he said. 'I found it very interesting, and most unlikely to be true. Your friend has more intelligence than you and – forgive me, but I feel this undeniable – is more the patriot. What we will attack is not just a case of vulgar profit, so common as to be of no account, but a form of villainy of great, of *prime* significance.'

Will should have blazed with fury at the calculated barbs, but his senses were all blunted.

'You offend me, sir,' he said, and Kaye almost laughed. 'But where is Sam?' he added. 'Where is Mr Holt? If he is still in Sussex, then —'

Kaye's colour heightened instantly, he was taken with real rage, not a simulation. He slammed his hand down on the chart-strewn table.

'Downriver, sir, to join us later, and damn your damned impertinence,' he snapped. 'He said you would not want this, he made that very clear. Mr Holt will do his duty, you will see.'

'But sir! You will not leave him on the beach alone! Those men are ruthless, violent, he expects a force!'

'He is downriver! I confide that he will join us, he might even come this night! There is no doubt about *his* patriotic feeling, no doubt at all!'

'' 'Fore God, sir!' shouted Will. 'I —'

'Silence, sir! Silence! I will hear no more! Have you no proper clothes on board here in your berth? Then dress yourself immediately, dispose yourself for duty, wash and shave! We sail on the ebb tomorrow morning and you will bear yourself with rectitude! Now sir – quit my sight!'

Outside, although the light was fading, the dockyard men and sailors were all active still. Will breathed deeply of the river air, his limbs beneath his clothes trembling so hard he thought they would be seen. The Biter was alongside the rigging wharf, starboard side to, and almost without a conscious intention he crossed the deck, swung legs across the bulwarks, and clambered down on to the dockside

That Sam Holt had betrayed him he would not believe. That he was waiting further down just made no sense. That there might be a message was possible, that he must leave one if there was not, his plainest bounden duty. Will strode through the yard along the riverfront until he reached the steps. He selected the two strongest-looking watermen, and offered them a half a guinea extra if they could make their wherry fly.

28

It was a hanging matter, what he'd done, but Will did not expect to hang for it. Unless he found some dire communication at Dr Marigold's that should delay him, he hoped he would be back betimes at Deptford, where he had no fear of anything save bluster from his commanding officer. Despite his clothes and travel-stained appearance he was recognised at the outer door and treated civilly within. Starving by now, he ate hot meat and oysters from a passing wench, and washed it down with ale. The heat was prodigious, the noise and music like a drug, but he crossed the court before the comfort overwhelmed him. Sam's description of Annette amused him as he waited at the doorway to the inner house: like a whip. Then her bed, mercifully, would not be a place for sleep, and sleep, oh sleep, was the only thing in the whole wide world to tempt him between the covers. Quick message, given or received, and he would be away.

Mrs Putnam, when she saw him, gave a squeak much younger than her years. She half rose from her table, and put her arms out as if she would embrace him, except there were three feet of deal between them. Her expression was between amazement and alarm.

'Mister Bentley! But so soon, how did you know? And those togs! Have you then left the Navy?'

'Margery, well met. Forgive me for the clothes, I am in haste.'

'I wager that you are! Indeed you are!' She bustled backwards from her seat, and did come round the table. Her face was positively roguish as she took his arm. 'Well, I declare! She said that you would find her out, but so quick, so very quickly!'

'Annette?' said Will. 'Has he sent a message then, already? Where is she?'

'No, not Annette, you gooseturd!' snapped Margery. 'Christ, do not tell me you've forgot!' This gave her sudden pause; she jerked his arm distractedly, then released it. 'But she's protected now,' she muttered. She raised her eyes to his. 'I'm talking of your Deb,' she said. 'But what mean you? Have you not come to search her out, to see her?'

There was a horrible excitement rising in his guts and nearly drowning him. It was so clear, that Mistress Putnam sighed with glad relief. Unceremoniously she dragged him down the passageway, past all the doors he knew that led to tiny rooms that whores lived in, into a quarter that he did not know. It was more opulent than the outer reaches, with fewer doors. Before one of these she stopped, put her finger on her lips, and listened.

'Lor'!' she whispered. 'How I wish that I could stay and watch. But as I'm paid to stop it happening, I'd best just fade away! Don't knock; go in and fear her senseless!'

She pushed him at the door and slipped off down the passage without looking back, but Will had to fight himself for some time before he could even touch the latch. When he did so, and it made a small noise, he removed his hand as if it had burnt him and, unthinking, gave a rap. For a moment there was silence, save for his panting. Oh hell, he thought, oh hell, it is Deborah within.

She was dressed as if for evening in a long pale gown, although it was too early in the normal way, and the chamber was bedazzled with the light from many candles. Her hair was dressed up on her head and William noted that her face, though touched with powder, was underneath it almost free from bruises – the first time, in fact, that he had ever seen it thus. Before her expression burst into wild delight he took in her beauty with a swoop of recognition, the full red mouth, soft curve of cheek and neck, luxuriance of hair, and eyebrows thick and serious. Then she sprang at him, damn nearly knocked him down into the passageway, and they tangled in each other's arms.

'Oh sir, oh Will!' she gasped, as they drew apart. 'Oh Will, you're here! Oh sir.'

The passage was still empty, but they got into the room. It was largish and full of light, and by whorehouse standards the top of luxury. For a moment it arrested him, he was taken by the drapes and mirrors, by the expensive smell of burning beeswax. The bed was huge, with posts and canopy, and there were two doors leading off, it was a suite. Then she moved in again, and face to face they held each other, each swamped and flooded with a similar relief.

'I'm here,' he said, 'but so are you, Deb. How? Why? How has it come about? I saw Sir Arthur, and he said— He said . . . that you were safe.'

He drew back, to hold her at arm's length and look at her. The colour in her pale brown skin began to rise.

'I am safe, Will,' she said. She moved her head, as if to show the room. 'As you can see. This is mine, I am the mistress here.'

There was an expression in his eyes that made her stop. Oh God, thought Will, she is protected. Margery said it, and this apartment is all hers. This bed is hers for lying with her benefactor on. The man who pays, and comes to sleep with her. Despite what Sir A had said – and he had said protection, too – despite it all, it could only be the magistrate.

'Will,' said Deb. Her voice was almost piteous. 'Please, Mr Bentley, do not take it hard. We can do it, sir! I will lock the door! Please do it with me, Will! I want to; please, I want to.'

The blush had spread right down her neck to the soft across her bosom. Her fright, or anguish, shamed him, for he knew he had no right. She was off from Wimbarton's house and all his evil men, but only to be made his city whore, for visiting. And Jesu, he thought, if it came to *him* to be her saviour then surely she would starve or end up in the gutter. Then, enveloped in her scent, the smell of her skin that he'd retained intact within his memory through all the days and rides, he had a rising urge to lie with her again, on this protector's bed, and damn his very soul!

'In any way,' he said, thickly. He gripped her by the shoulders, pulled her in to him. 'In any way, why should you be faithful to that rogue, that villain? What right has he to keep you to himself!'

His desire had become violent in a second, his need was powerful, and he bore her back towards the bed without thought for the door, or undressing her or him, or anything. But Deb resisted. Her face was shocked, she pushed back at him with both hands.

'A rogue? Why do you say that, sir? He saved me, he is a friend.' Suddenly, she understood. The blush increased and darkened, spread like a crimson burn across her face. 'Oh Will, not Wimbarton, it's Sir Arthur. Not him; your friend and benefactor.'

The shock was like a blow. He let go his grip on her and Deborah, unbalanced, sat on the bed abruptly. Will, too close, stood back. He stared at her, and she had to turn her face away.

'He rescued me,' she said, voice faint. 'He bought me from the magistrate, I think. He—'

'*Bought* you! How bought you? Before God, Deb, do you mean Sir A, Sir Arthur Fisher?'

'But not for that, though! Not as a whore, Will, he is too old. Oh listen, listen to me!'

She covered up her face as if in tears, and Will drew further back. He saw she was in tears, they were wetting through her fingers, dripping on her cheeks. Strangely, he still felt desire, his stomach was hollowed out with urgency, but he also was ashamed by it. In a movement he spun to sit beside her on the bed, and put his arm around her shoulder. Deb put her hair into his face and neck. For some moments neither spoke. He listened to her breath shuddering, held her, squeezed her with one arm. Slowly his lust subsided, and her tears.

'It was what you told him,' she said, at last. 'After Wimbarton came to steal me and Sir Arthur made me go. I told him they were lying and Dennett was dead and buried but he thought I was a lying sluttish whore, in league. Then you came back to his house and told them too, you said I'd said that I'd seen Dennett shot and it was true and afterwards the master *did* believe it, Mrs Houghton said, he was ashamed at what he'd done to me. Oh Will, oh Will, I cannot do the words together, can you follow what I want to tell? It was you, it was your words saved me from that Wimbarton, that *pig*.'

She cried again, more copiously but less racked with pain, and William held her, and stroked her hair and face. As far as she knew the story, it emerged, Sir A had listened to what Will had reported, and possibly had been struck by fear and guilt. When the storm of grief about his nephew had begun subsiding, he had contacted the magistrate and tried persuasion, a hint of investigation by the law, and finally good simple cash. He had bought her back, although not to live with him as Wimbarton had assumed, but because – according to the household women – of his great Christian conscience. But still, Deb said sadly, he truly thought that she was fallen, worthless, bad. He saw her once, for a matter of five minutes, and asked her where she would like to go.

'I could not stay in his house,' said Deborah. 'He did insist on that, he said it would not be seemly and in any case he trusted neither Wimbarton nor his violent men. He said that if I stayed they'd kidnap me one day, if I even so much as walked out of the purlieus, but I think in truth his reasons were for shame, people would get to hear and think he'd bought me for his harlot. Then he said there was a friend in Hertfordshire, an old man, an even older man than he! I was to sit, and do some tatting, go to church on Sundays and grow old, I guess. And still he'd pay me,

I was not to fear for starving or the streets.' She smiled at William, she was composed once more. 'Had I dared to, I would have asked to wait for you, then gone and been your friend, wherever. But I think he feared that, too, for your sake. I think he feared I'd be a clog on you.'

She needed it, so William took her hand and squeezed. Some of her candles were guttering, giving aromatic smoke. She glanced at them proprietorially, they pleased her, he could tell. Sir A was paying well for her, however little she gave him in return. He was a strange philanthropist.

'How came you here, then? Surely he does not know the house, or what sort of place it is? Sam and I took care to keep it privy when we used it; it's not much like his holy man's in Hertfordshire!'

Deb bounced up off the bed and nipped some of the candles out between her thumb and fingers.

'I said 'twas safer here. No, don't make that face, 'tis true in some ways, the old Herts party I'd have murdered out of boredom or just run mad and jumped into a river, would I not? I said I knew a house in London, quite respectable, where I could lodge with women to look after me. That's true as well – there's Mistress Putnam, Margery, there's even Mrs Pam to kick my arse if I get saucy. And Dr Marigold, I could tell him with great truth, had plans to bring me on, give me an education, which is also so, and all the time he got the cash none could molest me. The clincher was, no one would ever find me in this teeming rabbit hole of London, no Wimbarton or his yokel ruffians, and the mountebank, sweet providence, is dead. That left only one I knew would come here, although the dear old man, of course, did not. I say I knew, but in truth I only hoped. 'Twas you.'

She was standing facing him, toying with the ribbons at her breast that laced her gown across. She did not seem lascivious, but his mouth went dry, the way she smiled at him so very sad, and sweet.

'But,' he said. 'But maid, how got you here, who brought you? You did not make Sir A?'

'Hah! No, Tony brought me, whoever else? He brought me with a sack of sovereigns, and dealt with Dr Marigold himself, I guess. Sir Arthur made him swear he would be secret with my whereabouts, and Tony is a man I'd gladly trust, would you? What other steward, I wonder, would have found it such a place and not insisted that he test the bed with me? Or not gone back to his master and said I was a whore again?' She caught the look that slipped across his face. 'Will.' She said it earnestly, like a solemn child. 'Will, since I've come here, I . . .'

She stopped, thinking of Wimbarton and all the things she'd had to do with him. She wondered if Will knew, or guessed, and if he'd think it shameful in her, or just a shame. She dropped on to her knees in front of him, and put her arms around his legs, then laid her head upon his thighs. Ten minutes later they were almost naked, Deb in a fine lawn shift, Will in his shirt, when a man opened the door they had not bolted, and entered with a long-nosed pistol. Deb, who knew she'd seen an apparition, locked in fright and could not scream, but croaked. When Will turned, he was looking down the barrel of the gun. It was held by Marcus Dennett.

There were men abroad for William in the London streets this night, but the mountebank had not been one of them. His target was Deborah, as it had been for a long and weary time, since indeed, he had struck Milady with a cudgel in the face and been shot for it. The ball had caught him at the join of neck and shoulder, and was still inside him somewhere, for it certainly had not come out that he knew of. It must have glanced a bone on going in, considering the pain was so severe and he had bled a deal, but since recovering he'd had no pain. Sometimes, absent-mindedly, he checked his stools, but so far had found no lead.

In the chaos and confusion after the firing he could have

got away with Deborah, a matter that he cursed himself for rather often. But truth to tell he had been badly hurt, and for near an hour afterwards could hardly stand, or talk. Wimbarton had proved himself a man of steel exceeding quickly, and his men had cleared the women out, beating a few to make them hold their tongues about the episode. Milady, when the smoke had cleared, was gone, and Marcus Dennett never saw her on earth again. In later days he feared to go near the Wimbarton estate or household, but he heard that she'd been buried and he wondered how she'd died. The steward Jeremiah, who had conveyed him twenty miles away hand-tied to a horse when he was fit enough to jog, had told him very plainly that he would hang if he was found in the vicinity again, there was a murder warrant out. He should count himself lucky, the ex-soldier added, that Mr Wimbarton had not ordered him to kill him on the spot, which he would have much preferred to do. Then Dennett, penniless despite all he had done for the good magistrate, was cut from off the horse, kicked in the injured shoulder for good measure, and told that he was free to go and starve.

Without a pretty maid to earn his bread for him, without his wagon home for sleep and shelter, without even a pack of cards to gull the stupid, Dennett fell to brooding and self-pity. He quickly decided that Deborah was to blame for all misfortunes, and further, that she had plotted it beforehand, she had had a scheme. The first long night, freezing in a shallow cave scraped in a rain-soaked banking, furious with hunger, he convinced himself that she would soon become a courtesan to some very wealthy man, she would soon have money of her own, in cartloads. So that was two people had cheated him out of what was rightly his. The difference was that Wimbarton was powerful and dangerous, and Deb a silly little whore. The thoughts of what he'd do to her gave him a meaning and a purpose back again.

It had been a hard time though, even for a man as strong

and single-minded as the mountebank. When he'd risen in the morning to steal his breakfast he had been almost savaged by a farmer's dogs, in the middle of that day he'd dined on hard bread thrown out by an innkeeper's wife for her pig, and he'd laid his head at nightfall in a draughty barn with only rats for company. As things got worse his determination that Deb should pay grew stronger. On the third day he was back in Wimbarton's area, building a shelter in the woods where Sam and Will had come across him first, and at nights began to rob food from lonely cottages that he'd noted long before as dog-free and owned by the old and vulnerable. He frequented roadside ale-houses much like a wraith, and heard quite soon that Deb somehow had ended at the local baronet's, but then back with the justice of the peace. The rumour mill came up with several reasons, which rendered down in Dennett's mind to this: she was a concubine, possibly a shared one, and the men who used her were both exceeding rich. *His* maid, *his* money, *his* chance to lead a full and happy life. And then he learned she'd disappeared one day, gone northwards, and the steward who had took her had returned alone. To the north was London, there was no other place, it was obvious. Deb was a whore and whores would gravitate, that was their nature, it could not be changed. Whatever else men knew London for, they knew it for its whores.

He did not relish London, Marcus Dennett, because in parts of it he was known for things he'd done before, well known but not well looked on. Inevitably, these were the parts where Deb would be – indeed he guessed that Dr Marigold's, from whence he'd torn her off the night poor Cec had died, might be the very place he'd find her – and the chance was high he could be taken by the law, or shot like a dog. He had no doubts, though, that he would hunt her down and claim her, and little fear. He was secret, good, and fast, and if she were to be at Marigold's, he already knew the ground. He heard the news she'd gone at a public house one night, and by two days later he had burgled his way into a store of cash – not big, but adequate – and tried to steal a horse from the stable of a coaching inn six miles up the high road. He'd failed in that, but got a pistol from a drunken groom, and a good thick coat, for winter was starting to chase off the autumn with a vengeance. For the rest of it he'd walked, and hidden in the daytimes, and asked questions clandestinely when he'd got to town. It had cost him dearly to get into Marigold's this time, but he'd opened up Deb's door with utter confidence. Until he'd seen her face above a shoulder, and a naked bum.

For a long and aching moment, Will Bentley looked at the gaping barrel, bereft of speech. His head was cocked round across his shoulder, and underneath him Deb was rigid as a plank. She was making a noise, a sort of mewing, which he realised was the sound of shock. He could not believe it, either, because the man there was the mountebank, and the mountebank was dead.

'Then Christ,' said Dennett, voice firm and confident, and not without amusement. 'Young Deborah is the queen of harlots, and she's got a paying guest! Continue, sir, continue. You can give the fee to me!'

Beneath Will, Deb began to squirm, and he heard a roar of anger rising in her chest. He moved his hand to stop it at her mouth and dropped his head to mutter urgently into her ear. 'He does not remember me. Be silent and he may not shoot.' It occurred to him that Dennett could only really see his arse, but he made no move to cover it.

'This is mortal rude in you,' he said. 'Sir, this is not a harlot's bedroom, but is fairly rented. Dr Marigold will hold you guilty for this work. His men go armed, you know.'

Dennett had closed the door when he'd come in, but deftly leaned back and slid the bolt across.

'She is a harlot and she's mine,' he said. 'You may finish

what you came for, sir, then instead of payment you may walk outdoors with us and I will take your horse. Am I not generous? She is a runaway and will be soundly beaten, but in the meantime — Ah, that is the way, Deb, wriggle about a bit, it's what these gentles like!'

Deb's fear had turned to fury, mixed with shame. Underneath Will she writhed and arched, however hard he tried to keep her down in safety. One leg got free and lashed across the bedside, missing Dennett's pistol by a hair's-breadth. This enraged him, and from treating it as some sort of bedlam lark, he let out a savage snarl. He lunged towards the bed, grabbing for Deb's ankle, the pistol in his right hand held above his head. Deb, touched but not caught, rolled herself convulsively away from him, displacing Will from off her, exposing herself quite naked from where her shift was pulled up to the waist. The mountebank, ignoring Will entirely, then leapt for her throat, bringing his gun hand down to clout her across the cheek and temple. As his hand came back for another blow, Will seized his wrist from behind, to be dragged across both Deborah and the mountebank by the unexpected strength with which he twisted his whole body round to face the new attack. Milady's wound almost unmanned him then, for as he jerked his arm to bring the gun to bear on William, he let out a sharp cry of agony, and his face drained white.

The barrel was in Will's eyes once more, at a distance of a span or less, and the mountebank, composed of teak and wire, had broken the grip upon his wrist. Will, having no other course, went for the pistol with both hands to push it clear or wrench it free, while Deborah, on her feet now, launched herself across the bed with both fists clenched and struck Dennett on the right side of his head. All three of them, from the momentum, crashed on to the floor, Deb roaring, and William found he had the pistol to himself, held crosswise like an oar-loom, while Deborah clawed at Dennett's hair and neck. In a second the mountebank was upright, had kicked her in the face with booted foot, and produced a six-inch knife from inside his riding coat. He did not come forward though, but stood and panted as if to get his strength. The gun, now pointing properly, exploded in Will's hand, and jumped, and jetted smoke and flame and lead at point-blank range, into Dennett's throat. Will looked at it, ears ringing, finger on the trigger still, for what felt like several seconds, and could not believe. Surely, he had not intended that?

'He's dead,' said Deborah. This time there was no doubt of it, his neck and chin were smashed. 'Will, you've murdered him. Jesus, he would have killed us both.'

Outside the room, already, there was screaming. Amid the wails the word 'murder' recurred, clear and regular. Momentarily, they were both transfixed, Deb's shift torn, and blood-stained from her mouth, Will panting and struck with horror, in his shirt. Murder. He had shot a man down, almost in cold blood. He had had the gun, the fight was over, he had shot and killed. He heard the feet along the passage, he heard screams.

'This was not your fault,' Deb shouted at him. 'Will! It is not your fault, he had a knife, he would have killed you with the gun! Will! Mr Bentley! Sir!'

Will shot the bolt back and opened the door before Marigold's bully-boys had cleared a way along the passage, and he pulled his breeches on, and got his coat in hand. Deb had seized a robe to augment her nakedness, but in the first rush of people, some to gain the room, some to pull them out, the robe was torn away. Will, to his shame, resorted to waving the gun in an aggressive fashion, and it did enable them to force their way along. But down below them in the inner court there was a separate commotion which would prove fatal to their chances of escape. The men abroad in search of William were from the Biter, a minor Press gang all his own, led by men who knew his haunts and predilections. As he and Deb ran out into the night, he came face to face with Jem Taylor, Tom Tilley, and Behar, with about three others moving in the shadows.

His gun was empty, theirs were not. But in any case, he could not have used it, under almost any circumstance.

They saved him from attention of the law, but he had no arguments they'd listen to to let him find his own way back, or deal with Deborah. Some of them were drunk and all of them were wild with joy at his predicament, which in their eyes – not knowing that a man was killed – was merely marvellous. They pushed the whore off, and grabbed and squeezed at her the while, and the more he bellowed at them the more they laughed. Taylor disarmed him casually, Behar tripped him when he tried to run to Deb and help her fight some others off, then, brutally because he was resisting them so fierce, they dragged him through the arch and out into the narrow road that would take them past the Fleet down to the waterfront.

'Oh sir!' screamed Deb. 'Oh sir, oh sir, oh help me!'

'I will be back, Deb! I will be back! If Sam comes, tell him not to go back down the Adur way, there's deadly danger!'

'Now come on, Willie,' boomed John Behar in his ear. 'Enough of whoring for a while! Slack Dickie has a crying need of you!'

'Please God,' yelled Deb, then went into a wilder scream. Will, twisting in his comrades' grasp, saw the denizens of the gay house flooding round her. One had a cudgel and he took a strike, another went in with his fist raised like a hammer. A murderess, a murderess! He heard the cry.

His last sight of her was of the maid at bay, head lifted back, hands held out towards the mob like talons, mouth open in a hopeless shout. One breast was visible, the shift was rent, her tormentors saw her as a luscious target. As his own men pushed and dragged him round the corner out of her sight, Will thought his heart and brain would burst. And still they whooped and roared with joy.

On the row to Deptford, they lashed him to a thwart. Before they'd fully left the staging, he'd tried to jump and swim, to Deborah.

29

The Biter slipped downriver in the early morning mist on a good breeze, light and cold, from the north west. William was up on watch in proper naval clothes at last, shaved and washed, but hollow-cheeked from lack of sleep, and anguish. Holt was not on board of course, and he had no belief at all in Kaye's continuing insistence that he was to meet them in the estuary. How, Will had protested; and Kaye had offered him a flogging for his impertinence. Bentley had come back in ropes, he'd said, and would finish up in shackles in the hold unless he held his tongue. He had deserted, and should thank his lucky stars for tolerance.

Will had been thrown up on to the deck still lashed, but the idea he'd run had never held much water, try as Kaye might with it. Strangely, the men who'd captured and tormented him changed sides on this, and reported that they'd released him from the clutches of a 'tasty, tasty tart', and that he'd been already dressed – albeit in long-toggy clothes – and ready for the off. There had been some type of rioting apparently, said Taylor, which had made the case exceptionally confused, but Mr Bentley had shown no signs of wanting to desert. The boatswain's *sangfroid* and disingenuity were marvellous to behold, but tore Will's heart. Not only was Deb abandoned, but he'd killed a man like Kaye had done, and would pay as little price. In some ways, to be manacled in the darkness of the hold would have been a kind of blessing.

Kaye needed him, however, for the coming fight. Will's dressing down had been in public on the quarterdeck, with the Navy men and Gunning's preparing Biter for the sea. Savaged, he was sent below to prepare to do his duty, which to begin with was the arming of the company and the readying of the carriage guns. When he emerged to start, Biter was swinging off the wall by action of the wind and tide, aided by dockyarders in two pulling boats and a set of warps at stern. Gunning was sober and superbly competent at con, headsails and fore were backed, then smartly filled, and in five minutes they were into the centre of the running ebb, clearing down the cordage and preparing to set more sail.

Two hours later, with Lieutenant Kaye below to 'rest or sleep' – or 'podge it up the neger boy' as Will heard Gunning mutter coarsely to his helmsman – he was standing at the weather rail watching the Essex shore slip by when Kershaw moved to join him from the lee. William, whose torment had been eased by working with the gunner, had fallen back towards despair, so welcomed the distraction. Duty was the whip, the spur, the chain he had been contemplating, and he wondered how one would ever come to terms with it.

'Mr Kershaw,' he said. 'Good morning, sir. Now tell me who you spy for on this day.'

His bitterness surprised him, as did the question that had slipped out. He had not intended rudeness. But the necessary apology was stillborn on his lips. Kershaw was not insulted, it appeared. The ghost of amusement curved his lips, but overall his face was calm and sombre.

'Your friend will not be joining us,' he said. 'He is not downriver waiting, that is a lie. We are going to approach a Frenchman that Lieutenant Kaye has intelligence about, off the North Foreland. Sam Holt has been abandoned to his fate.'

The wind was blowing chill, but still quite light. Will stared across the rain-washed marsh and woods, a featureless and unhuman landscape. Inside him was an awful loneliness.

'Go on,' he said.

The thin, stooped man was not shy or crushed today.

His swinging moods, the fear and gloom that sometimes overwhelmed him, could hardly have been guessed at.

'He got a message through,' he said. 'Two messages – one for Kaye and a word-of-mouth to me. He gave the time and place the gangs were going to meet and do their Adur run, and said that he would stay there, not return. He gave some indication of the numbers under arms, and warned it would be very stiff and bloody. He said that Kaye should tell you.'

'How know you this?' A pause. 'Are you Kaye's confidant?'

'I spy,' said Kershaw, blankly. 'That is what you think, so I'll confirm it. Sometimes I do not know whose side I'm on, is all. Black Bob gave me the writing to his master. He gives me everything of Kaye's. He hates him.'

The Biter lurched, as the helmsman pulled her round a point or so nearer the wind to keep the channel. Kershaw's thin, bony hand touched the rail for balance. The marks of torture were horrible upon it.

'I was not told,' said Will.

'Indeed. Holt's word-of-mouth was that I should, if possible, get the message out that he was safe to Dr Marigold's establishment for you. One Annette, who could be trusted. I could not make shift. Or, let's say, shall we, I did not. In excuse, I was told it was not essential, at a pinch you would know, or guess. In truth, I had become afraid of Kaye, for which I stand ashamed. I could say I did not know by then that he'd decided to avoid the Sussex venture, but that would be another lie. My message *should* have been, for you to run to Sussex on the instant and save Holt's life, get him away. However stiff and bloody it will be down there, he is now abandoned. He has been left to face it quite alone.'

'They have to know he's there first,' said Will, robustly. 'We planned to spy the leaders out if we could not get up a force to take them. He's pretty good at secrecy, he knows the area like his hand. When we do not turn up in Biter—'

Some look in Kershaw's face caused him to stop.

'What?' he asked. 'Surely they could not guess him out? The only way they'd know is if— What, Slack Dickie would betray him? But how? But why?'

'I do not know,' Kershaw replied. 'Leastways, I don't know if he'd sink that low, or if he thinks it that important. The how would not be that difficult, would it? If you know certain people.'

'What, the smugglers? Mr Kershaw, what is it you mean? Are you suggesting Kaye is linked up with them somehow? He is a Navy officer! And he agreed! He would have . . . he was taking the Biter round to apprehend them, save that this Frenchman thing came up. I do believe he thinks that is a more important venture, to move against the enemies of the Crown.'

Indeed, he thought, he has told me to my face. He has called me unpatriotic over this very thing. Kershaw, three feet from him, remained unmoving, face unreadable. If Kaye is tied to them, Will thought, and my uncle is tied to Kaye, then what means that? Impossible! Whatever else Swift is, he's honest. And *he'd* ignore a hundred smugglers, if he could kill one Frenchman. They are the enemy.

Kershaw watched his face as if he read it. He said quietly: 'The French ship we're seeking is very fast, I've heard of her. Two dipping lugs, damn near as long as we are, she moves like shit from out a goose and goes to windward like a knife. Kaye gathered information from the time you saw him at the Lamb. I heard him speaking with one man that I knew of old. The Biter may come up with her somehow, if she be taken by surprise, but if she runs . . . She was built of fir, in Kent, by Englishmen. She was built for speed, you know, not honesty. The man who skippers her knows these coastal waters as well as I do; better. Mr Bentley, I make one prediction only, for I cannot answer any more. Whatever reason Kaye has given you for attempting it, we will not get near to her, or catch her under sail, we cannot. And Mr Holt is on a Sussex beach alone. I have said too much.'

He walked away towards Mr Gunning at the con, who was conversing quietly with the helmsman. Will ached with tiredness, soon to go off watch, but he tried to struggle with what Kershaw had implied but would not say. Kaye's move against the French lugger was a blind, a cover, because he did not want to land at the Adur, and he had made it impossible for Will or Sam to seek out any other aid in time. The move against the French would do no harm in any case; the lugger was a match for them, would show them heels. But even less than half successful as a venture, it occurred to Will, it would do Slack Dickie good in their lordships' eyes: to spy out, find, attack a vessel full of men who should be chained in jails and prison hulks. The irony, that Sam should have put him up to it, by telling of Céline. And now might be a sacrifice.

The last part, in his cot a half an hour later, kept Will awake, but not for very long, because he felt he could have died for lack of sleep. The part about why Kaye should want to protect the villains on the beach – if he did – why he might let Sam be killed – if true – he could not hold to with his mind at all. He saw Deborah in her torn shift, face racked with fear, surrounded by a baying horde. Deb could be dead already, dead many hours, dead to him for ever.

Like all the other things he faced, there was nothing he could do, at all, about it.

From the very first part of the action against the Frenchman, it looked to Will as if Kershaw had got it wrong. The engagement was undertaken fast and brilliantly, a combination of fine seamanship, and bravery, and luck, with Kaye elated to the point of bloodlust. His tactics were excellent, although they did cost several men. The French lost more, however, including their pilot-captain. It would be an extremely close run thing.

They'd gone right round the foreland before they picked

up signs of their quarry, and Kaye himself, after poring over Gunning's chart, had climbed up to the maintop to look forward through a glass. This had caused some cynical amusement in Will's breast, for he had decided Kershaw's version would be right in outline, if not in detail. Slack Dickie with a spyglass, keen, did not ring true. Indeed, he'd climbed down again disconsolate, with nothing seen. It was a half an hour later, with the daylight almost gone, before a cry went up.

It was the absence of good light that let them bring it off. Lieutenant Kaye, instead of piling on, ordered Gunning quietly to shorten sail, and made as if to bring Biter to and snug her for the night. From a distance she looked like a merchantman, a tubby, snubby collier from the north. The lugger, lying offshore a half a mile, must have studied them, but decided there was no danger there. She had two boats alongside, disgorging men it seemed, and an empty one, a yawl, was heading for the shore. Impossible to tell if they were starting the loading job or finishing, but Kaye was in the mood to wait and see. Within five minutes, his brig was almost drifting, under rags. The wind was freshening with the dark, and to the north west black, rolling clouds were piled. It might be a very dirty night.

Astern of the Biter, as was her way, she towed the cutter and two yawls, along with the captain's skiff, and he told Will off to see two of them hauled up close for manning. Will, with a strange sensation, ordered both John Behar and Tilley to head his crew, while Silas Ayling, who had been made up to boatswain's mate after Shockhead Eaton's death, took Jem Taylor's as his own. Naturally, with an action close to hand, Lieutenant Kaye stayed in command of Biter, with hands enough to man the guns and the boatswain to control them. Then Kershaw, who was standing awkwardly near Gunning at the binnacle, asked Bentley if he would take him with him, in his boat.

This struck Will odd, but Kaye, who'd heard it, waved an airy hand.

'No use to me, sir!' he told the midshipman. 'Take him and welcome! Drop him overboard!'

'Thank you, sir,' said Kershaw formally. Jesu, thought Will, Mr Kershaw, you were wrong. Kaye relishes this action, he is positively transformed.

'Mr Bentley,' said Kaye, 'the plan is this. When I send you and, Whatsisname, the boatswain's mate, you are not to board, d'you hear? You're to cut the chickens from off the mother hen, which, by loss of paying customers, will give them pause for thought. They'll have small arms, no doubt, but their boats will be jam-packed and yours will not. Run rings round them, pick them off like birds I do not care, they're only bloody Frogs. Meantime, I'll put some shots in the mother and try to slam her down. Then, if I lay alongside of her, you board too. Do you understand that?'

Slack Dickie insults a man without awareness that he's doing it, thought Will. God save me from the very rich and stupid. He nodded rather curtly, and acknowledged with a crisp 'Aye aye, sir!' It was by no means a bad plan, when all was said and done.

By the time they'd drifted close enough, they could see their timing was exactly right. Two boats were pulling from the shore into the wind which, fluking near the foreland, was dead ahead and gusting stronger, but the last boat to have unloaded was being hauled on board. On the lugger's foredeck men were gathered at the anchor windlass, and the fore was being cleared for hoisting. Had the wind been lighter both sails would probably have been left up and brailed, but even with her muffled main still up the mast, the smuggler was starting to sheer quite wildly in the swell. It was almost time to go.

Lieutenant Kaye concurred. He gave the order and the men, with whoops, piled across the bulwarks and down into the boats, still shielded from the vision of the enemy. They were bristling with arms and could not be quiet for the life of them, which hardly mattered any more. As

Bentley, then Ayling, gave their orders to let go and stand by to hoist, Gunning, at a word from Kaye, roused his men to clew-garnets, braces, tacks and sheets, and to break out canvas with the utmost speed. Will's cutter dropped astern, the main went up, she blew off in a gust around the Biter, up helm and sail her off. In half a minute more they had the mizzen set, sheets trimmed, and were surfing across the waves towards their quarry. Ayling's crew were only slightly slower.

The speed and skill of Gunning's men was also most commendable, and must have shocked the lugger's people horribly. Kaye had the wind-gage, and was close enough to run down and ram if that had been his intention. Gunning spread everything, and the bulky brig, from slopping like a wicker basket full of fish, dug in her nose, and then her arse, and *surged*. Jem Taylor and the gunner cleared ports and ran out guns, with excitement sweeping the deck like wildfire. As he raced away, Will saw a small black figure approach Kaye on the quarterdeck, with a glass and bottle, and foreboding swept him. Do not celebrate too early, Dick, no, don't do that, he thought. Then he braced himself against the tiller and told Behar to ease the mizzen sheet.

Kershaw was beside him in the cutter's well, gazing intently at the scene ahead, his one eye shielded from the spray, and he first saw the flaw in Kaye's plan. He said something to Will, was not heard above the wind, then shouted it.

'They're not his boats! He will abandon them! Look, he's going to cut her free!'

Will glanced, and saw a seaman on the lugger's foredeck raise an axe above his head. At the same time the main began to shake and thunder with the brails let fly. The foreyard was already rising up the mast.

'Blood!' he shouted. 'They're shore boats! You have it right, sir! Tilley! Hugg! Get your muskets up! Get me a helmsman for a guinea!'

He had not thought of it, he did not know why, but nor

had Kaye. The heavy boats to bring out the French escapers were not going back to France, but were merely ferries. Clearly the most important people were on board already – and the bulk of others – and the rest were seen as extra cash, expendable if need be. Both boats were wheeling for the shore, with their sailors pushing and shoving at the landsmen to get them clear from off the sails for hoisting. On the instant Hugg's musket cracked, to no effect apparently, then Tom Tilley's, and shortly afterwards three more from Ayling's boat. Like firing from careering horses at a leaping hare, not any chance at all, except by simple luck.

From windward came the crash of heavy guns, as Biter hauled her wind to bring her starboard side to bear. Will saw shots pluming in the rolling sea, but the lugger was not hit. Her fore was almost up, her anchor warp was cut, her main hard in, and already she was forging ahead with extraordinary speed. 'Hah,' said Kershaw beside him, and Will knew exactly what he meant. The lugger was brilliantly handy, given men who knew her, and the Frenchmen clearly did. Once she had speed up, and with a bit of fortune, she might get clear of Gunning's rolling tub completely.

'He's wearing round!' said Kershaw, in astonishment. 'I wonder what his game is now!'

Will could not afford to look. He chose a target from the two ahead, then bellowed and gesticulated until Ayling understood and shaped up for the other one.

'Hold fire, men!' yelled Bentley to his crew. 'We'll go in close to get a good one, then I'm heading up.' To Kershaw he added, but maybe not loud enough to hear, 'If Kaye can wing her, we're near enough to go on board perhaps.'

'She's falling off,' said Kershaw, who had heard. 'He's coming round to pick them up after all, is he? 'Fore God, I don't know!'

As the lugger turned upon her heel, she fired off two guns at Biter, and one shot tore a perfect circle in her forecourse. The Frenchman, on a dead run, screamed down towards her ferries and the Biter's boats, careless of her chance to claw off and outmanoeuvre her attacker.

'He draws eight feet or less,' said Kershaw, laconically. 'He's luring Kaye on to the ground, the stoat. How much does Biter draw?'

Will did not know, but there was no doubt she was deeper, perhaps two feet or more. She'd squared up, and was plunging in a line straight after her prey, as if water depth was no consideration. Will felt sweat break out beneath his arms.

'Gunning knows,' he said. 'He knows these waters and he's very good, when sober.'

Tom Tilley grinned at him, having overheard. 'He's sober, sir,' he said. 'He hasn't touched a drop for days. Look, shall we fire? You can see the buggers' teeth.'

Shots cracked out from Ayling's boat, and a man in the nearest ferry slumped. There was a flash from near him, a ragged stream of smoke, and then a pistol-snap, barely audible.

'No,' said Will. 'We'll save it for the mother hen. She's coming round.'

The lugger was close in now, downwind of them and – just – the shorebound boats. She was going like a running bull, but as she reached the ferry the helmsman gybed, then luffed her sharply to kill her way. Men were jumping up like spiders on a web, with hands on board dragging them by clothes and limbs and hair. Sails flapping, head to wind, she forereached to the second boat, which smacked into her, its mainsail dropped, a huge confusion of men jumping to get out. Ayling's gunners let out a ragged fire at quite close range, and two or three men fell but were picked up again. The lugger began to drop astern with helm reversed, and as she paid off both yards were dipped most prettily, when she began to gather forward way with entrancing ease. Biter was bow on to her, with few guns to bear, but the Frenchman's all were clear to fire.

'She has to turn,' said Kershaw. 'She'll hit the bottom else. Ah – there she goes.'

As Biter swung hard round on to the wind, Will heard a ragged fusillade. The instant it was over, and before he heard the one that did the damage, the cutter received the most amazing blow, he felt her lift and smash beneath him. He was sprayed with something wet, not sea but something warm and heavy, and in front of him Behar's trunk sat at the mizzen sheet, blood weeping from his headless neck. Ahead of that, a swathe of crimson stretched out to the bow, with mangled men adorning it. This was all in silence, he was not aware of any sound at all. The bow, in fact, was open to the sea, its whole starboard side removed from just behind the stem. Before time was properly renewed, he watched the sea roll in and swamp the boat, but very slowly. Then he heard the screams.

The lugger, having done for her, damn nearly ran across the wreckage then. There were many men on deck, seamen and pick-ups from the shore, and some were openly aghast at the carnage they were bearing down on, and had caused. At the very latest moment the helm went down, she sliced up towards them, sails let fly and all a-shake. If she was life-saving, it was each man for himself, and some on board the cutter were past help anyway. Tom Tilley jumped, and Tennison and Wilmott, then Will, after pushing the crippled Kershaw into the reach of willing hands. The cutter crunched along the lugger's side; two screaming men rolled off and under, the water staining red. By the time he was on board, his soaked pistol held foolishly in hand, her sails were filled and sheeted and she was ploughing on.

The fusillade that had sunk the cutter had hit Biter, it appeared. Her forecourse was down, the yard cocked across the deck, the canvas covering and impeding men. She was athwart the seas and rolling heavily, as other men strove to clear the decks for gunnery and sailing. In common with all hands, William watched from the lugger's deck as she forged under Biter's lee at about a half a cable's distance. The action seemed all over, and although the French skipper could have put in another volley, he did not do so. But as the Biter rolled away from them, exposing her weedy larboard side, four of her guns were fired almost simultaneously, and by luck or judgement they caught the roll just right. First the flashes, then the strikes, then the reports. Will looked aloft and saw the top part of the foremast sag then break, the sail dropping like an enormous bat. From aft, though, came a burst of screaming. A ball had smashed the rail, missed the mainmast by inches, and killed and crippled, mainly from splinters. One of its victims was the pilot-captain, whose leg was severed at the groin. He bled to death in half a minute, without a word or cry.

There was cheering on the Biter and another, single cannon-shot, that went wide. But the lugger, with only her mainsail set, still forged through the water fast, and stayed close-winded. None of her fore hamper had gone overside to drag her back, and the helmsman, small, dark and saturnine, handed the spokes as if on a summer outing. Within a minute they were clear ahead of the Impress brig, and in five they went about on to the larboard tack to sail round her on the windward side to clear into deeper water before standing south.

Before that, though, the Biter men were rounded up as prisoners. There were only five of them, and it was not roughly done, perhaps as only Will had brought a firearm on board, and that quite drowned for all to see. The common men were separated off by common Frenchmen and had their sea knives taken off them, then they were herded forward as if to share a can – which, for all Will knew, they might. He gave his pistol up, politely and butt-first, and Kershaw indicated with his hand to show that he had nothing. As they went aft men were washing blood away, but the looks they got were curious, not informed by rage or hate. In the cabin, seated at the table with four men, was Céline.

'Mr Bentley,' she said. 'In less tragic circumstances, I would say well met. I do not understand how this came about, this sad *contretemps*, but now, it seems, you are our prisoner. I am sorry for that.'

She was vaguely as Will remembered her to look at, but of a different manner entirely. Small, dark, but with a heavy seriousness, as if she were in command. Indeed, the men who flanked her said nothing, although they followed the conversation as if they understood. He found her manner rather chilling; and her assumptions.

'You are in breach of English law,' he began. It sounded ludicrously pompous. One of the Frenchmen seemed to smile. Will said stiffly: 'In any way, the action is not over yet, not by a long shot.'

'And it would need a long one, *cher monsieur*,' said another Frenchman, his English almost accentless. 'The sad thing is that there were shots at all.'

We are at war, thought William, angry with himself. That's what I meant to say. But Céline was shaking her head from side to side, looking white and weary.

'Blaise Léopold is dead,' she said. 'There are dead on your side, also. Mr Bentley, we do not wish to chain you up. We need your word is all, yours and your colleague's. Monsieur . . . ?'

She was talking to Kershaw, who stood silently beside him.

'My name is Kershaw,' he said. 'You have my word. I knew of your Monsieur Léopold. I am sorry for his death. A fine seaman and navigator.'

They all stared at him. Céline's eyes, suddenly, were filled with tears.

'Thank you,' she said. 'He was. And Mr Bentley? Your *parole*?'

'You have it,' he said. His mouth was stubborn. 'But our action is not lost. Not yet. If it comes on hot again, the word is void. Is that agreed?'

Nobody smiled, but after a moment, there were nods.

'But it is lost,' said one of the Frenchmen. 'It is too late for you.'

The men on Biter, it appeared, were not of his opinion but of Bentley's. When he and Kershaw made the quarterdeck once more – as an act of courtesy it was made open to them – she was still just visible in the gathered gloom, and she was making canvas. Their vision of her, and hers of them, was made possible by a rising moon, which the Frenchmen must have cursed, and the fact that the north-wester clouds were running down the coast but, by some quirk, were disinclined to roll out across the sea, obscuring the light. It was a spring-tide moon, almost full, and in the next hour it climbed into the sky like an enormous lamp, imparting stark beauty to the rolling seas that were breaking white into the distance. By the end of that hour the English brig, her damaged gear replaced or repaired, had grown a full suit, including studding sails. It was going to be a race. Things might not be lost completely, after all.

'She is a stiff-built tub,' said Kershaw, with a sort of grudging admiration. 'Not many of her size could carry that press in this wind.' He glanced at Bentley with an odd gleam in his eye. 'How long before she carries something away, do you reckon? Those Deptford riggers are infamous, you know.'

Will, upset and irritated by the whole damn circus, thought levity was out of place, so did not answer. It was hard to tell at such a distance, but to him it seemed that Biter was gaining fast. On the foredeck of the lugger, men were working hard at rigging a jury mast.

'Mark you,' said Kershaw, 'if we should stay in close, it won't be many hours before our brig will need deep water, will it?' Again the strange look. 'Or have you not studied the charts for hereabouts?'

The sense of irritation grew. Will had not studied any charts for much too long and, strangely, somehow felt that these 'were not his waters'. He countered with a question he thought rather pointed.

'Mr Kershaw, how square you this with what you told me earlier? That Lieutenant Kaye would not bring off this action? That somehow it was a blind to leave poor Sam alone?'

'I did not say that, I think.'

'You did, sir! Quite plainly, sir!'

Kershaw shrugged his one good shoulder. He was very calm, and very confident, no trace now of his normal nervous reticence.

'I do not imagine Kaye would be so venal as to want him dead deliberately,' he said. 'Although he might, if the stakes were high enough. That is, if Mr Holt were like to see there enough people he might later know. No, what I meant was Kaye had chose to do this run, to attack this lugger on information he had received, because on the face it was an act of duty and of bravery, that would not in actual fact come off. While on the beach at Sussex, men he might have had an interest in would be unmolested, save by your lonely friend. What I chose not to tell you, sir, was why. A case, let's say, of loyalty divided.'

'And?'

'And what? And was I wrong? Look at those French sailors there. In half an hour, let's say, they'll have the foresail up again. Will Biter hold her then? Will you take a wager? But Mr Kaye looks increasing patriotic, don't he? He's fighting to the very, very last.'

'No,' said Will. 'I'm asking for a further explanation. Of "loyalty divided". Or what you chose not to tell. It is my uncle, isn't it? You are suggesting my Uncle Daniel and Lieutenant Kaye are . . . are what? Are something to the smugglers? Are involved in what is to happen on the Adur beach? I do not think so, sir. I do not think so.'

Instantly, the moon went behind a thick stray cloud and they were plunged into total blackness. When it lifted, thirty seconds later, Kershaw had moved to weather and was talking to two of the Frenchmen who had been in the cabin with Céline. They were talking intimately, and William wondered, sickly, if their conversation were in English or in French. Then, on the foredeck, a cry went up, hands clapped on to the halliard, and the forward lug began to rise. Another spell of blackness, longer than the last, and when the pale moon glow came down again, the sail was risen. As it was sheeted in, the lugger was lifted by a rolling crest, and drove vibrating through it, throwing white water wide from both sides of her stem.

The mast up near its break was badly sprung, so no attempt had been made to extend it to its proper height again. It had been fished and tightly parcelled, and a block stropped on to take the halliard. Perhaps fifteen feet of height was lost in all, so the sail was reefed to the second set of points. With the wind astern she balanced badly, and when she'd settled down was nowhere near her proper speed. Will, on his own by choice for some long time, stared at the Biter in the milky moonlight until she shimmered in his eyes. She was carrying her canvas well, despite the wind felt as if it were growing all the while, but it was impossible to tell if she was losing ground or gaining. At this rate, the chase might last for ever.

In his concentration he did not hear footsteps, and he jumped when Céline spoke behind his ear. Her voice was strong and calm, but rather troubled.

'A stern chase is a long chase is what French seamen say,' she said. 'Or is it the English, I get mixed sometimes. Do you think she's catching us?'

He looked at her with curiosity. She had a strong face, with deep, dark eyes. She was very serious, which he found peculiar, in a woman. Although, he remembered, Mary Broad was like it, also. Not like women were supposed to be. Then he thought of Deb, and his stomach clenched with pain and fear. Deb, he knew, was very likely dead. Most likely.

'You do not reply,' she said. 'I don't know why I tell

you this, because you won't believe me. The Navy do not chase us normally because they know. We are not in the normal way of smuggling. This boat, her captain Blaise Léopold, God rest his soul. Sometimes we bring Englishmen from France. Sometimes we carry English people there. But you don't believe me.'

He had heard this before from Mary, and in truth he knew no lónger if he believed, and did not care. He thought of Sam alone on the beach, and he thought of Deb, whose whereabouts God only knew. The night was wearing on, and he was full only of doubt and pain. A cork in a maelstrom, that's how he saw himself. He was tossed and thrown about, and whoever had control it was not him. He felt hopeless, forlorn, alone. He would not reply because he could not.

'She's getting closer,' said Céline, still calm and quiet. 'Do you know these waters? Do you know the Goodwin Sands? Look there, up out to larboard. Look, there ahead. We need poor Blaise now, this was his element.'

The tide was running south, and fast, the wind was north-westerly and brisker all the time, the black clouds spreading from the coast. The sea they ran in was rolling comfortably, smoothed by the blast but still whitecapped and flecked with foam. But up ahead ran seas that made a complement to the lurch of fear her words had wrought in him. He did not know the waters, but he knew the Goodwins by repute, as what seaman did not, however ignorant of detail? By ill repute. The killer sands.

'Ah,' said Céline, at his side. 'He has agreed it seems, he is on deck again. Now, sweet lord, we must give thanks for that.'

Will turned, and all his fear that Kershaw was a traitor was confirmed. With two others of the officers he had emerged from the after scuttle and taken up position beside the helmsman. He had no chart in hand, but pointed out across the starboard bow.

'Now treachery,' breathed Bentley, but the woman responded sharply.

'He will save your life,' she said. 'Would your Captain Kaye do that? Or that of your luckless friend he has abandoned? Even now he'd drive us on them, if we allowed him opportunity. If we stand clear he will come up with us, what's more. Mr Kershaw has been persuaded to give us all some chance, that's all.'

True it was that Biter was drawing close. In the increasing wind she still could hold her canvas, while the lugger, with too much astern and not enough ahead, was developing a tendency to yaw and wallow. But Will had seen the brig brought on like this before.

'It is a trick to lure him on the sands,' he said. 'The Biter draws at least two feet on us, and Kershaw knows it. It could be bloody carnage.'

The helmsman altered course at the Englishman's direction, and the people, when they'd tended sheets, were set on to clearing boats. There were three on board the lugger, two of twenty-five feet or so, one of twenty-two. The foreyard, in dropping, had damaged one of the larger, although she still looked seaworthy enough for reasonable seas, short distances. The seas around them were getting worse as the water shallowed across the banks, though. Over to larboard they were breaking on the sands, like insane waterspouts. As a lifeboat, Will considered, she would be of fearsome little use.

On a rush of anger, he left Céline and strode across to Kershaw, who was staring out ahead.

'Sir! Are you in league with them? Have you no shame, sir! If Biter goes on ground, there will be your comrades dead! Give up the con! I order you!'

He was ridiculous, and it engulfed him. He was powerless, and it cut him deep with shame. But Kershaw's face was fixed and tense, the muscles in his jaw standing through the skin. He did not reply.

There was a black squall coming up astern of them, and to starboard there was also broken water up ahead. Only dead before the stempost was the surface relatively flat, although even here the sea was soupy with the sand that hung in it. The moon was sinking, its light less strong, with the forward-reaching cloud fronds almost up to it. Each person on the quarterdeck eyed the squall in silent fear. Suddenly, Will hoped desperately Kershaw had got it right. Below them was the bottom, they did not know how far. The tension in his guts was horrifying.

'She is firing!'

It was Céline who'd shouted, who had seen the flash. At the instant came the report, ragged in the wind that also tore the smoke away. And the Biter, helm hard down, was rounding up to stop her headlong dash.

'Kaye's warning us,' said Will. 'A warning shot.'

'Mr Gunning,' Kershaw said, as if in conversation. 'I said he knows these waters, he is a seaman born.'

'I hope you do, sir!' said Bentley heatedly, and as he spoke the lugger struck, with a stagger and a lurch that threw men – and Céline – off their feet, and with an appalling, tearing crash brought down the damaged foremast, which toppled forward almost slowly, like a felled tree in a forest, its square black sail spreading out to shroud the waters up ahead.

In the confusion on the deck, Will found his head was close to Kershaw's, and, most bizarrely, Kershaw smiled.

'Ah, that I do,' he said. 'Indeed.'

For a moment, the hull under them was firm as any jetty, but the sensation did not last for long. The wind, which may have paused in the seconds before the squall hit them, tore down with screaming intensity as the night went irrevocably black. The seas, which had lifted them along quite easily, began to strike, and pour, and rend, and swirl across the afterdeck, bursting up as driven, bitter spray as each new wave struck the stern. Will scrambled to his feet to be knocked over instantly, and shot along like garbage in the flood. He hit the mainmast, grabbed on to it, then grabbed Céline as she swept by, coughing and retching water. With the squall came rain, in gigantic,

403

stinging lumps, and out of it, when the sea voided itself into the waist, came Kershaw crawling also.

'Let's get that mainsheet cut,' he said, and snaked off to leeward, smiling like a dog. He's mad, thought Will. He's gone completely mad.

Whatever, Kershaw was too late to free the sheet, because the weight of wind in the mainsail broached the lugger, as she lifted to a sea, right round to larboard till she lay along the troughs. In a lightening of the black, Will saw the damaged boat, half full of men, lifted bodily and neatly overside, where she landed bottom downwards and bobbed as safely as a duckpond toy. Without hesitation, they made shift to ship their oars, and pulled back towards the lugger to pick up other men. By now the deck was thronged, despite appalling danger from the seas that raked it.

For a minute or two Will was lost, drowned in another comber, and the world blacked out. Then, as lightning began to flicker, he watched the smallest boat lift off the waist-deck, scattering the men who'd cleared her from a mess of fallen gear, and swing along the lee side, still inside the bulwarks but afloat, then come for him as if a charging bull, unmanned and empty, heading to cross the taffrail and away. But as she passed him, Kershaw caught her bow-line in his only hand, swinging himself around a mast-stay to take a turn with it. As the yawl's stem jerked and the hull swung in an afterwards arc over the side and in again, Kershaw let out an awful, cut-off scream as the stay bit deep into his stomach, enough to break his back. The gunwale hit Bentley low across the groin, dissolving his sight into a flash of agony, and when he saw again, the boat – with him inside it on the bottomboards – was ten feet or more beyond the lugger's stern. Almost in it, by some miracle he could not guess at, was Kershaw draped across the bow, his trunk inside, legs out, and, clinging to the starboard side, Céline and a French smuggler.

'Help me,' said Céline. 'My arm, my arm.'

But Will, try as he might, could hardly move, so violent had the blow across his stomach been. He got to them, and took her shoulder, but he had almost no strength at all to pull. The Frenchman, whose face was pale and desperate, used all his failing energy to get her higher from the sea, then, having looped her arm into the boat, lifted her leg until Bentley could pull her knee on board. Five minutes later, when Céline lay in the bottom vomiting water, the Frenchman gave up the fight, released his hold, and slipped beneath the waves. Kershaw, although he seemed to cling there, was already dead.

30

The lugger had been built of fir for speed and lightness, not long life. Over the next short, endless minutes in the lightning storm, Will saw her breaking up as she was pounded on the Goodwin Sands. He should have gone to her, to aid the desperate men, but there was nothing he could do but wait for his own death. His legs were numbed to uselessness, Céline was sitting on the bottomboards in swirling, slopping water, incapable, and Kershaw never moved. Will shipped one oar over the stern to try to get her prow into the wind and stop her filling, but the dead weight at the stem, and Kershaw's trailing legs, made that impossible; she rolled, and rolled, and slowly filled. It would be a short time only before she was waterlogged and sank.

The blackness of the squall was of a great intensity, but the lightning play, for a time, was almost constant. In it, he saw the Biter's boats run down on the lugger like so many jackals, but not to rend, to save. They came down under rags of sail, filled up with men, then sailed off across the wind to where Gunning had placed the ship, upwind of the banks but towards the Kentish coast to give an angle they could fight to. As the lugger's mainmast went overside, as she was pounded into pieces, pass after pass was made, and many men were saved. Kaye's operation, Bentley knew, was cool, and brave, and brilliant. Whatever Céline said about their lordships' attitudes to the lugger's secret work, it seemed inevitable that he must be lauded for it. As he himself, inevitably, would drift to leeward to smash on the shoals, or merely be swamped, and drown.

In one long flicker, Céline was moving. She rolled on

to her side, got on to hands and knees, then went forward. She kept her body low, pressing to the thwarts when she came to them, until she reached the bow. Her weight, with Kershaw's, made the many gallons in the bilge rush forward, so the gunwale came alarmingly closer to the broken surface. Will shouted, but she did not hear, and suddenly stood up, thrust her head close to the broken man's to check, then seized him by the shoulders, lifted, and pushed. Another shout, this one of horror and astonishment, still no response. For one instant, he was face to face with Kershaw, then he was gone. No impression of expression, nothing, just a blank. Then Céline twisted, and launched herself back towards the middle, and the yawl rode easier.

'Was he dead?' said William, to the roaring wind, but Céline was feet away, bailing with a canvas bucket, going like a foundryman. She was in a sea cloak, on her knees, feet sticking out of it and one shoe lost. The water shot across the side in a pulsing, constant stream. Jesu, thought Will; we might get out of this.

Down to the lee there was still clear water, or clearish anyway. Over to the eastward the breaking seas were worst, but to the west the boat looked to be beyond the vilest jumble. The lugger was lost to sight by now, although Biter's top hamper still appeared in flashes, which were growing fewer by the minute. The squall was passing, although the wind was still extremely hard. Somewhere in the dark – not all that far – there lay the coast of Kent. For the first time, it occurred to him that they could get to it. Acknowledging its pointlessness, he unshipped his oar from the quarter and joined Céline down in the bilges with another bucket, despite his wrenching stomach pain. She did not speak, but he got a flash of smile. She had her tongue-tip gripped between her teeth. In five minutes of intensive labour, the bottomboards stood proud.

Céline was an expert sailor, and they got the masts up almost without a difficulty. Shipping the rudder was the hardest – he had to grip her round the waist while she plunged head-under several times before the pintles and gudgeons were engaged – then they rested for a while, driving under poles. With wind and sea astern it was more comfortable, and in the east the sky was lightening. The clouds had retreated to pile above the land once more, and they both prayed for sun, and quickly, before they froze to death. Best part was when she rooted in an after locker, to produce cold cured bacon and a brandy bottle, put there – although she'd only guessed and hoped – when the boats were readied earlier, in case of a disaster. They ate like ravens, but drank sparingly, and that for warmth. Typical free trade trick, she mouthed, holding up the spirit. I would give my nose for a tin of good fresh water.

The yawl would carry half a main, when they decided time had come, and as they hoisted Will realised just what a weight there still was in the wind. It had veered round to the north and was blasting clear and chill, and the sailing, for a time, he found exhilarating. This troubled him, because there were many other things that he should think about, but he recognised his brain was tired almost beyond the point of reason. The lift and surge of each passing roller, the juggling of mind and tiller to keep her on her course and safe from broaching, this was enough for him for the moment. He could not even face steering in towards the land, bringing the sea from its comfortable set on to the beam, where he would have to fight or guard against the breaking tops. Céline slept, sitting head down in her cloak, and it occurred to him as in a dream that she would end in France if the boat kept on like this. With wind astern it did not chill them, and the sun climbed hot and naked so that he gently steamed. He woke up with a dreadful jerk, as the yawl went into a broach. But Céline had plucked the tiller from his hand, and she heaved it hard to windward. She was smiling down at him.

'You are tired, you must sleep. I'll wake you when we reach the Sussex beach.'

'What?'

She was joking with him. The thought had not occurred to Will. The Sussex beach? Where were they now? How far?

Maybe she was not joking. He stared at her but did not know. He tried to take the tiller back but she pulled him forward so that she could have his place. Will did not resist her strongly. There was an emanation off her of command.

'It was something that your friend said. Kershaw. Whose body I tipped overboard. Who was he, Will?'

'He was not my friend, he was— He was a spy, I think. Do you think he put the lugger on deliberately?'

She shook her head.

'I do not know. He knew the waters. He told me your Captain Kaye had come on us because he saw an opportunity. Some English lord had said he must take smugglers, so he needed an excuse. He knew of us from his spies, other spies.' She laughed, briefly and not with enjoyment. 'There are so many spies, aren't there? You English love them very dearly. He came on us, his very splendid cover. And left your Samuel on the beach.'

'But you are smugglers! If his intention was protection of the breed, if he loves smugglers—'

Her next laugh silenced him. Céline shook her head.

'He does not love smugglers, he is part of them,' she said. 'But only part of some of them, of course. I thought that Mary had explained, maybe? No? No, Isa Bartram is a suspicious man. Or perhaps she feared that it might hurt you. It—' She stopped. 'No, we are smugglers, in our fashion, but Kaye does not stand to gain or lose by us, there is no business link, however tenuous. He could attack us, kill us, capture us, the outcome would be all the same to him. But those men on the beach, whom he was set on to knock down— Well, suffice to say he did not want to do it. Does not. But could not, under any circumstance, admit. He got word of us, we were convenient, a sacrifice.

409

Although their lordships, as I've said before, might not be so sanguine as to what he's wrought.

'Yes,' she added, abruptly. 'I do think Mr Kershaw put us on the sands deliberately, out of some sense of duty I would guess, misguided duty, possibly. He thought Kaye ought to do his duty also, at the very least to rescue Sam. He thought from where we were, a rescue would be feasible. Do you tell me seriously you did not know this? It is tonight the gangs are running to the Adur, it is tonight the link takes place. Kaye could have done it, what you and he and this Navy lord agreed, but he used us as a blind, the timing fitted perfectly. If I understood your Mr Kershaw right, he thought that you and he could, also. At least could go and aid Sam on the beach. It may be that we cannot make it, the beach is many leagues. But do you tell me it was not what you intended?'

'What time is it?' asked Will. 'How many leagues?' And then, inconsequentially, 'Bobby Beaumont, that was the lord. Lord Wodderley.'

'We should turn west,' said Céline. 'The sun is past its peak, but with this wind I think there should be time enough. The landing will not be till after dark, the boat is good, and we are good enough. But you, Will, must get sleep.'

He nodded, and his head was throbbing with dull pain. How many days, he wondered, since he'd had a proper rest. Oh many, many days.

'But you could sail to France.' He said it without thinking, the thought just came. She nodded.

'I could, but then I won't. You have to trust me, Will. Remember Mary and the Bartrams, though. I am not a business associate, but the links are strong, what good to me if I betrayed them? They do not want this thing tonight to happen, that's how Sam and you were first involved. Was it not Sam's kinsman that they killed?'

Yes, true, thought Will. Sam, at the worst, is there to watch, to spy out the participants. God's blood, if he achieves it, and then we pick him off the beach, the job is done! And if he's attacked, and I am there to help him —

That gave him pause, for in the boat he had no weapon. But he believed that he did trust her, and somehow that gave him comfort. She was, in truth, a most extraordinary maid.

'You can handle her alone?' he asked, then humphed at his own stupidity. 'Pardon me. Young women, as fine seamen, are unknown, almost, where I come from.'

'You live at Petersfield,' she said laconically. 'It is a long way from the sea. I could sail a boat at six years old. Before you go to sleep, sir, take the helm. I need the bucket.'

'But the bottomboards are dry.'

'And I, sir, need the bucket. Take the helm.'

Dr Marigold, whom Deborah had never seen before, saved her life that night. After Will was dragged away from her she fought like an animal, but had no doubt at all that she would die. The mob was overwhelming, fired up with lust for blood, but for her body also. She received many blows from fists, and scratching tears from women's claws, but she was also bitten on both cheeks and on her neck, and her bosom was squeezed and torn. Between her legs a stick was thrust, and hands, and – had she gone down – she would have died of crushing, rape, and suffocation.

He was a short, fat man with powdered face and powdered wig, and something of a dandy. He was, to Deb, a face beyond the crowd, who stood out because he was flanked by three enormous flunkies holding burning brands as torches. His mouth opened as he shouted, but that was lost within the general roar. She lost sight of the face as someone tore a tuft from off her head and blinded her with pain. A blow to her chest, and she was falling backwards, to the gutter and her death. It stopped very shortly after that. She hit the ground, and rolled and tried to spring on to her knees, then upright to face them, but her tormentors had pulled back. Instead of bellies, fists and snarls, she had the yard in front of her, setts slippery in the glim. And this short, fat person with a garish face, and dandy clothes, and a pistol with silver chasing that he waved about without aggression, but to miraculous effect. In thirty seconds she was bleeding there alone, except for her rescuer and his men. In the shadows there were figures, but they did not stay to watch, they disappeared.

'You are a trouble to me, wench,' he said. 'Mistress Margery said that I must save your life, and indeed, two corpses in my house would be an *embarras de richesses* for one night. Now you must go. I give you half an hour.'

A wild idea to follow Bentley came to her, but she was naked, beaten, and did not know where to go. The vision in one eye appeared blurred, she could not rightly see.

'But . . . but I have protection here. Sir Ar— No, I cannot give his name. And Dr Marigold.'

'I am Dr Marigold. I had hopes of you, but I fear your looks are gone. That gentleman who pays for you gave me discretion, as is normal. He will not complain.'

'But, sir—'

But Marigold had turned, and Marigold was gone. One of the flunkies gestured with his torch, lasciviously, and in its gleam she recognised Mrs Putnam. Some minutes afterwards, in a cloak, she was led to the older woman's room, and given brandy and some washing water, and – shortly – some of her own stouter, outdoor clothes, brought by a girl from her own suite. The body, Margery told Deb, was gone from out of it, as soon would every trace of her inhabitation also be. She showed a purse with money in, that she would donate from the goodness of her heart, but implied the maid had brought the trouble on herself. When Deb – a shadow of her spirit stirring in her – challenged that, Mistress Margery sighed, and said it was the times, the times. Which, strangely, reminded her of old Sir A, and made her cry again.

'He says I've lost my looks,' she said. 'That Marigold.

But I have never seen him, how should he know? Oh Margery, it is not true though, is it?'

'The times he's looked at you, only your face was bruised, maid. Now you're bruised all over, and you're scalped in parts, as if Virginny savages had got at you. Nay, your looks will grow again, don't fret, the reason he wants rid of you is scandal, a thing he can't afford here, in any wise. That's what it boils down to, maid, just money, like everything in this world we live in, where all are money mad. You have brought scandal here, you must allow, since the very moment that you came. That mountebank attacks the house and kills that thin girl, what was her name again, that Cynthia, and now he's dead and in the Fleet or in some limepit if I know Marigold. Just because he looks a fop, dear, don't mean he ain't a man of hardest stone. Cecily, poor Cecily, see, I ain't forgot her, bless her soul. She cried to me the day before she died, of a town called . . . Stockport? And a river with an ugly name, the goitre, or some such. Now, what was it?'

'The Goyt. The name is bad but it is very lovely. The Goyt, the Tame, the Mersey.' Deb had dried her tears, but they still leaked down on her cheeks. She sniffed, hard, and shuddered. 'But can he throw me out? What will Sir Arthur say? My good protector?'

'What the hell he likes,' said Margery. 'No skin off Dr Marigold's appendages. Look, there's a bit of money there, go find yourself a lodging, some cheap house. Or even wander home, back to the River Goitre. There's not enough to take a coach but carters will do a little trade in my experience, and you're safe enough from pimps and whoremasters in your current state. Go home and fright your ma to death, she'll box your ears but probably forgive you, as mas must do. You could try your "protector", I suppose, but you'd be a fool, in my opinion. It's not every maiden that Marigold kicks out for bringing murder to his house, I can tell you that much. This "Sir Arthur" would be good indeed if he did not merely bar the gates to you,

413

when he could have you hanged for certain. Listen – in a month or two you'll have your face again. Get some good cheap lodging and when you're right you can go whoring for yourself. That's the best way up the ladder, maid. Do that.'

Deb, silent but no longer tearful, contemplated her future, but saw only Will Bentley, being dragged away to join a ship. She was the maiden in the song, in all the songs, the maiden weeping on the shore, her sailor gone away.

'Where is the Adur?' she asked Margery. 'What is "the Adur way"?'

The matron shook her head.

'There's a River Adur down near Shoreham and Portslade. I left Sussex when a kid, but I'm pretty sure of that. The Arun, the Adur, and the Ouse, through Lewes. I was born at Burgess Hill, I couldn't stand the quiet. Why, do you know—'

But Deb's face cut off reminiscence. She stood, distracted, and said she had to leave, which was quite right, her time was more than up. Rain spattered on the window, and it was cold outside, but she thought she would go there, to Sussex and the Adur, where – she pretended that she hoped – she might find Samuel.

'How will I get there?' she asked Margery. 'There is someone I must give a message to.'

Mrs Putnam's eyes were full of pity.

'Maiden; maid,' she said. 'Stay in London, where you might be safe. Don't go out on the roads alone at night, or you will die.'

When Deborah left the house, she took a wicked little knife the woman gave to her. It might serve equally, to save her life, or end it.

Sam Holt had been betrayed, but the chaos of the landing and the night came close to saving him. In any way, he'd been in his home country for several days, had spoken to people, had spent cash – Sir A's – and knew the secret house as clear as day and had a vantage point that should have been impregnable. He had seen men he had known since early days as respectable, upstanding pillars of the eastern community, and had seen one man arrive from Hampshire – one man of several of a similar type and order – whom he had recognised. He had only seen Will Bentley's father once before but he had no doubt, however much it saddened and alarmed him. Now Christ, he thought, how do I tell my dear friend that?

Will Bentley, in the yawl out in the ever-wilder Channel, was moving, through Céline, to sad awareness of his own. She had awoken him as the weather had deteriorated, suggesting that they might be better off, in fact, to up and run for France, which was at that point not so very far away. She couched it in the nature of a jest, but when he was wakeful and aware, Will could see merit in it, from a seaman's angle. The northerly was blasting fiercer, with a heavy sea running offshore, confused by a counter tide. The surface was broken and ugly, with gouts of heavy water rising abrupt from any quarter, threatening to swamp. Had he not been so dead with exhaustion he would have woken naturally, and within a minute he was bailing hard. The boat was good, though, with another reef to take, and when he'd emptied her he dropped the sail and she rolled safe and comfortable in the troughs while they tied the last one in.

'She'll do,' he said. 'We'll work her closer in to get some lee. You could have run me off to France but did not, and I thank you for it. If you wish to go on shore in England, rather than risk your life out here, I would be proud to take you, if not pleased. By which I mean,' he added, flustered, 'by which I mean, you are such a . . . by which I mean, your help is very vital, and that is a pleasure, very great.'

She was laughing, her brown face frank and easy, although drawn and pale with tiredness.

'You are such a gallant boy,' she said, 'so *galant*. I am old enough to be your sister, is that English?, and that is how I treat you, I could not dream of leaving you alone. No, she will serve, or "do", as you put it, and I am as determined to help Sam Holt as you are. And Mary Broad, and Kate, and Isa and the rest. It is you that—'

Will had been thinking that his sisters were both younger, and not in any way at all like this young woman. But her breaking off alerted him, and the way she turned her face away.

'What? It is me that what?'

'Oh, hoist away!' she said. 'Let's see how well she takes it, and work her in towards the shore. We cannot be so many miles from the Adur, I spoke a clump of fishers while you slept and they were out of Pevensey.' She grinned. 'I played the part of boy at tiller, my master sleeping, my accent West Sussex way. They maybe thought that we were of the trade, but being taken for a woman would have been much more unwise, I think!'

They got the close-reefed sail up and sheeted and the yawl lay to the seas much quieter, taking spray but no more solid water. She was tearing through the sea at a terrific rate, and would probably handle in a full gale if one came on. Will took the helm while Céline broke out more bacon and – to his joy – produced a water breaker she had found. It would have served several men a half a week had the yawl become a lifeboat, so they did not stint. In the fading light, and not far northwards, they could see the Sussex coast in its wreath of cloud. Whatever happened, shore and safety, of a sort, was achievable.

Will came back with his question after they had sailed another mile or more, and he had thought the implications through. He did not ask Céline what she had meant to say, because she had stopped herself from finishing. He harked instead to Richard Kaye, and something she had said earlier, before he'd slept.

'Mary Broad,' he started. 'She knows something about

416

Slack Dickie – Lieutenant Kaye – that she would not tell for fear of hurting me. That was your implication, I believe? Some leagues ago?'

Céline's eyes were calm. She decided in a second, and she nodded.

'So Kaye, I take it, is some way involved with smuggling, and somehow involved with the men behind the Hampshire men, who would take over?' he continued. 'The men who want to link up with the East Sussex men and Kent men, whom Mary and her fellows see as villainous? He agreed to help in mine and Sam Holt's venture, then attacked your lugger so our attack would fail without him being seen reneging? Have I got it right thus far?'

Céline nodded once more. She looked to weather, and eased her sheet a fraction.

'But Kaye's no friend of mine, but is to Daniel Swift, my uncle. And throughout my times with Mary Broad, and Hardman, and the Bartrams, they would never venture any names. It was "shadows" this, and "shadows" that, the men behind the bitter changes, the men behind those two most dreadful outrages, the men who murdered Charles Warren and Charles Yorke. Am I to believe they are both implicated, Kaye and Daniel Swift? That as well as being Navy officers they are traders with the enemy!'

A sudden heat had come on him, on the last words he had seemed to choke with it; but Céline stayed deadly calm.

'Not with the enemy,' she said. 'Kaye is an English patriot, full blood. He fell on Léopold's boat because of that, because we are French, we *are* the enemy. It was legitimate.'

'And that is sophistry! If you are right he does business with the enemy, he is a backer of the trade! What is the difference?'

A creaming crest rose sharp beside their hull and Céline headed it, then delicately tweaked the stern to weather. It lifted her and the aft end both, then dropped them in a foaming gush as the wave roared under them.

'What is the enemy?' she replied, with the tiniest of smiles. 'This year France, next year Spain or Holland. Perhaps the enemy is the government, in every land? Certainly the enemy is those venturers who take a different stance, or play by different rules, or fight for their own territory like our Hampshire friends. Of course Blaise Léopold was not the enemy in one sense of the word, he brought home English prisoners of war for you, but being French we could be named as such for Richard Kaye's convenience. Of course France is the enemy, but trade is trade and must be carried on despite the mad rules of our rulers, so we are not the enemy, likewise for Richard Kaye's convenience. Did not your "good King Charles" have a cousin who was King of France? Did he not borrow gold from him to use to fight a war against him with his certain knowledge? That's what our history says. Convenience, at bottom it is all convenience. Even killing, when necessary, is a convenience, is it not? As it is for governments, so it is for us.'

'So Richard Kaye is one of the men behind the villainy that led to Yorke and Warren being killed? As a convenience . . .'

More crests arose to windward, were handled, ridden, used. The boat and woman were in perfect tune. After each manoeuvre, sweet and delicate, she gave a little smile.

'I must be honest with you,' she said at last. 'The Hampshire people do not know. The names they were suspicious of, *we* were suspicious of, were kept from you, were not mooted to you, because Mary in particular feared your hurt. Remember, Jesse was her husband. You are held in very high . . . regard.'

His voice betrayed his bitterness, his confusion. 'Convenience, also – or is that sophistry? Had I known, I maybe would not have joined the hunt, how could I have? We were looking for the murderers, Sam and I. We were not expecting to be used. Naive. Naive.'

Cold spray hit his face but he held it there and did not look away. Céline eased her sheet. The yawl was staggering to a stronger gust.

'We did not know for certain, but we had to know. No one could come up with a better way. And there are other men you know of. A doctor of your area. The Petersfield Recorder, we think, but have no evidence direct. Men, even, of your family. Will, we do not know, we may be wrong. Sam Holt and you were setting on for it, but Kaye sank all our hopes. You may call this convenience if you so desire, you are cynical: if we can rescue Sam he may know more, he may have certainties to tell us.'

'Men even of my family.' Bentley's voice was bleak, he was clearly wrestling for understanding. 'Daniel Swift is Kaye's protagonist, but you did not state his implication, you do not answer me. But Kershaw was Swift's man and he sank Kaye's hopes in a way, and told you it was because Sam Holt was abandoned and betrayed. If Kershaw was Swift's, how can you say that Swift is of the shadows? Oh Jesus Christ, there is that schooner building on the Thames!'

This to himself, as the memory hit him. Swift's own ship, on the stocks, his own fast private ship. And what was she for? Taking herring? No. Céline, hunched in her boat cloak, raised no question of his silent perplexity.

At last she said: 'We all must rise, Will, that is the bottom of it. This war won't last for ever, maybe, and no man can finance a good run off his own back, can he? This landing on the beach tonight might involve four hundred men or more, and money to finance such ventures is not lightly raised. I don't know why Kershaw wrecked our boat, or even if he did, on purpose, but if he was Swift's man he knew you and Samuel as well, and maybe changed his loyalty, is that impossible? And maybe Swift is loyal to the King, and Navy, but knows he has to live, and thrive, and

rise, whoever is the so-called enemy or even – horrors –
if there is no one to fight at all, and he is on the beach!
Men are ambitious, Will, although you do not seem to be.
Maybe Kaye skewered your hopes to stop you learning
things you would have found too indigestible. Back to
convenience, although that's too warped to contemplate!'
She laughed, briefly. 'No, you've come against reality,
brother. It is a bloody business, this life we're leading. All
of us.'

Did his father have a share in the building schooner?
Had not Swift said that?

'But you do not know?' he asked forlornly. 'You think
there is involvement, but you do not know for sure?'

'We do not know,' Céline agreed. 'For certain.'

Sam Holt had been betrayed, but the violence of the
weather, his good hideout, and Bentley and Céline con-
spired to get him off the beach alive, if only just. Ten hours
after that the question was an open one. When they sailed
into calmer waters he was on the bottomboards, face white
and tinged with blue, hair caked in blood, unmoving. As
they ran the forefoot on to mud, Céline gave way to tears.

They had reached the Adur beach in full dark, with
the moonlight patches less frequent than the night before.
From a mile away Céline had discovered two luggers of
the trade, both French, one of which she thought she
recognised. They were anchored well off, with small boats
going in, but the landing was extremely difficult because
of the rising storm. When they approached the beach
themselves the prospect was daunting for a yawl of light
construction. The free trade men were using heavy beach-
boats, and had dozens of hands to hold and haul them. If
they put the yawl within the breakers, she would likely
smash to pieces.

There was the sighting problem, too, for the gang had
lookers-out on shore and ship, and would hardly tolerate
intrusion. While a single small boat could pose no threat

it would not be welcome, although they were handier than the heavy landing vessels and could get away if chased. Dark-sailed and unexpected, they hoped, simply, not to be seen. Indeed they were not, for some while, but ranged up and down the beach in indecision. They were here, the landing was on as they'd expected – what could they do? They were unarmed, one woman and a man, and Sam, alive or dead, was – where? If they put the boat ashore she would stay there, of that they had no doubt. She would go to pieces in the surf, and in any way, they could not get her off and out again; they were too few. For fifteen minutes they hardly spoke; they backed and filled, and went about, and ranged. They were both beset by growing hopelessness.

It was being sighted that was the salvation they were praying for. As they swooped in close, in agony as to what to do for best, a shaft of moon broke through, a cry went up, and a volley of shots went off in quick succession. At the same instant, a lone figure broke from his cover behind the men firing at the yawl, who had, in fact, been beating through the undergrowth in search of him. He hared off down the beach towards the eastward – the yawl was sailing west – and Céline, as if she had not seen, put her about, ran off the beach against the rolling waves, then sliced along it to reach the point that the running man was heading for. The limping man, in fact, for Sam had received one ball already, in the leg, when flushed out of his hideaway and into thicker cover.

By the time they'd reached the point of no return, where the waves were breaking and they could not go, Sam had reached the edge and was plunging out to meet them. The batmen and the musketmen had seen him also, and were racing down upon him like a dervish horde. Some had discharged their pieces, others were in the line of fire, but it was too much to hope he would get away unscathed. Before he was waist-deep he took a ball below the shoulder, and as he swam close enough for Will to seize his coat to drag him across the gunwale, another hit him in the neck. Sam, whose mouth was open for a greeting, snapped it shut, went blank about the eyes, and folded into the bottom like a boneless heap. He was bleeding. Céline bore off, then gybed her round without a hand from Will, and ran offshore like an arrow into the seething blackness. There could be no pursuit.

It was forty miles or so to Langstone, but both knew that there was no alternative to going on. As they made their offing Will lay with Samuel in the bottom and tried to save his life. For some minutes he was not certain there was life to save, but he rubbed the pallid face with brandy, substituted his drier, warmer coat and cloak for the soaking shoreman's togs, and dribbled some spirit between the icy lips. At one point Samuel coughed, then gagged, then came to life and smiled the faintest smile. 'Ho, Will,' he said, 'fine life upon the sea, what?' then slipped off again. But his face got warmer, and from time to time he moved. Later, Will took the helm and Céline lay beside Sam, and wrapped both in her boat cloak, and rubbed his cheeks and hands. From time to time she moved, to lift her head and smile towards frozen Will, hunched beside the tiller, one hand upon the sheet as he fought to keep the yawl afloat in the violence. From time to time she got up on her knees to bail.

They could not go ashore, if for no other reason, because of the level of the seas. The wind was hard offshore still, which gave them some sort of lee, but the Sussex shingle beaches had breaking surf never less than a cable's length in depth. Even if they had found a landing – and Will had little idea of where they were within a mile or five – the chances were they would have ended in a lonely, isolated spot, and found not even a shepherd's hut to shelter in. Also there were offshore shoals, there had to be, it was in nature, which if they found would mean their ending. By morning light, he hoped, they would see Selsey, which he could recognise, and after that he knew the waters intimately, and they would fetch. Had it not been for his intense cold, Will would have dreamed of landfall in Langstone Haven which – he realised it then, and not before – he loved. The very strangeness of this thought brought him to his senses, for he was drifting off, cold or no cold. The yawl was falling off, a gust caught her with the sheet not free to run, and she lurched and took a swipe of green sea inboard as the lee side dipped. Will thrust the tiller down, let fly, and woke Céline with his frantic shout. The water washed Sam's face while she plied the bucket.

Worst was off of Selsey, where the tide was running hard against them, contrary with the wind, which was bitter now, and stronger, from the north east. The tidal rip was terrible, the wind fought it relentlessly, and Céline was letting fly, and sheeting in, and letting fly almost without cease. The halliard was led underneath a thwart and made up in a jam so that she could release it with a jerk and lose the sail if need be, but by the grace of God – as she said it – that necessity was spared them.

And then, with the sun burning down the Channel after them, and round the Bill, and the sea miraculously sane again, if still exceeding wild, Will saw the South Downs leading him along the coast, and the point where they appeared to drop away to nothing, which was where, when coming from the east, he knew he'd find his landfall at the Langstone entrance.

'Céline,' he said. 'It's there. Follow the line of hills. Perhaps two hours. I think the tide's turning west, it's easier. We'll come to Mary's at high water. How's Sam?'

He was lying flat on his back on the bottomboards, swathed in black, nothing of him visible to Will. She sat beside him like an eastern doll, one small area of pale skin peeping from her hood. A small hand emerged from out her cloak and gently touched his face.

'He's not so cold. I hope this sun can chase the clouds away. I hope that he can live.'

'What shall we do?' said Will. 'When we come to Langstone?'

The question was meaningless, but both knew what he meant by it. She was a spy, a smuggler, an escaper, a Frenchwoman. He and Sam were deserters maybe, mutineers or heroes, God knew what. They'd set out to uncover murderers and they had been sucked into a swamp. All three of them could hang, in probability. In truth, he realised with a sudden swoop, he was a murderer himself, of that there was no doubt. And probably, he thought, I've killed Deb, too.

'It is too hard,' she said. 'Too *compliqué*. I'm tired, I want to sleep and cry, and say hallo to Mary and the children. I think that things will go on as before. That is what I think we have to do.'

Go on as before. But everything he'd learned about and found. About Swift, and his society, and even – she had said – other members of his family, whom he would have to ask after; not now. And his position in the world, an officer of the King, a gentleman. Fighting to uphold the right. And honour.

'You can't change anything,' said Céline. 'You do know that, don't you, Will? You will change nothing, so you will have to change. You understand that, don't you? Will? Will?'

Great crimes had been committed, that much he knew. By all of them possibly, certainly by him. And by them, the others, known and secret, oh yes, by them most definitely. The water danced before him, green and whitecapped, leading him to Langstone entrance and the way to home. He was tired, bowed down with great exhaustion in the gleaming chill. Great crimes had been committed, that much he knew. Céline declared with confidence that nothing could be done.

Oh God, he thought, if Deb is dead and Sam should die. Oh God.

'Understand?' he said. 'I am not sure that I do.'

And when at last they ran the forefoot on to mud, Céline gave way to tears.